PRAISE FOR CHRIS PANATIER

"Panatier's world – wracked by war and held together by weary patriotism – seems all too close at hand, and his characters are as real as your next-door neighbors. His unlikely hero, Willa Wallace, takes on mankind's oldest foes – poverty, prejudice, greed, and things more calculating and predatory – in this exciting and genre-challenging debut from Angry Robot Books."

R.W.W. Greene, author of *The Light Years*

"With *The Phlebotomist,* Panatier has created a unique, intricately imagined vision of a divided society, where cash-for-blood is a booming trade and society is split by government sanctioned exsanguination. Rich, bold and visceral, this is a layered, post-apocalyptic book you won't escape from easily, and one which left me genuinely squirming in my seat."

Gemma Amor, Bram Stoker Award-nominated author of *Dear Laura* and *White Pines*

"A compelling dystopian thriller that presents a fallen world and proceeds to dissect it with sanguine enthusiasm using its refreshingly unconventional heroes."

Indrapramit Das, author of *The Devourers*

"A terrifying tale of governmental manipulation and control, set against the kind of global health crisis that used to be a futuristic "what if" but is now very much a "what might be"... equal parts fascinating and horrifying, and never not entertaining."

Dan Hanks, author of *Captain Moxley and the Emb*

"In *The Phlebotomist,* Chris Panatier g
protagonists – a plucky grandmoth

and a teenager with swords – we didn't know we needed, and sets them in a near-future world that terrifies because it feels so possible. Nuclear disaster? Check. Constant monitoring by Big Brother? Uh-huh. Invasion of both men's and women's bodies for the Common Good? That, too. At once grounded in legit science, and also so totally imaginative that you have to find out what happens next, this book will take root at the base of your brain, threading its tentacles into your spinal cord and requiring you to keep turning pages until the bloody end."

Jessica Hagemann, author of *Headcheese*

"A clever, inventive fantasy with a horrific twist that explores whether we are more than the sum of our parts."

Tal Klein, author of *The Punch Escrow*

Chris Panatier

THE PHLEBOTOMIST

ANGRY ROBOT
An imprint of Watkins Media Ltd

Unit 11, Shepperton House
89 Shepperton Road
London N1 3DF
UK

angryrobotbooks.com
twitter.com/angryrobotbooks
Time to Bite Back

An Angry Robot paperback original, 2020

Cover by Chris Panatier and Glen Wilkins
Edited by Gemma Creffield and Robin Triggs
Set in Meridien

ISBN 978 0 85766 861 5
Ebook ISBN 978 0 85766 862 2

Printed and bound in the United Kingdom by TJ International.

9 8 7 6 5 4 3 2 1

To my mother and her sisters.
To my wife, her sister, and mother.
To my sister.
To my daughter.

Doom is a flood that waits for the rift.

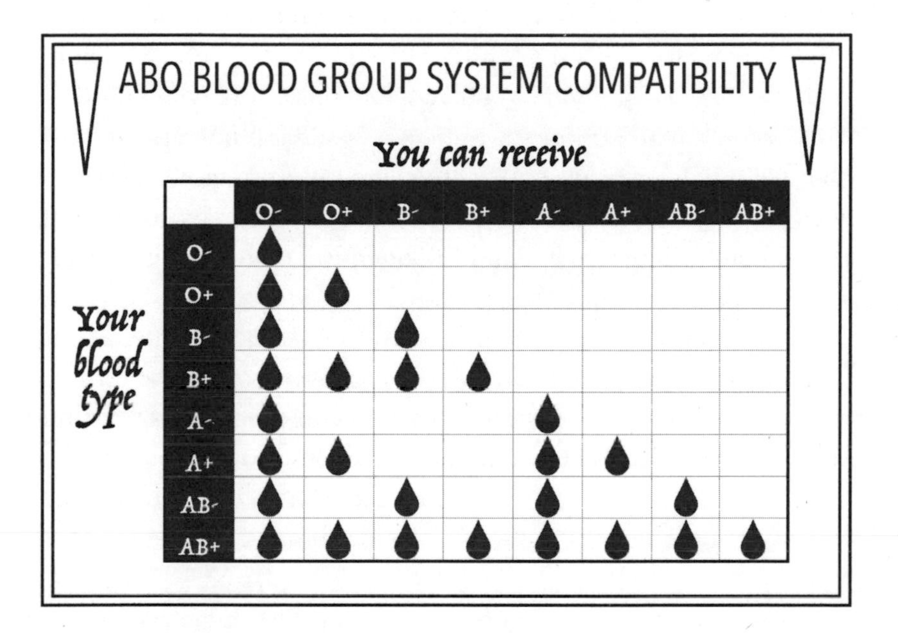
ABO BLOOD GROUP SYSTEM COMPATIBILITY
You can receive
O-
O+
B-
B+
A-
A+
AB-
AB+
Your blood type
O-
O+
B-
B+
A-
A+
AB-
AB+

CHAPTER ONE

HYPOVOLEMIA

A state of decreased intravascular volume, including as a result of blood loss.

The sun was barely up, but the hour didn't keep folks from scrambling in to sell their blood. Early bird donors packed into lines that stretched to the entrance, their collective anxiety like a vapor that flooded Willa's nostrils when she walked in behind them. After so many decades on the job, she could almost discern the iron tang of it. That they were a mixture of types was obvious by their dress, with some low- and midbloods sprinkled in among the usual O-negs. Willa double-checked the time in case she'd somehow arrived late and glanced around for the station manager. "Claude?"

"Over here," he called, rounding the corner from the big freezer.

Willa held her arms open toward the growing mob.

"Price boost," said Claude.

"Again?"

"Check your PatrioCast," hollered Gena from down at Stall D. "Came down thirty minutes ago."

Willa slipped on her reading glasses and brought up the alert screen on her handheld touchstone:

▽ PATRIOCAST 10.19.67 ▽

Residual ionizing radiation since Goliath causes latent spike in chronic diseases
To answer demand, Patriot offers the following incentives for units donated above the Draw. Valid through 10.21.67:

ONEG: +40.75
OPOS: +34.64
ANEG: +18.75
APOS: +16.67
BNEG: +5.7
BPOS: +5.13
ABNEG: +1.71
ABPOS: +1.45

▽ *Patriot thanks ALL DONORS. Your gift matters!* ▽

Patriot called it the Draw, but the people called it the Harvest. It came every forty-five days, a reaping of blood from every person sixteen and up. But it wasn't the Harvest that had Donor Station Eight packed to the gills. It was the chance to sell. For those feeling blooded enough to give beyond the minimum, Patriot was a willing buyer – that was the Trade.

Willa hung her jacket and donned her black lab cloak, then brought Stall A online. She buttoned the cloak and pulled its hood snug to her head as the various scanners and probes hummed to life. Each stall had two lanes, corral like, so phlebotomists could handle a pair of donors simultaneously if they were dexterous enough to manage. Willa was.

All of Patriot's collectors carried the title of "Phlebotomist," a point of unvoiced contention for Willa, since she was the only one who'd ever actually been a genuine phlebotomist. Sure, the others could pull a blood bag, spot-check it for authenticity, and drop it in the preservation vaults, but they wouldn't know the cubital vein from the cephalic. Especially Gena. Decades before the world went sideways, Willa had been trained in the old ways of venipuncture. Not that it mattered. True phlebotomy was an antiquated practice, irrelevant, like driving a car, another thing she used to be good at. The new ways were undoubtedly more efficient. It was for the best, after all. People in the Gray Zones needed the blood.

Willa's first two donors, a man and a woman, stepped into the lanes and lowered their shoulder-zips, exposing ports in their skin onto which blood bags were connected through a small siphon and needle junction. She quickly removed and processed the man's bag, then turned to the woman.

The man interrupted, "I got extra," and presented a second full bag from a satchel.

"Where'd you get this one, Tillman?" Willa asked. He was in so often that his sourcing had to be black-market. Most likely blood muggings. The cash-for-blood trade had created an unseemly underground economy, and it was booming.

"It's mine, *reaper*," he answered with a devious grin.

He knew that she had to take the blood if it scanned clear. It was company policy to accept any blood offered, so long as the phenotype, or blood type, matched the donor's profile. That didn't guarantee it was actually the donor's blood – far from it – but it gave Patriot a veneer of deniability if they were ever accused of being a market for questionably-sourced product. She ran it over the needle probe, which analyzed for phenotype, as well as other immunoreactive antigens and antibodies, the organism of origin, diseases, and the percentage of red blood cells in eryptosis, or cell death. If the readings were off, the bag would be rejected.

The probe cleared the unit and she dropped it curtly into her booth's cooling vault. Tillman smirked and scanned his touchstone for credit. "See you tomorrow," he said.

"You'd better not," said Willa.

She rotated to the woman. "Sorry about that, ma'am."

The woman was rough, wearing her thirty or so years like fifty. She held her sleeve open loosely, eyes drooping. Willa sighed and reluctantly removed the blood bag from her port. "Ma'am?"

The woman's eyelids fluttered as she struggled to say something. Her head flopped forward and she collapsed against the stall, her thin legs and arms in a tangle.

"Claude! Gelpack!" Willa rounded her station into the narrow corral. "Ma'am?" She tapped the woman's cheeks.

When Claude arrived, Willa traded the woman's blood bag for the gelpack, a small syrette filled with carbs and epinephrine used to jumpstart folks who sold more than their bodies could give. She broke its cap, pushed the two tiny needles into the skin on the inside of the woman's arm, and squeezed the contents into her basilic vein.

Claude looked at the woman, shaking his head. "Crazy. An A-neg in here trading like a lowblood."

Willa applied a small bandage over the wound and gave a touch of pressure. "How do you know she's A-neg?"

"Just a hunch." He leaned into the stall and scanned the bag on Willa's console. "Mmhmm. A-neg."

"The incentives are too high, Claude."

"I hear you, Willa Mae, but…" he dropped the bag into her vault and took the chance to whisper "…what can you do? Rules are rules." He gave a helpless shrug.

Willa helped the woman to a bench along the wall opposite a screen tuned to the Channel. She let her eyes blur over it while the stranger went in and out of consciousness on her shoulder. Back before the war, before Patriot, the medically recommended wait between donations was fifty-six days. This was to ensure that people fully recovered between donations. The absolute earliest that the human body could replenish a unit of blood was twenty-eight days, with many people taking up to three times that. The Harvest had lopped eleven days from the interval, mandating one donated pint every forty-five. If you wanted your government food rations, you showed up. If you didn't, you starved.

The Harvest alone was enough of a strain. But Patriot had gone a step further, offering cash to people willing to sell even more than the Harvest minimum. Of course, people were drawn in. Robots had taken most of the jobs and the Trade was regarded as something like basic income. Except folks were paying for it with the fruit of their veins. It never ceased to amaze Willa how much people could adapt, walking around in a constant state of hypovolemia just to get a little more coin, wearing symptoms so long that they eventually became character traits. Weakness, fatigue, confusion, clammy skin. Eventually anemia or shock ended the cycle. To Willa it was like state sanctioned Russian roulette, and folks were just spinning the cylinder.

Claude looked at her sideways. She was violating company policy by vacating her stall, but Claude tended to give her wider berth than the others. She had quickly worked her way up to Stall A – the equivalent of first chair in an orchestra – and had never relinquished it. Her gaudy production numbers brought her a certain amount of leniency.

The woman's hands lay folded against the bench like possum claws; skeletal and dirty, the dwindling meat beneath the skin a ticking clock. Willa had seen it all before, a cycle of destruction that churned through the districts to touch every family.

The woman straightened as if she'd been suddenly plugged back in.

"Ma'am?" Willa asked with a gentle touch to her wrist.

"What do you want?"

"You passed out. You've given too much."

The woman's pupils tightened on the screen, where a scrolling chyron flashed yet another incentive bump and she sprang from the bench. Willa latched to her arm instinctively. "There's no need. You're A-neg. The price will be the same tomorrow. Please, don't."

"Get off me," she growled. Willa knew it wasn't who the woman really was, but the Trade had a way of exposing the nerves. Ripping her arm away, she returned to the back of the line.

Willa stepped into her stall and got her line moving. She processed bags, checked for fakes, but her eyes stayed on the woman. In short order, she was next in line, a new bag on her port, filling red pulse-by-pulse. "I'm feel good," she mumbled in anticipation of Willa's objection.

"No, you don't," said Willa. "That's the gelpack talking. It's just adrenaline. Please don't do this."

The woman leaned heavily on the side of the stall. "You haffto I got kids."

She was technically correct. Willa did have to. Grudgingly, she removed the half-full bag and processed it. It was a brutal thing, the blood trade, but here she was stuck on the receiving end of it; a cog in a runaway machine.

Just before close, a notification glowed orange on her display. She deactivated her stall, sending glass barricades across the lanes and flagged Claude in Stall B. "Coolant."

Claude summoned Willa's donors to his line and they grumbled their way over.

Willa angled a panel open and dipped her hand into her cooling vault. Her toes curled anxiously inside her orthotics. It was warming. "How much room do we have in the big cooler?"

"Topped out after lunch."

She had almost fifty liters. Blood couldn't be transfused after four hours in warm conditions due to bacterial proliferation. It would go bad long before morning if she couldn't get it cooled and her pay would be docked. "I'll call a technician."

"Good luck with that."

Willa tapped the support button and sat helplessly as donors side-eyed her from the long lines in front of Claude. *Sorry* she mouthed.

Closing time came with no technician responding. Normally, all of the vaults would be taken to the distribution hub after hours, but with no way to cool hers, it had to go now. She wheeled the vault, about the size of an old hotel refrigerator, from under the console and unhooked the cables from the processing interface. Having taken all of the extra donors, Claude's line was still out the door.

"I'm taking this to SCS," said Willa.

"Sorry, Willa, I'd do it, but..." The station supervisor couldn't leave with donors present and Patriot didn't turn away willing supply.

"I know," she said. "When you're done... do you mind... can you fetch Isaiah from school?"

"Sure. He's at the same spot?"

"He is. Thank you, sweetheart."

"My pleasure," answered Claude, swiping blood bags from the donors nearly as fast as she.

Outside Station Eight the sky was purple on one side and orange on the other, with clouds like gray icing layered between. The type of weather Willa described as *soon-to-be*. Mid October cool, soon-to-be cold. She shivered preemptively and hailed a taxi drone.

Drone rides were an absolute luxury in the blood districts and Willa felt guilty in summoning one, even if it was necessary to help her ferry the vault. After half a minute, a taxi drone in mustard yellow broke from the low-hanging clouds.

The sight of a drone descending from the sky to land right in front of you was something Willa would never get used to, even though they'd been around for decades. They seemed alien. Aside from helicopters, things that could fly were supposed to have wings. And drones were *not* helicopters.

To Willa they looked like flying gumdrops. Aside from some aerodynamic ridges that pinched out from the sides, they were rounded at the edges and slightly narrower near the roof. The motors were mounted in an array around the top rim, giving them a crownlike appearance. They were called "ducted fans," though the term meant little to Willa. They resembled giant rolls of toilet paper with propeller blades tucked snuggly against the inner walls. Independent articulation allowed them to control not only lift, but direction and altitude. With small alterations to the blade shape over the years, they were hummingbird quiet. Another eerie feature.

The taxi landed and the door swept open from the bottom. *Welcome aboard CROW FLIES*, it said.

"Patriot Distribution, SCS," said Willa. "Quickly please."

We will arrive at Patriot Distribution, Southern City Segment, in two and a half minutes.

Once she'd buckled into the bench and secured the vault to the cargo clip against the wall, the drone lifted off. A screen around the inner perimeter created a false three-hundred and sixty degree window, interrupted only by an actual window, set like a porthole in the door. She'd flown in plenty of drones but, much like their appearance, she had never gotten used to them – how they felt, how they took away all control. She longed for the solid predictability of a steering wheel and the responsiveness of an accelerator. Before the war, before the Harvest, before Patriot, when the asphalt was still good and cars could be afforded, Willa owned the roads, collecting tickets like blue ribbons. Speeding – her one real vice. But that was then. Nowadays, a car would appear every so often near the business district, but only the rich had money for such extravagances.

The drone traveled through the early evening glow in electric silence, toward the rough geographical center of the Southern City Segment. This was one of four such segments that made up the city, along with North-by, Crosstown, and Eastern. Each had a distribution center that collected the day's take from the donor stations in that segment. Totals from each were then shipped by transport drone to Central City Collection – CCC – downtown. Set in the middle of an urban forest, Triple-C was a sprawling complex that Patriot media proudly termed "the Heart" because it was the central hub for the circulation of blood to the Gray Zones. *From our heart to yours,* so it went.

Willa put her hand to the side of the vault, anxious over the precious cargo warming inside. Her anxiety was double since she didn't know when the coolant had actually gone out. It was possible the entire load was bad, and a single day of lost pay could break her.

The drone settled and Willa quickly unclipped the vault. *You have arrived at Patriot Distribution, SCS,* said the drone. *Will you be needing continued service?*

"No, thank you," she said, her heart already pounding like a countdown.

Have a most pleasant evening, then.

"You too." She rolled the vault onto the concrete apron in front of the building. The drone sped away.

Set off from the more densely populated residential areas, SCS Distribution stood alone at the center of a magnificent hexagonal concrete expanse, surrounded by a wall with trees stretching up behind it. A single road led out and into the blood districts. As far as she could tell, the place was empty. No people or other drones. Just a speedloop tube descending from the building's outer wall and into the ground at the far side.

The transports had not yet taken to the sky, and until they'd all departed, she had time to deposit the vault. She wheeled it heavily to one side of the huge polygonal building where a cutout in the thick concrete had a processing interface that looked like an old automated teller machine.

Willa's orthopedics slipped on the moist concrete as she struggled to roll the cooling vault to the connection point at the far end of a ramp.

Her bangs wicked away beads of sweat as she wrangled the vault. *You're too old for this*. Finally, with her legs about to give, a loud click signaled the vault's successful connection to the interface and it absorbed into the building. She rested against the wall for a moment, letting the cool cement sooth her nerves. Above, the blood transport drones began to filter from the building. They were wider and shorter than human transport drones, more utilitarian, and less refined – shaped like giant cigar boxes with ducted fans powerful enough to carry up to six cooling vaults apiece. Their only embellishment was the phrase BE A PATRIOT illuminated on their bellies.

She felt for her touchstone at the end of its lanyard and navigated to the screen that would register if the blood had gone through. It still read 00.00. She'd gotten the blood to distribution but wouldn't receive credit if it had spoiled. Holding her breath, she watched the numbers and willed them to change. They had to change. They had to. Afraid to blink, her eyes started to burn.

... 47.52 liters

Relief. A stay of execution. Only two and a half liters rejected.

She exhaled and stood up. Aside from the exiting parade of blood drones, she was alone. The air smelled like rain. She pulled up the hood on her reaper's black and began walking. Maybe she'd get home before it really came down.

She stopped after only a few steps, thinking that she'd heard something like a distant mosquito. It became more pronounced, a high-pitched whining that seemed to emanate from the squadron. One of the drones had fallen below formation. Even if it cleared the wall, she could see it wouldn't make it over the trees. A tick of panic came at the loss of such a large amount of blood, especially after she'd exerted so much effort to save a single vault. She briefly envisioned herself running underneath to try and catch it. Much as she disliked the Harvest, the Gray Zones needed every drop. Willa drew up her touchstone and alerted Patriot Emergency.

The motors on the drone struggled as it sank, with one exploding in a torus of glowing shrapnel. It hit the compound's outer wall and smashed to the ground, sending prop blades into the hull and gashing the steel. Vaults tumbled onto the pavement as the twisted carcass came to rest. Willa felt herself drawn through the debris field, but stopped short of the drone, still showering sparks. Calm down, she thought, there's no one in there.

A metal ring rolled lazily to her foot where it toppled over, and silence returned. She took stock of the scene and began toward the wreckage, careful to avoid the red slick of donor blood that would soon coat the asphalt. But as she neared the drone, her stomach twisted.

There wasn't any.

She triggered her touchstone's light and flashed it over the ground. Not so much as a drop of red, and no bags whatsoever. Had they remained inside the vaults through the crash? Had they all somehow held? Their poly construction was strong, sure, but those fan blades… it seemed impossible. Nearby, a dented vault laid open on its side, one wheel still spinning. She knelt to look inside.

Suddenly a white light blanched her vision. Willa turned into the beam eyes closed, her touchstone held aloft. "Willa Mae Wallace!" she yelled. "Station Eight, SCS."

The light descended from the sky and settled nearby. She cracked an eye just enough to make out the shape of a Patriot security drone silhouetted against the backdrop of the outer wall.

"Step inside, please," came a voice.

Willa took a final glance at the carnage and headed for the drone. When she was clear of the glare, the door opened to reveal a nice-looking man standing inside. He was in his early forties with a tanned face and a full head of brassy hair. His beige suit set off a bright pink tie and matching pocket square that immediately made Willa think of country clubs – if those still existed someplace. Her eyes were drawn to a gold pin in the shape of the letter "P" with the stem plunged through an anatomical heart that rested against his lapel.

"Yes, well, the newer insignias are terribly bland, are they not?" He spoke as if already in mid-conversation. "I suppose I flout the corporate message by remaining loyal to the original logo after a rebrand."

"I've seen you at our station before, I think," Willa said, "but I'm afraid I don't recall your name."

"Jesper Olden." His voice had the velvety timbre of wealth. "Patriot security. Please, step in from the cold." He took her hand and helped her inside.

"You don't look like security," she said, forgetting herself, then quickly added, "I mean – my apologies, it's been a long day. You just don't see people dressed like you many times in the year. Especially not out in the districts."

"No offense taken, Ms Wallace." He tapped the control screen. "We should have you home in fewer than two minutes."

"Oh, you don't have to do that, sir, I'm OK walking." But just like that, Willa felt the drone lifting off.

"Nonsense. We don't need you getting hit on the head by a defective drone." He gave a tepid chuckle. "Think of the liability."

Willa smiled weakly. Liability? The court system had long ago been largely dismantled, now used only to settle financial disputes among corporations and wealthy individuals. Regular people didn't meet the net worth threshold to utilize the system. His choice of words was perplexing. Maybe he was just using outdated vernacular as a matter of habit. Perhaps he was so out of touch that he didn't even consider how ridiculous the reference had been. He stared blithely out the window and Willa decided that must be it.

"Well," she said, "thank you for the ride." She stepped to the opposite side of the passenger compartment and took a seat. Relief was immediate. She'd always stored anxiety in her feet.

Olden considered the viewscreen. "Ah, there they are. The diagnostics on the crashed drone, see?" He gestured to some figures that Willa couldn't make out and gave the rest a cursory review. "Did you hear or see anything odd? Did you note anybody in the area before it went down?"

"I didn't see anyone else," she affirmed. "It just fell, that's all." There had been at least one empty vault in the wreckage but she had a gut feeling she wasn't supposed to have seen that.

"No one saw you there?"

"Not anyone other than you, Mr Olden."

"Wonderful. I appreciate the effort you made to get your take processed, especially this close to our Patrioteer conference." Willa knew about the conference, an annual two-day meeting for upper management to do whatever it was upper management did. Jesper played with the screen. "Let me credit you, let's say, five hundred as bonus for your effort. Is that fair?"

"Oh, Mr Olden, you shouldn't do that," she protested, uncomfortable accepting unearned lucre.

"Don't be foolish, Ms Wallace." He tapped in the amount. "That drone could have killed you."

"It was nowhere near–"

"Willa. May I call you Willa?" he said without really asking. "I insist on it. Patriot insists on it." He brightened. "You could buy Halloween candy this year. Five hundred would cover the entire segment, I'd bet. You'd be royalty."

"It's too much, Mr Olden, I'd prefer you didn't give me any money." The amount was more than a week's pay, and easy money came with strings. Aside from that, Halloween hadn't been observed for at least twenty years.

"And I'd prefer our drones not endanger top performers." He tapped the display. "Now let's not have any further discussion of the matter. *With anyone*."

"I'm just happy to do my job."

"I assure you, Willa, we appreciate it." He flattened his suit jacket. "Ah, here we are at your stack. Do you feel well enough to return to work or will you need some days off?"

"I'm fine," she said as the door opened. "I'll be there tomorrow."

"Lovely, then. A good evening to you and to Isaiah."

She shivered at the mention of Isaiah. It always surprised her when Patriot managers voiced little details about her life that she considered private. She halfway assumed that the executives received prompts from their implants whenever they spoke with low level workers to make them seem more relatable or friendly. But she never got used to hearing strangers mention her family members out of turn.

The drone lifted away and her touchstone signaled the arrival of the money. An influx of five hundred would have had her rejoicing and thanking God out loud if she'd actually earned it. Entering her apartment stack, it felt like a chain.

She greeted Isaiah with a suffocating embrace that made him lose whatever game he was playing on his old viewer and he grumbled an objection.

Claude, who had come over to keep an eye on Isaiah, politely passed on a dinner invitation. She couldn't blame him. He was a station supervisor and didn't have to eat from The Box like everyone else. The Box – a literal box of prepackaged food – was provided by Patriot to residents of the blood districts who maintained one-hundred percent participation in the Harvest. The idea had been sold as a way to streamline subsistence programs. Instead of going to the store and picking out groceries for yourself and your family, the government picked them for you. Processed mystery meats and condensed dairy, sickly sweet canned fruit cocktails, powdered grains. On lucky weeks, a handful of oat cubes or tea. Many lowblood families relied on The Box completely. With her job, Willa leaned on it as a supplement, but few were able to live entirely Box free. She'd pass on it too if she could.

She and Isaiah ate genmod pasta prepared with a splash of black-market vinegar, topped with the last of some dehydrated poultry cubes that she'd managed to stretch over a full week. She stirred her bowl until they puffed into something that resembled the meat they had once been, and took small bites, chewing deliberately to make it all last. Isaiah devoured without ceremony.

A thought occurred to her, curiosity in the wake of her encounter at SCS, that she might tune to *The Patriot Report*. The show, which aired in place of the local news, touted Patriot's blood collection statistics and good deeds. Willa considered it a painfully tacky program, tortuously drawn out to thirty minutes in length, and cast in the mold of an old lottery-drawing segment complete with a shiny host yammering on through billboard teeth. The company served a vital role but bragging about it in such an ostentatious fashion left a bad taste. The fringes of the country were at war. People were suffering.

Swallowing her disgust, she turned it on, drawing Isaiah to the screen like a moth to a porchlight. Another reason she rarely watched anything.

"Isaiah, please," she said, yanking him back a reasonable distance. "It's nothing good."

Tanned darker than a roast turkey, the host was flanked by two scantily-clad assistants who held up digital posters announcing the statistics for every precinct within each of the four city segments. Willa did a double take. Setting her dinner to the side, she paused the screen and quickly added the figures. Southern City Segment was reporting a full take, highest in the city.

Impossible. With a crashed drone – carrying what were most likely empty vaults – SCS should have been dead last. They were either mistaken or they were lying. She reached for something to write with and jotted down the numbers, thinking she'd discuss it with Claude, but her pen scratched to a halt. Jesper had been clear. She couldn't tell Claude, couldn't tell anyone.

CHAPTER TWO

PHENOTYPE

The observable physical properties of an organism, determined by the combination of that organism's inherited genes and the environmental influences upon them. Within the ABO blood group system, phenotypes are expressed generally as A, B, AB, and O.

Sleepless nights were the norm. Only now there was a new reason for her insomnia. The crashed drone and its incongruence with *The Patriot Report* had Willa's mind aquake. Why would they offer her such an obscene amount of money to stay quiet? Why would they lie about the number of units they'd collected?

The morning's cool light filtered in from the window. She sighed deeply, opting to lie in bed just another minute to let her bones acclimate before forcing them into action. She rolled to the side and reached to the nightstand for her hair. It was just thick enough to look good, but not so heavy that it went crooked whenever she knelt or bent over. It was hot pink, her favorite color, but she chose it so that Isaiah could always find her in a crowd. It also didn't hurt that it looked good against the reaper's black. She rotated it until the mark on the band fell in line with the center of her brow and pulled it snug. It'd been thirty-seven years since Chrysalis first took her real hair. When it had finally begun to grow back, she found she actually preferred a bald head.

A well-kept straight razor was cheaper than shampoo anyway.

She twisted up from her bed underneath the apartment's lone window, taking care to keep her nightgown from hiking, and put her feet in her slippers. Across the room, Isaiah snored soundly in his nook. The apartment's second room was technically his, and he wasn't a baby anymore, but she felt better being able to see him from her bed.

In the kitchenette, Willa dropped a pair of oat cubes from The Box into a pot to boil, then doled them into bowls and began eating as Isaiah stirred. He rose zombie-like, climbed into his chair, and spooned the bland porridge into his mouth, eyes still closed.

"Good morning, 'Saiah."

"Gramrrr," he mumbled back.

"We say 'good morning' in this house."

"Good morning, grandma," he said.

"That's it," said Willa, cleaning the last chunks from her bowl and taking it to the sink.

From a carton over the counter she grabbed a fresh blood bag, tore the security seal, and peeled away the shrink-wrap. She removed the backing paper, flicked the cap from the needle, and slipped it into the port implant on her upper bicep. Her eyes wandered to Isaiah as she pressed the sticky bag to her skin and pulled on the tiny tab that triggered a chemical coolant pod inside. At sixteen he'd be subject to the Harvest.

They walked hand-in-hand down the street of their largely B-positive neighborhood, known as B Plus. Even though she was AB-positive, she could afford the modest upgrade in location on account of her job. B Plus was lowblood to be sure, but anything was better than AB Plus. Her daughter, Elizabeth, had hoped to send Isaiah to school in B Plus because of its success in placing children into the few available trade practicums, and Willa made just enough, with the extra blood sale here and there, to afford it. She remembered the days of her youth when college had been a goal of most parents, but nowadays it wasn't something that regular people thought about. College was for another class altogether – the upper crust – those in wealthy neighborhoods like Capillarian Crest, far removed from the blood districts. And rich enough to bribe their way out of the Harvest.

Willa sent Isaiah up the steps with a kiss and stayed on the sidewalk outside the school to make sure he made it to the teacher waiting just inside. He disappeared behind the glass and she watched until his shadow's shadow had faded. All she hoped for was to stick around long enough to shepherd him to adulthood. That had been her promise.

Back in Stall A, shorter lines told Willa that prices had dipped, and with the lull in donations she dwelled on the five hundred sitting in her account, lead-weight money she had no way to un-take. She never accepted anything from anybody unless she'd earned it, and the years had taught her that there was no such thing as free money. Sometimes a buyer simply paid in advance for a future thing unnamed. She scoured her mind for Olden's motives, for what he might ask of her in the future, but other than keeping her mouth shut about the crash, she came up empty.

Her touchstone sounded, and with nobody standing in line, she took a break to glance at it.

▽ PATRIOCAST 10.20.67 ▽
Safety Reminders!

Never trust a blood bag given to you by someone you do not know.
It could be CONTAMINATED.

Before affixing a new blood bag, wash your port with hot water and PatrioCleanse™ antibacterial soap (Free at all donor stations).

Blood-borne pathogens are HIGHLY CONTAGIOUS!
Do not associate with anyone who is ill.

If you become aware of a sick individual, you can help them! Tap the PatrioCare™ icon and Patriot will deliver them to one of our convalescence facilities for treatment. Remember, preventing the spread of disease is a four-step process:

Sequestration
Diagnosis
Inoculation
Elimination

▽ *Patriot thanks ALL DONORS. Your gift matters!* ▽

Protecting the blood supply was vital to helping those inside the Gray Zones and so Willa was generally supportive of the measures taken to do so, even if they tilted toward heavy handed. She'd escaped Chrysalis and most of its aftereffects, but not without help. Acute radiation syndrome – ARS – had been widespread in all directions of the blast. In managing the crisis, the government had drawn a miles-wide circle around ground zero. The radiation levels for those within the ring who had survived the initial blast were deemed untreatable. Those on the outside of the ring with signs of ARS received platelet transfusions in the hope that their bone marrow cells would repopulate. If they did, the patient recovered, if not, they met the same fate as those inside the ring. Willa had been outside the ring. The transfusions had saved her life.

All of that didn't mean she was blind to reality, however. Over time the consequences of Patriot's strict policies had begun to pile up. Fed by an accelerating cycle of fear that someone's cold or flu might actually be hepatitis or HIV, neighbors started reporting neighbors. You couldn't get the police to AB Plus, but news of infection would have the authorities outside the house in minutes. Even without confirmatory testing, Patriot scooped up the afflicted and transferred them for treatment. Sometimes they didn't come back. Rumor had it that Patriot quarantined those who failed to recover in a remote settlement on the city's edgelands. Willa wasn't so sure. The real problem was paranoia, and no one could eradicate that. Eventually, people learned the drill: if you were sick, draw the curtains until you weren't.

Willa's vault was cooling blood again and the lines brought no drama. The monotony and repetition was a respite from the outside world – the struggle to live and provide, the state of her once great country, bomb anxiety, Isaiah's future... She got lost in the contours of each blood bag she collected, let the cold liquid inside salve the tension she stored in her arthritic fingers. A job could do wonders for one's mental state, regardless of its complexity. Completion of a task was good for the soul.

At close, Willa exited the station into a heavy mist. She briefly considered summoning a brellabot to keep her dry, but that meant money. Besides, she'd kept on her reaper's black, which was surprisingly weather resistant. She flipped up the hood. Based on the latest forecast, fallout drift was negligible.

Situated in the middle of a large O-negative district known simply as O Minus, Station Eight was the busiest precinct in the segment. As universal donors, the O-negs enjoyed the highest demand for their blood, which meant it fetched the top prices.

What Patriot was willing to pay for blood was dictated by a few factors Willa understood and a few she didn't. The biggest key was compatibility, and thereby the proportion of the population that could safely receive one's blood. The O-negs could donate to just about a hundred percent of the population, barring rare cases, while O-positives were donor compatible with around eighty-five percent of folks. As such, those with the O antigen were deemed "highbloods". A-negs could donate their blood to about forty-six percent of the population, while A-positives hit at about thirty-nine percent. This solid, but by no means high, donor compatibility meant people with the A antigen were "midbloods". At the bottom of the barrel were B-negs and B-positives, at fourteen and twelve percent donor compatibility, and below them were AB-negs at four percent and AB-positives at three and a half. Their blood was worth the least. The Bs and the ABs, then, were "lowbloods".

Willa's route toward home took her from O Minus into the midbloods, their borders delineated by an uptick in poverty. Finally, she traversed the southern tip of A Plus, across a thin finger of O Plus, and into the lowbloods.

Hardly a neighborhood and more like a slum, AB Plus was the place she'd come from – and eventually escaped. Folks with the AB-positive antigens were the opposite of O-negs in just about every way. They were universal recipient. Willa mused that the term carried such a pleasant connotation if you needed blood, but not if you had to sell it, which of course everyone did. As donor blood, AB-positive was a bad match for anyone but other AB-positives, which accounted for only three percent of the population. So demand for it was miniscule. The real kicker was that since AB-positives were compatible recipients for the other seven blood types, should they need blood, they didn't even require their own type. Where the Trade was concerned, AB-positive was redundant. An unlucky mistake of creation. A sick joke. Willa half wondered why Patriot bothered to collect it at all.

The worst part about the whole thing – from the Harvest, to the Trade, from cash-for-blood donations to neighborhoods segregated by blood type – was that it didn't have to be like this.

Back when phlebotomists were valued for their skill and knowledge rather than to serve as glorified button pushers, Willa had real training. She *knew* blood. Understood that it wasn't just one substance, but a blend of four distinct components, or fractions, with each one serving a different, vital purpose. And importantly, patients rarely required all of them at once.

In the old days, fractionation, also known as apheresis, was the process by which only some of these components – red blood cells, plasma, platelets, or white blood cells – were removed from a donor's blood. Depending on the need, be it trauma, a leukemia diagnosis, or any number of other maladies, fractionation allowed for the selective collection of blood serums rather than all or nothing.

Before the Harvest, fractionation was standard practice. In one sitting, whole blood was drawn, centrifuged into fractions, the desired component removed, and everything else sent right back into the donor. An anticoagulant introduced into the system ensured the blood didn't curdle before the donor got it back.

And that was the problem. The synthetic anticoagulants used in blood transport and preservation were unsafe for introduction into the body, making them ineligible for fractionation. Transported blood, for instance, had to be processed to remove synthetics prior to transfusion into people. The only anticoagulants that were safe for use during apheresis were made from crops that were contaminated by fallout. Absent an anticoagulant, fractioning simply wasn't an option. So whole blood made the Harvest.

Willa drew to a stop in front of a lopsided ranch-style home, its siding sloughed in places exposing the pink swirls of century-old batting and rotten studs. A bay window in front still held glass in the center pane, and there, collected like a gathering of starfish, pressed the tiny hands of maybe a dozen children, their eyes shining from behind.

Higher up in the window, the blinds opened enough for another set of eyes. Likely one of the few adults occupying the home, with shared responsibility for the children inside. That's how it was in AB Plus. Automation had killed off the jobs, so parents turned to the Trade, doing what they could to provide, tripping along the tightrope of hypovolemia until they eventually made one donation too many.

It was an inescapable cycle for those in the lowbloods. Even choice of mate was an exercise in self-preservation. Since blood type is inherited, the only way to maintain an O-negative bloodline was to have kids with other O-negs. An O-neg wasn't going to pair with someone without it and risk downgrading the blood of their children. For the same reason, the midbloods avoided lowbloods. They might even get lucky, as the laws of genetics allowed the rare O-negative child to midblood parents. But an AB mother would never give birth to an O child, regardless of the father's blood type.

And that's what got her, the truth of the world these children had yet to appreciate. Born with the wrong blood into a world organized according to it. Relegated to damnation through no fault of their own.

Willa looked to the sky and wondered when the last time a catering drone had been inside the jagged border of her old neighborhood. Months probably, maybe longer. Elsewhere, virtually all commerce was conducted via drone, especially in the business districts where they saturated the sky like starlings. They were even thick in the air over much of O Minus, where run-of-the-mill drone services could be afforded. Not in AB Plus. These people still walked miles to pick up The Box when it was issued every two weeks.

She considered her touchstone. The five hundred sat in her account like a swollen cyst. It was true that she and Isaiah could use it, but she wanted it – and all the questions that came with it – gone, excised from her conscience. They'd always gotten by before the five hundred, and they would get by after it.

A tap brought her touchstone to life. "I'd like catering service please," she said.

State star level: two through five.

"They don't have one-star drones anymore?" Willa asked, perturbed.

One-star foodservice level selected, confirm?

"Confirm."

How many dining, please?

"One hundred."

Confirmed. Debit four hundred and eighty-nine. Confirm?

She smiled. "Confirmed."

Willa glanced back to the window of the house from where the eyes gleamed and gave a little wave. The starfish twinkled back. Above them, their guardian, scrutinized her. She understood. Nobody wandered into AB Plus to take in the view. You were either trouble, or stupid, or both. Willa just hoped the drones came before somebody decided to blood-mug her. With her luck it would be Tillman, who come tomorrow would waltz in to Donor Eight looking to sell her own blood right back to her. She took solace in knowing that he wouldn't get much for it.

She waited, kicking her toes at the sickly grass that stuffed the sidewalk cracks. It was an uncanny feature of the blood districts. They were woven together by contiguous patches of gray-yellow grass, agglomerated like land masses that crossed sidewalks and streets alike. It was everywhere, twining its infirm way across empty lots, abandoned salvage yards, and childless parks beset by naked trees.

Green and blue landing lights appeared in the distance, four sets in all. Commerce drones were distinguishable from those built to transport people, taking on the form that best served whatever they carried. The approaching catering drones looked like flying charcoal grills. They descended from the low clouds and landed smoothly on the sidewalk to either side of her. Their ducted fan stalks folded seamlessly into the body panels and she bounced her touchstone against their interfaces to verify her identity. Segmented domes slid open to reveal a three-hundred and sixty degree buffet of steaming bins: rice and beans, corn bread, pickled vegetables, and some sort of cheap white fish. A drawer presented degradable bowls and biopolyware.

Willa signaled an invitation to those inside the nearby homes, but the eyes stayed put. Understandable. She'd have had the same response if she were the one behind the blinds. Give them a minute, she thought, an empty stomach will always prevail.

She laid a filet in the bottom of a bowl, buried it under hot beans and rice, unwrapped a fork, and gently folded the mixture so as to allow the steam to escape. She set her backside against a drone and dug in. Up and down the street, the windows framed constellations of eyes, and she could tell from the shuffling behind each that the empty bellies were winning.

CHAPTER THREE

INFUSION
To introduce a fluid solution into the body through a vein.

"What're you looking at, Everard?" asked Sasha, one of the youngest.

Everard let the blinds snap shut as he pondered. "Crazy woman just standing out on the street."

"How do you know she's crazy?"

"She's standing in the middle of AB Plus, 'Sosh," said Everard. "That and she's got hair brighter than bubble gum."

"What color is bubble gum?"

"Pink."

"Can I see?"

"No," he said, shooing her away. Now, what in the damned hell was a woman – and an older woman, at that – doing loitering in the roughest patch of AB Plus? He reopened the gap in the old blinds again and watched as she messed with her touchstone. Couldn't be a spy if she had a touchstone. Either that or she was a top-notch spy with a jailbroke handpiece. Still, pretty brazen to go 'round out in the open looking like a circus performer. Then again, what was the saying? *Hiding in plain sight*?

The padding of feet told him the rest of the children had gathered to see what the fuss was about. "Y'all scoot," he said, taking Honey under the arms and bringing her back to the living room. "Come on, stay away from there."

He set her into an old beanbag and turned back for the window, where all the children had shoved themselves beneath the blinds to get a view outside. He rushed back to the front. "Goddamit you guys, what'd I tell you?"

"She looks nice," said Jack, an older boy about second grade in age, though no one knew his exact years.

"Git," said Everard, trying to herd them away. They scattered momentarily only to recongeal into clusters at the window's edges. He opened the blinds again to see the woman staring directly at him. She did a friendly little wave. *Who was this person?* All around him the kids shouted greetings as they returned the salutation.

"What's she doing here, Everard?" asked Jack.

"I don't know and I guarantee you she don't know either. One can shy of a sixer for sure, Jack... she's probably crazy."

He kept watching. She let her touchstone hang free on its lanyard and pushed her hands deep into the pockets of her coat. That pink hair. Odd as it was, it seemed familiar to him, though he couldn't place it. Was that a reaper's outfit? She waved again and then glanced to the north. Drones.

Worse than a spy. She was Patriot. They'd come for him.

"Quick!" he ordered. "Everyone into the back room!" He corralled the children. Years of vigilant living had hardened their discipline in times of emergency, and they moved to their safe places largely on their own. Returning to the window, he opened the slit in the blinds as four large commerce drones landed just off the old crumbled sidewalk. The woman tapped her touchstone to each and the shells on top slid open to reveal... food? "Holy shi–" he stopped himself. "That red beans and rice?" He felt like he was having a bad trip, but he hadn't been 'shrooming in twenty-five years.

Furniture shuffled in the other room as the children reemerged from their hiding spots, with Everard too flabbergasted to stop them. He hadn't seen commercial drones over AB Plus in, well, ever? And four of them full of food? Something like that cost more money than he'd know what to do with. With that kind of money, the woman had to be a criminal. A criminal dressed like a Patriot station worker. Only a pro would be so brazen. He felt a mixture of wonderment and admiration at the stunt.

They all watched as she took a bowl from a compartment and began scooping heaping blobs of rice and fish into it. Then, standing out in the open in the middle of AB Plus, the woman in the pink hair began eating dinner.

"She's eating food!" hollered Ryan, as the others exclaimed various theories and pontifications about the woman who'd brought food drones into the most desolate place in the city. She took another bite and began gesturing to the houses, then signaled Everard to come outside with her. "She's inviting us, Everard! Can we go?"

They were all hungry. They were always hungry. Everard couldn't remember the last time he'd had anything more than a nibble of the meals they made for the children. His ribs jutted out so far the kids could hang from them. He turned from the window. "You stay put. Get me? I don't know what this is all about. Anything happens, you get in your hiding spots and send word to Lindon, yes?"

The children nodded.

"Good. Lock the door behind me." He took a pocketknife from his cargo shorts. "Octavia," he said, handing the tiny weapon to the oldest child. "You the man o' the house." She nodded.

"But she's a giiiiiiiirl," one of them squealed as Everard left the room. He heard Octavia give the boy a dressing-down and the whining stopped.

He went to the dark entryway, flipped a series of deadbolts, and cracked the door. The woman saw this and addressed him.

"It's OK!" she called. "Come out here before it gets cold. Bring those kids. Get them fed." She took an exaggerated bite. "You too, come on," she hollered toward the neighboring homes.

Everard looked down the block at the other houses. No

movement, though there would be soon if he didn't make a move first. They'd give him a short grace period out of deference for who he worked for. He rubbed the stubble of his shaved head and gave his beard a pull. He opened the door slowly.

"Come on," the woman called again.

He moved cautiously forward, knowing that the neighborhood was just as interested in his response as they were in her. As he stalked down the weed-covered walk, he tried to place her. She definitely wasn't from the neighborhood. Clothes were too clean and in good repair. She was well fed. He tried not to assume too much from the Patriot lab coat – she'd probably stolen it. He shouldn't have been susceptible, but he found himself charmed by the pink hair, the cheerful way it popped against her dark skin. When he got to within a few feet, he eyed her and the food with equal suspicion, at the same time unable to hide his own desire for it. Turning back to the children in the window, he signaled for them to stay put, then back to the woman said, in his most indifferent tone, "Who're you?"

"Willa," she said. "I'm from here."

"Willa," he repeated, thinking on it. "None from here can afford a food drone, much less a quartet of 'em."

She shrugged. "Nevertheless, here they are," she answered, holding the bowl toward his face. He inhaled reflexively and felt his mouth go swollen with saliva. She noticed.

"Stop waiting. Call those kids out here, take this."

Everard allowed her to place the bowl into his hands. The warm, fragrant steam filled his nostrils and suddenly he was a kid again, celebrating Thanksgiving on the bayou. He gave in, shoveled a mouthful. It was like waking up in a better time. Nostalgia hit him like a shot of adrenaline and he felt his chemistry change. He spun to the door. "Come on, come on out! Hurry on."

All ten children poured from the home. They reached him and stood quietly in line, a learned behavior, taught for their own good.

"Grab a bowl, each of you," he said, handing them out. "Lynn,

Ryan, Octavia, Jack: help the tikes first, unnerstand?" The older children nodded and went to work doling servings to their younger compatriots. None took a grain of rice before the smaller children had their bowls.

Restraint inside the other homes failed as doors erupted with a similarly diverse ragtag compliment of children, galloping ahead of the few adults who tried to herd them. Everard finished his bowl, which Willa graciously reloaded with a mountainous spoonful.

"You got money," he remarked, swallowing. "You highblood or employed?"

"Employed."

"Doin' what?"

"Phlebotomist," she said.

So she *was* Patriot. *"Reaper."* He grunted with a note of disdain. "Patriot know you're doin' this?"

"It's not illegal," said Willa.

"Yeah, well," he said over a mouthful of hot rice, "something good happens in AB Plus, it's usually 'cause it's illegal. Speakin' of, how'd a reaper come into the funds to buy all this?"

"Production bonus," said Willa. "I didn't catch your name."

"Everard. Everard Oladc Augustus Alison."

"That's a mouthful," she said extending a hand. "Willa Mae Wallace."

"That's an old name."

"I'm an old person."

He grinned through his chewing. "You ain't look old in that hair."

"Well, I'll consider that a compliment," she said.

"It was," Everard answered, filling his mouth again. "Tryin' to bring back All Hallows' Eve?"

"Afraid not," she answered. "Chrysalis got mine. I wear this so my grandson can find me if we ever get separated."

He nodded, understanding. "Hmmph. Smart."

One of the drones closed its cargo panels and lifted off. A group of better than forty children had cleaned it of food, piranha-like, in minutes. The other drones left shortly after, but the population of the street remained to revel in the glow of good fortune.

"You kids gather," said Everard. They assumed a single file line, bowls in hand, along the uneven and broken concrete of the sidewalk. "This is Willa Mae Wallace. She brought us this food tonight. She's lowblood just like all you. And guess what? She has a job." Their faces lit. "Hardly has to sell any red neither. That's because she listened when the teachers visited. She studied hard. Read those books. And now she makes her own coin, y'all unnerstand?" The children nodded eagerly. "Now, each of you tell Ms Willa thank you."

One by one, each child shook her hand. Everard felt a tinge of guilt at what he had said, but told himself it was the right thing, to give them hope. Otherwise, there was nothing.

CHAPTER FOUR

ANTIGEN

A substance that stimulates an immune response in the body. There are over 300 known antigens found on blood cells, with those in the ABO blood group being the most immunoreactive, and therefore most important to screen for.

Willa put the kettle on as Isaiah sawed logs. The boy could sleep through anything – an inconvenient fact, in her opinion, as the trauma of previous evacuations rekindled. Forty years had passed since she'd slept in a way that allowed her to forget she was trying to sleep. Lying in bed ten miles from ground zero, she'd been dreaming when Chrysalis bloomed, but the blink of light had burnt through her lids like a camera's flash.

She still saw it whenever she shut her eyes, the mushroom cloud that came with no warning and no explanation. In the years that had followed, the government gave a smattering of possible reasons. Rogue nation-states, terrorism, sleeper-cells, et cetera. Even the name evolved over the years until the citizenry settled on a moniker that described the bomb's effect on their way of life. Chrysalis. The thing that changed everything.

The bombs that followed were the natural sequelae of the first, with the country now engaged in a never-ending war with someone, though the authorities were cagey about saying who. They justified their surreptitiousness under the umbrella of protecting intelligence, and with the press largely dismantled, the public had long given up in pushing for answers. Whoever was in charge now – whether it was the shell of the once elected government, or its largest private contractor to which it had gradually ceded power – kept information to a trickle.

Since Chrysalis, sleep had been a fit of wakeful vigilance. Regular PatrioCast notifications kept the prospect of extinction fresh, feeding her mind's anxiety over another burst of annihilating light. In contrast, the depth of Isaiah's own sleep troubled her – he was a slow riser, and she worried on the lost seconds that might mean the difference between life and death. As if on cue, her touchstone lit up.

▽ **PATRIOCAST 10.21.67** ▽

Northwestern Gray Zone Update – Traumatic blood loss: up. Acute illness down. Radiation sickness stable. Anemia of chronic diseases climbing for the following cancers: lung, bladder, ovarian, thyroid.
Total Units Required last 30 days: 2,874,234
Total Units Provided by Patriot: 2,874,234

Northeastern Gray Zone Update – Traumatic blood loss: up. Acute illness stable. Radiation sickness climbing. Anemia of chronic diseases rising for: stomach, lung, liver, colon, breast, gallbladder, esophageal, bladder, ovarian, leukemia, thyroid.
Total Units Required last 30 days: 10,120,098
Total Units Provided by Patriot: 10,120,098
#Lives Saved Estimate last 30 days: 50,000
#Lives Saved Estimate year-to-date: 190,000

▽ *Patriot thanks ALL DONORS. Your gift matters!* ▽

Willa went to the hallway and pulled on her aubergine rain boots. A small mirror hung on the wall catty-corner to the door. It was easy to avoid, and she usually did, but it seemed to call to her today, so she faced it.

There was Elizabeth, her daughter, gazing back. She always did, just looking older than when the Trade had finally taken her: skin pulling down on those high-up cheekbones, crows' feet creeping, ear lobes stretching. They'd resembled twins more than mother and daughter – friends and strangers alike had made that clear. The mirror showed Willa, but she never saw herself, only what Elizabeth would have become had her years not been stolen – had she not been failed by her mother.

A knock at the door.

Willa broke from the imagined reunion, stepped back into the main room to check on Isaiah, then went to see who was paying visits during breakfast time. She placed her touchstone on the door, which brought up the outside view through an external camera. A man and a young woman, both in suits, stood smiling. The woman gave a wave.

"Ms Wallace? We're from Central City Collection. Just hoping to follow up on the incident from night before last."

They were Patriot. And from the Heart, no less. "No need," said Willa through the door. "I'm totally fine."

"We won't take much time at all," said the woman. "Just some necessary paperwork I'm afraid, seeing as you're an employee."

Willa didn't like them coming to her home, but Patriot did as it pleased. The lines of privacy had been pushed backward for years now, and there was no reclaiming lost territory. "Just a moment," she sighed.

"Not a problem, Ms Wallace. No rush."

"Isaiah," she said, nudging his head, "get up, go get dressed."

The boy rose semi-conscious from his pallet and walked into the bathroom on autopilot. Willa did a once-over of the apartment. She wasn't sure why; she'd done nothing wrong. She kicked some trinkets underneath their reused-crate bookcase and flipped down the four manual locks on the apartment door.

Upon opening the door, her eyes went to the visitors' lapel pins. They were identical to those the company phlebotomists had been given, with the new, friendlier Patriot insignia – the letter P impaling a valentine-style heart, rather than the vintage, anatomically correct organ as worn by Jesper Olden.

"May we?" said the woman. The request was perfunctory, a formality understood by all three individuals.

"Of course, Miss…?" prompted Willa, stepping aside.

"Scynthia Scallien, Patriot logistics, and this is Mr Hunter, Patriot security," she said in a disarmingly courteous way.

"Please excuse my place. I live here with my grandson, and he–"

"Isaiah?" said Scallien. "He's almost ten, is that right?"

Willa felt her throat tighten. "Yes, that's him."

Seeing her tension, Scallien said, "He was enrolled in PatrioTot, just a few years back, Ms Wallace."

"Right," said Willa. Isaiah peeked in from the other room and Scallien gave a playful wave. He trotted out, ever intrigued by new people.

Hunter smiled grandly, offering a hand. Isaiah took it proudly and gave it a robust shake.

"Very strong, master Isaiah!" Hunter crowed. "You might be a boxer some day!"

Isaiah made fists and considered them, smiling. Hunter shadowboxed some and Isaiah dodged the fictional blows.

"Isaiah," said Willa. "'Saiah! That's enough, now."

"It's not a problem, Ms Wallace," said Hunter, presenting a lollipop from somewhere in his black trench coat. He gestured to Isaiah. "Is it OK?"

Willa swallowed hard. She hated taking anything from Patriot, but how could she object? She'd taken the five hundred, after all, and this Hunter person seemed harmless enough. She nodded and Isaiah snatched the candy and made to scurry away. "Hey now!" she hollered. "What do you say?"

He turned around. "Thank you, sir."

"Very welcome," said Hunter.

"Don't eat that now, you save it for after supper!"

"Yes, Grandma," he called back, headed to his room.

The kettle began its low whistle and Willa went to cut the burner. "You all are lucky, kettle's hot. Please, sit down. Mint tea?"

"No thank you for me, Ms Wallace," said Scallien. "Hunter?"

"I'm fine, ma'am. Just came from the Pantry."

"The Pantry. Years since I've eaten there." Willa poured herself a mug. "Do they still have that *croque madame*?"

"They sure do," he answered. "Had it this morning."

Willa could almost taste the sandwich – the toasted bread, the ham, melted swiss, fried egg on top...

"We needn't be long, Ms Wallace," said Scallien, taking a seat and steering things back to business. "We just wanted to drop in and see how you were doing after the accident." She found her own touchstone and set it on the table, an unspoken signal that the conversation was being recorded.

"Accident?" Willa said, returning to Scallien.

"Has it been so long already?" laughed the woman. "Two nights ago. Outside SCS Distrib."

"Oh, no, ma'am," said Willa, pressing harder than necessary against the tea bag on the rim of her cup. "I wasn't hurt. Honestly. It didn't come near me. I don't get all the fuss. Mr Olden himself gave me a ride home, you know, and I'm embarrassed to say he deposited five hundred in my account. I told him I didn't need it."

Scallien doodled a fingertip over the surface of the table, considered an image only she could see and smiled. "Already spent it though, right Ms Wallace?" she said, raising a playful eyebrow.

There it was, ice in the air.

"Is that a problem?" Willa asked. "If it is, I'll pay the money back."

"Of course not. We're pleased to see that you were able to make use of it," Scallien answered with renewed warmth. "Interesting choice though, letting go of that kind of money so quickly. I could imagine a hundred things you might spend it on." She looked around the apartment.

Willa felt the woman judging their home and suppressed the urge to say something.

"Anyway, we assembled some docs," Scallien said, gesturing to Hunter, who placed a screen onto the table. "Standard stuff. As with any settlement, there's a mandatory arbitration clause should there be any subsequent disputes, and of course, an NDA for you to sign."

"Settlement?"

"What did you think that five hundred was for, Ms Wallace?"

Willa felt like she was being slowly dismantled. "Like I said, ma'am, I wasn't hurt."

"And we're all thankful for that. You're a top performer at your precinct. A real profit center." Scallien's words, while whitewashed in company-speak, were now delivered with what seemed like genuine happiness at Willa's wellbeing. The hot and cold, casual schizophrenia of her manner made Willa dizzy. "And the NDA is a non-disclosure agreement that we'll require as a retroactive condition precedent to the monies advanced," Scallien continued, redirecting Willa's attention back to the screen. "Like I said, very simple. Boilerplate, really."

"Non-disclosure of what? That a drone crashed?"

"The fact of the crash, yes. Can't have word of something so embarrassing come out in the weeks right before Patrioteer." She flashed through the pages on Hunter's screen and pointed to a line there. "*Each and every, all and singular*. That means the agreement covers anything you may have witnessed appurtenant to the accident."

"Like what?"

"I don't know, Ms Wallace, I wasn't there."

Willa felt she was being shaken down by ambiguities and suggestion. With Patriot, even casual interactions felt like interrogations. "You mean the fact that Mr Olden took me home?"

Part of Scallien's face smiled and part of it didn't. "I meant what I said, Ms Wallace. Any. Thing. You-may-have-seen. Is that clear?"

The woman's vague allusions had Willa wondering if Scallien knew it was possible she'd seen the empty vaults. But she dared not probe, and simply answered, "Yes."

"Wonderful." Scallien stood and put her hands on her narrow hips, suddenly jovial. "We can't have people hearing about how you get paid if there's a drone crash, can we? Every phlebotomist in the city would race down to distribution hoping to get bonked on the head."

"But it didn't–"

"Yes, yes, I know. You've said. Completely unharmed. Lucky for you, eh?"

Willa forced herself to summon a weak smile and nodded.

"I will shoot this to your touchstone so you can have a lawyer look at it."

A lawyer for someone in the blood districts? In O Minus maybe, but not outside of it. "No," said Willa, "that's alright. I'll sign."

"Great. That's good to hear. Much more efficient."

Hunter scrolled to the bottom of the viewer and handed it to Willa. She'd long ago realized the futility of reading documents before signing them. Nobody had a choice on contract terms. Negotiation? A myth like civil rights. She squiggled her signature.

"We'll be out of your hair, now, Ms Wallace," she said. "And what hair it is."

"Thank you for hosting us," said Hunter.

"And remember the non-disclosure," said Scallien with a conspiratorial tap to the side of her nose. "Not a word. About any of it."

"I understand."

"I hope so. Violation of the NDA warrants liquidated damages." She exited. Hunter, seeming less of a cold fish than Scallien, shook Willa's hand and the door closed behind them.

Willa held her mug and stared at the door. Liquidated damages?

Isaiah emerged from his room, a giant towel wrapped up over his chest. "Who were they, anyway?"

"Nobody, sweetheart," said Willa. "Go get ready for school." She considered her tea, but no longer wanted any.

CHAPTER FIVE

HEMATOCRIT
The proportion, as measured by volume, of whole blood that is made up by red blood cells.

Everard made the long trek toward Donor Eight, checking and rechecking the blood bag stuck to his arm underneath his old beige windbreaker. The wind was biting some today and he lamented the decision to keep on the cargo shorts rather than something that might cover his pale and largely hairless calves. The terrain changed as he crossed from the low, to mid, to high-blood neighborhoods and so did the people. While even though the O-negs were "poor" by historical standards, they seemed at least to give half a damn about how they looked. It made him self-conscious and he felt for the unshaven scruff under his chin and neck. He threw his hood up, curled himself against the cold, and lit a cigarette.

Nearer to the donor station, he checked the blood bag another time and lit a new cigarette with the stump of the old. He flicked the butt into the street and cased the surroundings for po-po, then tried to remember all of the Locksmith's instructions about what he was supposed to say and how he was supposed to act. He didn't like associating with non-criminals. He didn't mind being sordid himself – it was all he'd ever known. It was the corruption of otherwise innocent folks that made him nervous, made him feel guilty. Especially now that they were going to involve this Willa Wallace who'd shown up in AB Plus with food drones like some pink-topped angel. The worst part about being a criminal wasn't comeuppance by other criminals, or even getting pinched. It was the collateral damage. Shrapnel taken by bystanders. He nervously checked the bag again and told himself it was for the greater good. Because it was.

Inside, he scanned the lines trailing back from each of the booths and spotted her immediately. Against the drab grays and burgundies of the station, she was a right scoop of ice cream. He hopped into her line and waited, noting at the same time that hers seemed to move double the speed of the others.

It came to be his turn and it took a second for her eyes to show their recognition. He'd hoped not to startle her too bad, but it was too late for that.

"Mr Alison," she said, blinking a few times as she adjusted to the shock of seeing him there in front of her.

"Ms Willa," he said. "Hey. Just bringing in some red."

"A bit far afield, aren't you?" she asked, her voice betraying the slightest anxiety. He had to give her credit, she covered well for an amateur. A less experienced person than himself might think she wasn't nervous at all. He was nervous too, of course. Hid it better than she did, though.

"You know DS6 is just outside of AB Plus," she said. "What brings you over here?"

"It's cold but the sun's out. Good enough reason as any to take a walk." He undid the zip on the arm of his jacket to expose his blood bag and allowed Willa to remove it. She considered his face passively while processing the bag in a fluid sequence of practiced motions. Everard let his eyes follow the bag as it passed over the ever-important needle scanners, but didn't allow himself to swallow too hard. The few seconds it took for her to process the blood felt like forever.

She looked up at him, her brow creased.

He swallowed too hard.

"Your hematocrit is high," she said.

"It is?" He swallowed again. An audible gulp this time. He was only forty feet from the doors and his flight instincts were doing a calculus. "OK," he said, trying to keep cool, "what's that mean?"

"Could be a lot of things," she answered. "You're probably just dehydrated."

"Dehydrated?" he asked, but only out of a desire to stall so he could better case the situation.

"Dehydrated," she repeated, then paused like she was waiting for something.

A countdown began in his mind. Something was wrong with the blood. He was going to have to book it. He pivoted a foot, planting it to run.

"I need you to touchstone in, Mr Alison." She gestured to a small interface on his side of the booth.

Touchstone in. Right. It meant the blood had cleared. Relief warmed him like a blanket. "Heh, yeah," he said, "guess that walk didn't wake me up like I thought it did."

She made a passive chuckle as he dug for his touchstone. "I keep mine on a lanyard," said Willa, holding it up from around her neck with a smile. "You might think about doing the same."

"You got me there, Ms Willa," he answered, finally prying his own device from out of his jacket. He tapped the touchstone to the interface.

Willa checked a readout on her side of the booth, then looked back up and her smile showed a hint of bewilderment. "B-neg?" she remarked.

"I know," he interjected, "I could probably live closer to the mid-bloods with bourgeoise sauce like that, right? It's the kids, though, see? I take care of them–"

Willa glanced at her line, which had begun shuffling with agitation. "I'm sorry, it's not my business. I was just surprised to see your phenotype coming out of AB Plus, that's all."

"Yeah, I gotchu," he said.

"Enjoy the rest of your day, Mr Alison."

He leaned in some, but without being too obvious, whispered, "We got to talk."

"I'm sorry, about what?" Her cool was cracking. "I can't. I'm working right now."

"Later then," he said, moving through. "I'll see you." And then he was out the door.

Underneath the heavy steel awning of the donor station entrance, he exhaled like he hadn't taken a breath the whole time he'd been inside. He snapped a cigarette from the soft pack and lit it as quickly as he could. The smoke warmed his lungs and calmed his nerves. He'd done it. Was he supposed to be happy?

The return trip home was marked by conflicting emotions. He'd scared her, that much was clear. Hadn't meant to, but there was no way to do what he had to do without disrupting the balance. He wished they could have chosen somebody else, someone who wasn't as good as this Willa seemed to be. But it was the right decision. She was the person they needed, like it or not.

The blood bag though. It had cleared Patriot's system. He straightened some from his usual hunch, and allowed a small amount of pride to drip through his veins. The Locksmith had been right.

CHAPTER SIX

VASOCONSTRICTION

The narrowing of blood vessels due to the contraction of their muscular walls, resulting in decreased blood flow.

Willa glanced to Claude, who, in the trough of a mid-shift stupor, had failed to notice the conversation she'd just had with Everard. It'd probably knock her count down by four or five units for the day, but she'd still process dozens more than the other phlebotomists.

She could still see Everard out on the street through the glass smoking a cigarette. What had that been all about? Probably angling to get more money. These were desperate times, especially in the lowbloods. She would have likely done the same thing if their roles were reversed. She hoped that's all it was. At least he was B-neg. He could fetch good value for it. Help those kids.

Willa opted to walk home, even though it meant crossing through the risky lowblood neighborhoods. She viewed each day after Chrysalis as a day that she shouldn't have had in the first place – the fact that she happened to be far enough from the blast had been a matter of pure luck. Ever since then, she'd only worried about herself to the extent that it would affect Isaiah. So even though walking home after work took her through AB Plus, making her a target for blood muggings, each trip was drone fare saved. That meant more for Isaiah after she was gone. External threats like those who would rob an old woman were one thing, but she was also mindful of her fading verdure – achy bones and flagging energy. Aside from the curse of lowblood, she had good genes, but even those only bought you time. She just hoped there would be enough of it for her to see Isaiah become his own man.

At an intersection a block ahead, a man stood casually against a pole that held a loose string of defunct traffic lights. Anyone hanging idle outside was almost certainly a threat, and Willa changed her vector in order to turn east one block before she normally would. Seeing this, the man straightened from his post and followed. Another glance and she felt a jolt of regret as she recognized who it was, his oversized cargo shorts an unambiguous identifying feature. She had purposefully avoided going down his street – in fact, she'd gone four blocks wide of it. But here he was.

Willa continued on, hastening her clip to a point just shy of trotting. Doing her best to look unbothered by his approach, she kept her eyes in front and her feet moving.

The top of a gentle rise with another intersection came into view. Everard's foot beats hastened and she could hear his labored breathing. "Ms Willa," he called from behind. "Hold up."

She turned to see him take a last puff of his smoke and flick it onto the ground before making the final jog to catch up with her.

He came up alongside at the top of the walk, a fresh cigarette already planted in his lips. "Evenin', Ms Willa."

"Everard."

"We got to pow wow," he said, sparking it.

"I'm sorry, I don't have time," she said. "I need to be home."

He took the cigarette in his fingers, flicked the ash and blew the smoke out with the wind. "So, you'll be a little late, that's all."

"Good night, Everard," she said with a polite dip of her chin as she turned north.

He placed a hand on her bicep. "We're gonna have our chat," he said. "You'll be home after." His grip startled her, not because it was tight or painful, but because it wasn't. A gesture that in any other context might have been interpreted as comforting – friendly even – was different here; a delicate warning, a diplomatic favor that told her not to press any further, lest she call forth stronger persuasions. Relenting, she turned down her mouth and gave a small nod. Maintaining his latch, Everard steered her back the way they'd come with enough authority to let her know it was his show now.

"Can I know where we are going?" she asked, determined to keep her composure.

"Jethrum's Diner."

"Everard, I don't–"

"I just want to talk, that's all. Can't talk business on an empty stomach."

"I only have enough for myself and Isaiah."

"What I'm offering will help yourself and Isaiah."

"I don't understand." She twisted in his grasp.

He let go. "Sorry about all that. Just keep walking."

"What's going on? What do you want? Please."

"When we get some food, I'll spill."

They traveled without speaking for another eight blocks to what was once a food kitchen, now the closest thing AB Plus had to a restaurant. They couldn't serve food for free anymore, and what they did serve was heavy in potatoes, fatty cuts of mystery meat, and local fungi. Everard urged Willa toward the door. "Two dinners," he said to the man at the front, "she got it."

"Just one," said Willa. "I'm not hungry." She bumped her touchstone to the interface.

They sat at the end of a long line of picnic tables with real metal cutlery set out. Willa watched Everard visit each of the four serving stations where he piled potatoes, greasy meat, and a wilted green of some sort onto a plate, then topped it with a blackened crust of bread.

Returning to the table, Willa watched as he dove in, growing angrier at the gambit, whatever it was, and its effect in making her late home. "I'm telling Isaiah I'll be home soon," she said, typing a message. Then she sat, fuming silently, until Everard finished sopping up the residue with bread bark. He licked his fingers clean.

Willa said, "I am going to get up and leave if you don't make yourself clear."

"You ain't leaving," he said. And she saw in his face that while he preferred to do things without resorting to violence, he was well capable of it. "Look," he continued, "no need to make a scene, alright?" He glanced around at the dozen other patrons in the place. "All these folk think we're friends. Just out for a bite after selling some red."

"Get to the point."

"Got a proposition. I ain't here to take advantage of your good charity."

"The food in your belly says otherwise."

Everard laughed as he wiped his mouth. "Well, you right on that count."

"Go on."

"You heard of the Locksmith?" he asked.

"Of course I've heard of him," answered Willa. "I caught him on a bag hack years ago."

"That must have been satisfyin' for you," he said, taking a toothpick from a shot glass in the center of the table and going to work.

"Everard, what do you want?"

"Not what I want. What *he* want."

"And what is that?"

"Simple…"

She saw it coming. "No."

"You ain't even heard what it is yet!"

"I don't need to hear it. I know what you want."

Perhaps he wasn't used to people resisting and he stroked his beard with annoyance and sucked the air through his teeth. He leaned forward. "Just a few bags to start. Handful a month. You pass 'em, we touchstone your cut. Never bother you again."

"He knows I can't do that. *Won't* do that. It's impossible anyway."

"People are suffering, Ms Willa."

"I know that. I'm in it."

He canted back for a belly-laugh. "You a reaper, Ms Willa! You're above it. You ain't in it."

"No, Everard. Just no. Look, I won't say anything. Just leave me out of it. I've got my grandson to take care of."

"Nothing I can do," he said with a shrug.

"Sure you can! Pick someone else."

"You who the Locksmith picked," said Everard. "Not somebody else."

"Why?"

"You're smart," he said, moving the toothpick to the next tooth. "Like him."

"If he's so damned smart, then he should know I would never do anything to put my grandson at risk." She pushed her chair back and got up to leave.

"Say no and we just run all our hacks through your stall." He played with the toothpick, then dropped it in his bowl. "Patriot'll assume you're in on it either way."

Willa glared down at him, wishing she'd never come back to AB Plus. "My record is perfect," she spat. "They would never believe that."

He leaned back in the folding chair and put his hands behind his head. "Oh really? You the one out here in public just bought dinner for the Locksmith's first lieutenant."

She leaned over the table between them, bringing herself eye-to-eye with the man who threatened to take away everything. "If I see you anywhere near DS8, I'll have the police called."

His face broke into a crinkled smile. "And what makes you think it'll be me?"

Willa crossed her arms. They had her at every angle.

"Besides," he said, "I don't think you want to be callin' no Five-O."

"Why's that, Everard?"

"You already in on the scheme."

"How do you figure?"

"I come through your line earlier today, Ms Willa."

"So?"

He snorted lightly through his nose. "I ain't B-neg."

With that, Everard rose from the table and pushed his chair neatly in. "Thanks for the dinner, Ms Willa. Think it over a few days. I'll be in touch and you can tell me what you want to do." And then he was gone.

Willa stood statue-still in the spot where she'd made her big stand against the gangster blood hacker, chastened and with a full appreciation that she was powerless to stop what was coming. Numbness spread as her mind set the stage for how it would all play out. If she refused the Locksmith, his hackers would run their scam through her booth, implicating her anyway. She could cooperate and end up fired and imprisoned when their efforts eventually failed. Or she could turn them in and reap the consequences of those who tattle on organized crime. Either way, life as she knew it was over. Her small act of charity had doomed her and thrown Isaiah's future into question. She'd been targeted by the Locksmith because kindness, in the end, was weakness.

CHAPTER SEVEN

$C_6H_9NA_3O_9$
Chemical formula for trisodium citrate dihydrate.

The first sign of a bad transfusion is a sense of impending doom. It is an actual, articulable sensation felt by the recipient of mismatched blood that is so clear in the mind that medical personnel are trained to ask about it – or were trained to ask about it, way back when Willa was coming up.

There are other symptoms, of course: fever, chills, discolored skin, flank pain, shortness of breath, etcetera, but it was the feeling of impending doom that had always stuck with Willa. It seemed to make cosmic sense. You behave carelessly with a gift as precious as blood, and the consequences ought to be equal to the good it can bring. And since the only cause of a mismatch was human error, Willa had always supported Patriot's exceptionally strict testing and safety requirements.

Being AB-positive, and therefore a universal recipient, meant she'd never get the wrong blood, but now she understood the sensation she'd learned about. Impending doom. That hackers routinely tried to compromise Patriot employees was nothing new, and Willa had known it was a matter of time before they came for her. Now she'd gone and hastened their arrival by flying in food drones to feed one of their soldiers, foolishly advertising wealth she didn't have, and then let herself be framed.

She wanted to believe Everard was bluffing. All logic said he had to be. She'd handled his blood bag, scanned it. The phenotypes in the bag matched his touchstone. Everything checked out. No system wide hack had been reported, which meant it could only have been a bag hack – a counterfeit bag – and his bag had been completely normal.

Or maybe not... Maybe Everard was telling the truth. If anyone could pull off such a feat, at least by reputation, it was the Locksmith. He would be playing a long game: use a single hack – if indeed it had been a hack – to make it look like she was in on it from the beginning, force her cooperation, enable them to ramp up the volume of their operation. Would she know when they began running it through her stall or would Everard's associates simply show up in her line one day? Everything she had worked for seemed pushed to the precipice, teetering there until it either crashed to the ground or she figured out some way to pull it back.

Her touchstone pinged. A notification for a deposit of two hundred and twenty-three. Reality hit like a hammer punching the nail in on the first strike. Two hundred and twenty-three was half of four hundred and forty-six; the day's bid for a single unit of B-negative. She shook her head in disbelief. She'd run their counterfeit bag and now they'd paid her a cut. They had her.

Crossing into the lowbloods, she felt propelled upon a cresting wave of disgust. What had become of the world? The little girl that she'd once been could never have imagined her own future, that she would become a "reaper," taking blood from people to give it to the government. How had the human body become a property to be mined, so that she could now be made a pawn for a hacker looking to cheat the system?

It came back to Chrysalis, of course, because everything came back to Chrysalis. It had changed the world so drastically and all at once, that what came after – a new way of living in the name of national defense – was expected, embraced even. Changes came, always in the name of the Greater Good. Changes in everyday life, like the subtle expansion of surveillance and police powers. Like the restrictions of rights, after few had questioned it and even fewer opposed. Incremental steps that, looking back, had amounted to gradual surrender by the people of what little freedom they'd had left. When another bomb came, this time on the East Coast – Kannikin Redux – the government's course seemed to have been validated. But then it took a further, final step, across what should have been a red line: the Harvest. Willa wasn't formally educated, but she was a student of her own six decades, and from that she'd identified a pattern: tragedy begat patriotism, patriotism begat opportunism, opportunism begat poverty.

And poverty begat blood hackers looking to compromise unfortunate phlebotomists.

She'd lost her way along with everybody else, went right along with it when her blood bank had been commandeered by Patriot years back – not that she'd had any choice. Willa never stopped loving her country, and she wanted to help those suffering in the Gray Zones, yet she couldn't shake the feeling that the Harvest and the trade were doing more harm than good. They'd become locked in a perpetual loop. Wouldn't the country be stronger, better able to defend itself against whoever kept it pinned to the mat, if the population were strong and upright, veins full?

Willa watched Isaiah blissfully spoon a gruel-like "Hearty Grain Stew With Beef Flavoring" into his mouth and thought about what it was like to have eaten real beef stew back in the day and how much she missed it. Watching the boy eat she considered what a gift it was to have no frame of reference. After finishing his meal, Isaiah hopped from his chair, skipped to his room, and then bounced back to the table. Willa collected the dishes and brought them to the sink for a rinse.

The water gurgled from the tap and she ran a sponge over the spoon and bowl, and her mind turned back to Everard. If he was serious – and if he truly worked for the Locksmith, then he was – she'd have to quit. Better to have no job at all than to end up in prison, or worse. She'd saved some money. They'd always figured things out before.

A sound, like the crinkling of plastic, tickled her eardrum. She turned to Isaiah.

He'd unwrapped the lollipop that Hunter had given him and was about to put it in his mouth.

"Hold on now," said Willa, walking over. "May I have a lick of that before you eat it?"

"Sure," said Isaiah, happy to share in the wealth. "You can even have two licks."

Willa smiled at the boy's generosity and took the candy. It wasn't that she necessarily thought there was anything wrong with it, but Isaiah was all she had, so she forgave herself some paranoia. She touched the candy to the tip of her tongue.

Now, there were a lot of things that Willa hadn't experienced in the decades since the bombs started falling: riding in a car, going to see a movie, sleep, a glass of wine. But there was another, the absence of which she had long stopped missing, lost to the years. What was once as common and ubiquitous as water or air before it disappeared from the world altogether soon after Chrysalis. Sugar.

Her tongue felt like it'd been struck by lightning and saliva poured into her mouth. Gone was the sickly-sweet and lingering film that came with the artificial sweeteners that had become the norm. There was no mistaking the real thing. And Isaiah had never had it. A child who'd never had sugar! Her smile bloomed as she leaned forward, eager to share the new experience. And then she stopped, and her joy evaporated.

There wasn't supposed to be any sugar anywhere. Fallout had destroyed or contaminated most crops, including sugarcane and corn. Everyone knew that. So how did sugar end up in a piece of candy? Her stomach knotted.

"I'm so sorry, baby," she said, locating the wrapper. "There might be something wrong with this. It could be dangerous."

"What?" he said. "I can't have it? Are you serious? You had some!"

"Isaiah, I want nothing more than for you to be able to eat your lollipop. But we don't really know the people who gave it to you, right? I tasted something that I don't trust. It might not be safe."

She could see him working through his disappointment, fighting to hold back tears. "OK, Grandma," he said, still eyeing the treat as she dropped it into the trash.

By the time she got Isaiah to bed, her brain was churning. Once his breathing took on the even meter of sleep, she left his side and went back into the kitchen and dug the candy from the garbage. She placed it onto the counter and stared. How was it that Patriot had anything, much less children's candy, made with sugar? And why? The sugar was contaminated. Radioactive.

Unless it wasn't. Scenarios unfolded as she envisioned a world where sugar had made its return. What if the fallout was no longer a problem? It had been eight years since Goliath. Maybe it had all dissipated. It had to go away sometime. Of course, all of that had to do with half-lives and whatnot, stuff she didn't have any clue about. Claude probably would. It was nice to think that sugar might be worked back into the system, and that they might be able to afford some from time to time to sweeten things up. All of the different foods they could add it to, the thought was like reopening a mothballed amusement park. A little glimmer of normal coming back.

Willa straightened from the counter and turned back to the room. Something nagged. A thing that she'd once known but had forgotten, squirreled away in the dusty crannies of her memory. Sugar was important for another reason, she was sure of it, but try as she might, she couldn't suss it from the cobwebs.

She went to the bookcase underneath the window. Careful not to topple the few struggling herbs on top, she ran a finger across the books stacked neatly inside. Years back, when everyone else had tossed all of their paper records and uploaded their lives to the Cloud, Willa had taken the opposite course, retaining the most important volumes from her life in tangible form. Control was autonomy, so why hand it over to an invisible chamber in the sky? She remembered her incredulity as friends and acquaintances had jumped to save everything digitally, storing it all in the ether. Willa had asked them what would happen if somebody decided to deny them access to their files, their records, their photographs – their lives; why they had so much faith in the benevolence of things they couldn't see. They rarely answered with anything more than a retort about her own paranoia. After the third nuke, Astrid, when the Cloud was finally sealed for national security reasons, she'd known she'd been right, but took no joy in it.

War and transience had whittled her physical collection, but at least she had some evidence of the life she had lived. Two photo albums, a coverless dictionary, missalettes from the year of her confirmation, and a plastic folder with Isaiah's birth certificate safely tucked inside Elizabeth's. Underneath the rest, she found her old phlebotomy technician's workbooks. She flipped through one of them, its paper made soft by the years, and came to the chapter entitled APHERESIS. This was fractionation, the lost practice of separating whole blood into fractions: plasmapheresis, plateletpheresis, etc. The practice, if resurrected, would allow Patriot to pull just the components of blood it needed without taking everything at once. It had the potential not only to end the Harvest and the Trade, but it could knock the legs out from under a caste system based on the tumbling dice of heredity. More importantly for Willa, it would render blood hacking – and blood hackers – obsolete.

She turned the pages, scanning quickly over the paragraphs with a finger. Halfway into the chapter was a two-page layout of the fractionation process, a diagram showing the connection between donor and the extracorporeal unit where a centrifuge separated the blood. One line ran from the donor's arm into the apheresis machine. A second tube carried the unused serums from the machine back into the donor. Between the donor and the unit was a flag that identified the location where anticoagulant was added. A footnote identified the chemical. "Trisodium citrate." She'd forgotten the name, but that was it, *citrate*. It was the scarcity of citrate, an anticoagulant, that prevented Patriot from being able to fraction the blood.

Her heart thumped as she flipped to the index and found the entry for it. "Trisodium citrate: A salt of citric acid derived through fermentation of molasses with yeast."

Molasses.

Molasses came from sugar.

Patriot had sugar. A million questions came to mind. If they had the necessary ingredient for the anticoagulant, then why weren't they fractioning? Did they not know that sugar was back in production? Who was making the lollipops? She needed to get through to Patriot. And they needed to listen.

Early the next morning, Willa swooped into Donor Eight like a gale. Claude, who had the responsibility for all of the pre-shift equipment checks, wandered in from the cooler with a bag of A-neg. A small red dribble ran over the backs of his gloved fingers.

"Oh my God, are you OK?" Willa exclaimed.

Claude almost leapt through the ceiling. "No, no – Willa, I'm fine," he said, presenting the leaking bag for her to see. "These new bags – the suturing at the needle siphon is weak. I've notified Patriot. Just back there trying to clean out the bad ones." He looked at the clock. "Since when do you show up for unpaid minutes?"

Willa pursed her lips, happy, trying not to be too excited. "Claude," she said, "why don't we fractionate?"

"No anticoagulant. You know that."

"Right. Nukes took out the sugar. What manages to grow is contaminated."

"Yeah," said Claude. "What's up?"

Willa dug into the bag that hung crossways over her chest and held up the lollipop in its wrapper.

Claude considered it a moment. "What's that?"

"Candy, Claude."

"OK, and?"

"It's made with sugar."

He snorted. "That's impossible."

"I haven't tasted sugar in almost forty years, Claude," she said. "*This* is sugar."

"How do you know it isn't some new sugar sub and it's just really good."

"First of all, there has never been a sugar substitute I would call *good*. And if you had seen little girl Willa you wouldn't doubt my ability to recognize it. This is made with sugar." She shoved it toward him. "Go on, have a taste."

Claude waved it off. "No. This is nuts."

"Patriot doesn't grow the food, right?" she asked.

"I don't know, honestly," said Claude. "Maybe they do, they do everything else."

"Well whoever made this put sugar in it. And Patriot needs to know, don't they? Either there's radioactive sugar on the market that's got to get recalled, or sugar is back in production because it's clean." Willa got closer, excited. "If I'm right – and I am – that this is sugar and it turns out to be clean? Then it means we can make anticoag and reinstitute apheresis now."

"Best keep all that to yourself," he said. "You go spreading that around, it'll be your job. I won't be able to keep them from firing you."

Willa was baffled. "Why?"

"Because it's nuts. First off, there is no sugar, and if you start spreading a crazy rumor that we can split blood again, we'll have a riot. It will throw the entire program off."

"But what if I'm right, Claude? Think about how we live." She pointed through the front doors. "Think about how everyone else lives. The Harvest is killing people."

Claude softened, aware that Willa's daughter had been among those taken. "You think you know these people, but you don't know them like I do. One, they'll never give you the time of day."

"Ah. Well. I thought you might, um, run it up the chain," said Willa. "You could take credit for it, I don't care about that. Patriot is a huge bureaucracy. Maybe the food people don't talk to the blood people."

"I'm the supervisor of Station Eight in Southern City, Willa. Have been my whole career. They don't care what I have to say either." He looked at the cameras on the wall and lowered his voice. "But second of all: you think they want anything to change? You think they want things to be easier on the donors? Willa: listen to me. Drop this now. For your own good."

Willa knew Claude's *we're done here* tone and let him return to the cooler. But she wasn't about to let it go. The clock said ten minutes until open. She went outside, brought her touchstone to life.

▽ BEGIN PATRIOTEXT CONVERSATION ▽

W. M. WALLACE: Mr Olden, it's Willa Wallace, Station 8, from the other night at SCS distrib. I would like to ask for a short meeting with you to discuss an important issue that might be very helpful to the company.

A parcel service drone zipped by while she waited for a response. Her touchstone dinged with a reply.

JESPER OLDEN ▽: I'm sorry, Ms Wallace, I do not have time to meet with you. Have an excellent day.
W. M. WALLACE: I apologize for the bother. It's just about the non-disclosure agreement. I needed to tell you something.
JESPER OLDEN ▽: What do you need to tell me?
W. M. WALLACE: We need to have a conversation. Besides, you probably don't want me typing it out. I will if you want though.

No immediate response. She prayed that her gambit would work and checked the time. Two minutes until open. Donors began to collect outside the doors.

JESPER OLDEN ▽: Connecting you with an associate. She will handle. Good day.
SCYNTHIA SCALLIEN ▽: Hello, Willa. I will be at your precinct directly after close today.
W. M. WALLACE: Thank you ma'am. I will be here.

▽ END PATRIOTEXT CONVERSATION ▽

Willa quickly messaged a neighbor she trusted to get Isaiah safely home from school and headed back inside. She felt like pacing, but her stall kept her stationary. She teetered back and forth with anticipation. Nerves. Nine hours to go until Scynthia Scallien found out she hadn't been summoned to talk about an NDA. Willa wondered how long she'd have to discuss her idea if the woman stormed out, or worse, wrote her up. She banished the thought of termination from her mind. Certainly that wasn't in the cards?

As the day wore on and she relaxed a measure, only then did her thoughts turn to the AB Plus blood hacking syndicate and her limbo within it. They wanted her to pass blood for them, presumably their own AB-pos as highblood. During their impromptu dinner the night before, Everard had suggested that he'd already done it, bringing in low blood as B-neg, a slightly better phenotype in terms of price than AB-pos. Even though he had invoked the Locksmith, Willa still thought it likely that his claim was bluster. Sure, they'd sent her some money, but that didn't necessarily mean they'd pulled it off. If anything, it was just another point of pressure to get her to join their scam. Executing a bag hack was next to impossible anyway, even if a phlebotomist was in on it.

For every blood bag removed, there was a highly regulated process that had to be followed in order for blood to be accepted.

Before a donor could receive credit, the phlebotomist removed the bag and felt it for imperfections or alterations. This was more of an art than anything else, but over time, each phlebotomist knew exactly how a bag should feel; its weight, thickness, pliability, balance. Willa had done it so many thousands of times, that her fingers and hands were sensitive to the tiniest deviation from standard. Next, the donor's blood bag was pressed against a reflective square from which a sterilized needle-probe emerged in a random spot to pierce the resealable poly. It registered blood type, temperature, antibodies, diseases and organism of origin (it wasn't unusual for people to try and pass animal blood). And then the test repeated. Two probes for each bag. If any of the data read outside of parameters, the blood was rejected and incinerated. If it checked out normal, it received a laser-etched label and a blood-type designation before going into cold storage.

As security systems improved, so did the skills of those trying to fool it. Desperation was a mighty fuel for innovation, which meant that AB Plus was crawling with hackers, trying to trick the system to get better value. Willa understood their plight – she shared their curse – but their deception could lead to bad transfusions. It could kill. And she couldn't be a part of it.

All the more reason her meeting with Scallien had to go well.

CHAPTER EIGHT

IMMUNOREACTION

A defensive reaction to the presence of a substance which is not recognized as a part of the body.

The front door coded open at 5:30 sharp. Seeing Scallien now for the second time, Willa found herself mildly amused by the young woman's airs. Gliding elegantly atop stilted heels, she wore a trim black dress with a white scalloped collar, set off by an old-style Patriot insignia pin. Her gait was smooth, with no wasted movement, as if every step had been choreographed and rehearsed – a corporate robot in high fashion programed for upper management.

"Ms Wallace." Businesslike.

Willa straightened. "Hello, ma'am, er – Ms Scallien," she said. "Thank you for meeting with me."

"Of course," said Scallien. Then lowering her voice, "Now, what is this business with your NDA, please."

Claude came in from the freezer and froze when he saw the young woman.

"Mr Vergenne, good evening," she said, smiling powerfully. "Give us a few minutes, will you?"

"Sure," he said, and disappeared around the corner.

"So," Scallien continued, raising an eyebrow that temporarily eased the strain of a taut, golden ponytail, "about the NDA."

Willa had practiced what she would say, how she would broach the sleight of hand she'd performed in order to get the face-to-face, but decided to adopt a direct approach. "I have to apologize, Ms Scallien, I needed a meeting with Patriot management and this was the only way I could think of to get it."

Scallien's smoky eyelids cut across her inky irises and she folded her arms. "You told Olden this was about the NDA."

"It's not. I'm sorry."

"So you lied. To your employer." Her mouth spooled into a churlish grin. "To a Patriot board member."

Willa felt quicksand. "He's a board member? I didn't know. He told me he was head of security."

"Security is a board position at the Company, Ms Wallace. But I am not concerned with Patriot's organizational tree, I am concerned that you lied to one of its branches." She flashed a mechanical smile and turned for the door. "Good evening."

"I'll be brief!" shot Willa. "I have vital information for the company. I have this!" She held up the lollipop and her breath. Scallien ceased her retreat and tilted her jawbone inquiringly. "Make it quick."

Willa set the lollipop on the shelf of her stall.

Scallien inspected it, her face twisted with confusion. "Is that the candy Mr Hunter gave to your grandson?"

"Yes," said Willa, feeling her nerves.

"Why is it here on the counter?" She leaned further. "Why is it open? Did someone begin to eat it already?"

"That was me."

"Why is it here?"

"Forgive me if I am overprotective. I lost my daughter, and –"

"Make your point."

Willa poked the candy. "This was made with sugar."

Scallien smirked, shook her head. "I'm sure you're mistaken."

"With all due respect, I know what sugar tastes like, ma'am," said Willa. "Try it yourself."

"Sugar isn't harvested, Ms Wallace, and if it was it would be quarantined for radiation."

"Well, this is sugar. And it's sitting right here."

"This is not a conversation I ever envisioned having," Scallien scoffed. "Shielded agricultural space is reserved for necessary food crops. Sugar is not one of them. Why are you wasting my time with this?"

"Because either you're handing out radioactive lollipops–"

"I assure you we are not," Scallien interjected. "Everything goes through the becquerel scanners."

"OK, great," said Willa. "Then that means *somebody* has untainted sugar!"

"You're going to have to tell me why that matters."

Willa paused, half wondering if Scallien was just playing dumb. She finally filled the silence, "Molasses is made from sugar."

"Molasses?"

"It's how they make sodium citrate, ma'am."

The air seemed to cool around Scallien as she processed Willa's point. "I see." She shut her eyes and pinched the bridge of her nose with her thumb and forefinger. "This is just too rich for me. So you think you tasted sugar in a piece of candy and that means that there must be giant fields of sugar or corn or sorghum out there somewhere that we could use to produce molasses to make anticoagulant?"

"Exactly."

Scallien laughed. "But that would mean that we've chosen not to do so even though an anticoagulant would allow us to fractionate. The thing that is missing from your tortured conspiracy theory is… why? Why would Patriot purposefully avoid fractioning if we could do it? What are you accusing us of, Ms Wallace?"

For the first time in their back and forth, Willa caught a hint of defensiveness in Scallien's voice. There was something to it. She pressed on softly, "I'm not saying that's what you're doing. I'm saying maybe Patriot wasn't aware of it and I– I'm just bringing it to your attention. If I'm right, Ms. Scallien, it would change everything. The Harvest, the Trade, all of it. Patriot could end so much suffering."

Scallien didn't respond at first, and the air seemed to stop moving.

"Wishful thinking is a powerful intoxicant, isn't it, Ms Wallace? There is no sugar in that candy."

Willa thought of a question and didn't mean to voice it aloud. But it came out anyway. "How do you know? I mean – how can you be so certain, just standing there? Are you a sugar expert?"

"I'm in logistics, Willa."

"But..." Willa said, hesitating and unsure about the decision to wander into a cross-examination of her boss's boss, "You had no idea I was going to bring up sugar when you came in here and now you seem to know all about it."

Scallien's agitation cracked through. "Do you really think Patriot wouldn't notice if the key to fractionation was growing in a field outside of Alliance?"

"Is that where they're growing it?" Willa snapped.

Scallien's eyes burrowed into Willa's.

"I'm sorry. I was out of line," Willa said. "I was just concerned that Patriot might be unaware of the... situation." Her voice trailed off. Scallien assumed a flat expression, but Willa could see a new set of wheels turning.

"OK, alright," said Scallien in an amicable tone. "Let's do this: how about I take that for testing, then? If it comes back positive, then we'll know we have an issue. If not, then we'll just forget the whole episode. How does that sound?"

It sounded like Scallien wanted the candy. And immediately Willa became acutely aware that it was the only evidence she had to prove the company had sugar. "It's fine," Willa said, quickly trying to deescalate. "I'm sure I was just mistaken. I'm getting older, anyhow. Could be that." She forced a chuckle. When she reached for the candy, Scallien's hand fell upon her own.

"If you don't mind," said the young woman. "We'll test it. Get you an answer."

"You can just taste it for yourself, right here, if you want. Surely you recognize sugar."

Scallien's grip over Willa's hand tightened and her smile spread wide. "I'm afraid I don't like candy."

"Just taste it," Willa said.

"Give it to me," growled Scallien.

"You know I'm right," said Willa.

"Nonsense."

"Then why are you trying to take this from me?" The uncanny strength of Scallien's contracting grip made Willa wince. "Are you trying to steal the proof?"

Scallien wrenched her fingers between Willa's, ripping the candy away.

"I know what I tasted," said Willa.

"I'm sure you do."

"I'll tell Jesper, then," said Willa. "He should know. Everyone should know." She brought up her touchstone only to have Scallien swat it away. It snapped from its lanyard and spun across the floor.

"Ma'am?" Willa said, bewildered.

Scallien dropped the candy into her purse and squeezed the clasp. "You're not telling anyone anything."

Claude came in from the back room. "Ms Scallien? Willa?" he said. "Everything good out here?"

"Leave us be, Mr Vergenne. Ms Wallace and I are just having a little policy refresher."

He considered the touchstone lying on the ground. "Are you sure?"

Scallien cocked her head toward him mechanically.

Claude held up his hands in surrender and returned to the back room.

Scallien took up her own touchstone. "I'll write to Jesper myself. Tell him everything."

"Good," said Willa.

The woman smirked. "Not for you."

A direct threat for her job. The idea that the woman would threaten her livelihood, something they could take away on a whim – the act of holding that over her head, the humiliation of it – it was all too much. Life had always been a tightrope and the strands were snapping. "Tell him that I know your secret," said Willa. "Tell him the truth is out."

"That's exactly what I'm telling him."

Willa watched Scallien tap away like she was ordering takeout. "Ask him why Patriot doesn't fractionate while you're at it," she added.

Scallien rolled her eyes.

It wasn't adding up. In the space of days Willa had been witness to two anomalies that, on the surface at least, seemed unconnected. Yet something about it all made her think they were related. What did a crashed blood drone and sugar in a lollipop have to do with each other? The only thing that they had in common was Patriot's desire to keep them under wraps. But why? Maybe Scallien would put it together for her. Willa worked up the courage as Scallien typed, then finally got her words out.

"That drone was empty."

Scallien's eyes became slits. "What did you say?"

"I'll bet you they all were," Willa added for good measure. "That's why you wanted the NDA."

"Drones…" said Scallien, working to calm herself in the face of Willa's accusation, "…drones travel empty all the time for scheduled maintenance."

"There were eight drones, one from each donor station," Willa said, "and the one that crashed empty just happened to be the only one traveling for maintenance? That's a mighty big coincidence, ma'am."

"Well, it's the truth. And I am about done with this inquisition."

"Why pay me off then?"

"Bad PR, obviously," said Scallien. "News of a drone crash would hurt confidence in the blood supply."

"Drones crash," said Willa. "You don't go paying people off every time that happens, do you?"

"Not unless it happens the weeks before Patrioteer." She went back to typing. "Think about the optics of a drone crash just as the regional higher-ups are getting to town for the conference."

"The drones are just for show, aren't they?" continued Willa. "There's nothing in any of them." Speaking so openly was dangerous, but voicing her mind was like taking a deep inhalation of fresh air for the first time in thirty years. She knew better, but the levee was broken.

"You're in violation of your NDA right now, Ms Wallace."

"So it's true then."

The tiny woman's body seemed to flex like a coiled snake. "No, it's not true, but leveling baseless allegations against your employer puts you in violation of your agreement. Section 2, paragraph thirty-six, clause DD, subpart one."

"Well, then they lied about it on *The Patriot Report*, Miss Scallien. They reported a full take for SCS, but you and I know that didn't happen."

Scallien dropped her chin, leveled her eyes. "Nobody lied on *The Patriot Report*."

"Without that drone being full, they did."

Scallien was resolute. "Nobody. Lied. On *The Patriot Report*."

Oddly, Willa began to think the woman was telling the truth. If *The Patriot Report* was correct, then the blood was going out from distribution another way. "The drones are empty then. All of them. The blood must go out through the speedloop."

"Fine, Ms Wallace," Scallien allowed casually. "The drones are decoys, a distraction for would-be poachers to protect the actual transport vector. They also double as a flying advertisement for all the good we bring to the world. Now are you satisfied?" She read something on her touchstone and typed a response. "There. Now you know all the company secrets. I hope you're happy with the price you've paid for them."

"All the secrets except why you don't do fractionation." Why not throw it out there? She was losing her job anyway. "I still don't understand that one."

Scallien looked up from her screen and put a slender finger to her lips. "Shhhh."

It was too much. Rage burnt up from her stomach. "The lowbloods have nothing," Willa seethed. "You know AB-pos is universal donor for platelets and plasma, right? But they can only donate those if you fractionate. So why aren't you?"

Scallien didn't answer.

"I'm AB-positive," Willa continued. "My daughter was AB-positive."

"So I'm informed." Scallien said, her tone darkening.

"The Trade killed her."

"Do you think that makes her special?"

The comment caught Willa blind. "I think she was a person. Just like you."

"Now that's where you're wrong, Ms Wallace. She wasn't just like me. And neither are you." She stopped typing to twirl a finger in the air. "You lowbloods love to prop up this ludicrous notion that people are inherently equal, when one look around should disabuse you entirely of the proposition. But it's something to put under your pillow at night, I suppose."

"It's how you keep us unequal," said Willa, making the logical point. "Patriot doesn't want to fractionate, because it would level the playing field."

"Playing field? You think we're on a *playing field*?" Scallien sneered. "We are in the *sky*, Ms Wallace, soaring above you, watching while you scrape by to play a game we created, unaware that you can never win. We don't fractionate, Ms. Wallace, because it doesn't work."

"Of course it works!" said Willa, almost jumping out of her shoes. "I did it my whole career before Chrysalis."

"Not for us," said Scallien, tapping her breastbone with a finger. "We need whole blood."

"What do you mean 'we'?" asked Willa. "Almost nobody needs whole blood."

Scallien sighed. Not a tired sigh or an exasperated sigh. A sigh of relief, of a weight lifted. She glanced back down at her touchstone and then back to Willa. "You've been terminated, Ms Wallace."

"You said 'we' need whole blood," said Willa, sidestepping the fact that she'd just been fired. "What do you mean 'we'?"

Scallien reached over a glass partition into the stall and scanned her thumbprint. Around the perimeter of the room, the wall cameras drooped. She set her touchstone face down on the counter, then oddly, stepped her feet out of her heels. Such an everyday gesture, but so entirely deliberate and out of place. It was the type of thing friends did to get comfortable before sitting down for a heart-to-heart. Only Scallien didn't. She came toward Willa, stalking like a jungle cat.

Confused, Willa pushed out from her booth.

Scallien began sawing her jaw back and forth, in the fashion of someone nursing a toothache.

"I said what did you mean by 'we?'" Willa's voice was higher with panic, louder from the adrenaline that dumped into her veins.

Scallien moaned, flexing her torso side to side, stretching her ribs. "I mean," she roared, "*We*!" Then her mouth fell open, the jawbone having come free of its hinge.

"What the hell?"

Suddenly, Willa was on her back. She reeled in a fog of confusion, imploring her mind to relay what was happening, but it was preoccupied by the primal task of surviving. As if separated from herself, she recalled the scene in which Scallien had screeched and thrown her body into her own with a force that belied her tiny stature.

Detached, Willa watched her hands as they pushed against the ravenous face, and she marveled at the tiny curved needles that had appeared in the woman's maw. Sweeping down from behind Scallien's lovely, but normal, white teeth, they glinted gold, pulling taut the tissue at the roof of her mouth like the venom-filled fangs of a cottonmouth.

Time slows down in the face of death – because that's what this was, Willa's death. Scallien's intent was almost tangible, its malevolence distilled and pure like a pungent vapor rising from her skin. After seconds, or even minutes – Willa couldn't say – the fog of shock began to twine away as if blown from a distance, and Willa returned to her body, emerging into a melee as her mind caught up to real time. The teeth gnashed. The golden barbs stretched long from the root as if reaching for a drink. Willa put an elbow to Scallien's throat to keep the mouth at bay, but the tiny woman was strong.

Or perhaps Scallien was not a woman, but rather possessing the shape and features of a woman. The fangs, the expression, the gape of her mouth, the wet strings slavering from it, were those of something else entirely. Scallien strained against the elbow pinned to her windpipe, oblivious to her own gagging like a dog choking after prey at the end of a chain.

Willa screamed and scratched and pushed against the animal force bearing down. Something else had come to occupy the space behind Scallien's eyes, something that felt like instinct. Drive. A sound bubbled, and a word gurgled from Scallien's throat, guttural, drawn out and visceral. *Eeeye-kooooooooor.*

Willa's hold was failing. Scallien – whatever she was – would prevail and Willa would die. She remembered holding Elizabeth as she'd faded, promising to guard Isaiah with her life. From whom would Willa seek the same promise now? There was no one. She was alone.

Willa's arm slipped to the floor and she was pinned. Scallien pressed downward, her breath hot iron, growling the same word over and over. *Eeye-koor, eeye-kooor*. Inching her knees forward and onto Willa's arms, she hunched into a sinister curl, leaned low to her face, and savored.

Over Scallien's shoulder flashed the shadow of reaper's black.

The sound that came next was like nothing Willa'd ever heard before, like an aluminum bat to a waterlogged coconut. The metal cooling element in Claude's hands struck with enough force to cave in Scallien's head, and she collapsed to the side motionless. Willa scrambled to the wall and made a ball of herself against it.

Waves of adrenaline pounded with nowhere to vent, and

her heart felt pressed to her ribs. Mere breaths later, tears burst, cascading down her cheeks and chin as her body heaved, keening. Her only thoughts were of Isaiah and of how he'd almost lost his only family.

"Willa?" It was Claude. "Willa?"

"Claude," she croaked, unable to stop the torrent. Her entire body shook with each gasp, every sob.

"Are you OK?" he asked, checking her over.

Willa fought to suppress the tremors of shock and fear that continued out from her core. Finally, she managed to look up into her boss's face, and almost smiled from the dumbness of his question. Beaten and scratched, but not mortally injured, she looked herself over and nodded in the affirmative.

"You have to leave."

She was too busy staring at the very small and very still body lying on the tile to really hear him. "Claude," she said, "there's something wrong with Scynthia."

His face didn't share her shock. "No," he said, stepping over to the body and its spreading slick of hemorrhage. "She is what she is."

"She's possessed, Claude! Did you see her? You saw her, right?" Willa wiped her face. "She was going to kill me!"

"It looked that way," he answered, letting the cooling element clank to the floor.

"What is going on, Claude?" she snorted, jittery with endorphin aftershocks. Why did he seem so casual about her near murder?

Claude knelt and glanced at the big clock. "I think you have an hour or two, maybe, before they miss her. Go get Isaiah and find somewhere to hide."

"Hide? What is happening?"

"Just listen to me, you need to get Isaiah and run. Now."

"She… she tried to kill me, Claude, in case you didn't see. We need to call security."

"She got *permission* to kill you, Willa," he said, reaching for Scallien's touchstone.

Willa looked at the body sprawled on the floor. "What was that in her mouth?" she asked of herself.

Claude rolled Scallien onto her back and held the touchstone in front of her face, at which point it unlocked. "Like I thought," he said, holding it out for Willa, "look."

JESPER OLDEN ▽: Update?

SCYNTHIA SCALLIEN ▽: She knows about the sugar. Pressing about fractionation now.

JESPER OLDEN ▽: That's unfortunate.

SCYNTHIA SCALLIEN ▽: Blabbing about empty drones. So she did see.

JESPER OLDEN ▽: A shame. Proposed resolution?

SCYNTHIA SCALLIEN ▽: Liquidated damages.

JESPER OLDEN ▽: When?

SCYNTHIA SCALLIEN ▽: Now. The Old Way.

JESPER OLDEN ▽: You've gone gold then.

SCYNTHIA SCALLIEN ▽: Yes.

JESPER OLDEN ▽: A genuine *vrae*. Proud of you.

SCYNTHIA SCALLIEN ▽: Thank you Jesper.

JESPER OLDEN ▽: Well then. You have Claret approval. Make sure to follow remediation protocol.

Willa read and re-read the exchange. "Liquidated damages?"

Claude helped Willa to her feet. "You have to go now."

"Where?"

He went over toward the hallway that led to the cooler and retrieved her touchstone. "Go outside, summon a teller drone, withdraw as much as it will let you. Then leave this here." He handed it to her.

"What?" she exclaimed. The prospect of going anywhere without her touchstone was almost as unsettling as her near-death experience. And in practical terms, it wasn't very different. Without her touchstone she would effectively cease to exist. Patriot assigned one to every citizen. Gone were driver's licenses, photo identification cards, or any other tangible way for one to verify who they were. Touchstones were the singular and all-encompassing source of personal identity. Instead of checking someone's ID, people tapped touchstones. If the touchstone worked when you tapped it, then it was yours and it said who you were – a person's face was irrelevant. Without one, you evaporated from society. Willa placed a hand over hers and swallowed hard at the idea of willfully abandoning it. "I... I don't think I should..."

"You aren't getting me. You have to be offline," he said, hefting Scallien by the armpits. "Are the locks on your apartment digital?"

There were few segments of life left where conversion from manual to mechanical or analog to digital wasn't entirely complete. Whereas touchstones had become essential in order to navigate daily life, digital door locks were still optional equipment, and it was there Willa had stood her ground against "progress." If you could control your own locks remotely, then who else might be probing when you weren't home? "No," she answered, making a lock closing gesture with one hand.

"Good. Go get Isaiah and then trash your place. Leave it unlocked. Throw off the scent."

"The scent for whom? What is happening, Claude?"

"Patriot is going to come for you."

"What are you going to do?"

He dropped Scallien unceremoniously, letting her head whack the tiles. "I need to grab some supplies and I'll find you. I think I'm fired too."

"We'll make for AB Plus."

"Go."

CHAPTER NINE

4 MPH

The speed at which blood circulates in an adult human body; equivalent to average walking speed.

Willa waited outside anxiously for a good two minutes before the banking drone landed, and then withdrew the daily maximum. Eight gold-colored triangular coins, each worth one hundred, dropped from the dispenser and the drone departed. She ran back into the station, hesitated for a regretful second, then hurled her touchstone over the stalls.

She ripped the pink hair from her head, shoved it into her bag, donned her hood, and set off at the quickest clip she could maintain. As rain began, she blazed a new route across the corner of A Plus, through the grounds of an abandoned school and a warehouse park. She wondered how long it would be until they came for her. Maybe they were already on their way. She picked up her pace.

At the door to her apartment and panting furiously, she fumbled with her keys – nobody had keys anymore – but her manual locks meant her entry wouldn't be detected or recorded anywhere. She wondered how many more minutes she had to get packed and out of the building.

"Isaiah?" she called. "Isaiah?"

He wandered out from the bathroom, shirt off, his hair wet from experimental coiffing. "Grandma?"

"Get your clothes on right now, baby."

"Where's your hair, Grandma?"

"I have it," she said, trying to conceal her overwhelming panic. "Get dressed."

"Why?"

"We have to leave. Please do as I say."

She ran to her corner of the room, threw open dresser drawers, and loaded a duffle with a mishmash of clothing. She took up an older, shoulder-length black wig, gave it a toss and pulled it on. At the table she grabbed her workbooks, a small box containing some old – now antique – lancets and vacutainers, syringes, tourniquets and intravenous lines. Soap. Dumped it all in. She did the same in Isaiah's room as he looked on while fumbling with a shoe.

Here they were, evacuating, just as she'd always feared. Though not for the reason she'd thought they would.

"Where are we going, Grandma?" he asked as she cast about plucking socks and underpants from various piles, shoving them into his backpack.

"A little trip across town, that's all, baby. Few nights."

"But why?"

"Get your zip-up," she said, pointing it out. "We gotta get out of here while it's still raining, alright?"

"Why?" he said, knotting the other shoe.

"My Lord, 'Saiah! Just grab your things, I'll tell you on the way."

"But where–"

"Later!" Willa snapped. "Get your stuff, now!"

Isaiah complied, only now seeming to process the moment's urgency, and selected some of his favorite shirts. Willa smashed an ancient lamp in the sink. She pinched the ten or so silver triangles from amongst the shards, yelping as one sank into the meat of her ring finger.

"Grandma!"

"I'm OK, baby, I'm fine," she said. "Just a little poke." She showed him the finger with a tiny sphere of red growing at its tip, then sucked it away. She dropped the coins into her bag with the others. All that she had.

In the kitchen, she slid a stack of peppermint tea and some biscuits, as well as some remnant oat cubes, into the duffle, then went to flipping the rest of their lives out onto the floor, emptying drawers and scraping cubbies.

"Toothbrush!" she hollered.

"Got it," said Isaiah, emerging from his room, backpack strapped on secure, jacket underneath. "Why are you making a mess?"

"Make it harder for people to figure out where we might have gone. Throw them off the scent."

"Is someone looking for us?"

"Yes, baby."

"Who?"

"Some people your grandmother upset."

"What'd you do?" his voice was shock with a hint of wonder.

Willa noticed his prized view-screen and headset pinned under his arm and knelt before him. "We have to leave this here, so no one can follow us on our trip. Trust me, please?" He released the screen and she placed it gently on the table. Finally, she threw on her coat, yanked on the aubergine boots, and said a quiet goodbye.

Outside, Willa thanked God that the rain was still coming down and that the evening streets were busy. Nearby, a man flicked his touchstone and looked to the sky, no doubt summoning a brellabot. Isaiah in tow, Willa marched toward him just as the drone arrived. She could have brought down her own old-school umbrella to avoid having to rent one, but it was bright orange and pink and not designed for anonymity.

"Pardon, sir? I lost my touchstone. Can I buy your brellabot?"

The man's eyes were cold – most peoples' were – but they flowed down to Isaiah and softened slightly. "Sure," he said, "but it's double. Fifty."

"Good, because I don't carry anything smaller," Willa said coolly, dropping a silver triangle into his hand. She accepted the drone's control beacon – a small black puck with a blinking yellow light – and clipped it to her lapel.

Off they went under the cover of their drone, into the early evening sea of brellabots. Umbrella drones were a marvel of technology, each with a miniature array of ducted fans mounted above the traditional fabric canopy – the science fiction version of a child's propeller beanie. They walked along as their brellabot slipped side to side and bopped up and down to avoid colliding with others as they passed. Despite having to move around so much, the dance between them was coordinated, orchestrated with seamless connectivity between each so as to keep their humans dry.

"Grandma?" Isaiah asked as he shuffled along.

"Yes, baby."

"Where are we going?"

"We are going to stay with some friends."

"We have friends?"

"I hope so."

"Why are we going to stay with them?"

"We need to hide."

"Why?"

"Because your grandmother discovered a secret that she's not supposed to know."

"What's the secret?"

Willa looked down at him. "The kind of secret that gets you in big trouble if you know it," she said, putting a finger across her lips.

She walked with purpose, steering them in an endlessly twisting and random course, down thoroughfares and alleyways, into food stands and sundry shops. Eventually, their route took them deep into O Plus with its glass storefronts and sit-down restaurants. They even found the Pantry, and Willa bent to scan the menu, if nothing more than to see the entry for the sandwich she used to treat herself to back before everything happened. There were club sandwiches, French dips, Italian cold-cuts, but no croque madame. Well. Maybe they'd turned it into one of those off-menu specials. Willa looked at the people inside, Os most likely. They weren't wealthy by any stretch – they would have been lower-middle class in the previous version of the country – but could afford the occasional night out.

Isaiah, who had walked without complaint for miles, was flagging. What better place to lay low and recharge than a restaurant they couldn't afford, somewhere would-be pursuers would never think to look. They needed to save their money, but they needed to stay alive more, and Willa wasn't all too clear on who or how many might be after them. "What do you think, Isaiah?" she asked. "Want to eat here?"

"Do you think they have hotdogs?"

Willa unclipped the beacon from her lapel and held it to the umbrella's underside where it stuck like a magnet, signaling the drone to take off in search of another customer. "Let's find out."

They found a seat inside, a booth between two other booths, set on the opposite side of a short wall from the door. Willa slid all the way into her side of the table while Isaiah savored the experience, spreading out on the wide red seat. A young woman brought water, which Willa downed before she could even walk away. Isaiah looked on with new bewilderment at his grandmother's behavior.

The server reappeared. "Can I get you anything or do you need a minute?"

"Noodles and franks, please," said Isaiah with a huge smile.

"Noodles and franks, got it," said the server. "And for you, ma'am?"

Willa wasn't hungry. Her stomach was hollow, but she felt no desire to fill it. The idea of eating seemed so unimportant with everything that was happening. "Uh," she said, "soup."

"Soup. Got it." And the server was off.

Their food came quickly, and Isaiah set into his noodles like a big cat with a fresh kill. Willa watched this, admiring not for the first time the ability of her grandson to adapt to sudden changes in his life. On the surface, at least, children so often went along with whatever was happening to them. Part of it, she knew, was that they didn't fully comprehend every situation and so didn't react as harshly as someone who did. In the short term it was helpful, especially when you had to move fast, but she worried on the long-term effects. At some point it all had to stop.

Less than half an hour later, they exited. Willa had forced herself to drink down her soup, while Isaiah slurped up a bowl of ice cream. Standing under the restaurant's awning, she scanned for anyone that might be coming in with another umbrella. A young couple, highbloods by their clean, styled hair, approached.

"Sorry to interrupt you on your night out," said Willa, doing her best not to sound anxious. "This is my grandson and we–"

"Take it," said the man, handing over the beacon without so much as a nod or eye contact.

Isaiah gave a shrug. "Free drone!"

"Yes, what luck."

Willa glanced around for anything suspicious, but not knowing what that might actually look like, pressed on. Their route remained circuitous though she knew the end point. At almost ten o'clock, they crossed the boundary into AB Plus. Elsewhere, cameras would have been a concern, but Willa recalled with no small amount of pride that the lowbloods could be relied upon to keep theirs in a constant state of *vandalized*. Willa unclipped the beacon and offered it back to the drone.

Watching it fly away, Isaiah asked, "Where are we, Grandma?"

"My old neighborhood," she answered.

"Oh," he said, taking it in with the new perspective. "Why?"

"To find someone who can help us, I hope."

She hustled them across wet asphalt and swampy grass until they were a stone's throw from the home of Everard Alison. He stepped casually onto the front patio as if drawn out by a premonition of their approach and lit a cigarette. He jutted out his chin and smirked. The gesture said *I saw you coming, I'll always see you coming*. Willa led Isaiah off the curb and across the way.

"Taking me up on my offer, then, Ms Willa?" he called as they splashed up the walk.

"Nope."

His face darkened, the smirk erased. "Then best git on," he grumbled.

"We need shelter for tonight, that's all."

"I ain't got food for two more mouths, Ms Wallace," he said.

Willa stepped into his personal space, lowered her voice and whispered, "I haven't asked you for food, have I?"

"Matter of time," he answered with a shrug.

"I fed you," Willa said. "Twice. Some people would do well to remember the kindness of others."

"Ain't about kindness. It's 'bout I ain't got food for two more mouths."

"We brought our own," she said, adding, "And if you can't afford food, you can't afford these." She flicked the smoking butt straight from his lips.

"Hey!"

"It's late. You want to stay out in the open or are you going to let me and my grandson inside?"

Everard sighed. "Were you followed?"

"You said I was smart, remember?" she said.

He raised his eyebrows and held his arm to the side in resigned welcome. "The Locksmith'll want to talk to you anyhow."

"Good. I want to talk to him."

The air inside was warm but stagnant. Children huddled together throughout, little teams in their designated areas, each with a pile of blankets and a few toys, some tattered books.

"Where are their parents?"

Everard turned, gave her a look, and she had her answer.

They came into a tiny kitchen with a small table and four chairs. Willa pulled Isaiah close.

"Empty veins," Everard said to no one in particular.

"Is the Locksmith here?"

A muted chortle came from his throat.

"OK," Willa said, "where is he?"

"Calm down," Everard said, filling two cups from the tap. "Sit for a spell." He gave his beard an easy scratch.

Isaiah poked her sleeve and gestured to a nearby group of kids. "Go ahead," she said, giving his cheek a stroke. "Stay where I can see you."

"That's good advice. With so few parents around watching, kids get misplaced."

Willa turned back to him. "Why would you say such a thing?"

"Because it's true. More missing kids outta AB Plus than anywhere."

"What?" Willa said.

He nodded somberly. "A handful go absent every month."

"I had no idea."

"And why would you?" he sneered. "Like I said, you ain't in it."

"Who's taking them? Where are they going?"

"Somewhere else, I guess," he said, sticking another cigarette to his lips but leaving it cold. "Why these few here ain't really 'llowed out of doors."

A tall man ducked into the small kitchen through a back door making Willa flinch. Everard made a gesture that let her know the man was expected, a friend. He was tall, dressed in a fitted, but years-worn, gray denim suit. The collar of his shirt seemed whiter than it was against his dark neck. "Ms Wallace?"

"Yes." She stood. "You're the Locksmith?"

He shook his head no. "I'll take you." He turned for the door through which he'd arrived.

"Isaiah?" said Willa. "Come on, baby."

"He can stay here with the others, he'll be safe," said the man.

"You have a keen sense of humor," said Willa. "But I'm taking my grandson." Isaiah came in with a one-armed action figure on loan from another child.

The man looked at Everard, who shrugged helplessly. "She already made me quit cigarettes."

"Somebody needed to." He waved her over. "Come with me, then."

Directly through the screen door in the back, across ten feet of yellow grass, was a shed slapped together with old 3D-printed corrugated panels, a cheap building material ubiquitous in the lowbloods.

"I'm not going in there," said Willa.

"It's not what you think," said the man. He opened a section of panel revealing a second door that Willa recognized as belonging to a taxi drone. The shed was a tiny hangar, built snugly around the craft. The man opened the door and ushered them inside.

"Where are we going?"

He gave her a look that made her suddenly conscious of her naivete. They were taking her to visit a notorious hacker and probably weren't keen on giving out the address.

"Won't we be traceable?" asked Willa, strapping Isaiah onto the bench seat.

"This drone's fugitive. Hasn't been on-line for months," he said, strapping himself into a utilitarian pilot's seat secured by an arm to the wall. "It's ours." He tapped Isaiah on the top of his head. "Hold on sir, this cab's a bit faster than what you might be used to."

"He's not used to anything," said Willa.

They lifted straight up through the hinged roof, and stormed low over a range of ramshackle homes. Isaiah hooted at the thrill of acceleration.

"Patriot can't see us?" Willa said, still unsure.

"They could see us if they had their eyes open," he said. "But without a digital signature we might as well be invisible."

"I didn't catch your name."

"Lindon."

"Willa."

"I know."

The trip covered only a few minutes and perhaps four or five miles, and the drone decelerated over another backyard shack. It snagged a series of wires as it dropped down inside, drawing them through pulleys that closed the roof overhead. Still in AB Plus, the new house, chipped paint and all, was a clone of Everard's, just in olive drab. Lindon opened the drone, allowing Willa and Isaiah to push out from the shed and into another wasted backyard.

Above them, a trellis woven tight with defoliated vines led from the shed to the screen door on the back of the house. The inner door opened as they reached it, and a short, stoutly built woman with an explosion of curly, burnt orange hair greeted them. She pushed a pair of dark-lensed welding goggles onto her forehead. "You're Willa," she announced.

"Yes, ma'am."

"You're Isaiah," the woman continued, extending a hand that Isaiah promptly yanked. "I'm Janet."

"OK," said Willa, "where is–"

"Come in, come in," she continued, nudging the goggles farther up and into her huge hair. She was solidly in her fifties, maybe five years Willa's junior, with dark freckled skin – that particular shade of deep tan that could be just as much from years spent in the sun as inherited.

Inside they found a quaint kitchen in robin's egg blue, with a kettle vibrating on a portable burner. It was clean and tidy, unfilled with children, and so well ordered it felt in stark contradiction to the world it occupied. It was domesticated, charming.

"You work for the Locksmith?" asked Willa.

"You could say that," she said, her patched dress of many layers twirling as she spun. "Let's go."

She led them to a door no wider than a broom closet, opened it, and began down the stairs toward a basement. About half-way down, she stopped, lifted a broomstick with a hook in the end from behind the hand railing, and extended it high above to a ceiling hatch directly over them.

"Oh, that's sneaky," said Willa.

Janet drew down the rope, opening the hatch and lowering the wooden stairs. "Up we go."

Isaiah spirited into the space. The day for him, Willa noted, had been the most exciting of his entire life. She followed, cautiously creaking herself up the steps. Once all were clear, the woman closed the hatch and flipped a light switch.

The room immediately transferred Willa to the days of her childhood.

All around, on shelves and tables, crates and TV trays, were radios, oscilloscopes, old televisions, arcane telephones and analog recorders – some even dating from before her birth – stacked atop one another in piles, or wired together into novel contraptions. Laptop computers and pads that had gone extinct when Willa was still in school lined wooden shelves around the perimeter. Miles of wire ran between them, which was, in a way, more unusual than the collection of dusty electronics. Nothing had used wires for four decades. Here, though, an entire era of computing power existed on a circulatory system of copper and plastic. A drafting table in the corner had the appearance of a workstation that one might use to build model airplanes, complete with precision razors, glue, soldering iron, and vintage hair dryer. On a shelf just above the table were bins upon bins of siphons, empty blood bags, and needles.

Isaiah couldn't believe his good fortune. It was a wonderland, and he went to prodding whatever he could reach.

"Stop that," Willa said.

"He's fine," said Janet. "You can't hurt that old stuff."

The operation was impressive, though Willa got the impression the equipment wasn't just a collection. There was a vague logic to it, how the machines were stacked and wired together, though Willa couldn't comprehend how it all worked. To think, though, that a single man had put so much effort into cracking the skin of a behemoth like Patriot was inspiring. "This is all his work," Willa said to herself, caressing the keyboard of the very model laptop her parents had owned when she was little.

"He's quite prolific. Doesn't sleep much though," Janet said with an exaggerated yawn. She leaned back into an office chair and wheeled to the drafting table. Pulling down the goggles, she said, "Care to see what I'm working on?"

"Sure," said Willa. "You help him?"

"Help him?" she said. "Willa, dangit – I *am* him!" She waited a beat for Willa to blink. "It's alright, sweetie. You're supposed to be surprised. It means my little ruse is working."

"But I caught you before at DS8. A bag-hack. You did time." Willa's brain was skipping now, trying to make sense. "You were a man," she said, her confusion growing, "taller too."

"I was?" exclaimed Janet, slapping her legs and putting her hands up to the goggles like binoculars. "Are you telling me that there are copycat hackers out there?" she laughed. "Let us file our complaint with the local magistrate!"

Isaiah laughed along, infected by the woman's jocularity.

Still putting the pieces together, Willa pointed at the begoggled woman. "You're the Locksmith."

"I'm the Locksmith," she said arms out wide. "But you can call me Janet."

"That's your real name?"

"It's what you can call me, heh."

"Janet," said Willa, hesitating.

"Well, if you prefer, call me 'The Locksmith', then, or 'The', or 'Locksmith', or 'Lock'. But don't call me 'Smith'."

"Lock!" said Isaiah.

"Lock it is," said the woman, tossing a thumbs-up and a wink to Isaiah. "Anyways, I'm glad you've decided to take me up on my offer." She stood and scooped up a blood bag rig. "Check out this design, Willa. The inner bag for the decoy blood is nanoceramic and totally flexible. Patriot's needles can't penetrate through it and into the main chamber. They bounce right off the inner wall of the decoy pocket."

Willa shook her head. "I doubt that. The needle probes are inconel. They'd penetrate nanoceramic."

"Oh yeah?" Lock raised her eyebrows and sniffed. "Everard came through your line two days ago. You paid him for B-neg."

"So it's true? He really did?"

"Yeah. He really did, Willa. That bag was full of his own AB-positive. Those needles might be strong, but their moorings are suspect. Flexible. They didn't pierce through to the main chamber. So, per my design, they assayed the decoy pocket."

"Which you filled with B-neg," said Willa, completing the puzzle.

"Correcto," said Lock, beaming.

Willa had actually been hacked. "But – I would have felt the pocket," she said, trying to rationalize it and feeling guilty that she'd failed at her job even though she now had no job to go back to.

"Look, I only half expected it to work, but it did," Lock said, tendering a bag filled with water. "Tell me you'd be able to feel that."

Willa flopped it over her fingers as she had with thousands of other bags. "It's very good," she said. Because it was.

"Right?" said Lock, inhaling deeply through her nostrils.

Willa, still troubled by the hack she'd failed to stop, thought it through aloud. "OK, I get the bag, but Everard had to touchstone in. It would have reported his actual phenotype and the discrepancy would have been flagged."

Lock cocked her head to the side.

"What?" asked Willa.

"Well, did it?" said Lock. "Flag a discrepancy?"

"No, it didn't. Why not?"

"Cause I'm a fucking hacker, Willa!" she laughed, plopping back in the chair and twirling back to the desk. "Touchstones are the one piece of hardware that Patriot puts in our hands. I hold something long enough, I'll crack it." She set her hands on her hips. "Wow, a real-life reaper up here in my workshop. So, you ready to do this thing?"

Willa shook her head. "I can't. They fired me today."

Lock's face went stormy and she snatched away the bag with a finger strike. "Fired you? Then why are you here?" She marched to the attic door. Isaiah, who was playing with an early cellular phone, observed silently.

"You can just use these bags. They're... really good," said Willa. "You don't need a phlebotomist on the inside to help you."

"That bag took me weeks to get just right. Mass production will mean errors and I need someone on the inside to help with the fudge factor," Lock said. "I don't have time to wait. I'm trying to feed my kids." Lock's face lost its exuberance and she seemed to shrink from the larger-than-life persona she'd inhabited back into the five-feet of space she actually occupied. She opened the door and gestured for them to exit. "Go on," she said. "Lindon will take you back. Not a word, of course. Or... you know... bad stuff."

Willa took a step toward the hatch but stopped. They were trying to do the same thing, after all, just on different scales. Lock was trying to hack the Harvest while Willa had tried to break it. "I know how they really move the blood," she said. "Where you could get enough highblood for every family in AB Plus to sell before they'd discovered it was gone."

Lock sighed. "I know where it is too. But I haven't been able to commandeer a blood drone. I can get a signal up, but I don't have the encryption to assume their navigation."

"The drones are empty."

Lock let the door slam shut.

CHAPTER TEN

ANALYTE

A substance or sample being analyzed, identified, measured, or otherwise tested.

"Empty." A question in statement form.

"Empty."

"Where's the blood, then?"

"SCS distribution has a speedloop tube."

"How do you know that?" asked Lock.

"I've seen it."

"No, how do you know they put the blood in it?"

"I figured it out."

"You figured it out? Why didn't I figure it out?"

"I saw a drone crash," Willa continued. "That and they basically admitted it right before they…" She covered Isaiah's ears and mouthed, *tried to kill me*.

"What?"

"I violated my NDA."

"You aren't killed though."

"We ran. This was the only place we could come. I'd met Everard before. He seemed like a mostly good person."

Lock sat heavily onto a stack of ancient computer monitors. "All of those drones, all these years… they've been empty?"

"I don't know for how long, but I'm guessing it's been that way for a while."

"Why? Why would they send up empty drones?"

"Extra security is what they said. Makes sense."

"Nah. Nah, it doesn't make any sense," said Lock, rubbing her brow. "If someone wanted to get their hands on an entire day's shipment, they'd need to take down all eight drones intact. It'd never happen. If what you're saying is true, then Patriot is vulnerable if someone gets hold of a single speedloop pod. And that doesn't make sense to me."

Willa shrugged. "How could anyone hijack a speedloop pod at anything but the debarkation point? Nobody knows the routes."

"That's true… Do you have proof about the drones?"

"Just my own eyes."

"Well, Willa," said Lock, "I can't make a move based on what you think you saw one time with your eyes or anyone else's."

"The blood is not in the drones, Lock. And when I guessed that it went out by speedloop, Patriot didn't dispute it."

"Oh, wow, Patriot didn't dispute it," Lock rolled her eyes. "Well, I've hit a dead end. I have no phlebotomist on the inside, and without that, no way to care for these kids aside from sending folks through on piecemeal hacks. One of these days, they'll catch us."

"I am telling the truth. If you can get into the speedloop pod, you can get to the blood."

"I want to believe you," Lock said, standing and shaking out her arms like a ragdoll. "But I don't make a move based on word of mouth. I gotta see it with my own eyes."

"Before three nights ago," said Willa, "I'd never seen one crash. You might wait around for eternity before another goes down."

"Hmm… before another goes down eh?" Lock palmed a board between the rafters a few feet up from where the roofline met the plywood floor. Dust and tufts of insulation puffed from the joints and she coughed it away. One edge of the board slipped down and a large rifle rolled from the void into her hands. She caught it heavily and shuffled to a dusty couch underneath the attic vent where she dumped it onto the cushions. "I guess we'll just shoot one down."

"Can I come?" asked Isaiah jumping up.

"I like him," said Lock.

"No," said Willa, then turning to the woman, "Shoot one down?"

"Probably lots of other ways to ground one of those bad boys, but this way is quick and we can do it remotely. A clear line of sight to the impact zone, the rifle does the rest." She pointed to the gun. "MK13-Mod9. That's mark-thirteen-block-nine in civilian. Only two-hundred forty-two inches of vertical correction at a thousand yards, so."

Willa's expression went flat. *Who was this person?*

"Bottom line, if the drone's empty, we'll talk. If it's full, you and Isaiah there will have to go."

"Where are we supposed to go?"

"Not my problem. You saw all those kids in the boarding house?"

"I did."

"They're mine. I'm responsible for *them*. You're responsible for *you*."

Willa and Isaiah stayed in the Locksmith's attic that night. Willa took off the aubergine boots but left the rest of her clothing on. Exhaustion meant sleep came fast. Before dawn, Lock nudged them awake. They got themselves together over tea and bulk protein chew. Near the end of the meal, Lock dropped a bowl of strawberries and blackberries in front of them. Fresh berries? Willa went to inquire about the source of the delicacies, but Lock said don't ask, so she didn't. They waited the rest of the day out, during which Willa explained everything that had happened to her, including Scallien's attack. She left out a few of the possibly hallucinated details.

About one hour before the blood drones would be leaving SCS

Distribution for their trip to the Central City Collection, the Heart, downtown, Willa, Isaiah, Lindon, and Lock took the rogue taxi drone back across AB Plus to Everard's boarding house.

Isaiah ran inside to greet the other children and Willa followed after. "I'll be back in a little while, baby. Be careful and listen to Mr Everard while I'm gone."

"I got those crumbsnatchers covered, don't you worry," Everard chimed from the adjacent room.

"Be good, 'Saiah," Willa reiterated to her grandson, hugging him, "and always keep your eyes open."

Lock waited at the door, where Willa joined.

They entered the drone and Lindon secured the shed door behind them. "Lindon isn't coming?" Willa asked.

"We don't need him," laughed Lock.

"Doesn't he need to shoot the drone?"

"Girl! Lindon can't shoot! My-oh-my," she said. "I figure I'll give it a go."

"Give it a go?"

"Can't be too difficult, right?"

Willa wondered. The woman could hardly wield the massive gun. And standing on end it was almost taller than her.

Lock settled in front of the nav screen. "I like that pink hair of yours," she said, steering the drone out of the shed and over the homes.

"How do you know about my hair?"

"I know all sorts of stuff. You still have it, I hope." She messed with the screen. "I assume we're going somewhere just northwest of SCS distrib?"

The woman did have a knack for subject changes. "Uh, yes," said Willa. "They'll be flying right at you if we land to the northwest."

"Alright, then, it's a plan," she declared, setting the drone on cruise and hefting the rifle. "This guy has a pretty legit scope so it shouldn't be too hard to hit one. We'll park in line with their vector and wait until they're over those empty lots in AB Minus. Then I'll just shoot one head on." She mimed firing the gun. "Boop."

After a short while, Lock angled her eyes out the small porthole window. "Hold on. Comin' in."

She selected a landing spot on top of an abandoned warehouse and set down between two large HVAC units. The drone itself looked something like an industrial condenser. Only the halo of ducted fans ringing the top differentiated it from the surrounding equipment. They stepped out onto the roof of the building. Lock walked to the back side of the drone with the butt of the rifle atop one of her combat boots.

"Help me get on top of this thing," she said, leaning the MK against the drone.

"On top of the drone?"

"I'm most accurate from prone position," she said.

"I don't think I could lift you."

"No need. I'll just step on you."

"How about I make a hand basket instead?"

"Well it'd be easier for me to step on you, but whatever suits."

"Easier for you," mumbled Willa, weaving her fingers together and offering the foothold.

Lock hoisted herself while Willa helped push her to where she was able to wrench the rest of the way up. She crawled onto the drone's roof just as a squadron of red lights came into view over a distant line of trees. "Gun me," said Lock.

Willa took the rifle by the handguard and brought it gingerly into Lock's waiting fingers. Rolling onto her back, Lock pulled it over her chest and flipped down the bipod from under the barrel. She set the rifle straight, reached into her pocket and drew a single, very large, round. It clicked into the chamber and she brought the bolt down with an experienced hand. "Straight ahead shots against oncoming bogies are notoriously tough to range in. I might have to fire twice to get my drop." She messed with the elevation knob on top of the scope as Willa observed with a mixture of shock and amusement. Lock set her eye to the optics. "OK, well, fire in the hole and all that."

Droplets of water exploded from the taxi's body panels with the rifle's report. Willa turned her eyes to the drones. The leader of the formation slumped to one side and began losing altitude.

Lock peeked over the edge at Willa, gave a wink and a thumbs-up. "First try."

"Where did you learn to shoot like that?"

"Semper fidelis, my dear. Long gun specialist, dishonorable discharge, Year of our Lord 2038, pleased to meet you."

"You were a Marine?"

"I were," answered Lock, her eyes following the wounded drone until it dropped into the woods just shy of the intended clearing. "Well that was a miscalculation wasn't it? Let's get over there before the cavalry. Here, take the MK."

Willa accepted the rifle, regarding the weapon with an even mixture of respect and unease. "Why were you dishonorably discharged?"

Lock slid down from the roof. "Trumped up some charges for refusal to follow orders, can you believe it?"

"What orders?"

"Illegal ones. My CO wanted me to smoke a POI – uh, Person of Interest – off the books."

"You wouldn't do it?"

"And now my whole life is off the books." She shook her head. "Ironic isn't it?"

They climbed into the drone.

"Didn't they shoot the person anyway?"

"Heh. Not likely. I was the only one of 'em could have made the shot. Bastard lived. Whoever he was."

Leaving the drone's door open, Lock lifted them off from the warehouse roof and over an expanse of empty lots to the wreckage. "I see it, let's get lower."

But Willa could already see what she knew to be true – there was no red slick, no debris field of donor bags, just vaults strewn about like tin cans. One lay sheared in half. She pointed it out to Lock, who nodded *good enough for me*. She slammed the door down and they rocketed from the trees before any sign of security showed on the horizon.

Lock patted down on the big pockets of her dress and leather jacket. “Heh,” she laughed, “that was lucky.”

“What was?”

“Forgot my second bullet anyways.”

CHAPTER ELEVEN

Marasmus
A state of severe malnutrition.

Willa secured herself to the bench while Lock twirled side to side in the pilot's seat. Willa felt struck by this woman; an excommunicated Marine who ran blood hacks from a hoarder's attic full of bygone-age ephemera. She wondered how such a person could possibly exist. Lock caught her staring.

"You alright, Willa?" she asked.

"Yes. Yes, I'm sorry. I glazed over for a minute there." She gathered her thoughts. "Your hideout–"

"Which hideout?"

Willa paused, confused. "The one in the attic, the one we met you in."

"*A* hideout," Lock corrected with a smirk.

"You have more of them?"

"Who would have just one hideout? What if somebody found it? Then it'd no longer be a hideout and you'd be S-O-L." She fluttered her fingers.

"S-O-L?"

"Jesus, were you ever a kid? Shit-outa-luck. *S-O-L,*" she chuckled. "Anyway, got hideouts all over, Willa."

"OK, but, the one you let us see... it's full of all those old computers and telephones and whatnot. Why?"

Lock sighed.

"What?"

"Short question that calls for a long answer."

"Tell me."

"Human Nature would be the subject heading," said Lock, gazing back out the window. "Yep, no matter what the technology, any hack always comes down to human nature in one way or another. Some people think the technology is where the magic happens, but that's short sighted. Most hacks are a matter of social engineering. Always have been. Most the time the tech never even enters the equation. But when it does, the tech is just... the medium... that's all. Humans are still at the head and tail of it, even if the humans at the tail are long dead. Get me?"

Willa did not.

"Weaknesses in technology are predictable because human beings are predictable. Bottom line? People don't care about old stuff." She tapped some instructions into the console and spun in her chair so they were face to face. "For example: how much time did your parents or grandparents spend explaining old technologies to you?"

"What do you mean?"

"They never sat you down and said, 'Willa, let's learn about how rotary telephones worked', or 'the internal combustion engine was a real marvel, let's spend an afternoon discussing it', or 'let's talk turn of the century sewage infrastructure', or 'hey Willa–'"

"I get it."

"The same rule applies to any trade. Software, hardware. No exception. Old is irrelevant. People have no desire to look backward in time and learn the workings of obsolete technology just for fun. Hobbyists, sure, but nobody listens to them. No, people focus on the present and hustle forward with the rest of the rats. These quantum computers now, they'll be the big thing until the next big thing. But do you think their designers and programmers ever got the hankering to learn how one solid state CPU built in 2020 talked to another of the same vintage? Hell no, that's boring shit, Willa. Why would they do that? That technology is stone aged."

"OK," said Willa, starting to follow. In a way, the same thing had occurred with phlebotomy. The new technology, blood bags and needle-probes and all of that was so advanced and easy, that the old techniques had quickly vacated the collective conscience, forgotten even by those who used to practice them. But it wasn't just phlebotomy for Willa. It was everything, really. At some point the world and its shortcuts seemed to have passed her by, moving on like water as she stood stubborn in the stream.

"Point is," Lock went on, "technology is like history: get far enough down the line and people forget, or worse, don't care. Technology outstrips itself, again and again and again. All the high-powered functionality is way up here," she said, holding her hand up toward the drone's ceiling, "but they've forgotten to give attention to the old boring stuff down here in the weeds with us," moving her hand low. "Take Patriot's operating system for example: that OS is top of the line quantum computing, the damned thing does calculations based off of the ability to observe the state of matter cross-dimensionally. But see, that central brain still has to talk to all the old systems throughout Patriot. Why don't they modernize the whole infrastructure? Well, one, it's cheaper and easier not to. And two, because nobody out in the districts can afford hardware that talks directly to any of the new systems. Don't even think they could buy it if they wanted to. It's almost like Patriot wants it this way. So what you get is layers of tech – vintages so to speak. There's still decades-old software that surrounds and buttresses the new systems. It's like… concentric rings in a tree. As you move out, the systems get older, and that makes them more permeable, susceptible to people like me. I bet when you were trained back in what, '20, '25, any hospital you visited still had those old dot matrix printers, right, even though it'd been invented seventy years before that. Well, only computers of a proximate vintage could talk to those iron-aged sumbitches, so they kept them around way beyond their obsolescence out of a combination of laziness and cost savings. That hardware at the periphery of the hospital's system would be like the outer ring of their tech. That's my entry point for Patriot: the outer ring."

"All the old computers in the attic, then–"

"Not a collection for when I'm feeling nostalgic. Our tech is so ancient nobody looks for it anymore – they wouldn't know how. We don't need to fly under the radar because there is no radar. Patriot is over there doing all their big important work, all the while I'm out here having a heart to heart with the outer rings through dialup. Well, not really dialup, but you capiche."

"So, the computer hacks you've done... you've done them with all that stuff in the attic?"

"Don't get the wrong impression, Willa, even the outer rings are tough to penetrate. Getting just one ping on their system takes me fifteen attics' worth of Cretaceous hardware, all chained together. We push a single line of code up the ladder from the local level, the donor stations read all the blood as O-neg for ten minutes, and then it's over."

"All of that for ten minutes?" Willa said, almost sad that such great effort garnered so little in return, and regretful that as a Patriot employee she'd rejoiced when the hacks were smothered.

"If we get the word out in time, we can run a thousand donors through that window," Lock answered.

"Weren't you concerned about mislabeled blood getting to the Gray Zones and hurting people?"

Lock looked at Willa in a way that was part bewilderment, part patronizing. She pointed to the homes flowing below them on the view screen. "That's AB Plus, down there," she said. "We're trying to survive – literally trying to save kids. And you're worried about some strangers in the Gray Zones – who are all probably gonna die anyway – getting a bad transfusion? You shittin' me?"

"They're innocent people, though."

"So are we, Willa."

Willa looked out the window as the homes, outdated and in

disrepair, rushed by. What had seemed so important only days before, the things that had concerned her as an employee of Patriot, had been rendered irrevocably irrelevant. Her hard wiring had been ripped away. Obsolete, just like the outer rings.

The drone set down in the shed behind the boarding house. Lock stepped out first and halted. She held her fist up like a soldier taking point.

"Something doesn't feel right. Everard usually waits at the back for me. Hand over the MK."

"But it doesn't have any bullets."

"Sure it does. In the stock."

"But you said you forgot to bring more–"

"You gotta stop listening to what I say, Willa!"

"I'm not just waiting here!" said Willa. "I need to check on Isaiah."

"He's fine, I'm sure. Stay put. I'll be right back."

"No, I'm coming."

Lock slammed the rifle across the drone's door, barring Willa from exiting. "You are staying right here," she said, all pretense gone from her voice. "I got kids in there too. My rules."

Willa nodded and the former Marine headed down the walk and into the home.

Willa stood inside the drone, nervous, praying that Isaiah was all right.

Lock burst back through the screen door, strutting with bravado. "Look what we got!"

Trailing behind was Everard, and stumbling before him, with his hands pinned behind his back–

"Claude!" Willa called, running to embrace him.

"Willa–"

"Shut up!" said Everard.

"Whoa, whoa, now," said Lock, separating Willa from him. "You know him?"

"Oh, they know each other," said Everard.

"He's my friend, my, uh," she hesitated, "coworker."

"Down at Donor Eight," added Everard, grinning like a trophy hunter.

"What's he doing here, Willa?" asked Lock.

"Probably trying to find me," she answered, looking back to him and taking note of his haggard state.

"Going door-to-door, matter of fact," said Everard. "Can you believe that? Got some balls on him."

Lock kept her gaze on Willa, reading her, looking for any sign of foul play or shenanigans. "Well," she said, "he's brought us a gift."

Everard flung a bag from his shoulder onto the ground. "Go ahead, Willa. Check out what we got."

"It's OK," said Lock. "Open it."

Willa knew the contents already. The bag was a Patriot-issued portable cooling vault for emergency blood transport. She knelt and unzipped it. "Claude?" she said. "Is this all A-negative?"

A weak nod.

She ran her hand through and eye-checked what had to be forty or fifty bags. All A-negative. "Why?"

"What kinda idiot steals anything but O-neg?" Everard hooted.

Claude's eyes expressed a sadness that Willa had never seen in him, their aperture telling of his hope to find her, but at the risk of succumbing to some vulnerability.

"Mr Claude here has presented us with an offering of modest value," said Lock. "A-neg's well enough in demand. Alright, let's bring this soiree inside-of-doors." She zipped the cooling vault and shouldered it.

Claude followed the bag as it went by. Willa scanned him over. *What was he up to*?

Inside, Isaiah had barely noticed her missing, now surrounded by a crowd of tiny admirers, rapt as he retold the tale of his journey across town just the day before, complete with brellabots and hotdogs eaten in a restaurant. Seeing Claude, he rushed over and hugged him. "Claude!"

"Isaiah," Claude said, with a gentle smile. "Hey, buddy."

Willa gently pried Isaiah away. "Past your bedtime, baby," she said. "You and Claude can hang out in the morning." Then turning to Lock, "Can we stay here, tonight?"

"Oh, I insist," she said with a colder, inhospitable tone. "Any vacant pallet will do."

Willa went to getting Isaiah settled in an adjoining room filled with children, and did a visual check on Claude, who sat motionless at the small kitchen table looking evermore fatigued. After the children's chirping died down, Willa sat with him, across from Lock and Lindon, who were in fervor about where to spend the blood.

"Donor Eight is obviously off the table," said Lock. "Would be funny to sell it back to the place he stole it from, though."

"Shouldn't go to Six neither, half my folks been busted in there," added Everard from the folding chair by the door.

"Safest bet is to send everybody segment-wide. A sudden clot of A-neg through one station would be suspect, especially since this one just stole a vault of the stuff," Lock chuckled and pointed at Claude. "Claude: what's the incentive on A-neg today?"

He inched his head from the table. "It's… it's not for sale."

"It's good as sold, Claude," she said. "What's it up to? Seventeen-ish?"

He nodded, then looked at Willa like he needed to tell her something.

"You have his blood, is he allowed to go now?" asked Willa.

Lock gave Willa a cynical smirk. "This bag keeps blood for two days, is that right, Claude?"

"Hmm-mm."

"Theoretically," Lock said, "he can leave once we've laundered it. But I still want to know why he came here in the first place."

"I promised Willa I would find her," he answered. "That's it."

"You found her," said Lock. "Now what?"

Claude turned to the window, his shoulders twisted and narrow.

"Claude, are you sick?" asked Willa.

"Just tired," he answered.

"Eat something then," said Everard, dropping a colander full of blackberries onto the table. Willa pushed it over but Claude waved it off.

"Ungrateful." Everard swiped the bowl and brought it in to the children.

Lock took in the situation. "I'll get the A-neg to my guy Jethrum tomorrow morning. He can offload it," she said. "So, tomorrow plus a week or so to let any additional surveillance this one's triggered blow over. Then he can leave."

"That's too long," muttered Claude.

Lock sneered. "That's the way it is, reaper."

Willa sat with Claude late into the night. She sipped tea while he didn't so much as look at the cup she'd made for him. He didn't seem well, like he had the flu, slumped with his head down on the daisy-print tablecloth. He'd likely been up for two days straight, just like her, on the run from Patriot since he'd killed his boss.

The children were all asleep, as well as the various adults including Everard beside the front door, and Lindon in the folding chair at the back. Lock had gone off on some errand, to another one of her hideouts, perhaps, or to negotiate a deal for Claude's blood. Willa straightened, felt her back pop, and went to the sink for some water. Bringing the glass back to the table, she scooted her chair right next to Claude, rubbed his shoulder until he straightened. "Hey," she whispered.

He raised his head and looked at her with sagging eyes.

"Claude, my God, what's the matter?"

"Shhh, don't wake them," he said, nodding to Lindon.

"Drink," she said, pushing the water over. "You've got to be parched."

He glanced at the water and pushed it away. "I came here to warn you."

"About what?"

"They've put out a PatrioCast on you… you and Isaiah. All of us now."

"Well I suspected that, Claude."

"Descriptions too," he said. "You got rid of the purple hair… good." There seemed to be more, but he didn't say it.

"It's pink," said Willa, trying to lighten the mood. "You look awful. We can find you a doctor. Lock has connections."

"Too late for that, now," he groaned.

"No, it isn't," Willa said, trying to make it the truth.

"I need to tell you–" He doubled over, pushing through a wave of pain, though Willa could see no external injury.

"Tell me what, Claude?"

Then he looked at her in a way he'd not in all the years they'd known each other. A look that pierced every layer of who he was to the outside world, Claude Vergenne: the fifty-three year-old, single, quiet, nondescript, supervisor of Patriot Donor Station Eight. Now he was just a person talking to another person. Then he whispered, "I'm going to die soon."

"Die? No, you're not," Willa's voice cracked and she went to stand. "You're just tired! What'd they do to you?"

Claude squeezed her arm and yanked her close. "Be quiet and listen to me!" he growled.

Her eyes welled from the pain of his grasp, but more the shift in her friend. "OK."

"I didn't steal that blood to sell it."

"Claude, I don't understand what's going on." She wiped a tear from her nose.

"It was to give me enough time to find you, that's all. Now I've found you." He paused and took in the room as if seeing it fresh for the first time. "I can't go back out into the world anyway. And I'm not going to get what I need the Old Way."

"The Old Way?" She pulled her arm free and shifted in her chair, a kernel of fear taking root somewhere in her core. "What were you doing walking around with fifty units of A-neg, if you weren't selling it?"

"You remember the blood bag yesterday?" he asked. "The leaking one."

"Yes," she said, recalling it. "The bad suturing."

"Yeah." He paused, allowing her to piece together what he was saying.

"Oh my God," Willa said, her gears turning. She remembered his shock when he'd seen her arrive. The bag he'd been holding was A-negative. He'd played it off like he'd been startled by her showing up early. But that wasn't it at all. It was because he'd been caught. "The bag… it wasn't really leaking was it?"

"No."

Willa stiffened, tying it all together. "You… you were drinking it?"

He nodded.

Time stopped. Everything crystalized. Claude was the same thing as Scallien. And suddenly her brain was screaming, imploring her to be as far from him as possible. After what had happened before, her instincts came on strong and potent, like ammonia. She felt her calves and hamstrings tensing automatically – her body going through its involuntary pre-flight coil. She glanced to Lindon, wishing he would come awake. Could Claude move as suddenly, as viciously, as Scallien had? Could she get to Isaiah before he got her? Could she get them both out of there?

"Willa," he said, placing a hand near to her on the table.

But she wasn't listening. She was panicking. Indecisive. Frozen.

"Stop that," he whispered, seeing her distress. "Look at me. I'm weak."

She looked at him. At first she saw nothing. Her brain was elsewhere. Then her eyes regained their focus. He was still just Claude. Same as he'd always been. And he was right. He could barely hold his head up. She knew in her heart that the man she'd always known would never hurt her. She just wasn't sure if that was the Claude seated next to her now. Trying to assume the best, she fought her fear, doing all she could to push it away, to swallow the scream that welled up from the atavistic place within that recognized a predator.

"I came here to help you," he said.

Her head was spinning, with one word flashing again and again. A word from her youth, from books and horror movies, posters on the wall and Halloween. It was the stuff of fantasy, not the real world.

Her voice croaked, "So, you're... you're a–"

"Basically."

Willa took the reins of her mind and forced it to slow down, to silence the alarms going off while she processed. "And what happens if you don't eat?" she asked.

"Already happening."

She didn't want to say the word, tried not to think it, but here she was, scanning the room for a duffel bag full of blood. Blood that she would feed to her friend if she found it. Then again, what if they didn't? What would he do then? Would nature compel him to fall upon her and drink his fill? She shriveled some. "We'll get you your bag."

"The other woman. She has it," he said. "Doesn't matter." He dropped his head to his wrists again. "I'm dead anyway."

"No, no. We'll figure it out." Willa cased the room, her attention divided between the vampire at her side and her desire to save his life. She had so many questions, turned to ask them, but he had nodded off, as if his own blood had drained. What would Lock and the others do if they knew the truth? What was the truth, anyway?

"Claude," she said, rousing him. "Claude."

"Hmm."

"Can I... can I... I want to... help?" she asked, pulling up her sleeve and sliding her wrist over the table.

He pushed upright, considered her crepe-paper skin and smiled weakly at her kindness. "Wrong type... you're the wrong..."

"Wrong type?"

"I'm A-neg," he said, muffling a cough into the crook of his arm. "I can only... A-neg, O-neg. Anything else would kill me."

"What about him?" she asked with a chin-tick toward the sleeping Lindon. It was callous, but Claude was her friend, and he was dying.

"I won't do it the Old Way." He crossed his arms a little tighter, as if smothering discomfort, and glanced at the sleeping man. "Besides, even if he wasn't sick, he's AB-negative."

"You can tell type just by looking?" She wasn't sure what Claude meant about Lindon being sick, but that seemed less important.

"Smell." His eyes fluttered and his head looped to his chest and back up again.

"Claude." She placed an arm over his back in a lopsided embrace.

"Hmm."

"What do we do... Claude?"

His head rested on the table, facing toward the window. It took all his strength to turn and face her. "I brought you proof."

"Proof of what?"

He remained there with the side of his face on the tablecloth, his body slumped and precariously balanced in his chair, his breath shallow. His eyes opened against the weight of mortal stupor. "Of who we are," he said. "The inside pocket..."

"Claude?" her voice rose higher as she saw him slipping away and she pressed her face into his shoulder.

"...of the cooling bag. All of us..."

"What, Claude? All of us what?" She squeezed him. "Oh, Claude."

"Scallien." His final exhalation made the words. "All... like her."

Willa felt the moment that death took him, his back where her cheek lay, at once rising with breath and then not. She wanted to reach out and catch his life, put it back inside of him. She pressed her weight upon him – this person who had been her only friend, who had saved her – and wished for her body with its warmth to revive him. But his skin was already taut, the flesh beneath it like hardened wax. With cool light filtering around the blinds on the kitchen door window, Willa laid her head beside his and prayed that it was all just a dream.

* * *

"Rise and shine!" hollered Lock, bursting through the kitchen door with a bowl of fruit. Lindon jumped to attention and Everard cursed something from the front room. Willa stayed where she was at Claude's side.

"What's going on?" Lock asked, setting the bowl on a countertop. "Hey," she paused, "is he dead?"

Willa did not answer.

Everard entered, but stopped cold upon seeing the corpse. "Whoa! He stroke out or something?"

"What the hell happened?" said Lock.

Willa sat up and put the heels of her palms to her tear-streaked face. "He died."

"I can see that!" Lock said. "How?"

"He starved."

"Come again?" Lock said, stepping closer as if she hadn't heard. "How could he have starved in a day?"

"He…" she tried to put it delicately, "didn't have any food."

"There's food here, Willa." Lock gestured to a freshly commandeered The Box resting on a shelf.

"He didn't have his food."

"*His* food?"

Willa struggled to formulate a way to explain what she knew, or thought she knew. "The cooler bag with the A-neg," she said. "He wasn't trying to sell it."

Lock's demeanor intensified. She spun a chair opposite Willa and sat. "What'd he steal it for then, Willa?"

Everyone had their eyes on her. How do you tell someone something that breaks reality?

"He was… He was something else. I don't understand it. Another one like him attacked me at work, a Patriot manager. She was… going to kill me," her voice wobbled. "And Claude saved me. He killed her. He was on the run, like me, and that blood was his lifeline. I think… I think maybe…" There was no easy way to say it. "It was his… food."

"Food?" exclaimed Lock.

"The blood?" Everard spat.

"Calm down," said Lock. "This is all bullshit. He probably just had a heart attack."

A line of children had gathered at the threshold between the front room and the kitchen. Lindon, who hadn't said anything to this point, ushered them back and away from the spectacle.

"It was a heart attack, Willa," said Everard. "A stroke maybe. Too much stress at work."

"Lindon?" Willa called.

He returned into the kitchen. "Yeah?"

"You're AB-negative, correct?"

His eyes popped. "How did you know that?"

She nodded to Claude. "*He* told me."

Everard nervously fumbled with his pack of cigarettes. "How he know that?"

"He could smell it," Willa said, feeling a sense of pride in speaking for her friend. "From across the room, he could smell it inside you."

The air went out of the room. Even Lock was at a loss.

Willa went on, "Claude said there's more of them. All of Patriot. The Harvest… the blood trade…" She cast her eyes to her dead friend. "I don't think it's for the people in the Gray Zones. I think it's for them."

CHAPTER TWELVE

HEMATOPHAGOUS
Feeding on blood; sanguivorous.

Everard had finally had it. "You sayin' he's Dracula?"

"I don't know what they are," said Willa. "All I know is he needed that blood to live, and he said he didn't want to get it *the Old Way.*"

"I think you need to leave and take him with you," said Everard, stuffing his cigarette back into the pack. "We been flyin' under the radar just fine by ourselfs. Who knows if he did something to lead Patriot or whoever to us."

"Agree," said Lindon.

Everard stormed into the next room and began loudly packing up Willa's and Isaiah's things. Willa crossed her arms and didn't budge, waiting for Lock's reaction.

Lock held Willa's gaze for several long seconds. "Stop." She glanced at Claude again. "What if it's all true?"

"You believe this?" asked Lindon.

"I don't *not* believe it," Lock answered, giving Claude a poke. "We already know the blood drones are a lie."

"What?" said Everard, reentering the kitchen. He let Willa's duffle drop to the linoleum.

"Yeah, I shot one down," said Lock. "Empty."

Lindon shook his head. Everard furrowed his brow and rubbed

his face as if he'd just been awakened from a deep slumber.

Lock went on, "Why'd he only take A-neg from the donor station? He could have grabbed O-neg just as easily."

"All that mattered to him was compatible blood," said Willa. "He wasn't looking to sell."

Everard leaned back against the wall, clearly trying to keep his distance from Claude. "Still don't make him a blood sucker," he said with some disgust as he considered the corpse. "Just a rogue employee carrying around a sack of blood who had an infarction in our kitchen."

"But he knew Lindon's blood type," said Lock, raising an eyebrow. "That's something."

"Lucky guess," Everard shot back.

"Everything Willa's said so far has been true," said Lock.

"May-be," he said, "but now she's tryin' to tell us he's a vampire. A *vampire*, y'all." Everard was genuinely incredulous, which surprised Willa. She would have believed him most likely of anyone to embrace the paranormal as an obvious explanation.

Lock stepped to the center of the room. "If this is all true, which I'm still not sure about, everything is turned on its head. I never liked the blood trade, but it had a reason for being. If it's all just a way for these… things to get blood–"

Everard interrupted, imploring her to stop. "We and these children survive here. 'Cause a your hacks. We can't risk everything based on the delirious ramblings of the soon-to-be-dead."

"Wait," Willa interrupted. "Where's the cooling bag?"

"Cellar out back," said Lock.

"He said he brought proof. Get it."

Lock grunted and rushed through the back door.

Willa finally noticed Isaiah nearby, transfixed by Claude's stillness. In all the confusion, she'd not thought to keep him away. "Claude died, Grandma? How?"

"We're trying to figure that out, baby," said Willa. The boy had already seen his mother fade from anemia and Willa felt a pang for introducing death into his life again. "I have a lot of questions too,

'Saiah." She held his cheeks and rubbed his temples lightly with her thumbs. "Sometimes we don't know why things happen the way they do." She shuffled him into the room to be with the other children. "Claude was our friend. I'm going to find out."

She reentered the kitchen just as Lock stomped back in with the duffle. She heaved it onto the table and ripped open the zipper. Willa pulled up on the top flap and sunk her arm to the elbow in blood bags as she fished around for the inner pocket. "Here we go," she said, her fingers grasping hold of something hard and pointy.

Then they all saw it.

"The hell?" said Everard.

It was gold. And a lot of it. A solid chunk, beautiful and rich in color, shining brilliantly but with liquid depth. It had shape too, and once the room was over the shock of treasure in their midst, Willa joined in their confusion as to what it could possibly be. It was an artifact or a sculpture of some type, a tiny jawless skull no bigger than a squirrel's, with vacant orbitals. Sprouting from below the eye sockets were a pair of golden tendrils that snaked out from the face, like forward-facing whiskers, their tips cambered to pointy spines, fine as fishhooks.

Willa set it on the table and zipped the bag shut.

Lock touched it, let her finger flow across the smooth dome on top. "Creepiest little knick-knack I ever saw," she said, poking at a tangle of tentacle-like outgrowths peeking from the underside, opposite the twin spines.

Everard put his hands on his hips, mumbled, "Satan's paperweight."

"OK. Alright. That's weird. Not sure it proves much, though," said Lock. "I mean, it's not worthless. We could melt this sucker down and issue our own currency."

Willa, meanwhile, couldn't take her eyes from the two slender barbs that ran down from the eyes. She recognized them. Those little needles at the ends had been meant for her, and she envisioned Scallien's face rendered around them as the memory of the attack rekindled. "It's her," she said.

"It's who, dear?" asked Lock.

"The one who tried to kill me. The one Claude killed. Her name was Scynthia Scallien. Patriot executive. It's from her… or, it was part of her," Willa said. "These were in her mouth, right behind her teeth," she pointed to the needles but did not touch.

"This whole rig was inside her head?" Everard gushed, his voice high with excitement.

"Well, those fangs sure were."

Lock used a nearby pen to flip it over and they all moved in for a look.

"Fangs are hollow, see?" said Everard flicking one with a fingernail. "Like a rattler. All pit vipers got 'em."

"So maybe she was poisonous too," replied Lock. "OK, well," she clapped her hands together. "We're going to need a new abode." She gathered the bag onto her shoulder and scooped up the relic. "Find somewhere to melt this down. Sell it, or something."

"You mean leave?" asked Willa.

Lock pointed at Claude. "Maybe you didn't notice the sanguivorous dead Patriot employee in the kitchen, Willa! The one who came here with a stolen satchel of blood containing the final remains of a murdered Patriot executive!" She slapped the table. "And *you*, a should-be-dead Patriot ex-employee. You were risk enough by yourself. Now three paths lead to our door. So. Time to va-moose." She took a quick inventory of the house. "The kids. Two loads. Lindon, take half to the Bahamas. Everard, bring the rest to Seychelles."

The men left the kitchen and went to organizing the children. Willa heard their voices throughout the house, rousing and gathering. She stood bewildered and finally got air into her throat sufficient to ask, "Where… Where are you taking them? I don't–"

"Bahamas," Lock answered. "Seychelles."

Willa shrugged.

"Sweetheart, you never use code words? You're missing out," said Lock. "They're safe houses, girl. Time to 'git."

"What's this one called?"

"Paradise Island."

Willa rushed into the front room and loaded Isaiah's backpack. "Where are we going now?" he asked.

"Somewhere just like this."

"I don't want to leave my friends."

"You don't have to. A bunch of them are coming with." She helped double-knot his shoes and shouted toward Lock, "Do you have a plan or something?"

"Sure, uh, yeah. Hey, can you come on in here for just a sec," called Lock from the kitchen, "I'll tell it you."

Willa took Isaiah by the shoulders. "You help those other kids get their things together, 'kay baby?" He nodded obediently, like he always did.

In the kitchen, Lock looked like she'd seen a ghost. "Claude's movin'."

CHAPTER THIRTEEN

AUTOLYSIS

The self-destruction of dead or dying cells.

He was moving, though not like a person moves; rather like something that had never lived. Like a scrunched drinking straw wrapper dabbed with water. Shrinking and expanding in different places at the same time. His face had melded to the skin of his forearm on which it rested. His back appeared sunken and slack underneath his windbreaker, its fabric drooped over shoulder blades like collapsed tent poles. His features dropped while his body began to slough from the bones. Bits of him drifted to the floor as if made of sawdust. Thickly clumping powder, still moist, poured from his pants legs, into and over his shoes. His sleeves dropped to his sides, drawn down by the weight of his disintegrating arms that spilled into miniature dunes across the tiles. At last, his neck and head slumped onto the table, becoming unrecognizable mounds of dust.

Willa and Lock shared the moment speechlessly. Willa leaned over and blew some of the dust from where Claude's head had been, gestured to Lock.

"What are you doing?" Lock asked.

"Pen," demanded Willa, blowing again. A fleck of gold appeared amid the remnants. Using the pen, she lifted yet another miniature fang-bearing skull from the wreckage.

"Lady," said Lock, "you know anyone that ain't a vampire?"

The thing was identical in shape and appearance to the one that had come from Scallien, but the pointy tendrils were shorter, their barbs less pronounced.

"Arright," said Lock. "Put him in the bag and let's go."

Accommodation inside the Seychelles was spartan, even compared to Paradise Island. There was a stove from which Lock siphoned gas from a neighbor, who was probably siphoning it from theirs. The weak flame barely heated a kettle, though something about being able to drink a cup of tea – even if dilute – worked to raise the spirit. Lock had earlier flown a sortie to an associate, the mysterious Jethrum, and sold off Claude's A-neg at what she labeled a usurious discount. Nevertheless, it earned them enough to feed both of the safe houses for a few weeks, if they were austere, which they always were. Willa didn't mind her belly growling so long as she had some tea, and she rejoiced that she'd remembered to bring some of the minty stuff along.

Isaiah and the other children continued to harass Everard in the shared space. He was a natural with them, knowing just when to be firm and when to let them burn off their cabin fever. Sometimes this meant allowing the children to dogpile and pummel him, during which he feigned protest, but couldn't suppress the joy in his voice.

"All these years of collecting whole blood," Willa said, testing the sides of her mug with her palms. "They told us it was because they didn't have the anticoagulant required to fractionate, but it was just because they only eat whole blood!"

"Apparently they eat a lot of it."

"What do you mean?" Willa asked.

"Well, your boy Claude, he bit the dust pretty fast like, didn't he?"

"Hey!" snapped Willa. "Claude saved me. He may have saved all of us."

"I didn't mean anything by it," said Lock. "My point is, how long could it have been since he ate? Not long, right? He had a whole cache of the stuff. Fifty-five total units. If they have to eat so often, then how much are they putting down across the board? How many of them are there? How many employees in Patriot? I mean, are we dealing with a couple dozen of these guys or thousands?"

Willa shrugged. "Patriot is big, it's everywhere. I don't know how many employees there are in total. But we collected a lot of blood. Millions of units per year."

Lock cleaned her goggles, reaffixed them to her forehead and yawned. "We know the blood drones are bogus. That's for sure. So the blood goes where that Speedloop tube goes."

"I suppose," Willa agreed, though the revelation was hardly helpful. They both knew the tube might as well have been invisible, as there was simply no way to trace its path. The advent of transport drones had brought with it many unforeseen consequences, not the least of which was the slow extinction of geographic directions, of maps, and even the end of memorized pathways from one place to another. Only the perpetually ambulant – the poor – still had to know and appreciate spatial relationships, learn the compass rose, and actually remember how to get from one place to another.

The speedloop, a frictionless, high-speed, high-capacity transportation system, was all over and largely underground, making its actual pathways impossible to know. Figuring out where it might emerge, or the origin of any single termination point, was impossible, absent spending the money to ride on it – an option not generally available to the low- or midbloods. The tube that Willa had seen running from SCS Distribution could end up anywhere, and it wasn't one you could simply buy a ticket to ride on.

"Do you have anyone over there at Patriot who could help us… preferably someone who identifies as human?" asked Lock.

"They all *identify* as human," said Willa.

"You know my point."

Willa shook her head. Her stallmates at DS8 could hardly be considered acquaintances, and what's more, they were mostly idiots.

Lock palmed Scallien's relic. "And the only two of these creatures you knew are now dead."

Willa nodded along and sipped her tea, then quickly swallowed a scorching mouthful as she suddenly remembered. "No!" she said, shooting up from her chair. "There's another one. He's a board member at Patriot."

"He's one of these?" Lock held up the relic.

"He has to be. I saw his PatrioText conversation with Scallien. He's the one that gave her permission to liquidate me."

"That's what they called it? Liquidate you?" Lock asked. "That's cold, Willa. What's the fella's name?"

CHAPTER FOURTEEN

AGGLUTINATION
When cells adhere to each other.

Willa waited in the middle of the concrete expanse, hardly believing that she had returned. By herself, she was exposed, vulnerable. Her situation stood in stark contrast to the last time she'd visited, then so keenly intent on doing her job, going beyond the call of duty to make sure the blood she'd collected got where it needed to go so that it could save lives. The thought that it was all probably a terrible lie had her brimming with rage and she briefly considered spitting on the SCS Distribution grounds.

She made her way toward the building, toward the same interface into which she'd delivered her vault a lifetime ago. She'd planned her walk so as to arrive at dusk, only a few minutes before the drones began their skyward march to the Heart. As the sun dropped behind the trees, they came single file from the roofline, the muffled buzz of their ducted fans hardly louder than an electric razor. A flock of grackles took to the air from a copse of pines behind the wall that ringed the perimeter. She followed the birds as they congealed into a disc with a slight depression in the middle, and thought immediately of red blood cells.

She counted the drones, read the words on each belly. Sneered at how they'd twisted a message she'd once been proud of. *Be a Patriot.* And even though she knew what was coming, she still jumped when the first one went down, careening into the concrete wall, its body disintegrating from around empty blood vaults. A second crashed down behind it.

They were past the point of no return now. Her heart was rocking. Her hands shook. And she realized that sweat had soaked into the shirt at her ribs – despite the cold – as anxiety gripped down. Her mind said run. But that wasn't the plan.

For the first time in days, she thought of what she must look like, or worse, smell like. She'd sponged off a handful of times over the tiny sink inside Paradise Island, but now with the prospect of seeing someone outside of Lock's crew, she felt doubly conscious of her appearance. She laughed aloud at the inanity of the thought and dug around in her bag for some lipstick. She twisted up a bullet of bold magenta and applied it in a clipped flourish, then smoothed down the pink hair that she had earlier re-donned. She capped the makeup and dropped it into her bag just as the lights of a security drone ascended into the sky from the center of the distribution building. Nervously, she flattened the folds of her reaper's black. Would it be Jesper or somebody else? She supposed it really didn't matter.

The drone landed nearby. Olden emerged and breezed around to where Willa stood. He extended an open hand, which she took instinctively. "We have a kill on sight order for you, Ms Wallace," he said, leaning forward to kiss her knuckles. "But I confess that my curiosity was too much! I simply couldn't help myself. I'm dying to know why our lovely blood drones always come crashing down in your presence. They aren't cheap, you know."

"They're fake."

"Well, of course they're fake, Ms Wallace. I commend you on your powers of deduction. Though to be fair, you had a little help from Scynthia, rest her soul."

"You send the blood out through the speedloop."

"You know," he said, carrying on like he did, "I've always had an open-door policy. If you'd had questions about our processes,

I would have happily answered them for you. At the cost of your mortal coil, of course. Secrets are secrets for a reason; you understand."

"And what's the reason?"

"Don't be coy in these last minutes, Ms Wallace, I suspect that Claude made everything known to you. Where is he these days? Carried off a rather large bag of A-negative from his precinct." Olden chuckled. "*That'll* be deducted from his paycheck."

Willa glanced toward the pines.

"Protecting him? I understand. He saved you from liquidation at the teeth of an ambitious junior executive." Olden removed a pocket square and wiped the corner of his lips. "Your loyalty is so admirable." He sighed, looked at the fabric. "Can I be honest with you? You just don't find that in our ranks. It's every man for himself, nowadays."

"You should hire more women."

He laughed genuinely, caught off-guard by her pluck. "But I suppose that didn't work out for either of us did it? You know, it's a shame I have to do this. You might have been upper management."

Willa scoffed. "That's a lie."

"I was being magnanimous," Olden said coldly, eyes narrowed.

"If you're going to kill me, can you at least tell me the truth?"

"About what, Ms Wallace?"

She shook her head. He could talk forever when he felt the need to pontificate on the way of things, but clamped shut when it came to answering a simple question, especially when he knew she really wanted an answer. "What are you?" she asked.

"What am I?" he asked, grinning. "Surely, you've figured that out by now."

"I want to hear you say it." She crossed her arms over her chest, looking directly into his eyes.

"Wouldn't you rather spend these last minutes talking to your grandson? You can use my touchstone," he said, handing it forward. "Here."

"Answer my question."

"Have it your way," he said, pocketing his touchstone. "But answer mine first – where is Claude?"

"Dead."

"Dead?" he asked, eyebrows raised. "And how?"

"You got your answer, now give me mine: what are you?"

"So strict!" he exclaimed, relishing the back and forth. "Come into the drone. I'll tell you on the way to your final destination."

"Do you think I'm an idiot?"

"Far from it, Ms Wallace!"

"I'm not getting in there with you. You'll liquidate me on the way. You want to kill me, you'll do it right here."

"Oh, stop being so dramatic." He stroked his lapels. "This suit is hand stitched. The fabric? Well, I don't really know where it's from, but I know it cost five thousand. I'm not going to risk getting it – ahem – stained. Second, liquidation is so... vulgar – an uncivilized way of taking a meal left to neophytes and hobbyists. Thirdly, you aren't my type."

Willa shifted uneasily on her feet. Shot another glance into the pines.

"Yes, do please stand back. Your impoverished milieu makes my stomach churn." He fanned himself.

"Pardon me?"

"The poor. They have a smell. Inside the nose of my kind it is the olfactory equivalent to rotting flesh. Just a whiff makes me want to wretch out my insides and have them purified by fire."

Willa shook off his insults. "You're avoiding my question, Mr Olden."

"Do you know," he said, placing the pocket square over his nose and mouth, "that every drop of blood in your entire body wouldn't buy a single component of that newly crashed drone?"

"Answer me!"

"Rich!" he exclaimed with panache. "What I am is rich."

"Rich?" she asked. It wasn't the answer she'd expected.

"So many centuries, so many monikers, who knows which was the original, biologically correct name."

"Vampires."

"*That* term," he said, tensing some, "we of course despise. No such thing. Fantastical creatures like unicorns and satyrs. I adore the smell of garlic, Willa. Love strolling about my estate on days when the *sun shines*. I own three tanning beds. I've tested the legends, naturally – bathed myself in holy water for Christ's sake – and guess what? Same as regular water. And how could we forget mirrors?" He framed his face with his fingers and smiled. "Do you think I could throw all of this together without one? But I digress. In answer to your question, Ms Wallace, we are both rich and also something else. And we are nothing without both. Most prefer the ecologically accurate taxonomy, 'Apex'. A crisp description, and entirely apt, but I prefer the oldworld nomenclature: 'Ichorwulf.'"

"Ichorwulf?"

"I know. A bit visceral, perhaps. Animalistic even – but it reminds one that you come from somewhere, and not to lose yourself in the present." His eyes flashed. "You're not losing yourself in the present, are you?"

"I'm not lost." Another glance to the pines.

"Perhaps. But so many are. Lost to convenience, the ease brought on by technology." He shifted and made his face look thoughtful. "I'll let you in on a secret, if you promise not to tell anyone."

Willa only sneered, her disgust for the man deepening.

"Well," he relented, "since you won't be around long to spread it, I'll tell you anyway. Do you know that virtually none of my kind would be able to detect your blood type by scent? That nearly all of them have completely lost their sense of smell? Decades of neatly labeled blood bags, prepared like baby food, coming from donor stations like yours, telling them what's what. Amazing, isn't it, how technological advancement works against us, how we are dulled, made stupider by our own achievements."

Willa found herself agreeing, but countered, "Claude hadn't lost his sense of smell."

"Claude was old school. Grounded. I liked him. His demise is a pity. I take it you sold off the stolen blood he was carrying?"

"The blood doesn't even go to the Gray Zones, does it?"

He let out a true bark of a laugh. Then composing himself, said, "The Gray Zones–" but he stopped, feeling the MK's cold muzzle pressed to the base of his skull.

"Take me to your leader," said Lock from behind.

Olden went rigid, sucked at his top row of teeth with his tongue. Willa felt an adrenaline surge at the success of their gambit.

"Mr Olden, meet the Locksmith," said Willa, smiling. "She's the one who's been shooting down your lovely drones."

"You can invoice me," said Lock.

Olden dabbed the pocket square to his forehead and adjusted a piece of hair that had come free. "You were stalling."

"You don't shut up."

"Can you blame me?" he said, mustering a salesman's confidence. "No one *converses* anymore. So, I see the dynamic has changed. How may I be of assistance to you ladies? Money? I can have a teller drone brought down. Twenty-five hundred sound appetizing?"

"You said your suit was five thousand."

"I did," he said. "How astute. Well, what would you say to ten then?"

"We don't want your money," said Willa.

"No?" He held his arms out to the sides. "You must want something."

"We'll be taking that drone," said Lock, nudging him.

"And your touchstone, please," said Willa.

He handed it over and Lock guided him into the drone with the rifle's muzzle pinned squarely between his shoulder blades. "Take it off network," she said. "Go on."

Olden brought up the screen and scrolled to a settings panel.

"Nuh-uh," said Lock, clicking her tongue. "Hardware disconnect, Mr Olden. Panel's right behind the display. Starboard side. I think you know that." He gave a respectful nod and smirked, opened a small door and unplugged the wire harness inside.

"Kill the circuit," she said.

He ripped a small unit from its mooring and tossed it on the floor, then smashed it with an oxblood wingtip.

"That'll do," said Lock, taking a seat. She eased the butt of the rifle onto the top of a combat boot while keeping the business end trained on Olden's head. "That's nice," she said, pointing out his Patriot lapel pin. "May I borrow it? Forever?"

"So," he said, loosening the pin and tossing it over, "what now?"

Willa pointed to the screen. "Show us where the blood goes."

CHAPTER FIFTEEN

EXSANGUINATION
The action or process of draining a person, animal, or organ of blood.

"Very well," he said. "Llydia?"

Destination, Mr Olden? came the drone's epicurean voice.

"The Crest."

Right away, sir.

Willa stayed quiet but knew Lock was thinking the same thing. Capillarian Crest was a real place, but for the denizens of AB Plus and the like, it held the status of myth: a large neighborhood, what would have been considered a wealthy suburb in the distant past, with beautiful mansions, rolling manicured gardens, and affluent residents unbound by the blood trade. That the rich could buy their way out of their obligation wasn't surprising – it was expected, understood. But now, sitting within feet of the monster who had recently given the go-ahead for her death, the truth insinuated itself into Willa's mind. The residents of Capillarian Crest didn't have to buy their way out of anything.

The drone jumped lightly into the sky, far more nimble and powerful than any taxi, and banked to the northwest.

"It will be eight minutes or thereabouts," announced Olden.

Eight minutes to destination, repeated Llydia. Olden gave a smug grin. Despite being inches from a sniper's rifle, this was not a man who feared for his life.

Eight minutes was an eternity in drone flying-time as the good ones had a cruising speed of close to two hundred miles per hour. Willa guessed Llydia was even quicker, meaning that Capillarian Crest was between twenty and thirty miles away, isolated from the rest of the city. On the screen, an expanse of green forest stretched to the horizon. No highways, no roads, not so much as a walking path to break the wilderness. The land rose and the trees seemed to gain height as well, until the woods gave way to an expanse of emerald grass and warmly glowing homes, spread out at first, but more closely situated further in. There were occasions in Willa's youth when she'd seen such homes in passing, from a distance. But now, decades later, they were alien. Nobody lived like this anymore. The arrangement of the homes struck Willa as they passed overhead and it wasn't until they began to descend that she understood why. There were no streets. They didn't need them.

"Llydia," said Olden, "go ahead and take me home, please."

"Home? Sorry, no. Cancel that Llydia," said Lock. "We're not going to your house. Do *not* land, Llydia!"

Olden frowned theatrically, now sensing he had the upper hand. "You say you want to know where the blood goes, yes?"

Willa's mind raced. Olden was playing a fast-paced game of chicken, upping the stakes and taking them out of their comfort zone to see who would be first to flinch. The drone set down on one of the sprawling lawns directly in front of a large, white house. And just like that, they were in the lion's den.

"Willa," said Lock, "I vote we just kill him now and take this nice drone."

Willa knew what Olden was, that he had given Scallien permission to murder her, that he'd landed at SCS distribution with every intent to finish the job. But he had a human face and she wasn't a killer. She tried to choke out a response as the door slid open.

"Willa?" urged Lock, her knuckles white around the rifle's receiver.

Olden smiled and winked. "You wouldn't do that in front of my family, now would you?"

Behind him, the glass doors to the home had come open and an exquisite woman with chest length blonde hair, strode down a path in the lush grass. Tall. Behind her, a girl, perhaps thirteen years old, followed. Olden pranced out to meet them. Willa and Locke exchanged nervous looks. If they didn't follow, they'd lose any leverage. Of course, standing in the middle of Capillarian Crest, they'd likely lost it already, and the drone was tied to Olden, preventing their escape. Willa quietly berated herself. They'd engaged the enemy without knowing how the game was laid out.

Willa followed onto the lawn with Lock close behind. The woman stopped and shifted so the girl was shielded behind her. Olden waved them off, smoothly as ever. "Nothing to trifle over, my loves. Some friends here for our evening meal. Quick now, run back inside."

As his family turned for the house, Willa and Lock sped their advance to keep up. With night falling, floodlights on the outside of the large, designer home sprang on as they entered.

They found themselves inside a magnificent foyer, glassed in on three sides and illuminated by an enormous crystal chandelier. The Oldens moved across the open floorplan and into the kitchen. Upon reaching an island at the center of it, the woman spun to face Willa and Lock. "No guns in the house, I'm sorry. Friends or no."

"Don't worry, ma'am," Lock opened the chamber and flashed it. "It's fully loaded."

The woman narrowed her eyes in disgust before Olden swept in between them. "Darling, these are my friends Willa Mae Wallace and this person here, with the large gun, is... well, I'm afraid I'm familiar only with her stage name, 'The Locksmith'."

"Lock's fine."

"Lovely," said Olden. "And Willa, Lock, this is my wife, Venya, and my daughter, Ellen." Ellen had moved beyond the kitchen proper, to the distant side of the room where she stood at a table in the breakfast nook.

"Hello, dear," Lock said, hefting the rifle. "Don't be afraid, now. This is just for show." The girl didn't react.

"Why are they here, Jesper?" asked Venya.

"They insist upon getting answers to some questions they have about the blood trade."

Venya's angular lips twisted and she pulled a tiny crease from her pencil skirt. "The blood trade? Jesper, are these Patriot employees?"

"Ex," said Willa. "As of yesterday."

"I haven't had the pleasure," said Lock. "Been told I'm unemployable."

Olden skirted the white marble island across from an immense refrigerator. "So, it was my thought that we could calmly discuss any issues that Willa and Lock have, here in our home." His eyes flitted to a particularly large chef's knife as he made his way.

"You reach for that steel, you're gonna have an issue with my MK, *'mkay*?"

"Haha," he said, steering away. "Let's find some common ground. Perhaps we should all sit down at the family dining table and go from there."

Venya pivoted on her heels with a sneer. Ellen took the seat by the window, between her parents. Willa trailed them to the table and settled opposite Ellen. Lock propped herself against a stool by the island, rifle at the ready.

Olden pulled his chair snug and clasped Ellen's hand on the table's gleaming cocobolo surface. "We are an open book. What all would you like to know?"

Willa saw the gambit. Ellen was the trump card. Olden had wagered her presence would prevent any violence. At the same time, she knew Patriot, and she certainly knew Olden. There was no way he would let them leave the house alive.

"Where does the blood go?" she asked. Although she had basically figured it out, they needed to stall while she tried to figure out a plan for their escape.

"Well that question has already been answered, hasn't it?" he said. "I've taken you right to it."

"Capillarian Crest?" Lock exclaimed.

"The name has a fitting ring, wouldn't you agree?"

"So, it comes here?" Willa continued. "For everyone that lives here?"

"Yes," he said, "we may export surplus, but what this city produces comes here. Patriot is a proximate producer. Buy local."

"We're foodies," said Venya.

"Tell me if I begin to bore you, but there is such a lovely symmetry to the system," he said, fanning his hands. "Donation precincts in every city, enough to drain the population in proportion to the number of – ahem – us."

"Bloodsucking vampires, you mean," spat Lock.

Venya stood, hissed, "How dare you!"

"Whoa now," said Lock, tapping the rifle. "No reason to get excited. Sticks and stones and all that."

Venya scowled and approached a mirror. She spoke into it while maintaining eye contact with Lock. "I exist. I am *Apex*, not some trashy horror movie creature."

"Ahem," said Olden to Lock. "Apologies, but we don't use the *V* word. On that subject we're a sensitive bunch."

Lock swept the rifle back to Venya. "Start existing back in your chair," she ordered, keeping the muzzle trained as the woman returned to the table.

"How much are you stealing from the Gray Zones?" asked Willa. "How much are you taking from the victims?"

"What Gray Zones?" asked Olden innocently.

"What do you mean *what Gray Zones?*" Willa asked. "The Gray Zones. Stop messing around."

Olden sighed. "Willa, you are not listening. There are no Gray Zones. Well – not anymore, at least. It began that way of course, and… evolved, I suppose. It's a truly amazing machine, what we've created." He waggled a finger toward the adjoining room. "You see the mantle, there, above the fireplace?"

Willa located the mantle, a heavy stone plinth with a rough-hewn front edge, over which hung a comically short ornamental sword. Resting on the mantle below the sword was a large, red book with gold lettering and filigree.

"Our annotated history," he said. "You are welcome to study it for as long as you like."

Willa felt the brick and mortar walls of her beliefs, of her very identity, beginning to shake and crumble. She'd assumed that these people, these creatures who ate blood, were merely piggybacking on the system. Skimming off the top to quench their thirst. But the truth went far deeper. They weren't stealing from others. They were producing for themselves. Her head reeled. Had she really worked her entire life, taking blood from those who couldn't spare it, allowing them to cash in their vital essence to make ends meet, not for the greater good, but for these things to devour? The words fell out of her like tears. "We're all just livestock."

"And what a noble place in the hierarchy you occupy… *sustenance for the elite,*" said Olden, fanning his hands as if his words were on a marquee. "Conveniently, we exist in roughly the same proportions as you do in terms of blood type. I am A-negative, so that is what I eat, or O-negative, of course, universal donor and so forth. Venya, my heart and soul, is actually AB-positive, universal recipient, which is convenient as anybody's blood will do for her." He looked at both Willa and Lock, raised his eyebrows, and added, "Which means you all have some common ground. How nice is that?"

"Y'all fuckers literally eat our blood," blurted Lock.

"Language," Olden admonished with a careless snort and head-check to Ellen. "So. This… is where the blood goes. This place, and thousands of others like it, in thousands of other cities," said Olden, shifting in his chair. "Check the kitchen vault if you care to verify."

Lock started to back towards it, but Willa stopped her in her tracks.

"Let me," said Willa. "You stay put."

"Yeah, smart," said Lock. "Hey Ellen, what blood type do you eat?"

The girl was stoic.

"A-negative, just like her father," Olden volunteered.

Willa went to the vault, swung the door open. The inside was filled with regular food: vegetables and fruit, milk, yogurt pods, lunchmeats, juices, sauces and condiments. "So, what exactly am I looking at? Where's the blood?"

"Appearances, Ms Wallace, in the rare case of visitors outside the species," said Olden, adding, "There will be a small switch, there, just inside the crisper."

Willa leaned over and looked through the window of the drawer.

"Feel free to squash the produce," Olden said helpfully. "We don't eat it."

The drawer opened smoothly, and nudging some leafy greens aside, Willa introduced her arm up to the wrist. "I can't feel it."

Olden began to stand. "If I can just–"

"No, you cannot just," said Lock. "Sit."

Olden obeyed, hands up in mock surrender, and leaned slightly forward.

Willa pressed her palm to the cold interior of the drawer and pushed it farther inside.

"That's it," said Jesper. "You're a natural. A bright future in *Refrigerator: Maintenance*."

Suddenly the door to the crisper closed, trapping Willa's wrist. "Hey!"

"Oh no!" Jesper whined sarcastically. "What's happening?"

The entire interior of the upper compartment of the vault, including the crisper and all of the shelves, began descending into the base as a single unit, pulling Willa's arm down with it.

"Make it stop, right now!" Lock said, aiming her gun at Olden.

"I wouldn't do that," he said.

Willa began screaming as her arm was wrenched downward.

Lock pressed the barrel into Olden's cheek. "Stop it! Now!"

"You asked to see where the blood goes. I'm showing you!"

Lock shouted orders at the vault.

"I'm afraid it only responds to family members," Olden added.

"What kind of locksmith gets stumped by a refrigerator?" said Venya, chuckling.

Ellen stayed frozen, struck motionless by the chaos around her.

Willa was on her knees, pinned against the front of the vault. Her arm felt like it was being slowly pulled from the shoulder.

Lock re-chambered her round and backed toward Willa.

Willa cried as the inner compartment settled heavily into the space where a lower freezer drawer might have been in a normal refrigerator. Her arm was wedged between the appliance's outer shell and the interior unit that had descended into it. Tears bled from the corners of her eyes.

"That is a *lot* of weight on that arm," Olden stated observantly. "I can't envision how long it will remain attached, though I am sure your tendons and ligaments will hold for a good while if they are any bit as stubborn as you are. But fret not. I have not forgotten that I promised you an answer to your question – Refrigerator?" he called musically. "Open the food drawer, please."

Amid all the pain, a soft mechanical noise brought Willa's eyes up the empty space that had been vacated by the shelved portion that now had her pinned. The back panel, where the refrigerator sat flush to the wall, dropped slowly down. Once clear, ten horizontal racks extended from a void, strung with Patriot-issue bags swollen full. Labels etched onto each by a needle-scanner from a donation stall just like hers delineated collection date, blood type and expiration. Almost all O-negative, with A-negative and other phenotypes scattered throughout.

"What is it?" called Lock, her eyes and gun still jumping back and forth between the gleaming Ichorwulves.

"Blood," Willa winced. "A lot of it. O-neg, A-neg… some AB-pos."

Lock moved closer to Willa and tried to budge the mechanism that had her trapped. At the sight of all the bags, Lock's voice came softly, as if the last touch of innocence within her had finally been snuffed. "People think they're giving their blood to help... but you people... you're just... stealing it from them."

"You would rather we pillage the townships and keeps for stray peasants as our ancestors did? Using a person for only a day before discarding them? You would rather be hunted? You would prefer mass murder?"

"At least people would know the truth," said Lock. "You've made everybody slaves."

"Oh, tsk, tsk. Please. Slavery carries such negative connotations."

The pain in Willa's arm radiated in pulses that gave the alternating sensations of severance and burning. She struggled to stay conscious and gasped for breath as her heart thrummed. Her head drooped low to where she could only see the three sets of shoes under the kitchen table.

Noting her incapacity, Olden smiled up at Lock. "Oops, look at that," he said. "Three against one."

"I'll shoot all three of you," said Lock.

"We're too fast for that," said Olden.

Lock sniffed, wiped her nose. "Fine," she said, swinging the gun to Ellen. "Come at me, I shoot the pre-teen."

Meanwhile, Willa's eyes blurred as thick tears dribbled from the tip of her nose. Through the salty film, a distorted scene met her sight, and she saw the slightest of movements beneath the kitchen table. It unfolded so slowly that she didn't know if it was actually happening or just an image refracting poorly through her straining eyes. She worked hard to focus, blinked away what tears she could, and watched the shadows. The gleam of a pointy red shoe tip, gently nudging down the heel of its opposite. A graceful foot with garnet toes pulling free of the vamp, moving lithe and dexterous to lay the stiletto on its side, then pulling the second shoe from the other foot. A hallucination? It felt that way.

Through her delirium, the removal of shoes seemed more than just a familiar routine that one might do when relaxing at home. The movement, somehow, was imbued with a significance that struck Willa as vaguely reminiscent. Déjà vu. From deep within, underneath the smoking remains of all she had believed and all she had worked for, came a vision. The small woman in the scalloped collar. The platinum ponytail pulled tight. The tiny murderess whose own demotion to bare feet had presaged her violence.

The second stiletto was placed to the side and Venya's feet settled together, her smooth calves tensing. Willa's voice came weakly, "Lock."

"Yeah, I'm here."

"Venya…"

Venya launched upward and away from the table, screeching, a flash of gold in her maw.

Red mist filled the air with the gun's percussion and the woman fell headless against the mirror. Ellen dove under the table.

Olden was on Lock like a bolt of lightning. They grappled backward toward the foyer, beyond Willa's periphery. The MK clattered to the marble and she heard the sickening thump of Lock's body hitting the ground. The sounds of hand fighting and struggle came clear, but she could not see it or do anything to help.

"No!" Willa gasped. She felt all of those she'd lost coming back to her: the friends, family, Claude, her own daughter, gathering in wait on the other side for this new entrant who had so quickly become someone she trusted; a friend. For a flash Willa saw herself as the common denominator in the death of so many, a cursed person, a *reaper* not only as government blood collector, but in the mythical sense. The last visitor. The one who guides the newly dead to the underworld. Now it was happening again. Her ears heard, translated the process of Lock's dying. Willa screamed and screamed, squirmed against the vault, powerless to save her friend.

"I can't say –" Olden spoke as he strangled the woman, "– that I loved her." Willa could hear Lock's hands slapping and grabbing, her breath only bubbles. "… so vain and boastful… overshadowing my own vanity and boastfulness."

"Let her go!" screamed Willa.

"I – am – free," Olden continued. "You have liberated me – leaving me with quite the mess, however."

Willa struggled against the vault, roared and fought to pull herself free, to see her friend. She owed her that.

The sounds coming now were abrupt, Lock's body running through its final reflexes. Airless coughs convulsed, her head bumping the tiles.

"You held on for longer than most."

Then choking. A gargling release. A thump. Silence.

Willa sobbed, her breath shallow, and her thoughts flowed to Isaiah. He was as safe as he could be, and with people who knew the truth. People who could help get the word out. Maybe they could expose the lies of Patriot and those it served, the *Apex*, these *Ichorwulves*.

Footsteps. Tears ran cool over her hot cheeks and her utter fatigue brought a measure of calm as death approached. Considering all that she'd been through, it was probably the case that she'd been living on borrowed time anyway.

"Willa?" said Ellen, kneeling down in front of her.

Willa flinched, unsure how to react to the vampire child.

"I think your friend is still alive, but she's unconscious."

Willa searched the girl's face. It lacked the animal intensity of her parents and her mouth bared no fangs. Confused, still panting for breath, she asked, "Where's Jesper?"

"He's over there."

Willa grunted, but couldn't bring her head around. "What's he doing? Is he – is he coming?"

"No. He's dead."

CHAPTER SIXTEEN

MACROPHAGE

A type of white blood cell and part of the immune system that consumes and digests foreign substances. From the Greek, big eater.

Everard explained the rules of the game again, then shuffled through the pack of cards until he located the Queen of Spades. He withdrew it from the deck and stuffed it back into the box.

"Why'd you take that one out, Everard?" asked Hali, who was eight.

"I told you. You gotta have an odd number of queens so whoever ends up with just the one lady is the Old Maid," he answered, leaning back against the front of the couch. "Any other questions?"

"Yeah," said Wren, sitting criss-cross on the stained carpet. "What does the winner get?"

"That's how you do it! Gotta have a wager. Right then," he said, washing his hands in the air. "What are we playing for?"

"Pizza!" exclaimed Sasha.

"Yes. Pizza!" Ryan added.

"Pizza?" asked Everard, underwhelmed by the stakes. "You could play for any-damn-thing in the world... uh, rocket ships or ponies, a trip to the storm on Jupiter, and all y'all want to play for is pizza?" He surveyed the circle. "Lynn? Wren? Isaiah? Got any suggestions more tantalizin' than that?"

Clearly happy with the idea of pizza, they each shook their heads.

"A'ight, suit yourselfs."

He dealt the cards around until they'd all been handed out. He fanned his own cards and evaluated them. "Now see," he said, plucking some from the array, "I've got a pair here an' I'm just gonna set that down." The kids just watched. "Y'all do the same, now, g'head."

The children went to work on their own cards. The youngest boy held up a pair of sixes.

"Yeah, just like that Wren. That's a pair. Set that down." He guided the boy's hand to the ground, then waited until the rest had finished sorting their cards. "OK, see, now I offer my lot to Jack and he picks one," he said, allowing the boy to select a card. "Good. Now, Jack, you offer yours to 'Sosh, nope – not face up, Jack. 'Cause see now she can just pick any card that helps her pair hers off, see?" He reached over and gently flipped Jack's wrist so that his cards faced down. Sasha selected a card from Jack, pulled a newly formed pair from her stack, and presented her cards to Hali. Feeling like the kids were getting the hang of the game, Everard stuck a cigarette between his lips. He didn't light it, though, on account of his proximity to nascent lungs.

When the game finally ended with Everard deemed the Old Maid, he stepped out back while the children pretended to devour their imagined winnings. He took the cigarette in his fingers and gave it a sniff down its length. There was nothing like the smell of a fresh one just before you fired it up. He slapped the filter against the back of his hand, put it to his mouth and flicked the lighter.

That first hit. Lord it tasted good. That old Willa was anti-smoking along with the rest of the planet, but he'd be damned if he was ever gonna give it up. Smoking was great. One of the last things in this shitass world that made him happy. Well, that and the kiddos. A smile glowed in the ember's light.

He leaned into the kitchen to check on the gang, careful to keep the smoldering butt outside the home. Having restarted a round of Old Maid without him, he felt his heart lift. Not just at their taking to the game so quickly, but because it might mean time for a second smoke.

He took a long draw and blew a ring skyward. The clouds were light and low against the early evening sky. A nip in the air seemed to warn of early snow. On the horizon a faint glow ebbed into being. He never wore his glasses – the prescription was decades out of date – but he wished for them now. He squinted, even set the smoke down on a rail so as to focus on seeing. Obscured by the clouds, the source grew brighter. Coming closer. A drone, no doubt. His pulse thumped in his ears. The color and hue of the glow shifted and altered with the changing density of the clouds through which it passed. Orange became amber became pink. A nervous dribble of sweat ran coldly from his armpit. He wished for purple as the pink began to darken. His mouth made the words. *Purple purple purple.* With the drone mere blocks away, the color shifted a final time, as hot pink faded not to purple, but to red. The color signature for Patriot drones. He took up the cigarette and did a few quick pulls.

Everard felt his body go tight, each sinew being drawn up and battened. Surely it wasn't coming for Seychelles. And if it was, surely it was only because Lock had hijacked it. She did stuff like that all the time, though she'd never shown up with an actual Patriot model. He stood paralyzed on the stoop; cigarette stuck idle in the corner of his mouth. Praying wasn't a thing he really did, but with so many souls under his care, *well*. He shut his eyes and pled with the Almighty to make the drone pass harmlessly overhead, to make it bound for some other destination. He opened his eyes just as it broke from the clouds.

He flicked the cigarette and screamed into the house. "EVAC!"

The children dropped the game and leapt into action as they'd been schooled to do at the mention of the word. Shoes went on, jackets were donned and zipped tight, the younger bundled and readied by the older. They ran to the cabinets under the sink, pulling out small backpacks filled with snacks, extra clothing, and water.

Everard turned back to the sky. The drone's vector was straight for them. Now the only hope, and a thin one at that, was that it'd been stolen and flown there by Lock and Willa. Maybe they'd commandeered a drone from that Jesper Olden. Right before it set down, he glanced back inside to see the children lined up at the front door just as they'd been taught.

The drone landed and doors opened on either side. A graphite and gold helmet broached the threshold. Everard retreated inside, locked the door, and blasted to the front of the house. He did a quick headcount as he undid the bolts on the front door and swung it open just as men smashed in through the back. "To your places!" he yelled, pushing the children out toward the street, hoping they'd remember their hiding spots throughout the neighborhood. A new soldier appeared out front, nabbing two of the children and striking out for the others. Some got past, some ran back into the house, pounding the floorboards and diving into any cranny that might conceal them.

He whirled inside only to find another soldier behind him. Everard leapt up, coiling his arm around the back of the man's head, locking his forearm across his neck and face. The helmet popped off. He lifted his feet and drew down with all of his weight. The man spun, striking Everard's tailbone against the door frame. Pain exploded up his spine just as the man's teeth sank into the meat of his arm. He released and dropped to the floor, then rolled to avoid a strike. Springing to his feet, he cracked the man's skull with the helmet, and followed with a flurry of punches. At the same time, soldiers flooded the home, collecting the children and dragging them away. Fire in his veins, he pummeled the man in a trancelike fury, registering half consciously the distant sound of his own voice coming through, a continuous stream of vitriol and hatred and anger and fear. The soldier's face became a bloody pulp and Everard felt a blip of pride at his skill in single combat after so many years of resting his mitts. Grabbing a handful of the man's uniform, Everard smashed a fist to his teeth just as he felt something clip his neck just below the ear.

He slapped his hand to the wound and crumbled to the floor against the wall. Time slowed to a crawl as he struggled to stand, only to feel the crush of a boot on his chest, pressing the air from his lungs. The home he'd protected was a blur of tiny bodies and wiggling limbs and fearful screeches – children facing new trauma in lives built from it. A backpack cartwheeled across the carpet, its contents tumbling out. A doll. A bag of crackers. Everard moaned with the sorrow of a parent who had lost, and tears spilled freely from eyes that could no longer see.

And as the room went black, they called for him.

CHAPTER SEVENTEEN

ANASTOMOSIS
A surgical connection made between two structures.

"Dead?" asked Willa.

The girl glanced over Willa's shoulder. "Yes."

Willa strained against the vault and Ellen quickly stood, said, "*Refrigerator, show Ellen's shelves.*" The racks of blood withdrew into the back wall and the interior chamber began to ascend back into place. Willa cried as her arm appeared, still partly in the crisper, her inner bicep torn and bleeding. It came free and she spun to the ground against the vault. Her eyes found Lock. And Olden.

Lock rolled to her side, coughing. Olden lay next to her, face down, the ornamental sword from the mantle lodged in the back of his head, its tip jutting out from under his chin. A runnel of black cherry followed the blade's edge to the floor.

"Lock," Willa groaned, "are you OK?"

Lock wheezed, "I'm–" coughing, "right as a – trivet."

Willa steadied as she regained her composure, shuffled on her knees toward where Lock lay. "How did you–"

"The girl," came Lock's rasping voice. "She did it."

Willa spun to Ellen. "You–"

The girl stood rigid as a soldier might. "They're *not* my parents."

"Not anymore, anyways." Lock said, caressing her throat.

"What are you talking about, Ellen? What do you mean they're not your parents?"

"He's not my dad, she's not my mom," she answered, rummaging through a purple backpack on a stool. "My name is Kathy and I'm from B Minus in Riversfork. We have to go now."

Willa heaved herself up and wrapped a kitchen towel around her arm. She took the ends up with her good hand. "Can you tie this for me?" Kathy nodded and snapped a crisp knot, pulling it down tightly on Willa's wounds. Watching the girl work, she said, "Riversfork is a thousand miles away. Why do you live here?"

"They took me from my district. *Adopted* me."

By now, Lock was standing and she limped over to pick up the rifle.

"What?" asked Willa.

"They can't have kids," Kathy continued, stepping into the slick of blood that had already taken on the appearance of wet sawdust.

"I don't understand," Willa said. "You mean, they literally can't reproduce?"

"Not like humans," Kathy answered, taking hold of the sword's handle. "They steal us from the blood districts in other cities, then adopt us." She placed a foot on Olden's neck and leveraged the blade from his skull. Willa grimaced as the man's face caved in. Lock grinned.

Kathy found the scabbard nearby, sheathed the sword and pushed it into the backpack up to the hilt. "Hey," she said, throwing open a kitchen drawer. "I need your help." She set a rectangular butcher's knife onto the counter.

Now Lock was grimacing. "Help with what?"

The girl set a cookbook face down and drew it to the edge of the counter. She stretched her right ring finger over the book cover and held the knife out toward Willa with her left. "You have to cut it off."

Willa was dumbstruck. "Cut what off?"

"My beacon," she said. "It's in the second joint."

She handed the blade to Willa. "Right there," she said, pointing to the finger's middle segment. "It's fused to the bone."

"Cut your finger off?" Willa said as she gripped and regripped the knife. "I don't know if I can–"

"You have to. And now."

Kathy ripped a dish towel from its rod and gripped it with her left hand. "Go," she said, steeling herself. "Please."

"There's no other way?" asked Willa, swallowing hard.

Kathy's face was no longer that of a child. "I keep my finger and they find me. They find you. Do it."

"Gimmie that," said Lock, going for the blade.

"No!" exclaimed Willa. "No. I'll do it."

Willa went to the range installed on the island, lit a burner, and sterilized the blade. She came back around to Kathy's right side. Lock set her hands on the girl's left shoulder.

Willa pointed to the finger. "There's a little divot right here between the joints. I'm going to try and hit it." She set the edge of the blade on the spot and hefted a large cookbook binding-down so as to concentrate the greatest amount of force in the smallest area. Not completing the cut would be worse than missing.

Kathy gritted her teeth and blinked her eyes in agreement.

Willa made a face at Lock. Taking the cue, Lock said, "Hey Kathy, you have any pets?"

Kathy turned to Lock, "Wha–?" And Willa hammered the knife.

Kathy collapsed to the floor, howling. Lock wrapped the towel tightly over the bleeding stump and pulled the girl's face to her chest. "OK, OK."

Willa didn't know whether to join in comforting the child or keep things clinical. "I'll dress it properly when we're back home," she said. She looked to the tiny finger laying on the cookbook. It seemed suddenly unreal, like it had never been attached to anything – a movie prop. Even the blood leaking onto the marble seemed fake. People don't just go around having their fingers chopped off.

Kathy growled to suppress the pain and began pushing slowly upward. "We. Have. To. Go."

"Whoa, hold a sec, kid," said Lock, giving her a gentle push back to the ground. She dug into one of her skirt's utility pockets and withdrew a small canister. "Open. This will help."

Kathy obeyed. Lock uncapped the lid from over a nozzle and spritzed the girl's mouth.

"What is that?" asked Willa.

"My own secret recipe. Little of this, little of that. NSAIDS, maybe some synthopiates, microamphetamines."

"Opiates?"

"It'll take a few minutes to kick in, but when it does, she'll be better than new. And stronger." Lock ran into the living room and called back to them, "Nobody else here we need to rescue?"

"No," answered Kathy.

Lock returned to the kitchen and scanned about the room. She pointed to several empty boxes folded against the wall. "Use those. Get the blood from the vault and I'll sort Llydia."

Willa brought the boxes over to the refrigeration vault.

"Refrigerator: open Mom and Dad's blood drawer," said Kathy, shuffling over.

"Kathy? Are you sure you should be standing?"

"Mmhmm. Fine," she mumbled.

Willa scowled at Lock, who headed toward the front.

"I didn't give her a big dose," said Lock, elbowing the door. "She'll be fine."

Willa gathered bags one handed from the top racks as Kathy used her one good hand to pull from the lower.

Willa was bursting with questions, but she knew she had to go easy given Kathy's state. "So, where are your real parents?"

Kathy's lips tightened and she began working faster.

"I'm sorry, you don't have to tell me," Willa added.

"Dead probably."

"What makes you think that?"

Kathy shrugged. "That's just how things go in the districts."

She had a point. "How did you get here?" asked Willa.

"Some they rounded up. Just came into homes and took us.

Others they got off the street. But the main way, especially with the young ones... was with candy."

"Wait, candy?" Willa asked, dropping three bags of O-neg into the box. "What type of candy?"

"Just, like, these red lollipops – I've tried them. They taste better than anything you've ever had. Anyway, they tell the kids to hand them out to their friends. The group gets bigger and bigger until they go back for more and that's when they're taken." She stuffed the last few bags into the boxes and sealed them. "All of the kids from Riversfork got split apart, so I don't know where they all ended up."

One-handed, Kathy folded up each of the poly handles on the sides of the box, pulled them toward the center and nudged it toward Willa.

"These are too heavy," said Willa, straining to budge it. "I can't lift it."

Kathy eyed the boxes and thought for a moment. She trotted into the foyer, kicked a large exotic-looking tree from atop a stand with caster wheels, and pushed it over to the refrigeration vault. "That tree was like five hundred years old," she said. "Jesper loved it." Working together, they lifted the boxes onto the roller each lending their good arm to the effort.

At the still-open refrigerator, Kathy dumped handfuls of cheese-tubes, yogurt pods, veggie snacks, and a pile of apples into her bag.

"Good thinking." Willa gave her wounds a gentle squeeze. "Anything else we should take?"

But Kathy was already at a wet bar opposite the kitchen appliances dancing her fingers over the unopened bottles. She selected one each of bourbon and scotch.

Willa held up a finger, confused, "What are you do–"

"Are these flammable?" Kathy asked.

"Why?"

"Just tell me," Kathy growled.

Willa considered the bar, clenching some at the thought of fire, but respectful of the girl's mission, whatever it was. "Well, sure.

But I'd try the silver bottle and the blue one," she said, identifying some of the ultra-potent stuff she'd regretted drinking as a young woman.

Kathy scaled the kitchen island, dowsed the floor in booze, and sent the bottles crashing. Willa backed toward the door as the vapors of grain alcohol cleared her nostrils. Kathy took up a blood-spattered kitchen towel and ignited a burner on the range. The towel flared and she tossed it to the merging puddles below.

Willa hustled the boxes toward the front as Kathy leapt from the island. The liquor accelerant ignited with a muffled whump. Kathy ran to the door and held it open as Willa pushed through.

Together they wheeled the blood across the lawn, allowing it to buffet against their shoulders and injured limbs. Kathy shot into the drone first, then Willa with the boxes.

Lock messed with the screen. "How much blood did you thieves nab?"

"We have to go, lady," said Kathy.

"Give me a sec, there, kiddo," said Lock. "I'll override old Llydia here soon. I'm still a mite foggy from dying a few minutes ago. Just let me focus."

"We don't have time," said Willa, pointing at the house through the open door.

Lock glanced up from the display and did a double take. "Why is the house on fire?" She looked at Willa and then to Kathy, whose face answered the question. "Alright," she entered a final series of commands and a new screen appeared. "I'm in. Llydia, take us to AB Plus."

I'm sorry, Miss UNAUTHORIZED, but only verified Patriot employees with appropriate clearances may pilot.

"Look, Llydia, I am authorized. Olden gave me a promotion. See? Here's his old touchstone, oh and look." Lock pushed her lapel with Olden's insignia pin toward the Llydia's camera eye.

I will consult the directory. Name and identification code please.

"Fuck!"

Consulting directory for employee last name FUCK.

"Guys," said Lock, glancing at the swelling conflagration outside, "I'm just gonna have to fly her manual-like." She pulled up on the barrel of the rifle and removed a round from the stock. "Ears," she said, bolting it. "Llydia, it's been genuine." She pressed the muzzle to the ceiling of the drone and pulled the trigger.

The confined quarters caused the blast to reverberate into their skulls and Willa almost collapsed from the bench. Smoke cleared through the newly formed hole in the drone's roof.

"R-I-P Llydia," Lock laughed, slinging the rifle and digging back into the circuit panel. "The brains are right in the middle of the ceiling on these things for easy maintenance. Not flyable now unless… ha! OK, here we go." Another panel opened below. A small joystick sprang free. "Whoa," she said, turning to the other two, "when was the last time you saw one of these? Just antediluvian!"

Lock pulled up on the joystick and they were off into the night.

On the descent from Capillarian Crest, they dipped into the wilderness to check for passing authority drones but saw none. "Eight minutes to destination," Lock quipped.

"Are we going straight back, then?" asked Willa. "Is that safe?"

"We'll grab our shed drone at SCS, then head over to Tahiti to get that blood on ice."

Turning to Kathy, Willa explained, "It's a safe house. They're all named after tropical islands that people used to be able to go to on vaca–"

"I know what Tahiti is," said Kathy.

"You do? How?"

"I've been to school."

"So, they – the Oldens – sent you to school?" asked Willa.

Kathy nodded.

"They raised you just like you were their own child?"

"Not raising. Training," Kathy said, passively considering her finger stump. "School, riding lessons, drama, violin, cotillion, speaking, Apex history, attack, debate. Everything. But I wasn't allowed to go anywhere, ever, without a chaperone hiding somewhere. And I always had to lie about who I really am. Even though the other Ichorwulves know the truth. They just play along with the lie."

A nauseating confliction sloshed in Willa's stomach. By all accounts, Kathy, and presumably the other stolen children of the Ichorwulves, had found a better life than they could ever have imagined from inside the blood districts.

"How long did you live with the Oldens?"

"Since I was seven."

"How old are you now?"

"Fourteen."

"Did they… love you?"

The girl's head whipped around; lips peeled back. "They don't love anything. Well, except keeping hold of their power. It's all they care about."

"Did you ever try to run away?"

"No," Kathy said, squeezing her backpack. "They would have killed me."

"So, when you say they were 'training you'," said Willa. "Training for what?"

"When we get old enough, they give us the Choice."

Lock glanced back from her piloting, asked, "A choice of what?"

"To become one of them," said Kathy. "And if we don't…" her gaze returned to the blurring trees outside, "they kill us."

"Some choice," muttered Willa, no longer conflicted.

"SCS Distribution just ahead. Taking us into cloud cover," said Lock. They accelerated upward and broke the moonlit overcast, then slowed to a hover.

"What are we doing?" asked Kathy.

"We got our taxi drone down there, just outside the wall. But it looks like SCSD is gonna be tricky," she said tapping the view screen, which projected a nighttime view of the building far below, where icons representing authority drones patrolled the area. "Well, we can't go crashing the party in Llydia, can we?"

"Won't they see us anyway?" asked Willa. "Aren't we on their radar or whatever?"

"Without a brain, she's not putting out signal. We're invisible unless they put eyes or cameras on us. And they got no reason to put cameras on us if they can't see us."

Willa considered the swarm of drones already polluting the air. "It's just a matter of time before they see us by accident."

"Willa, I only just commandeered her, y'know. When I get five minutes, I'll outfit her with a smudge."

"A smudge?" asked Kathy.

"Spectral cloaking device," said Lock. "To anyone watching through a camera such as what gives us this image," she tapped the display, "a drone with a smudge distorts the picture, makes it look like a bird fart. But until then, SCS will just have to wait."

Lock kept them in the clouds as they moved toward Tahiti on the southernmost edge of AB Plus and dropped them straight down from above into a roofless shed little different from the one behind Paradise Island. The house itself was brick, which meant it was far older than the rest. "This house is unstaffed, so it should just be me in there. You wait here. Shit goes down, just use the joystick. Drone goes where you push it." She looked at Kathy. "Sorry for cursing."

"You already said fuck earlier," said Kathy.

"I did?"

Willa nodded.

Lock began to push the boxes. "They both full?"

"Yes," said Willa. "Almost forty liters, probably. I'll help."

"No, nah, you keep by Kathy, I'll do these," she said, with another grunt.

Lock opened the door and pushed the cargo from the shed. Kathy turned and presented something from within her backpack. "Cheese?"

Willa couldn't remember when she'd last eaten. "Yes, please."

Lock returned shortly and slammed the shed door. Kathy extended another cheese tube to Lock who took it with a wink.

"Tahiti secure. Blood safe. I can send Lindon over from the Bahamas tomorrow and he'll launder it up," she said, plopping into the captain's chair and biting into the food.

Silence settled over them as they chewed, and Willa could feel all three of them decompressing. Willa watched Kathy, curious about the girl who had just killed her adopted father and only shortly thereafter insisted upon the amputation of her own finger. She was big for fourteen, nourished. Strong. Auburn braids framed a heart-shaped, freckled face. Despite the infusion of Lock's homemade narcotics, there was a confidence in the girl's countenance, in those focused ochre eyes. They suggested everything was going according to her plan, as if she'd always been ready to rid the world of the Oldens and had been simply biding her time until the opportunity arose. The amputated finger was a speedbump, a toll tax given willfully for freedom.

"Hey, uh, Willa?" said Lock, breaking from a reverie of her own.

"Yes?"

"How did you know Venya was about to attack?"

"She took her shoes off."

"She what?"

"Took her shoes off. Scallien did the same."

"They go barefoot when they eat the Old Way," said Kathy.

"You've seen that?"

Kathy took another bite and started chewing. "I've seen a lot."

"Why do they go barefoot?" asked Lock.

"I don't know," answered Kathy, "ask one next time it's about to eat you."

Lock looked at Willa. "I like her."

"Me too," said Willa.

"Let's get back to the Seychelles," said Lock. "ETA two minutes."

The door had been ripped clean from the hinges.

"Oh God!" screamed Willa, sprinting from the shed and tossing aside the torn screen. The kitchen was smashed to pieces, splintered wood and old silverware strewn throughout. The children's emergency go-packs sat at random spots across the floor.

"Isaiah!" she cried, pushing through the entryway to the small living room. She tripped through a smattering of toys and into the back room, also empty. Lock yelled something from the other kitchen, but Willa wasn't hearing. She was underwater. Drowning. Rushing back to the front, she noticed a pair of legs sticking out from behind the deflated old couch and scrambled over.

Everard's chest struggled to rise. Breath sounds came hoarse as the angle of his head and neck against the wall pinched his throat. Blood wicked out from defensive lacerations on his arms and hands into the filthy carpet. Willa struggled to pull him to a sit in order to free up his airway, revealing a gash on the side of his neck.

"Everard!" she exclaimed, slapping her hand to the wound. "What happened, Everard? Where are the children?"

His eyes were slits. A word croaked out, "Took."

"Who? Who took them?"

He only groaned in response.

Lock rushed in, put a dry rag to his neck to stem the bleeding, but the low pressure made only a trickle. "Kathy, go in the drawer next to the fridge and grab my suture kit. I got to sew our boy up."

Willa asked, "Do you have any blood in this house?"

"Nah. Fridge is out."

Willa knew the fix but had never performed it. "Lock," she said, "where did you hide our bags before we left?"

"Pantry."

"Kathy!" called Willa. "Fetch my bag from the pantry, please."

Kathy stormed through the kitchen, her own hand still in a bloody towel, gathering the requested items.

"Everard?" said Willa. "Double checking: you're AB-pos, yes?"

Head slumped to the side, he mumbled, "Mmhmm."

Kathy returned with the supplies. Lock pulled out a cutting needle, then rushed to the stove and sterilized it. She drew a length of thread, looped it through the still-warm stitching hook and went to work on Everard's injury. "Looks like they just nicked you, son," she said. "Any deeper in and you'd be the artist formerly known as."

Willa groaned through the pain of her own injuries and she tore her bag open, restacking the contents beside. On top of her workbooks, she piled gauze, needles, catheters, vacutainers, surgical tape, and syringes. She handed the tubing to Kathy, said, "Please boil this, quickly," then dragged over a chair from the other side of the room to Everard.

"Stay awake, kid," she said, garnering a weak grin. While he was twenty years her junior, he was at least forty years old.

Kathy returned with the tubing set out on a cloth. Willa popped an eighteen-gauge needle from a sterile pack and slid it onto a catheter. On the other end, she placed a cannula rig with a control valve. Tore a length of tape. She felt the antecubital space in her elbow crease and guided the cannula's needle into the cephalic vein. Kathy's eyes went wide. Willa nodded to the roll of tape. "Help me get this in place?"

Kathy ripped a piece of tape, set it over the cannula, and pressed it to Willa's skin on either side.

"What are you doing?" asked Lock, still sewing.

"Something that probably nobody has done in seventy years," Willa answered, twisting the valve on the cannula. "Anastomosis. Direct transfusion." Her blood pushed through the tube toward the needle at the base, which she handed to Kathy. "Keep it off the ground. When you see a drop, tell me."

"Why don't we just go back and get some of the blood we stole from Tahiti?" asked Kathy.

"He needs it now," said Willa.

"Can't risk flying Llydia again until she's disguised, anyway," added Lock.

"I see a drop," said Kathy, focused again on the tubing coming from Willa's vein.

Willa closed the valve, stopping the blood on the far end, and knelt beside Everard. She took the free needle from Kathy, then tapped Everard's forearm lightly at first, then with increasing urgency. "Lord, he's got no veins left." She would have preferred the cephalic, but it had sunken from its spot in the skin's usual topography. The median basilic, to the inside of his elbow was available, and she angled the needle in and nodded to Kathy, who secured it with tape. She sat in the chair and opened the cannula, starting the blood flow from her vein into Everard's. "Say a prayer."

"Are you some type of doctor?" asked Kathy.

"No, baby," said Willa. "I'm a phlebotomist."

CHAPTER EIGHTEEN

ANTIBODIES

A protein produced in plasma that is used by the immune system to attack pathogens such as bacteria and viruses. If a person has type B blood, it means they have the anti-A antibody. If type A blood is introduced, it will be attacked by the body as foreign.

"How's his pulse?" Lock asked, her voice faint.

"Stronger," Willa said, touching Everard's wrist. She turned to Lock, who sat with the line now running to her arm, supportively adding, "You're very brave, Lock." She checked the tubing. "Two units were the minimum he needed."

His eyes blinked open, no longer glassy as they'd been thirty minutes earlier, and followed the tube in his arm to the needle in Lock's and finally to her face, where she looked down on him heavy-lidded. He'd been resurrected.

Willa knelt down. "What happened to you?"

"They landed in the back," he grunted, eyes gently weeping. "I was out for a smoke. Hoped maybe it was you lot. Couple-five of 'em. I pushed the kids out the front and tried to hold them off. They did me and got the little ones."

"How did they find us?" asked Willa.

Everard sniffed. Shook his head loosely, wiped his eyes.

"We don't even know if they were looking for us specifically," said Lock. "Though it seems mighty coincidental."

"Came straight out of the sky. Landed here, purposeful."

Willa peeled the tape from Lock's arm and withdrew the needle. She held the tubing high, allowing the remaining blood to flow slowly through the tubing and into Everard, then clamped it when the pressure equalized and the blood halted inside the catheter.

"How you know to do all that?" he asked as Willa retracted the needle and pressed some gauze to the wound.

"She's a phlebotomist," Kathy answered.

He considered her practiced movements. "Never seen a phlebotomist can do this."

Willa wound the catheter and walked to the kitchen where she brought the water back to a boil.

"She's old school," said Lock, lightly rubbing her own arm.

"We have to go find the children," said Willa. "Now."

"How are we supposed to do that, exactly?" asked Lock.

Willa returned from the kitchen. "Kathy, when they took you, where did you go?"

"Central City, Riversfork," she said. "Do you have one of those here?"

"We do!" said Willa, getting closer. It was a piece of information. Patriot was a regimented place. They probably handled things the same in each city. "Lock, they're in the Heart."

Lock nodded, taking it all in.

"What happened there, Kathy?" Willa asked. "What did they do with you?"

"They fed us," she answered. "Gave us toys and games. We got to watch movies and play. In the mornings, they had teachers come in and they started little learning groups, reading and math... I don't remember them all. We thought they were very kind," she said, though her face was a grimace. "We'd been taken, but it was, like... relief. We didn't worry about food. We slept through the night. A lot of the kids started to think it was pretty great, and after a few days, a bunch wanted to stay."

"Just as they planned, I imagine," added Lock.

A hole opened in Willa's heart, emptiness crept in. She couldn't provide much for Isaiah, but he knew she loved him. But oh, the places his mind would go with a belly full of rich food, brand new toys, and comfortable, friendly surroundings. Would he want to come back home to the districts to live with his grandmother after all that? Part of her wondered if he'd be better off – at least he wouldn't be subject to the draw anymore. "Kathy? Did you want to stay?"

"My parents were probably still alive then, so no. I wanted to go home," Kathy answered. "But a lot of those kids had no parents. They were easier to go along with it. They told us it was a government evacuation to protect us. And we got to eat candy and play. There was a swimming pool."

"Love pools," Everard winced.

"How long were you there before being sent to the Oldens?"

"A couple of weeks, till I got picked."

"They actually came and picked you out?" asked Willa.

"Yeah," said Kathy, as if there were any other way for it to happen.

"We have to get to the Heart," said Willa.

"Willa," said Lock in a doubtful tone. "This is Central City you're talking about. *The Heart*. There's no way in. I've reconnoitered it before. So have my associates. It's the Great Pyramid of Khufu far as we're concerned."

"We have a Patriot security drone sitting in the shed outside! Can't we get in with that?"

"Llydia? She's offline, sure. They can't find her, but if they see her and can't hail her, they'll shoot her down. No. Taking a stolen drone into Triple C airspace is the most certain way to die."

"You don't know that," said Willa.

"Well by now they've figured out that Olden and his headless bride got charcoaled inside their abode," said Lock. "It's his security drone that's missing, so I'd venture that using same to fly yourself into the Heart would result in your multiple perforation via lacegun."

Willa didn't care to be reminded about laceguns. They were a relatively new horror in a world already full of them. Carried by all manner of law enforcement including Patriot security, they reminded Willa of the old toy guns she'd played with as a child that shot coin-sized, frisbee-like wafers rather than spherical or bullet-shaped projectiles. Where the toy projectiles bounced right off of your skin, the razor-sharp alloy of *lace* cut right through. What's more, slight alterations in angle and pitch meant that lace could change direction, following a target as dictated by the gun's programming. Since lace was paper-thin, even the stubby lacegun rifles could hold a few thousand rounds. "I don't care," Willa said, cracking. "I need Isaiah to see me. I need him to know I tried. I have nothing else."

"Willa," said Lock, taking the seat next to her and draping her arm over her shoulders, "listen to me now. I'm committed to this, but we can't just be a couple of old-lady kamikazes. We're too slow, they'd see us coming. You are wise, Willa. Our solution isn't going to come by force. It's going to come by experience and brains and patience."

"What do you think we should do then?"

"Well, see, I don't know yet. That's the patience part."

Later, Willa huddled near a candle set low on an empty bookcase and tried to focus on the problem before her, rather than the life-shattering consequences if they failed. Unable to bear any further separation from the children, Everard, bandaged and reenergized by Lock's mystery mouth spray, had taken the long walk to the Bahamas to check on them. Lock had urged him to stay on account of his wounds, but he'd insisted. And who were they to stop him? The kids meant everything to him, and he blamed himself for losing the ones that had been under his care. Willa understood that. Only, the place where Isaiah was, she couldn't go. Kathy lay curled asleep on the threadbare couch. Lock snoozed restlessly out at the kitchen table.

Willa thought she'd done everything possible to keep her

daughter's son safe and healthy since her passing. But what was it she'd kept him safe from exactly? Were her drills and evacuation plans just empty exercises against the threat of another bomb that was never to come? While she'd been worried over how to protect her grandson in the face of another attack, the danger had always been just beyond the door, signing her paychecks, eating the blood she'd been pulling from her neighbors. *So foolish, Willa. Kept your head down and did your job thinking that it would matter. And in the end, none of it did. They were going to come for Isaiah one day and you had no idea.*

She watched Kathy and wondered about her real parents. What if they were still living? She wished she could write to them, let them know that Kathy was alive and well, that she'd saved their lives. Probably leave out the part where she'd helped murder and cremate her adoptive parents.

In just days, Isaiah would be in Patriot's system, a child with a new name in some other city, just as Kathy had been "Ellen". Where would they take him? Maybe it would be a family with a lavish home, offering opportunities he'd never dreamt of. She slumped against the bookcase and stared into the darkness.

Across the room something flashed; under the couch, a light.

It was all the way under, back up against the wall, a tiny white LED strobing in the carpet. Willa knew it immediately. It had shined from Isaiah's nook in the corner of her apartment for years. His viewer. *But how could that be?* She'd told him they had to leave it behind so they couldn't be traced. She remembered putting it on their kitchen table. The little devil had managed to sneak it out anyway.

She crawled across the floor and reached under the couch. Kathy didn't budge. With the viewer in hand, she retreated to the corner and tapped on the screen, bringing it to life. It asked for a password. Password? Willa had forgotten how old the viewer was. His mother had purchased it secondhand. Passwords, and the technology that asked for them were relics, almost old enough to join Lock's attic-bound computer museum. Everything was biometric now.

Now, other than his decision to smuggle the viewer, Isaiah was the least deceptive, most straightforward kid she'd ever known. He couldn't be un-earnest if he'd tried. So, what password would that kid choose? Willa typed:

P-A-S-S-W-O-R-D

Password invalid.

OK, maybe she hadn't given him enough credit.

I-S-A-I-A-H

Password Accepted.

Willa smiled at the innocent sweetness of her grandson's encryption and dimmed the screen. A basic drawing program was open. Willa enlarged the sketchpad with her fingers. There, in shaky writing that reflected his surrounding chaos, was one word quickly scribbled. *Attic.*

Willa looked immediately to the ceiling, heart pounding. Was Isaiah up there hiding? Did he avoid getting caught? She sprang to her feet, ready to go find him, then stopped herself short. No, no. They'd been back for hours. The boy would have come out of hiding as soon as he saw her. She gazed into the slats of a vent just above, then back to the viewer, realizing what her grandson had left them: a warning. She rushed over to Lock, shook her awake. "Hell?" barked Lock.

"Quiet, shhhhh," whispered Willa, turning the viewer to Lock's face. "Isaiah wrote this. Found it under the couch."

Lock's face settled to stone and she glanced upward at the old-style ceiling vents for an air conditioning system that hadn't run since Chrysalis. She pointed upward and cupped her ear, Willa followed suit. Hearing nothing, Lock gently pulled the barrel of her rifle from the wall and unclicked the stock, withdrew a round and opened the chamber. "Waiting for us to go to sleep, I bet," she whispered back. "Talk normal like we're still up." And then in a louder voice, "I can't sleep, you want more tea?"

"Sure, I'll have chamomile, do you have that?" And then, quieter, "Let's just get out of here."

Lock whacked the side of her own head, whispered, "Yeah, no shit, Willa. Wake Kathy."

The girl was kid-comatose, and Willa prodded her awake with a finger to the ribs. Kathy rolled over and Willa whispered in her ear.

"Sorry, don't have chamomile," called Lock, "just some oolong."

Willa slung her bag and guided Kathy toward the back door. "OK," Willa answered, "that would be great. I just can't sleep."

Lock eased the back door just enough for Willa and Kathy to squeeze through. Kathy's pack caught hold of the broken screen door and pulled it outward. Willa saw it happen in slow motion and reached for the screen just as it released. It smacked the frame with a loud crack.

"GO!" screamed Lock. Willa and Kathy raced toward the shed and leapt into the drone. Lock ran too, but whatever exploded through the roof was faster, and it fell upon her.

It took a moment for her eyes to focus in the moonlight, but Willa soon realized she'd seen him before. The big, quiet guy that'd visited her house. But he wasn't quiet now. Surrounded by splinters of the wall through which he'd launched, he hunched over Lock, eyes rolling back, pinning her to the grass, shoes off. Willa ran from the shed.

"Mister Hunter!" she shouted.

He looked up, eyes focused on her. Lock seized the moment to jam her Patriot lapel pin into his neck. He screamed and pulled at the pin. The top of the "P" gushed. Lock pushed him away and rolled to her rifle, balanced to a knee and leveled it. "Move and die," she said, her voice nonchalant. "Where's your touchstone?"

"Come get it," he said, ripping the pin from his neck and tossing it to the ground.

Lock angled the rifle and fired. The man's right hand disintegrated and he collapsed to the side, roaring in pain. Keeping her eye on him, she palmed another round and chambered it. "I'm happy to keep shooting off body parts until I find it."

"In my back pocket!" he cried.

"I'll get it," said Kathy, emerging from the shed.

"Careful, Kath," said Lock, triggering the flashlight mounted to the stock. Without looking away, she picked up the lapel pin.

Kathy found the touchstone and retreated. Baring his teeth, the man pushed up from the ground and stabilized himself with the wounded arm tucked into his ribs. He got to his knees and pressed his remaining hand over the hole in his neck. He considered Lock and then Willa. "I remember you."

"Is my grandson at Central City? Is he in the Heart?"

He shook his head.

"Kathy, let me see that touchstone," said Willa, taking it in hand. She went over to him and put it in front of his face to unlock it. "How much money do you have, Mister Hunter?"

"However much you want… you're just renting it anyway," he said with a smirk.

Willa's fingers danced on the interface. "Good, well hopefully we get a loaded teller drone."

"They're coming for you," he said.

"You already did, bitch," said Lock, checking the bolt. "How'd that work out?"

A teller drone appeared from behind the roofline and settled a few feet away from Willa.

"Tell it to give you fifty thousand," she ordered.

"What are you going to do with me?" he asked.

Lock scoffed, "How about I shoot something off every time you ask a question?"

"Julius Hunter, Patriot ID hexadoublesixtythree," he called. "Withdraw fifty thousand from discretionary." A clinking noise came from inside the drone. "You won't be able to spend those without being noticed. No reputable business deals in tricoin anyway."

"Lucky for us, my associates are of negative repute," said Lock.

A small door opened and presented a tray with two enamel-red tricoins. Willa had never seen the denomination.

"Two twenty-five thousand coins, huh?" Lock said. "Well, that *will* be tough to pass, he's not wrong 'bout that."

"What are we supposed to do with these?" asked Willa, her own blood rising.

"I don't tell the drones what denominations to use."

"Are the children still at Central City?" asked Willa, pocketing the money. "How long until they're moved?"

"It doesn't matter," he said. "Even if I told you, there is nothing you can do to get them back."

"What type blood are you?" Willa said.

"Highblood to you."

"You look like a twelve-pinter to me," said Willa.

"What are you talking about?" he asked, standing in spite of his injuries.

"Siddown!" Lock ordered. He slowly dropped back to his knees.

"Most people have about, oh, ten pints of blood, but every now and then… big gentleman like yourself…" Willa dug around in her bag and presented the twice-boiled catheter and a needle. "Twelve pints of blood."

He started to laugh – loudly.

"Hey you. Shut up," said Lock.

He only laughed harder.

"What?" asked Willa.

Hunter stopped his cackling and removed his hand from his neck. The blood had stopped running from the wound and what was left had dried to a powder. Smiling, he ran his fingers together, freeing the red dust to flutter away in the beam of Lock's lamp. "Come and get it, I guess."

Willa dropped the transfusion kit back into the bag and let it slip to the ground. She gestured for the gun. Lock raised her eyebrows at Willa's sudden aggression. She re-bolted the MK and gave it over. It was heavy and scary. The barrel wobbled as she brought it level. "The Heart. How do we get in?"

He just shook his head.

"Answer me!"

"Humans can't enter. It's impossible."

"You'll help us, then," she said. "You'll help us get those children back."

"I won't."

Willa pressed the rifle's trigger just enough to dent her finger pad. She wiped an eye with the bend of her wrist and retrained the sights on the man's heart, wondering briefly if Ichorwulves even had them. She knew what she had to do. Whatever Patriot knew of their activities, they would know more if Hunter lived. She re-shouldered the gun and blinked away her conscience. "Lock, get Kathy in the drone."

Lock said nothing and moved with Kathy into the shed.

"It's OK, Miss Wallace," said Hunter. "I don't have family. I would do it to you if I was on your end."

She squeezed the gun everywhere but the trigger, backed into the shed.

"What are you doing?" Lock yelled. "Shoot him!"

Willa backed away. "Let's go."

"He has seen us, Willa. He knows we have Kathy. Think. We have to do it."

"No."

In one motion, Lock pushed Willa to the drone's bench and stripped away the rifle. "No!" Willa cried just as a shot peeled the air from her lips.

Lock cleared the chamber. She bent to retrieve the spent shell and glanced at Willa without judgment, but rather in the way a soldier might regard a civilian who had tried but come up short. "The touchstone," she said.

Still in shock, Willa let the dead man's device slip from her fingers and into the grass. Lock slapped the door switch and Willa stared at the man's lifeless body until the view pinched shut.

They left the Seychelles for good. And even though Willa knew they were headed to join Everard and Lindon, she felt completely lost.

CHAPTER NINETEEN

Ganglia

Collections of interconnected nerve cells in the brain associated with the relay of motor control, emotion, cognition, and learning among the cerebral cortex, thalamus, and brainstem.

The Bahamas wasn't far by drone, two minutes tops, but every passing second was torture, wasted without sight of a solution. Willa thought of all the children, prayed that the other safe house hadn't been raided. Lock steered Llydia with one hand and examined her rifle with the other, taking a moment to flick some stray blades of dead grass from the Pic rail. Turning back to the viewer, she said, "Did you know Olden's lapel pin is a needle?"

"I saw it was hollow," said Willa, still jittery from the latest murder.

"It's a needle though. Like an on-purpose, intentional, needle." Lock dug in her jacket pocket. "See?" She handed it backward to Willa. Kathy scooted in to get a look.

The pin had a fine coating of powdered blood, which dusted easily away. Behind the top of the "P" was a modified Luer connector, not unlike the hub of a large gauge needle. The P's descender, on close inspection, was a standard, short-bevel hypodermic.

"Fourteen-gauge lumen," said Willa. "For getting the blood out quick as possible."

"Fourteen is big?" asked Lock.

"Gauge works inversely. Higher the gauge, smaller the needle. A twenty? Small. Fourteen is just about the biggest."

"Jesper wore it every day," said Kathy. "I never noticed that."

"One wonders if he ever used it to get blood," said Lock, "the Old Way." She put it to her mouth and mimed sucking on it like a straw.

Houses blurred by, their rooftops in the night just gloomier shades of their daytime colors. Willa wondered how many might be owned or controlled by Lock and how much firepower she had aside from the sniper rifle. "Lock?"

"Yeah, Willa."

"I have to get my grandson from Central City."

"I got six in there too, don't forget. My grandkids for all intents."

"Do you have more guns... or weapons," Willa asked, struggling to speak in a parlance of violence entirely unfamiliar. "Grenades?"

"Good God, Willa, you're gonna make me crash if you keep up with your jokes."

"I'm not trying to be funny."

"Alls I have aside from the MK are twenty-six rounds sitting inside the original ammo box that I gave myself as a retirement gift when they kicked me out of the Corps."

"You only have twenty-six more bullets?"

"Yep. Speaking of which – Kathy, would you be a dear and fetch a round from the stock there? We're getting close to the Bahamas. Yeah, just flip the little – you got it."

Kathy handled the gun adroitly and clicked down the small door on the stock once she'd found the bullet.

"Just drop it in my pocket," Lock said, indicating. "Here we are. Cross your fingers."

They slid into the shed with a thump and Lock opened the door.

"Janet!" called Lindon, emerging from the back door.

Embracing her he said, "Everard made it, just barely. His dressings came open and he bled some. He's inside."

"And the kids?"

"We weren't hit." He looked to Willa. "I'm sorry, Ms Wallace. I really am."

Kathy exited the shed and Lindon went to her. "Lindon," he said, offering a hand. Kathy took it, gave it a jerk. "Kathy."

"Do you have a last name?"

"Not anymore."

"I'll look at Everard," said Willa, stepping through the screen door.

Slumping but conscious, an unlit cigarette hanging from the corner of his mouth, Everard raised a finger in salutation from the card table below a curtained window. Willa opened her bag and laid out her works as the others entered.

"What happened over there?" he asked

"Patriot left one behind," answered Lock. "In the attic. That old Isaiah left his viewer behind with a warning. If we had all gone to sleep, we'd… ahem, anyway."

"Viewer's how they found us," he spat.

"I'm sure it is," said Willa, easing Everard back in his chair and checking on his dressings. "I didn't know. I'm sorry." The blood had come through and soaked the front of his shirt from the neck down. She quickly went into her bag for more gauze and bandages. "Lock's going to have to stitch you again."

"No more goddamn needles," he grunted. "Just bandage."

"So long as you don't move," said Willa. She pressed the new dressings down as Everard groaned, and dropped the soiled ones onto the table.

Lindon gestured toward the next room where the children slept or softly murmured. "What's the plan?"

Willa used a clean bit of bandage to wipe blood from her fingertips and tossed it on top of the others. "We have to break into the Heart before they move the children, or we'll lose them forever."

"You can't get into Central City," said Lindon. "It's not even a possibility."

"I told her. It's impenetrable," Lock said.

"And there's only the three of us – four," Lindon said, noting Kathy. "No weapons. No resources."

Willa nudged Everard forward and wound a cotton stockinette lightly around his neck and secured it with a reef knot. "We got fifty thousand off of Hunter."

Everard almost undid his bindings and Lindon straightened, eyes wide, as if Willa had just levitated.

"Fifty thousand?" exclaimed Everard. "That much money could buy half of AB Plus."

Willa produced the tricoins. Everard and Lindon began laughing, though Everard eased up on account of his neck gash. "Where," he said with a huff of discomfort, "d'you plan on spending those?"

"Naysayers, the lot of you. Fifty k is fifty k," said Lock. "We can launder those at maybe twenty-five percent. They're worth something to us."

"And what do we do with twelve k?" asked Everard. "Walk up to Triple C, say 'Here's twelve thousand, please return the children you stole'?"

"No. We have to get the truth out to the districts about the Ichorwulves," said Willa.

"Ichorwulves?" said Lindon.

Lock snorted. "That's what they're called – or, what was it – oh, yeah, 'Apex,'" she said. "Think pretty highly of themselves."

"So, what the hell are they?"

"Well they ain't bulletproof!" Lock exclaimed, popping the butt of the rifle to the floor.

Willa tapped her finger on the card table. "If people stop donating blood, they won't have anything to eat."

"*We* are those people, Willa," said Everard. "AB Plus, the other lowbloods, they ain't giving up their meal ticket. We'll starve before the Ichorwhatsits do."

"We have to tell them the truth, Everard. They deserve that, don't they?"

"The truth!" he blurted. "What do you think people are gonna say when you come around spinning yarns about the undead? Get the door shut in your face is what."

"Everard's right," said Lock.

"We have Claude's skull thing, Scynthia's too," said Willa. "Maybe people will boycott the draw if they see those."

"Those could be anything, though," said Lindon. "Art sculptures."

Everard put off a visible tremor. "Brain crabs."

Kathy perked up. "What are you guys talking about?"

"The little souvenirs those Ichorwulves leave behind after they biodegrade," said Lock. "Little gold skull thing with pinchers."

"You've seen one?" asked Kathy.

"Seen one? We got two of them, darling," said Lock.

"Where?"

"In Willa's bag. Under the unmentionables."

"Can I see?"

"Sure," said Willa, burrowing into the duffle. She flopped some clothes out and withdrew the relic that had once been Claude. Kathy gasped and took it.

"You know what that is?" asked Lock.

"Yeah. It's a ganglion," said Kathy. "An *Apex Ganglion*."

"OK, what the hell's that?" said Everard.

Kathy turned it over in her hand. "It's like… like not quite a brain. More like a thing that… doesn't control them, really, more… pushes them. It makes them what they are. I can't really explain."

"A gang-leon," said Everard. "Gross."

Kathy looked over the table, then placed the ganglion with a clank onto the blood-soaked bandages piled on the table. It sat there, balanced like a nightmare arachnid paperweight, the long front tendrils almost like legs with a tangle of stunted ones at the back.

"Whatcha trying to do?" said Everard, leaning in.

"Watch," she said.

Everyone held their breath. Willa was afraid to exhale. What was the girl doing? Then they all leapt backward. Except for Kathy, who wore a satisfied grin.

One of the tendrils moved. Slowly it pulled away from the rags, then returned, like testing water temperature with a hand. The other side did the same. At the ganglion's base, the tiny branches lost their rigidity, flexing slightly so as to settle deeper into the gauzy dressings. The long tendrils at the front clawed at the cloth causing it to bunch up underneath the eye sockets. It wobbled, awkward, a land-borne crustacean learning to walk.

"What the hell's it doin'?" shouted Everard, who'd pushed himself away from the table to the wall.

"It's trying to seat," said Kathy.

"Seat?" asked Lock.

"Yeah, like, it's trying to sort of, take control. It thinks it's back inside. The blood, uh, wakes it up, I guess."

The thing stumbled forward.

"You've seen this before?" Willa stated more than asked.

"I saw a lot at the Oldens'. You should see what happens when you put them in a whole puddle of blood. They go crazy."

Lindon, who'd been frozen during all of this, finally spoke. "What exactly are we dealing with, here?"

Everard unhooked a long pole from the old blinds and prodded the thing. "So this gang-leon," he said, "eats a hole in your head and crawls in and then you get possess' and it gives you a thirst for blood."

"No," said Kathy. "It grows inside after you get turned. Then it seats."

Lindon put a hand over his mouth in a combined display of fear and disgust. "It grows there?"

"If you get bit," said Kathy. "Something like an infection. It takes a while for it to get fully grown."

Everard squirmed.

They all watched as the thing balanced in the darkening cruor, stumbling blindly in an instinctual search for a place to embed itself. Finally, it clanked over on its side. Kathy picked it up by the top portion, the tendrils and rootlike extensions still scanning for purchase, and set it on a shelf. Its movements slowed to paralysis in the absence of blood.

"That is some shit," said Lock.

Willa contemplated the thing, both disgusted and intrigued by it. "OK, Everard," she said. "What if I told you the truth about Patriot and the Ichorwulves and then showed you that? Would you believe me then?"

Everard was still locked on the ganglion, seeming paralyzed himself. He cleared his throat. "It's freaky, Willa. But I don't know if I'm skippin' the draw and risking starvation or jail 'cause I been presented with a gilt crawdad."

"They've got to be told about the lie. They've got to see what we've seen," said Willa. "Then maybe they'll boycott. At least the truth would be out."

Everard shook his head. "I don't know. Repercussions and whatnot."

"OK, well… we know the drones are empty," she continued. "Lock could shoot one down in public."

"Word might spread," said Everard. "But Patriot would just whitewash it on the *Report*. Technical difficulties, testing new drones, there a million little things they could make up."

The Patriot Report. The words signaled the germination of a thought. Willa stood. "*The Patriot Report*?"

"Control the airways, control the information. The way it's always been," Everard said, toasting an unlit cigarette to the Truth of Things.

Willa slapped the table. "That's what we do! We shoot down a drone *on camera* and put it on *The Patriot Report*."

"How do you do that?" asked Kathy.

Willa smiled big. "This is the Locksmith, Kathy. She's hacked Patriot's mainframe before. I'm guessing she can figure out a way to upload a little footage of some empty blood drones to the live broadcast of *The Patriot Report*. Right?"

Lock just shook her head. Willa couldn't tell if she was just skeptical or all out against it.

Everard fluttered his lips. "And what if you hijack *The Patriot Report* for one whole episode? Show a couple-a crash drone," he said. "All the sudden you think you're a master manipulator. Use that smart brains of yours: the only people that boycott are the ones that got *a choice*. You forget where you come from? AB Plus ain't got no choice. Neither really do the other districts, for all that matters."

Lock shrugged. "His analysis is salient."

Willa knew they were right. A boycott meant forfeiting the next meal for a lot of these people. For those who relied completely on The Box, skipping the draw even once meant being kicked out of the program and going hungry. The world in which boycotts influenced behavior hadn't existed for decades. But her brain wasn't sending forward any other options.

"We have to try," she urged. "We might have to do it more than once. I don't know how many times. But assuming we *could* do it, Patriot would lose patience even if we didn't hurt the supply. I know them. They need to control everything. Maybe we could leverage them to release the children."

Everard rolled his eyes.

"Well, does anyone else have another idea? Anyone?" asked Willa, frustrated. "We take down a drone and broadcast it. Lock, you could do that, right?"

"My dad operated HAM so radio's in my blood," said Lock. "But yeah: maybe."

"Even if it doesn't cause a boycott, people will know Patriot is up to something. And they'll know someone is out here fighting for them," said Willa. "At the very least, maybe Patriot holds up on transferring the children if they're under the microscope."

"Delay Patriot, figure the rest out later," said Lock. "It's half a plan."

"Half a plan better than no plan, I'll cede you that," said Everard, sweeping his unlit smoke like a conductor's wand.

"Hope springs eternal," said Lindon.

* * *

Willa lay on one of the children's mats staring at the ceiling, unable to sleep. Or maybe she was able but didn't have the want. *Of course* she didn't have the want. Even the idea of wanting to sleep disgusted her. She ran through the past twenty-four hours, her body feeling as if it'd borne the toil of two lifetimes: soreness and aches making themselves known in the quiet and stillness. The muscles of her arm burned. The lacerated skin of her bicep stung. She massaged it some, feeling guilty for allowing herself to feel any pain beyond the hole that had been stabbed through her heart.

She wanted to know things, to do research on Central City and Patriot and the Gray Zone lies, but without a touchstone, even with its censored content, she was entirely in the dark.

Helplessness was a punishment worse than failure. On this precipice where her life now teetered, all she had left to grasp was their long-shot half-plan that sat drawn out on scraps at the card table. It wasn't much, and if she was being honest with herself – it was riddled with contingencies and reliant on the predictability of an entire swath of people fueled by desperation. There was no way to know how they would react when shown the truth. Even assuming the plan got off without a hitch and they were able to broadcast, there was always a chance they'd be completely ignored. Nothing like this had ever happened before, as far as she knew, and there was no way to guess the odds. Certainly, they were against. But it was, as Lindon had said, something to give them hope, at least for now. *Hope.* A foothold that kept you from falling, even in the worst of times. Until it gave, of course, as all footholds eventually must.

And she remembered the old saying that she'd heard repeated by her parents, who were probably repeating theirs. *Hope dies last.*

CHAPTER TWENTY

Mitosis

The process by which cells are replicated. Refers specifically to the division of a cell that results in two identical daughter cells.

Never a deep sleeper, he woke with a start. Still aching all over from his ordeal, he was not as groggy as he expected he would be with only an hour or two or three of sleep. He slipped to the side of his pallet, put a cigarette to his lips. His hand scrambled for the lighter, located it, then stopped at his T-shirt on the way to his mouth to poke at the bloodstained pattern. He tapped at his neck. Felt no pain. Pressed harder. Those women were good at what they did, real modern healers. Would have made a fortune down in the low quarter of North-By where all your former Southern Coast residents with their mysticism practiced the sacrifice of perfectly good fowl by candlelight.

He pressed up, groaning some but again less than he thought he would have, and walked into the other room where the children were housed. It was pitch and so he went to where he knew the window was boarded, found the plank with one loose nail and swung it to the side, letting the moonlight spread across their faces. He'd not given any hint to the others of the degree of immense guilt that pressed down upon him like an anvil. It would be a form of penance, to have to look upon the faces of the children still safe and protected by the tall one who'd not let his domain be raided by those wolfs.

He mapped each sleeping face, Cali, Sundip, Honey, Gustavo, Octavia, Frederick, hoping they would cut his heart deeply enough so that the wound would never heal, providing a reminder in their gentle eyelids and tiny noses of the ones that had been taken, those whose kidnapping he couldn't stop. Lynn, Hali, Jack, Wren, Ryan, Sasha, Isaiah. He traced over them again. And again. Until he realized what he felt.

Empty.

CHAPTER TWENTY-ONE

ENDOCRINE SYSTEM

A chemical messenger system that exists between various glands and organs to regulate things like metabolism, growth, tissue function, etc.

Jamaica, the house where Willa and Isaiah had first met Lock, appeared unraided when they set down behind it. Willa dabbed at the new yellow paint on Llydia's exterior as they exited. It was still tacky and clearly fraudulent at close range, but from a moderate distance was no longer of obvious Patriot make. Secured with deck screws to the drone's posterior was Lock's smudge device, a collection of circuit boards soldered together like graham crackers stacked askew. At the back door, Lock presented a massive kingring from inside the leather jacket and fumbled through the keys like a jailer. Willa felt a kinship with this woman and her manual deadbolts.

Lock opened the attic above the basement stairway. As they ascended, every shadow seemed to take on the shape of a huddled Patriot agent, calmly waiting for them to make their return. Lock clicked a few lights and the shadows retreated like cowardly haints.

She ping-ponged about the room, bringing old monitors to life, clipping wire harnesses together, adjusting dials. "So look," she said, resuscitating a screen with a tough-love whack to its backside, "first thing, we need to get our signal ready to transmit to the hub. I'd bet we can cover maybe sixty or seventy percent of the city depending on how close we get our relay. If we're convincing enough, what folks don't see the transmission will hear about it via word-of-mouth."

Willa watched, inching one way and another in a subconscious effort to show a willingness to assist, but all of the technical talk was beyond her training. "What can I do?" she asked, finally.

Lock blew a curl of toasted orange from her face and surveyed the room. "Well, unless you know how to shoot, I'd guess you're gonna have to pilot the relay over to Central City."

"Fly… the drone? To the Heart?"

"Yeah, we can't hijack Patriot's signal from here."

"I don't know how to fly a drone!"

"It's easy. Like I told you before, you just pull the stick wherever you want to go. Pull slowly, go slowly, pull faster, go faster. It ain't the Blue Angels."

"Uh."

Lock took up a box from the counter. "So look, everybody is on PatriotNet – 'cause it's the only NSP. And like I told you before, their infrastructure is built on layers of ancient tech. They still use beta-beam, can you even believe that? So we're gonna intercept and retransmit it. MitM stuff." She grabbed a dusty piece of equipment from a shelf.

"What?" said Willa, head swimming.

"Man-in-the-middle hijack. Classic hacker move," Lock answered. "This here is our wireless hub. I'll be talking to it from Hawaii–"

"Hawaii?"

"Oh, yeah, we'll relay a signal from there later on. Our broadcast should be short enough to prevent detection for a spell, but a signal that big will eventually be noticed. Anyway, I can't give up Jamaica. I got less resources on the Big Island. Patriot can have it once we're done."

Willa tried to visualize the logistics. "So, you're talking to the hub from Hawaii. What does the hub do?"

"OK, right, so this box is our hub. It will sniff for Patriot's signal, and then spoof it."

"I'm sorry, I'm confused."

"Patriot's server will think our hub is the client. The client is, well, everybody watching on the other end – everyone in the blood districts. The client thinks our hub is the Patriot server. Nobody notices anything until our content goes out instead of *The Patriot Report.*"

"Won't Patriot notice?"

"Well, yeah. They'll have the signal down in a minute, maybe two. But that's all we need."

Willa just shook her head in disbelief. At the same time she noted her admiration for the lady.

Lock hefted a brick-sized chunk of hardware onto the desk and stacked the hub on top. "And this guy right here is your battery." A roll of duct-tape appeared from somewhere and she bound them together in an overkill of taping.

"What are you doing?"

"You're going to drop it straight out of Llydia, fly-by style," said Lock. "Return to the nest, you know, lay a malignant little egg."

"Drop it?" asked Willa. "Won't it break?"

Lock grinned as she went back to work affixing large chunks of polyfoam to the already bulging package. "I don't know if the kids still do it, maybe up in O Minus, but remember the egg project you did as a little girl? Where you had to keep your egg unbroken for a week?"

Oh, Willa remembered. Having to cradle an egg in a padded box of her own design and construction, never letting it out of her sight for an entire week, while the boys got to launch rockets and play sports. "Mmhmm. I remember."

"Well, this is our egg," Lock said, thumbing the hub. "And this right here, is our box." She clapped a pair of foam blocks and set to taping them.

This went on for some time with Willa helping Lock handle the growing ball of foam and duct tape, until they had a silver egg two feet in diameter. A small hole burrowed from the surface to the signal-box inside so it could be switched on when deployed.

In the late afternoon, Willa and Lock piled into Llydia along with the MK13 and the egg. "You drive," said Lock. Willa opened her mouth to object, but Lock cut her off, saying, "This is the only practice you're getting before you drop me in my spot. Best make good use of it."

Willa's hands went clammy and she wiped them on her reaper's black.

"Anytime now."

She strapped into the pilot's chair and took the stick. A gentle upward tug and Llydia lifted from the shed. Willa pressed forward and they angled away from Jamaica.

"Stick to the roofline – ugh!" Lock bounced and grunted as they slammed into the bricks of a leaning chimney.

"I'm sorry," said Willa, concentrating intently. "Do you want to take over?"

"Nope. No, I fully support you here. You have my full support," said Lock, fastening the seatbelt on the little bench and pulling it tight. "How are you doing navigation-wise?"

"I'll need help once we cross out of the diagonal." A reference to the line that ran southwest to northeast through the center of town and stood as a rough demarcation between lowbloods and highbloods.

"Not a problem. I'll give you a visual on the Heart and then you take me to Crosstown Distribution for Drone-Murder-Three-Point-Zero." She unfurled a piece of cloth to reveal a small camera with a homemade adapter and secured it to the rifle's Pic rail. "Bring us up now, Willa."

Willa pulled up hard and the drone rocketed silently skyward.

"Aaaaand hover, good. Just let the stick free. Alright, see over there?" She pointed to a spot out west, where the buildings and homes gave way to an area forested by towering redwoods. Miles within, at the center of the heavy green sat a large and brilliant white parallelepiped, a crisp cube cantered and twisted to one side. It was alien, otherworldly. The low sun cast its sides in gentle pastels of cream, rose and gold. Willa felt the breath rushing from her lungs as she could not believe that something so beautiful could still exist. She'd lived in the city her entire life and had only glimpsed the thing a handful of times, and then fleetingly and from a great distance. It simply wasn't visible from street level or the low altitudes of taxi drones.

"Hey?" asked Lock. "You got your bearings, then?"

"Yeah." She brought Llydia around and descended to the rooftops back at the center of Crosstown. Willa could feel Lock tensing as she took them over a building and threaded the drone between a pair of condensers. They landed hard on the roof. Lock hefted the rifle and exited, then scrambled up a ladder behind one of the environmental units with youthful agility. She checked her equipment and gave Willa the thumbs up, hollered, "Stay low!"

Willa closed the door and eased up on the stick, careful not to scrape the sides of the narrow gap into which she'd landed. Pressing the controls forward, she skipped over the landscape and toward the giant urban forest at the center of it. Soon, the homes, buildings, and other scraps of derelict infrastructure became less dense, broken by the nature surrounding the Heart like a veil that shielded it from the dystopia it had created. She slowed some and wove her way into the Redwoods. Neither she nor Lock had access to intelligence on the security surrounding Central City and so she cautiously felt her way in. At the same time, she knew she had to hustle to get back and retrieve Lock.

The trees were biblical. Old. Enormous. Majestic. Thick and more alive than anything else in the entire city; cultivated and cared for as if to guard what lay at their center. Willa proceeded slowly, feeling almost like her passage came at their pleasure. Weaving between them gave her some feel for Llydia and she began to intuit the drone's movements and propensities. Soon she was *handling* instead of just steering. As her confidence grew, she applied greater pressure to the joystick, and felt the old familiar rush of acceleration. She swung Llydia around and between the trunks as memories rekindled of her first car and driving too fast. The blistering speed and wild shifts in inertia made her heart race.

A break in the forest ahead showed the white monolith on fire in the sun's waning beams. Around it sat a variety of temporary modules, placed there no doubt in anticipation of the Patrioteer Conference. She relaxed her grip and allowed the drone to settle into a static position a few meters above the ground. She triggered the door open and surveyed the expanse. The air was quiet and fragrant with pine straw, and Willa marveled at the very existence of such a woodland paradise in the midst of the gray and desolate city.

All around was virgin wilderness. No sign of security, much less any type of technology – above ground anyway. She kept from landing, as Lock had warned her about the possibility of ground sensors. Being offline, Llydia was invisible to Patriot's monitoring software. They could only be detected by sight, and the Heart, for all its beauty, had no windows. The sun dipped below the trees. She had ten minutes to lay the egg and return to Lock. Her nerves calmed when she retook control of the drone and thrust the stick ahead.

Llydia dashed from the primordial wood, low over the thick clover lawn, then full throttle to the crown of the building. Rather than hover and drop the egg, Willa set down on the building so as not to stay airborne and visible. A lip around the roof's perimeter concealed her from below. She released the door again, took up the egg in both arms like a beach ball, and trotted across the roof toward the center where a spire of technology rose like the Eiffel Tower. The signal generator. The surface of the roof had a crisp waffle pattern and she teetered along a shoulder-width strip of concrete, almost spilling into one of the deep squares as she ran.

She reached the spire and stopped to consider where the best place for the egg would be. She could stab it onto one of its metal juts or she could drop it into one of the surrounding squares. The signal might be stronger on the spire, but the egg would be visible.

The problem was reversed if she dropped it. Lock hadn't given her any guidance on this. She reached into the egg and activated the signal.

A vibration in the air caught her off guard. She looked toward the far end of the building.

A security drone breached the roof's lip. Willa glanced to Llydia. Too far to run. She dumped the egg into the closest waffle square and half climbed, half tumbled into another, hoping she'd not been seen. The drone's approach brought a cloud of dust that filled her cutout. She stretched the cloth of her reaper's black over her mouth and watched the sky. The drone passed overhead but gave no indication that she had been spotted. Once it cleared, Willa peeked over the edge. It was headed right toward Llydia.

Out from the hole, she sprinted down the line, feet skipping along the roof like a roadrunner. The patrol drone slowed as it reached the limit of the roof and hovered just feet from Llydia. Willa cast about for something, anything she might use to distract it before Llydia was blown to kingdom come and she was left stranded.

The drone panned side to side, its four lacegun barrels protruding from its shell like noses, sniffing the air for trespassers. Realizing she couldn't make it back into Llydia without being seen, she scooted underneath and huddled down into another waffle square, waited for the drone to fire its guns.

No sound came. Instead, the drone banked over the roof and flew noiselessly back toward the opposite side. Why hadn't it fired?

Llydia was steps away. Willa peered out from the hole. The patrol drone reached the spire then flew in a slow circle around it. What was it doing? Had it detected the egg? She had to act.

Willa burst from her hideaway and hurled herself into Llydia, falling hard onto her ribs. She righted herself, grabbed the stick and yanked it up and to the side. She whipped the drone in a tight loop, screaming over the roof and darted directly in front of the Patriot drone.

Inexplicably, it showed no interest. *Why not?* Willa wove back and forth before it, doing her best to distract it before the egg was discovered. "Come on! Are you blind?"

And then she remembered the smudge. Llydia was cloaked. The patrol unit couldn't see her if it didn't know what to look for. It closed in on the hot square.

Willa nudged the joystick just as the other drone came around, effectively shouldering Llydia right into it.

The drone twitched to her as if it'd been startled from a lazy daydream. *Halt!* came a woman's voice through the open hailing frequency.

Willa yanked Llydia to the heavens. The jolt of momentum pushed her into the captain's chair. Through the display she saw the Patriot drone enter the same steep climb. Its pilot must have been able to follow the visual signature left by the smudge given that she now knew where to look. A stream of *Trespasser* and *Identify* and *Will Shoot* came blasting over the comm.

She wheeled Llydia into a dive. An alarm flashed red on the display just as a fusillade of lace bullets punched through Llydia's skin. Meters above the ground, she pulled hard on the yoke then thrust it toward the towering trees who before had let her pass. With no digital signature for the security drone to lock onto, its pilot would have to fly by hand to give chase through the forest. So instead of slowing among the redwoods, Willa accelerated, pressing the stick as far forward as it would go. The motors whined their stress. She felt taken back in time to the black vinyl seat of her old Camaro, sliding back and forth as she carved tight corners on splashy tires. She dipped and zigged, galloped over branches, and rounded trunks. The patrol drone followed, but Willa could tell by its movement that the pilot was struggling to navigate the gauntlet while staying on her. Ahead, through the last margin of forest, were the anemic lights of B Plus. More ordnance pocked her mount.

The patrol unit was faster, nimbler than Llydia. Once they were out in the open, it would have little trouble bringing her down. Willa kept the throttle at one hundred percent as they crossed into the blood districts. Down streets and lanes, between row houses and shuttered storefronts, she raced, weaving hither and to while the Patriot drone closed in, spinning out streams of steel-cutting lace.

Willa knew the streets from her youth, running and climbing through them with her companions, hiding from bullies when provoked. As a child she'd mostly escaped them, but had sometimes found herself cornered into unforgiving dead ends. It was the bricked-in alleys, the places with no way free, that she was certain to never forget; and decades on, they still glowed like beacons across the geography of her mind. An idea sparked.

She executed a series of breakneck left turns. Into narrow alleyways she flew, over and over, establishing a pattern that the Patriot drone began to emulate, even anticipate. Left-left-left, left-left-left. When she'd done it three or four times, she hesitated, swung left down a different lane, and pulled up on the stick as hard as she could.

Llydia leapt, narrowly dodging the patrol drone as it blasted around the corner and into the dead-end wall that blocked egress from the lane – a heavy bulwark of brick and mortar. The drone's aluminum-air battery pulsed like an exploding star and the shockwave carried Llydia skyward, motors sputtering from the pressure change. Willa righted the drone and checked the wreckage through the display – for survivors, she guessed, then wondered what she would have done had she spotted any. The explosion had been so powerful, so complete, that she saw nothing of the drone or any hint it had existed except for a wall that had been reduced to rubble. With no time to spare, she sped off for Crosstown Distribution and her sniper accomplice.

"What in the name of Pete took you so long?" hollered Lock as she clambered into the drone from behind the condenser on the rooftop.

"I was chased."

Lock examined the smudge. "This looks good, how'd they follow?"

"They were about to find the egg. I, uh, let them know I was there."

Lock gazed out through two of the many holes torn through Llydia's flank. "Did he getcha?" she chortled.

"Her," said Willa as they lifted off. "She chased me for a while until she stopped chasing me."

Lock set down the rifle. "So you got her. How?"

"Dead end. I pulled up," said Willa, weakly miming the chase's final seconds, a note of regret in her voice.

"Well, it was you or her, sweetie," said Lock. "I'm glad it was her."

They rose into the air. A mile or so away, the sky above Crosstown Distribution swarmed. Willa flew the drone in the opposite direction and leaned into the throttle. "Did you get your footage?" she asked.

"Oh, yeah," Lock exclaimed. "I wish Olden could've seen it. He'd have been piiiiissed. I dropped two more of those bad boys. All empty, of course."

"We're going to have to repaint Llydia again, I think."

"Oh sure. Now that they're looking for taxi-Llydia, we should turn her back into Patriot-Llydia."

Willa raced them back to AB Plus and brought the drone to a hover. "Where's Hawaii?"

"Oh, right," said Lock. She pointed to a street on the display. "Follow this one here for the next couple of clicks."

Hawaii was particularly dilapidated. It was a creamed-corn colored clapboard home with all but one window boarded over. With no shed, Willa put Llydia near its backside and killed the motors.

Lock unclipped the camera from the MK and leapt toward the house, then wheeled around as she rummaged for the right key. "I'll upload the footage, you cloak the drone."

Willa collected some chipped PVC panels from against a chain link fence and began layering them on top of Llydia so she'd be invisible from above. A worthless old spool of T-9 ethernet line and some moldy carpet padding finished the roof. Lastly, she scooted a dilapidated chicken coop into abutment with the drone's door. Satisfied that Llydia now looked like every other pile of junk behind every other house in the district, she went inside.

"Lock?" she called. "Hello?" She played with the light switch but there was either no electricity or no bulb in the fixture. It was too dark to say which. "Lock?"

"Yeah Willa! In here!" The call came from only a few feet away. Willa looked with confusion at the old refrigerator. "Open the door!"

Willa did and could see the back of the main compartment cracked open, exposing a secret passage. The irony of finding herself in such intimate contact with yet another refrigerator failed to amuse.

The door led to a void behind the wall, where one might have expected to find a pantry – and if this had been a normal home before Lock got hold of it, it wasn't any more. The space was cramped, but unlike the rest of the house, it hummed with electricity, the walls plastered with technology. It was the attic at Jamaica, only cozier.

Lock had the goggles over her eyes. "*Patriot Report* in five minutes, Willa. You excited?"

"Nervous," she said. "Did you get the upload from Everard?"

"Yep, right here," said Lock, shuffling some files around on a wizened laptop. "Just drop my footage right up in here... aaaaaaand cut."

"It's done?"

"That was the easy part. Now for the hijack." On another screen, Lock brought up three windows, minimized and arrayed them so she could see each. "Oh no," she said. "You turned on the egg, right?"

Willa's heart stopped. "Yes, of course I did. What's wrong–"

"Just kidding, that's us right here," Lock said, poking the middle window on the screen.

"Why do you do that?"

"Just introducing some intrigue," she said. "Lighten up."

"You think we need more of it?"

"OK, see," continued Lock, "like I said, they've kept their peripheral tech rudimentary because they know they've got to communicate with the substandard hardware had by the likes of AB Plus if they want to get their *Patriot Report* seen at all. So we're just sniffing for packets right now." She pointed to the window on the left.

"Packets?"

"Little collections of data. See this stream here? Lots of packets. Nobody else is generating that type of bandwidth. That's going to be Patriot." She selected the stream and clicked on it. "Sniffed you right out, bitch."

"What is that over there?" asked Willa, tapping the opposite window.

"That's the client," Lock answered. "Everyone else is already pinging the crap out of the server wanting to watch their beloved *Report*."

"Does this mean the egg is working?"

"Damned straight." She tapped out two quick lines of code that looked roughly identical, except that they were the reverse of each other.

"Are you spoofing now?" Willa asked.

"That is exactly what I am doing, Willa. I'm spoofing the shit out of these guys," Lock declared, spinning in her chair. "We'll make a hacker of you yet." She whirled back and finished typing on the old plug-in keyboard and hit "enter."

Tiny fans buzzed to life within the machines.

"Thirty seconds to showtime." Lock consulted her watch and waited. "Five, four, three, two," Lock said as she clicked an icon. "Engage."

The screen went entirely black. Lights came up gradually on a red curtain, with a draped cocktail table in front. On top, a solitary candle burnt.

"A little dramatic," Willa muttered.

"It's theater, Willa."

From off screen came Kathy, disguised as a game show host wearing a top hat, an ill-fitting dress shirt and bowtie, and over that, a hideous green sports coat.

"Greetings, and welcome to *The Patriot Report* for Tuesday evening, ten-twenty-five, twenty sixty-seven. I'm your host, Kathy. I don't have a last name because Patriot took it, but I digress."

"I digress?" interjected Willa.

Kathy continued, "We set new records in collections today. Love my people in B Minus. You guys really came through."

A piece of poster board appeared on the table next to her with Everard's daikon-pale fingers keeping it upright. On it were written the names of each of the four city segments: NORTH-BY, EASTERN, SOUTHERN CITY, and CROSSTOWN. Kathy uncorked a large black marker. "Let's add up today's totals! How much precious blood is each segment contributing to the Gray Zones?" She put a thoughtful finger to her lips. "Let's see, hmm, North-by: *Zero!*" She scribbled a big circle. "Eastern: *Zero!* Southern City: *Zero!* And last but not least, Crosstown: You guessed it: *Zero!* For a total of…" she grabbed the board and flung it off screen, "*Zero!*

"Oh, but Kathy," her voice thickened with sarcasm, "I watch me and my family's valuable blood fly to the Heart every night in Patriot's glorious blood drones!" She pointed to the camera. "Not so fast, fellow blood-slaves. Watch!"

The scene faded to a shot of the horizon. The camera wobbled ever so slightly and then the narrator, Lock, spoke. "In a moment you'll see the Patriot drones just over yonder wood on their way to the Heart. We're going to knock one down and look inside it together. While we wait, perhaps I'll introduce myself. I'm Janet, but my friends call me Janet – oh, more next time, there they are." The frame showed a line of lights ascending from distant trees. "We'll let them get over this field here," she said, tipping the gun downward. "OK, number one. Cover your ears." The camera went absolutely still as Lock took aim.

When she fired, the image jostled for an instant and she zoomed in on a faltering drone. "Ah hell, let's go for bonus points." She fired again, fatally wounding a second drone. Both plummeted, crashing near to each other. "Alright then, fellow citizens," she said. "Let's see what's inside." She zoomed in, way in, until she had a clear shot of crushed and torn blood vaults strewn across the ground. "Imagine that! Crashed blood drones with no blood splatter, no blood bags, no blood at all!" she yelled. "Worst piñatas ever!"

The scene cut back to Kathy, who renewed her commentary. "As you can see, there's no blood in those drones. If there's no blood in the drones, then where is all the blood that you, the public, so dutifully give? Not the Gray Zones, that's for sure. Because there *are* no Gray Zones. The places we call the Gray Zones think that *we're* the Gray Zones. Get it? Patriot is collecting the blood and pumping it straight to Capillarian Crest."

She approached the camera.

"Why, you ask?" She thrust Scallien's ganglion toward the camera, blurring the image in and out. "Because they eat it!"

She stepped back to the table and set the ganglion down. "These things live inside the rich, and inside Patriot management. Literally. Like, in their brains." She took up a blood bag and stabbed it with a pair of scissors, letting it bathe the ganglion in syrupy red.

Instantly, it began squirming. "The only way to stop them is to kill them," she said. "And the only way to kill them is to starve them." She lifted the ganglion, its tendrils and roots thrashing against the air like the legs of a crab pulled from water.

"So, stop feeding them," she said, allowing the ganglion's roots to slowly shrivel like a dead spider's legs. "Skip the Harvest. Boycott the Trade. I'm Kathy. You'll hear from us again soon."

The screen went black.

"Yeah!" Lock crowed and embraced Willa, then began ripping power cords and jerking cables from the walls by the fistful.

"What are you doing?" Willa asked at Lock's sudden flurry.

"Baby, that signal we just put out is gonna draw more attention than a backyard tire fire! Gotta take down the house." A drill appeared out of nowhere and she shoved the spinning bit directly through the keyboard of the laptop she'd been using, cackling, "Turn and burn, Willa!"

CHAPTER TWENTY-TWO

HEMATOPOEISIS

Refers to the production of the cellular components of blood and plasma, specifically new blood cells.

Willa watched Kathy sitting legs crossed at the kitchen table with a tin mug of tea and an easy demeanor. The morning sun came through the blinds, painting her in stripes like the nascent head of a crime family. "Do you think it'll work?" asked the girl.

"We'll know soon," said Everard, sparking his first cigarette of the day. "I can walk the bottom third of Southern and put eyes on the donor stations there, Lindon can take top segment and I guess–" He took a pull on the cigarette but convulsed into a riotous coughing fit.

"You're the last person on the damned Earth who still smokes those," said Lock. "Maybe your body is telling you something."

Everard tried taking another puff with the same result, carefully snuffed the butt, and put it back into his mouth unlit.

"So, I guess I'll take middle-Southern," said Willa.

Lock sucked on a lemon slice, strained it through her teeth like a pirate fighting scurvy. "I'll go with," she said.

By noon, Willa and Lock had made it to Station Four, the furthest precinct in middle-Southern. Even from several blocks away it was clear that their broadcast had had an effect. A protest had formed with hundreds of people carrying signs and banners, throwing rocks and other detritus. Patriot security were fighting a losing battle to keep them on the far side of the street, and the station became an island in a sea of people. High above, Patriot drones circled like vultures on a thermal.

"They're everywhere," said Willa nervously.

"If we turn tail now, it'll look suspicious," said Lock, guiding Willa forward. "Just chill."

They tried to look nondescript as they moseyed into the fringes of the congregation. The crowd, raucous and vocal, harassed the few citizens who braved the throng to sell or donate, even pelting some with red paint. What on most days was a steady stream of donors and sellers had dwindled to less than a trickle.

Willa wasn't sure what she'd expected, but she recoiled at the sight of hostile crowds shouting down their neighbors. Even though every person living in the blood districts was a victim of Patriot's scheme, their broadcast had – at least for the time being it seemed – further divided the people. Now there were two groups: those that held the line and those that crossed it. And even though Willa knew the boycott was best, she empathized with those who went in to get their money so they could eat.

There was another concern. She worried that the protests would be written off as mere escalation by activists who had been voicing their opposition to Patriot for decades. If all they'd done was flame the fire of the already suspicious, they risked marginalizing their message. She wanted people to believe what they'd been shown.

The scenes at Stations Five and Six were no different. They watched as a few would-be donators scurried away under a hail of castigation and garbage scraps.

Lock spoke up. "What's the matter with you, Willa?"

"They all seem like crazies," Willa said with a tinge of dismay. "We wanted people to believe us."

"We wanted people to stay home is what we wanted," huffed Lock. "Makes no difference to us if they're doing it to avoid the crazies or if it's because they actually believed Kathy. If they're on the couch, that's all that matters." She gestured to an ocean of anti-Patriot signage, buoyed on the crowd like ship wreckage. "So long as those guys stay fired up, people are gonna sit it out."

He made it halfway back across the bottom third of Southern City before he tried to light another cigarette. He knew he shouldn't, but figured to try yet again, as the nicotine drive hadn't let up any despite smoking's violent new side-effects. The reaction was more sudden this time, and he folded to retch the moment the heat hit the tip of his tongue. He continued in a fit, hacking and spitting, said *what the shit*, squeezed the soft-pack into a bow and hurled it to the ground. When the attack subsided, he unwound himself tall and stretched his back, looking around.

The headache, the goddamned brain-crushing headache. It felt like a hangover is what it felt like – though he hadn't fought a hangover for years and years. There were a few reasons for that. The first was his biblical tolerance for alcohol, and the second was because no one had been able afford the real stuff for at least a dog's age, and backyard 'shine turned him into a berserker. Maybe it was the pica. Everyone ended up getting some measure of it when anemia reached a point. Blood loses its metal and you start craving wads of old paper chased with dirt. A real affliction heard of by no one until the Harvest came on.

Eh, this felt different than that. He was hungry for food, just nothing seemed to satisfy. If he kept walking, he'd hit Station Seven, across from which was the little eggroll cart affectionately known as the Roach Coach, where he could load up on Vietnamese fried rice. He was sure the cart's proprietor, a tiny little pine nut of a woman by the name of Ametrine, owed him a favor, though he couldn't quite remember from what the favor was due, but figured he'd dig it out by the time he reached her.

* * *

Willa and Lock took a circuitous route back to the Bahamas with no drones tailing. It had been years since Willa'd taken a long walk that didn't end up at work or at home immediately after work. They'd been walking all day now, and she'd forgotten just how the extended activity could clear the cobwebs. It wasn't that it took her mind off her troubles. To the contrary, it actually made her focus on them. But it stripped away the static, all the interference she had no control over, leaving the root of the problem exposed for contemplation. As her feet found their rhythm on the concrete, her mind unraveled some, like a muscle relaxing. Light-headedness crept in and she realized that, aside from Kathy's cheese and a wedge of lemon in her tea, she'd barely eaten. Had it been days? Either way, she'd not remembered to, hadn't wanted to.

She wanted Isaiah back. A return to the way things were. They'd gotten by. The little apartment. Isaiah's school. The hallway mirror she'd so often avoided. How she missed that mirror now, and the chance to gaze upon her daughter reflecting back, to say hello again. They had taken walks together when Isaiah was stroller-bound. Willa imagined the sound of Elizabeth's footsteps in the dying grass alongside her and Lock. Rustle, scrunch, rustle, scrunch.

There was a time before. A time that felt impossibly distant, like an alternative reality. But even with the wars, Patriot and the Trade, there had always been family to lean on. There had been three of them. Now two. Or was it one? The thought of losing Isaiah was... too much. Her heart felt weak. Hollow as a glass bulb. She needed to focus on the task at hand.

But try as she may to shake away her fears, the more memories poured in to remind her of what she'd lost. Elizabeth's birth. Her childhood. The joy she felt in every molecule of her body just being around her daughter – and her guilt for bringing her into the world when she did. It was that world, after all, that had taken her away. She wished to talk to her again. Wondered what they might share.

More than anything she wanted for Elizabeth to see Isaiah, and the mature, sweet boy he'd become. The imagined footsteps in Willa's mind persisted – rustle, scrunch, rustle, scrunch. And then she heard them. A beautiful young woman in a denim jacket and black frame glasses had come up alongside them. When did she arrive? Willa wiped her eyes.

"Hi, Mom."

"Elizabeth?" she gasped. "Is it really you?"

"Of course it's me."

Willa worked her eyes open and closed a few times and tried some deep breathing. It couldn't be Elizabeth. Elizabeth was dead. She looked back to the woman. "I'm imagining you."

"Yes."

"My baby," Willa said, embracing the hallucination. It was like she was lucid dreaming; aware of the fantasy, but consciously deciding to back-burner her rational mind for the sake of the experience. "I've missed you so much."

"I know, Mom. I miss you too," she said, furrowing her brow. "You look thin."

"Hmm. Not much appetite." A tear tracked to her chin.

"What's wrong, Mom?"

Willa tried to keep from breaking down completely. "I'm going to get him back. I promise. I will. I'll do whatever I need to. Even if it kills me."

"Mom, it's not your fau–"

"It is!" cried Willa, jabbing her finger into her chest. "I lost him!"

"No you didn't. Don't say that. It wasn't your fault. You have raised that boy by yourself better than I ever could have dreamed."

They continued on past driveways overtaken by the cancerous yellow grass, staying near to the curb to avoid the crumbling sidewalks. Elizabeth stooped to pick a flaming yellow daylily, her favorite flower. Willa hadn't ever seen one just growing by itself in the open like that. Then, the lily was hallucinated too.

"We were together, Elizabeth. The three of us. We could have survived as a family," Willa said, her voice cracking. "Why did you have to go?"

The young woman pressed the flower to her nose and inhaled deeply, then plucked a petal. "Thought I was stronger than I was, Mom."

"Why didn't you tell me? Why didn't you ask for my help? I would have given you my entire paycheck, sold my own blood for you."

"You don't have to tell me that. I knew it then… I just thought I could handle it." She pulled another petal and let it drift. "I made a mistake I can never fix."

"I died when you did," said Willa.

Elizabeth put her arm around her and pulled her close.

Willa looked at her daughter and admired her skin; dark and deep like heartwood. She'd gotten it from her father – his one positive contribution. Her gorgeous skin always glowed, until she'd sold every last milliliter her body could manage, and it had yellowed with anemia. But now, as they walked together, the sickness was gone. She was the very picture Willa kept in her mind.

"Saw you flying that drone around," Elizabeth said, sniffing at the flower again. "I bet you're real proud of yourself."

Willa, recalling the chase, pushed her smile modestly downward. "Maybe some."

"And I thought that was smart, what you and Lock did with *The Patriot Report*. Oh!" She poked a finger into her mother's shoulder. "That girl Kathy? Where'd you find her? Wouldn't want to get in her way!" Another petal fluttered.

"I stay clear," said Willa. "A force of nature, that kid."

Soon they were laughing, an interlude like they'd had from time to time in days past, when good conversation could erase the world.

They walked together for another few blocks. Willa's voice pinched in her throat. "I'm lost now, Elizabeth," she said. "I can't think of the next step. Patriot will move Isaiah soon if they haven't already, and he'll be gone forever. I don't know how to get to him."

Elizabeth nodded her head in thought, her shiny black hair hanging down over her chest, the sides splayed like long bristles on the softest brush. "You already know the solution, Mom."

"No, I don't. I don't know anything!"

She released a petal to the breeze. "What did you always tell me when I came to you with a problem?"

Willa gave her a look. "I don't… I don't remember."

"You would say, 'Elizabeth, look inside first.'" Another petal.

"Look inside?" Willa repeated, remembering. She'd always wanted to teach her child to be self-reliant.

Elizabeth stopped walking.

"Sweetie, what is it?"

She held the lily with both hands to her chest. "It's time for me to go now."

"No, please. Stay and talk a few minutes longer. I'll introduce you to–" She turned briefly toward Lock, who was gazing blithely into the clouds, then turned back.

Elizabeth stood behind them, having stopped in the grass. Willa tried to stop walking herself, to turn around and run back for a final embrace, but her legs wouldn't obey. Her mind was trapped inside a body that wouldn't listen. She glanced back a final time.

"I love you, Momma." And the daylily's last petal fell.

Things were confusing, wherever Willa was. The light was a blackness that shone somehow bright and she tried to blink away the silvering that burnt her eyes, like staring into an eclipse only to be haunted by the afterimage. "Elizabeth?"

"Who's Elizabeth? I don't know any Elizabeths, sweetheart," said Lock, leaning over from above. "Is Willa in there?"

Willa's eyes slowly came back to focus, and she recognized Lock's giant hair as the freckles on her face rendered in their appropriate constellations.

"Are you OK? You passed right out, Willa. I dragged you for a city block before Lindon came down Boulware and saw me."

Sweat dripped from the rim of her goggles to hit Willa square in the cheek.

"Where are we?"

"Back on the island, dear."

Willa swiveled her head to a throng of children who'd gathered. They returned to the living room as if her regaining consciousness was anticlimactic.

"When'd you eat last?" asked Lock, taking a teacup of oats from Everard, who continued into the next room with rations for the children.

Willa stretched her neck side to side in hopes of clearing her head and Lindon helped her to sit. Lock sprinkled a handful of vibrant blackberries into the cup, then held it out to Willa in an attempt at spoon-feeding. Willa took the cup herself.

Warmth returned to her cheeks as she ate. The group agreed that the crowds and protests they had witnessed at the donation stations were consistent across the segment, and that there was no reason to think it any different in North-by, Eastern or Crosstown. It seemed like news of the pirated broadcast had made the rounds.

"How soon until we know if the boycott worked?" asked Lindon.

"Based on how fast that old Claude gave up the ghost," said Everard, doling out portions into crayon colored bowls, "they'll be hit by the dip in supply right quick."

"They're certain to have reserves, right?" asked Lock of no one in particular.

"Hmm," Willa muttered, "easier said than done. You've got relatively short shelf life on whole blood and you can't freeze it without adding in special polymers."

"And they eat all the time," said Kathy bringing over another bowl. "Six times a day, every other hour," she said. "We have breakfast and dinner. They have two o'clock, four o'clock, six. *The Evens*. They miss one or two and get hangry real fast."

Willa shook her head as if she'd just gotten the punchline of a joke told days earlier. "My God," she said, palming her forehead.

"What?" asked Lock.

"Claude," Willa answered. "He was always going back into the storage cooler at the precinct. I thought he was just a diligent boss, checking inventory or whatnot."

"Snacking," said Kathy.

"Seems so, doesn't it?" she said, taking another bite, and getting a punch of energy from the berries bursting in her mouth. "We collected a lot of blood. Although I can't say the same for all the precincts, I mean, Donor Eight is in a heavy O-neg patch. Either way, they must consume a great deal."

"They do," Kathy confirmed.

"Well then, they'll be feeling the pinch soon, you think?" said Everard. "Octavia, you share with Honey now," he added, motioning to two of the girls in front of him.

"Maybe they'll starve," Lindon suggested from over by the sink where he appeared to be cleaning vomit or some other such excrement from his shoe.

"They won't let that happen," said Kathy.

"They'll break the fiction first, I bet," said Lock. "Probably just start rounding people up buffet style if they run out. We may have actually just screwed ourselves."

"Great," said Lindon, "so if the boycott works too well, they'll just drop the whole charade and start killing people in the streets?"

"Maybe," said Lock, with an exaggerated sigh. "Econ *one-oh-one*. We've hurt the supply, and soon it will mean a spike in demand. How do we use that to our advantage? That will tell us the second half of our plan."

"We catch one of 'em," said Everard.

"And how would we do that?" asked Lock.

"Head into the business districts with a few bags, see who bites?"

Lindon rubbed his face in frustration. "That's your plan? Tie some blood to the end of a stick and see if you hook one?"

Everard crossed his arms "Not precisely… it could be another sort of trap. I'm scattershootin' here."

Willa suddenly began chuckling through a mouthful of oats.

"How hard she hit her head?" asked Everard.

"I think she's having another episode," said Lock.

Willa shook her head to assure them she was fine and quickly chewed through the remainder of the pasty grains, swallowed hard, and reached for a glass of water held by Lindon. She took a drink, cleared her mouth with a swish of her tongue. "Look inside first."

"Inside what, dear?" asked Lock.

Willa smiled, feeling Elizabeth's glow emanating from her own skin. "Inside us," she said, standing. "Inside us, inside this house, inside this entire neighborhood!"

"Right," said Everard. "Well she knows where she is at least..."

"AB-positive," said Willa. "Our blood."

"Our blood's inside us," said Lock. "Yes."

Willa steadied herself and stood from the floor. "It's poison."

"Say what?" exclaimed Everard.

"Poison?" Lock crumpled her eyebrows. "To who?"

"To the ninety-seven percent of the population that isn't us," said Willa. "We're universal *recipient*, right? Not universal *donor*. O-neg, O-pos, AB-neg, B-neg, B-pos, A-pos, A-neg: an AB-positive transfusion isn't compatible with *any* of them."

"Yeah," said Lock, "we all know that."

"For us – for people – the wrong blood means you get sick, maybe you die. For them–"

"The Ichorwulves," Lindon interjected.

"Drinking the wrong blood... it's fatal." Willa crossed her arms.

Everard straightened. "AB-pos. Our blood? It kills them?"

They all looked variably confused, except for Kathy, who seemed to perk up. "Venya was AB-positive."

"Yeah but she doesn't have a head anymore," said Lock.

Willa interjected, "Look, three and a half percent of the population is AB-positive. The other ninety-whatever percent couldn't receive a transfusion of AB-positive or they'd be at risk for a transfusion reaction. It's toxic to them."

"Hold up a sec," said Lock, shutting her eyes in thought. "Back up. How do you know that? How do you know it kills them?"

"Claude said something the other night. He told me he was dying without his supply. So I offered him my blood–"

"You what?" burst Everard.

Willa nodded. "Yes – OK. I did. He was my friend, I wanted to help."

"Jesus H, lady," added Everard.

"Anyway," Willa continued. "He said that I was the wrong type and that taking my blood would only kill him faster. It makes sense, right? A transfusion of the wrong blood could kill anyone. The Ichorwulves aren't that different from us, I guess. When it comes to blood, the same rules apply." She shook her head in disbelief that she'd not realized it before. "It's so obvious now."

Lock set to polishing her goggles. "Claude was pretty upset when we took that bag from him. It was all A-neg. His blood type," she said. "And come to think of it, the Oldens' supply was similarly curated."

Everard leaned in, puffed at his unlit cigarette and blew imaginary smoke over the table. "They eat the wrong blood, they die."

"How are we supposed to get them to drink our blood?" asked Lindon.

"Make them think it's not our blood they're drinking," Willa said.

"She wants to run a blood hack," answered Lock.

"Blood hack," Willa confirmed, while not failing to register the irony as a loyal former Patriot employee.

"It makes sense in theory, I'll give you that, Willa," Lock said. "Tell the computers to register AB-pos as the other phenotypes, the machines stamp on the wrong label. *Badabing*! – The Ichorwulves get AB-pos, thinking it's O or A-neg, drink it down and…"

"Bite the dust," said Everard.

"Right!" Willa exclaimed.

"Hold up, hold up," said Lock, shaking her head so vigorously that her orange hair churned about like a turn of the century car wash. "Sure, it's great in theory. But even if we could execute a hack on that scale – a city-wide hack – they know blood type by scent. Claude proved that."

"That's the thing," Willa responded excitedly, "Claude, Olden, they were the old guard. Ichorwulves are completely reliant on the way the bags are tagged at the donor stations. It wasn't always that way, but it is now. They got lazy, and it became too easy to just read the label. They've lost their sense of smell. Olden said as much."

"That's true," said Kathy.

All heads turned.

"Jesper and Venya, they were like, show-offs," said Kathy. "They knew all this old Ichorwulf history. Deep. Like, ancient stuff. And Jesper was big, you know, at Patriot. They'd have these dinner parties at our house all the time and they'd set out these giant wine glasses and fill them with different types of blood, even some Jesper said were diseased. And then they'd do these, like, smell tests. And none of the others could do it, not one. Not even the Claret. Just him and Venya."

"The Claret?" asked Willa.

"The Claret... they're like the top people in the company. Uh... board of directors, something like that. They'd fly in for business from some other cities – I don't know from where – for meetings and dinners and all that. Jesper would go from glass to glass, kind of bragging." Kathy mimed along as she spoke, "*B-negative, AB-negative, O-positive, A-negative, Ab-neg with factor V deficiency, A-negative with hepatitis, B-positive with leukemia, B-positive with polycythemia vera.*"

"Policimia whatah?" asked Everard.

"When the body makes too many red blood cells," answered Willa.

Kathy continued, "It'd get late and he'd get real serious and start lecturing the others – he'd actually get *angry* with them – tell them they should be ashamed about how they'd lost their way, lost what made them different – and better than us, than humans. That they should be schooled in the old ways. He'd speak about how traditions aren't just for show. They're gifts handed down by prior generations, like, instructions on survival. That you forget the lessons of history at your peril. He would always say *doom is a flood that waits for the rift.*"

"Heavy shit," said Everard.

"Bit dramatic, I'd say," said Lindon.

"You never met Jesper Olden," Lock answered back.

"Yeah," Kathy agreed. "Everyone would get really tense and then he'd just laugh it off and then they'd all laugh with him. But he hated them for it because it meant they were soft. He'd go on these rants after everyone had left, about how their loss of smell made them, like–"

"Vulnerable," said Lock.

"Vulnerable, yeah," said Kathy, standing up and cleaning away the bowls from the children.

"So, if we run a hack, they won't be able to smell the difference," said Willa.

Everard shut his eyes in cogitation. "So, we get a bunch of AB-pos–"

"Of which we have plenty," interjected Willa.

"Right," he continued, "and Lock does a hack to trick them to thinkin' it's bona fide highblood. They eat it and drop deader than disco?"

"What's disco?" asked Kathy.

"I'm sorry to bubble-burst, but that's impossible," said Lock, silencing the room. "You are talking about a city-wide hack."

"It's not impossible," said Willa. "You've done this before."

"Nothing this big. Not even close."

Willa felt she was losing the thread. "But–"

"Let me tell you why." Lock collapsed into a folding chair at the table while thinking out loud. "Remember: my hacks aren't centralized. We'd need to hit all eight precincts in each of the four city segments. That's," she counted out seven fingers, "thirty-two precincts. Most I've ever done was three, and I barely had the firepower for that, to be honest. I'd have to daisy-chain all the islands in our network, hit all the donor stations at once. And we're already down Hawaii." She shook her head.

"Can't your hacker friends help?"

"No one in town ever matched my output. And half of them have been pinched," she sighed. "Sorry Willa, it's impossible."

"What about another egg?"

"Oh, sweetheart," said Lock, sympathetic to Willa's lack of technical understanding. "We intercepted a piece of a signal. We weren't *in* Patriot. That's not this."

Willa stared at the flower print curtains pulled tight, imagined a window with Isaiah playing outside. "A bag hack then."

"A do what?" said Lock.

"That blood bag you showed me in the attic of… what house was that?"

"Jamaica?"

"Yes, Jamaica," said Willa. "The bag that you made. It was perfect. I couldn't tell it'd been altered. Everard passed counterfeit blood through *my line* with it."

"It was one bag!"

"You printed it, though, right?" asked Willa.

"The nanoceramic alone took my printer a day," exclaimed Lock. "We'd have to print a hundred thousand bags for the type of hack you're talking about. At least."

"How good a printer will twelve k buy?"

Lock's eyebrows shot up her forehead as she remembered the tricoins. "Three k would get the best," she whispered. "Maybe two and a half even."

"Then we'll get four of them," said Willa.

"Two would more than do the job. We can use the rest on food," said Lock, who seemed buoyed by the direction the conversation had taken.

Lindon finished a cheese tube and raised his hand. "So, we need a hundred thousand bags, a hundred thousand full doses of AB-pos, enough highblood to put into the decoy pockets, and a hundred thousand people to go along? That's all? Anything else?"

"The people would do it," said Everard. "It's free money. You could drop a bag of onion juice on the sidewalk and someone would try to sell it."

"We don't need to fill the entire bags ourselves," said Willa. "We just need to distribute them to everyone with the decoy pocket already full. People will add their own blood to the bag, then go donate. The needle probes will register the small amount of highblood in the decoy pocket, and the lowbloods will get paid for it."

"And where do we get decoy blood?" asked Lindon, irritated. "Just go begging for that much highblood? Tell people to trust us? Come on."

"Yeah, I mean, I have friends all over, but not thousands willing to hand over high-grade sauce," said Lock.

Willa rubbed her temples and tried to clear her mind. They had a viable course; it was just strewn with immovable obstacles. "Guess we'll just have to break in and steal it from them during the Patrioteer Conference," she said sarcastically.

Bowls clattered onto the counter and rolled across the floor as Kathy spun toward the room from the washbasin. "What did you say?"

"Patrioteer?" asked Willa.

Kathy's face was a knot of anger. "Patrioteer," she sneered, "is where they select the children."

CHAPTER TWENTY-THREE

LEUCOCYTE

Also known as white blood cells, leucocytes are immune system cells that attack disease agents and foreign substances.

Llydia zipped along over endless fields of late season silicorn. A new coat of purple paint, the designated shade for ambulance drones, lay in drip-marked brushstrokes across her hull and putty-filled bullet wounds. Willa piloted. Lock chaperoned the MK13. Kathy cradled her newly rounded belly.

For the second day in a row, they'd set out hoping to cross paths with a blood transport on the only road into the city. With Patrioteer just days off, and the boycott still in full swing, Patriot would need to secure a large infusion of surplus and then scramble it to Central City quickly and quietly. Squadrons of transport drones would raise questions. All of this pointed to trucking it in. And there was only one city close enough and big enough to supply what Patriot needed: Alliance.

The road was old and crumbling, hemmed in on both sides by vast stretches of golden silicorn. Without knowing exactly what shortage they'd created, they figured Patriot would need at least a few trucks to make up the difference and hoped to spot one as it made its way.

Forty miles from the outer boundary of town, Willa brought them to a long stretch of road with good visibility in both directions. It was like they'd been transported across the universe to an entirely different planet. There were no buildings, no homes, no infrastructure, no communication beacons, no blood trade, and, except for Llydia, no drones in the aquamarine sky. Willa swung them low and slow over a glistening swath a mile out from the road just as she had the day before. Anyone traveling the road would be blind to them on account of the towering cornstalks. Silicorn, a genetically modified crop bred to produce a silicon analog within its kernels, were more than twice the height of their namesake plant. She checked back and forth between the window and the display.

Lock straightened in her seat. "I packed the sabre saw, right?"

"Yes, Lock. It's right here," said Kathy, patting a duffle. "That's the fourth time you've asked."

Lock leaned over and adjusted the golden bangs on Kathy's new hair. "No one's gonna buy this," she muttered.

Willa looked at the girl. To say she was uneasy about involving Kathy, who was still a child, in an attempted heist was putting it mildly. It felt like a betrayal of what should be an innocent time – though for Kathy, that window had long since closed. Fearless though she was, it didn't matter to Willa that Kathy wanted to be involved, the point was that she shouldn't have to be. Willa mourned the world as it had once been, a world that strove to preserve the happy ignorance of childhood. But what choice did they have? They were flying in a stolen drone to hijack a blood transport because the world was run by vampires. She supposed it wasn't just the innocence of children that had been lost.

Willa considered Kathy's getup. The wig was too big, her legs too spindly. "They don't need to buy it completely, they just need to hesitate," said Willa, half trying to convince herself that it would work.

Lock shook her head. "I don't know. She's only fourteen."

"I look older though," said Kathy with an extravagant toss of the hair.

"Look!" Willa pointed to a distant rooster-tail of dust blooming up from the road. "That's got to be it." She dipped Llydia to the tassels and accelerated parallel with the truck's vector, flying to a point several minutes ahead.

She found a bend in the road where they could land unseen and set the drone down at the edge of the crumbling asphalt.

"Places!" ordered Lock, running outside. She unhooked a few panels from the drone and heaved them spinning across the road, cracked a flare and shoved it into the dirt just underneath Llydia's front quarter. Drones were more catastrophic-explosion risk than fire risk, but they were counting on the truck's pilot not having time to run the checklist on drone behavior in a crash-landing situation.

Willa took a blood bag from the duffle and for a moment saw the situation from the lens of only a few weeks prior, when her life had been humdrum and predictable. Now she was immersed in a world she'd not known existed, doing things she'd never conceived of doing. She opened a small knife and slit the bag gently, careful not to produce too large a hole, then held it high into the sunlight and let it drain over her face, chest and arms. She squeezed the last dribbles from the poly and chucked the bag into the field.

"Holy shit, Willa, you look like Beelzebub," said Lock. "Rub a little of that inside Llydia so it looks like you brained yourself genuinely."

Willa knelt at the door and gathered some of the blood from a glob under her chin, wiped it on the door. Llydia was the wrong size and shape for a medical drone but hopefully the color and badging would do the trick. Willa looked at Kathy, who sat on the bench staring off. "You ready?" asked Willa. Kathy rose and stepped into the road, her face inscrutable.

"He's about to come around the bend," Lock called, running into the crop rows with her rifle. "Remember to stay the hell out of my line of sight!"

Willa laid herself half outside the drone and half in it, trying to think of the most natural way to have fallen dead after a traumatic head injury. She settled on a rigid-looking, head turned, arms-to-the-side pose, as if she'd been dead before she hit the ground. She rubbed some grit from the road into her sticky face and tried to slow her breathing.

Lying still now, she watched Kathy take to the road. She was awkward in the kitten heels they'd given her to look taller and her swollen belly was pronounced against the wind, while her dress inflated behind to a diaphanous billow. Everything about the spectacle screamed that this was a child in costume. Except for her face. If they looked at her face, they would believe anything.

The roar of the truck's giant tires against the broken pavement came nearer and it finally rounded the corner. Tears summoned, Kathy stumbled toward it, waving wildly with one arm, holding her stomach with the other, yelling for the truck to stop. Willa feared they might try to drive right through her, but Kathy was unflinching – exactly as a stranded expectant mother would be. Just a few hundred feet from the decoy, Willa heard the truck's brakes engage, and it slammed to a halt.

Before it had even settled, Kathy was running into the plume of dust carried forward by the truck's momentum, screaming hysterically about her water breaking and her nurse being dead, how the drone had malfunctioned, how she didn't know where she was, and could they please help her for the love of God.

Inside the sleek gray cab were two men, the gold Patriot insignias on their caps tiny points of light behind tinted glass. Kathy hammered on the hood with her fists, stumbled toward the drone as she gestured to Willa's dead body, and screamed for them to call her another hospital transport. The driver's eyes ran from Kathy to Willa and back to Kathy. They made no move to exit the truck and instead the horn blared, sending an explosion of crows from the field. Kathy collapsed; ears covered. Willa cringed as her mind was transported back to the sirens that had once sounded the end of the world. When the horn died, Kathy sprang up and continued her ranting. Growing ever more impatient, the driver honked again, nudging the truck a few feet forward as Kathy reeled.

Willa could hear panic edging into Kathy's voice, not the feigned panic of her imagined situation, but the real deal. And Willa, like Kathy, was having doubts that the plan would work. The truck slowly pushed forward.

A bullet slammed into the window, striking the driver through his hat, and he slumped against the wheel. His partner quickly pushed him over and out the driver's side door, where he crumpled into an unnatural knot. The truck lurched and Kathy dove into a gulch at the shoulder. A second shot split the air and punched through the cab. The man's head flopped onto the dash and the truck began to drift. Willa lit up from her spot and crossed in front just as it passed, urging her legs to move faster as she chased the rogue vehicle. She gained ground until she came even with the cab and lunged for a utility handle just behind the door. Holding it with both hands, her feet dragged on the asphalt. The rig crossed the lip of the gulch and began to canter to the side. Any longer and it would topple. Willa pulled her feet onto the running board, jumped in, and smashed the brakes as she twisted the wheel back to the road.

Lock had burst from the field by the time Willa righted the truck and Kathy'd thrown away her baby, a duct-taped cushion inside a pillowcase. Willa tugged the second man from the cab. He was large, but she finally got his belly over the edge of the seat and gravity did the rest. She found his touchstone and pocketed it.

Lock pointed back down the road. "Get them into the field, stat! I'll take care of the truck." She leapt in from the passenger side with the sabre saw and started chewing through the roof of the cab. Kathy and Willa worked to drag the driver into the crop rows, a task they did after much toil and an uninterrupted string of cursing from Kathy.

As Lock's saw buzzed through the nanofiber shell of the truck's cab, they ran to the second driver, who was lighter than the other, and managed to get him off the road. Willa put her finger to his face, rubbed the blood between her fingers. Wet red sawdust. Kathy collected his touchstone.

Back at the truck, Lock had removed a roughly circular chunk of the roof and was busy securing what Willa recognized as a battery pack to it, the wires running to the disk of material.

"Where's the taxi?" asked Kathy.

"I called it from a burner and chunked it in the road ahead. That's where it'll land," said Lock, handing down the sabre saw. "Grab this."

"Patriot is going to notice the truck is stopped," said Willa.

"If they've noticed, they'll stop caring as long as it's moving again. Alright, take the brains here, Willa." She gave the electronics down from the cab. "Don't let that battery loose. It's transmitting. Y'all start walking down the road until you see the taxi." She began to shut the door, then pushed it open again. "Remember what we talked about. Rendezvous tomorrow at the predetermined coordinates. If for some reason I don't make it back, password is *vengeance*. I'm out." She slammed the door and the truck roared ahead.

Willa handed the hardware to Kathy. "Head up the road. That way it'll look like the truck is still rolling. Patriot will think its slowed due to poor road conditions."

A taxi appeared on the horizon.

Kathy began walking and the drone set down just ahead of her. Willa checked to make sure the bodies weren't visible from the road, then caught up with Kathy. They buckled the truck's brains onto the bench, and tossed both the drivers' touchstones inside.

Lovely afternoon, said the drone. *This is the fare going to Central City Collection, correct?*

"It is," said Willa, "but you can't go any faster than twenty knots and you've got to mirror this road and then only city roads after that."

That is substantially more expensive than a direct course.

"We've already prepaid for a custom route."

Indeed you have, said the drone.

"Remember to fly slowly," Willa added.

Please do consider a direct route. Economically–

"Bye, now," said Willa. "Thank you."

Thank you for choosing CROW FLIES.

The door closed and the drone accelerated to twenty knots as it traced the prescribed path.

Kathy and Willa trotted back to Llydia, reattached her body panels, and lifted off.

Willa hammered the drone away from the scene as fast as she would go. With the city coming up on the horizon, they steered wide of North-By so they'd come into AB Plus from an angle not obviously tied to the hijacking. It was probably an overcautious move, but they couldn't risk that someone might make a visual on them. Willa tried to focus on the display but ended up watching Kathy instead, finding herself taken aback by the girl's unflappable and businesslike approach to things. The kid was an enigma.

"What?" asked Kathy.

"Oh," Willa said, not even realizing she'd been staring. "I'm sorry, I just... *who are you*?"

"You know who I am," said Kathy, tucking the dress under her legs. "What are you talking about?"

"You don't act like any fourteen year-old I've ever known, is all. You seem... older than that."

Kathy narrowed her gaze at Willa, scrutinizing. "I'm not one of them if that's what you're asking."

"No, I never–" but the thought crept in now that Kathy had mentioned it.

"Apex age like anyone else, Willa."

"I didn't mean anything by it. You're just a unique kid."

"You think?" she answered sarcastically. "Stolen from home and raised by Ichorwulves for seven years? Groomed by them? You mean that's not everyone's experience?"

"Groomed? For what?"

Kathy seemed bemused, like it was obvious, like they'd been through it all before.

"The Claret, Willa."

CHAPTER TWENTY-FOUR

PICA

A psychological disorder characterized by a desire to consume non-nutritive substances. It often accompanies extreme cases of anemia.

He was getting hungry now and nothing would stay down. Not fried rice or lemons or protein foam or oats. Ice had worked for a bit, then that stopped. He couldn't even drink water. First, it'd been the smokes, now nothing sat right. His brain felt like it was changing seasons. His perspective twisted. He was suddenly apathetic about the whole effort, hijacking Patriot and all that jazz. It was hard to tell if it was due to delirium from lack of sustenance or genuine indifference. Whatever it was, he needed to eat.

How he felt hunger had changed. It was no longer an emptiness in the belly, but a yearning, a desire to fulfill a drive that centered itself deep within his psyche, like instinct. He paced the Bahamas while the children played, secretly tasting various materials for something that would trigger an instinct that would tell him, *Yes, this is your food, eat this.*

Just down the steps from the back door, he touched his tongue to a blade of grass, peeled some of the tissue-thin bark from a birch sapling in the far corner. Back in the kitchen, it was thread from the drapes, paint chips, the tine of a plastic fork. Nothing worked. In the children's room, he rummaged through the home's toolbox, a sorry mishmash of finishing nails, wood screws, liquid poly, a big hammer, a child's starter box saw, and a four-inch level. He smashed the plastic housing of the level with the hammer and withdrew the capsules of greenish fluid, eyed the oblong bubbles within. A quick check on the children and he pushed into the corner, biting a capsule and letting the fluid twine down his throat.

An explosion of spittle and phlegm burst from his mouth, coating the wall over the toolbox, followed by another round of rocky coughing. Reeling, he stumbled to a nearby table and propped himself up while getting control of the fit. He gathered the tablecloth – still stained from where Kathy had doused the ganglion – and pressed it to his mouth to muffle the sound. Each cough was thick, deep, and he could swear his rib meat was vibrating straight off the bone. He set his head to the table, heaving, trying to get calm. There was a visceral quality to his breathing. Wet. Labored. And he felt the twin forces of desperation and exhaustion pulling at each other – the prospect of starvation versus succumbing to it.

What else was there to try? Maybe he could weasel into one of the food markets over in the highbloods and start eating things till they kicked him out. Exotic fruits. Peaches maybe. There had to be something that satisfied. Plumes of his animal breath steamed the red-stained tablecloth and a pocket of vapor was created. An iron tang wafted from it like a narcotic and suddenly he was intoxicated. His pupils dilated and his pulse quickened. His mouth watered and his nostrils flared, their hollows filling with the potent aroma of life itself, an oasis for him among pools of dried blood.

CHAPTER TWENTY-FIVE

Pathogen
Anything, such as a bacterium, virus, or parasite that can cause disease.

The hardest part of the blood bag hack was getting past the two needle punctures that came at random, followed by the phlebotomist's own sense of feel. A would-be hacker had a choice to make: either enhance the inner bag's strength to prevent the needle probes from puncturing through the decoy pocket and into the large pocket of lowblood, or sacrifice inner bag integrity in order to get past the phlebotomist. In the first scenario, the phlebotomist wins, in the second, the needle. Only by sheer luck would a poorly crafted bag get past the needles and the phlebotomist, a thousand-to-one, or worse, proposition.

Now it seemed they'd solved the problem of the bag. Willa hadn't let on when she had first held Lock's attic prototype, but she knew as soon as she'd touched it that no phlebotomist would suspect a thing. And if Lock was also right about the strength of the decoy pocket, that it would rebuff the needle probes, then they were on their way. They just needed highblood to fill the decoy pockets, and now it seemed they had it.

On the day after the heist, Willa and Lindon flew to the set of coordinates Lock had provided, leaving Everard and Kathy behind to watch the children back at the Bahamas. Dressed in a new coat of ubiquitous yellow, Llydia set down in a strange urban wilderness, under strict instructions not to exit the drone until Lock came to meet them.

Willa considered the display and took in their surroundings through the tiny window, but couldn't place their location. It was densely, and diversely, wooded, though the ground was less dirt and more crumbling asphalt, with faded parking stripes and an old shopping cart corral. Taking the place of toppled lampposts were towering softwoods, Trees of Heaven, maybe, hackberries, and some conifers. In the distance was a building, spread long and low, painted in battleship gray with a single bold blue stripe sandwiched between two red ones running its length. Further to the southeast, along the border of the parking lot were countless modular homes, the type used for temporary housing after floods or hurricanes, piled on top of one another, white, with green-black moss infecting their seams and corners. Willa had a distinct recollection of them from her youth, when they'd been deployed as field hospitals and morgues at the height of the coronavirus pandemic.

At this point in her life, Willa assumed she'd been down every street in the blood districts, knew every neighborhood and the buildings within, but this place wasn't ringing familiar. She processed her confusion and her lips formed the shape of a question to be asked, "Where–"

"Bad Blood," said Lindon, staring out.

That was it. Bad Blood. The place where people went and never left. A camp for the infected. The place where those with bloodborne illnesses came to live until they died.

"Lindon," asked Willa, "you know this place?"

"Sequestration – Diagnosis – Inoculation – Elimination," he said, tapping a rhythm to the window.

Like a flashbulb, Willa recalled what Claude had told her – that he could smell that Lindon was ill. "You're sick, aren't you?" she asked gently.

"Mmhmm. HIV."

Willa nodded and turned back to the display. What could she say? The world had decided that anyone with HIV, AIDS, Hepatitis B, Hepatitis C, malaria, coagulation disorders, syphilis, or any of a number of viral fevers, weren't worth saving. That it would be better to let them die out in a leper colony in the parking lot of a petrified big box store.

Lindon gave a muffled snort, his mouth curling upward. "Years ago, Janet – er – *Lock*," he said with a sardonic eye roll, "caught me trying to steal pharma that she had her eye on. We'd picked the same depot to raid. She almost blew my head off. No joke. Been together ever since." He smiled. "I help her out, she helps me get meds for my family who live here."

"Your family lives here?"

"Not blood, but we're all family in this place," he answered, massaging the stress out of his long fingers. "When I joined on with her, I thought maybe someday we would be able to break this system. I had just come to terms with the fact that it wasn't going to happen. And then you came along."

"What are we doing here?"

"Lock's calling in a favor," said Lindon. He gestured to the display as the woman came into view, emerging from a tunnel of trees. "Here she is now."

Lock, goggles down, knocked on Llydia's window. "Open up, no drones overhead," her voice came muffled through the glass. "I think you all made it without a tail."

Willa triggered the door and they stepped out. The air was greenhouse wet and sweet like wisteria. Warmer too. It felt like spring, not autumn.

Lock wheeled and began toward the building sprawled out before them. "Lindon acquaint you with your whereabouts?"

"He did," Willa answered. Her eyes drank in the alien landscape. The old parking lot opposite the modular homes stretched to the northwest until the trees obscured its full reach. Small swatches of a concrete wall showed through the gaps between trunks. The prefabricated homes were a color that had once been white, with solid plastic steps leading up to a single thin door at the center of each. Flanking the doors to either side were squat, horizontal windows. Willa thought they looked like faces; screaming mouths between suspicious eyes. The houses in the blood districts, while small and mostly decrepit, had been, at least at some point, homes.

"Apparently the factory modules were never supposed to be lived in long term – that was what people were originally told anyways," said Lindon, sweeping his hand to the expanse. "But I guess it was good enough for Patriot, so..."

"Easier to get people to go somewhere if you tell 'em it's temporary," said Lock, kicking a crabapple.

"Wasn't it obvious when it happened?" Willa said. "Mass relocation? How many times throughout history have we seen this play out?"

"Zero times if you don't know your history," said Lock, wagging a finger. "Edit the history books. Keep the populace ignorant. By the time you figure out what's happened to you, you're living behind a fence. *Oops.*"

Willa saw how it all must have unfolded, with years passing before the intent of the settlement became fully clear, especially to those who remained outside its walls. For decades, Patriot had touted its "convalescence centers," where the sick were supposedly treated, and Willa loathed herself for ever believing them. Over decades, the company had gradually sacked away an entire segment of the population under the theory that any pathogens would eradicate with the deaths of their hosts. Of course, diseases were nomadic things and naturally cropped up in the districts, so Bad Blood always had an influx.

"I mean, Patriot pretty much telegraphed what they were doing," Lock went on. "How's it go? *Sequestration, diagnosis, inoculation, elimination*? Just move that *S* to the back and you get 'DIES'. I mean, come on, folks, they literally spelled out their intent."

Looking around, though, the reality of Bad Blood didn't quite match Willa's conception of what such a place would be.

Small touches here and there showed how each module had

been tailored by its occupants: makeshift awnings, vine covered trellises, washbasins, even flowerboxes with living flowers. In some places the units had been pushed together, connected in twos, threes, and fours, horseshoed around open areas that embraced communal spaces. Further back, Willa spotted a number of vintage drone shells overturned as water collectors with distribution pipes spreading out toward the clusters of homes. She traced one of them to a quadrangle of gardens, in one corner overflowing with branches hanging heavy with pomegranates. Overhead, vine-covered cables towing pirated electricity ran to the modules, illuminating their windows with illegal light. Willa noted with a touch of cheer that Bad Blood seemed no worse off for its lack of contact with the outside world.

All around, shades tugged to the sides and doors cracked open. Parents and children, entire families intact, emerged, cheeks and bellies full. They stood confident but also protective, not just of their families but of their home – this settlement where they had been sent to disappear, now their sanctuary within a dying city. Seeming almost at ease, they lacked the drawn angst and blank despondency of their corollaries in the districts. These people had built something where there was nothing. They had been forsaken and were better for it.

"Now you see the source of my secret cache," Lock said, finger flicking toward one of the small gardens. "Only place to get quality produce."

And there Willa had the answer to Lock's mysterious bowls of fresh fruit.

"They're pretty self-sufficient here, as you can see, but if I can do a little hocus pocus on a pharma drone or dial up some direct current for them, skim some electrons, then I get to forage."

The watchers looked from the steps and patios surrounding their modules. Willa followed Lock around to the side of the big building and they arrived at a heavy steel door with an analog knob and deadbolt. Lock knocked and after a few seconds it pulled open from within. A man with a lazy blue eye pinched his face into the crack of the door. "Hey Janet," he said. "Password?"

"You ask for the password before you open the door, John," said Lock, pushing it wide and breezing by with the others in tow.

"Oh," he mumbled, shutting the door and bolting it. "I still need to know the password though."

"Vengeance!" hollered Lock without looking back.

Heading in, Willa felt a rush of nostalgia. She'd shopped at stores just like it during her formative years. They sold groceries in the front half and everything from housewares to clothing and garden supplies in the back half. The concept of "stores" at all, much less one of this scope and selection, was surreal now. The idea that someone could go to one place, buy a gallon of cold milk, a bag of apples, school clothes, and a vacuum cleaner, bordered on obscene. To think that not only had such luxury existed, but that people had taken it for granted, was the peak of absurdity.

It hadn't really lasted, in the grand scheme of things. The megastores arrived and strangled out the small shops, then the internet wiped out the megastores, and then Patriot killed everything. If you wanted something now, you bartered, took your chances on the black market, or hit the local Patriot sundry shop. They already had your blood, why not also the money they'd paid you for it? Full circle.

Willa followed Lock past dozens of dusty checkout aisles. All of the old fluorescents were burnt out or broken with the exception of a small grid of lights in the far corner near the refrigerated section. "Is this where the truck is?" asked Willa.

"It's where the truck isn't," answered Lock, sending a shopping cart rattling to the side. "It's been parted out so Bad Blood can use its bits. Our price of admission."

The contents of the shelves, and in most places the shelves themselves, were long gone, as anything useful had been stripped and repurposed within the settlement. As they neared the back section, the unmistakable hum of refrigeration compressors vibrated lightly through the air.

John came up alongside Willa. He was short and stocky with

haystack blond hair, and had on a tucked-in flannel shirt, making him look like a diminutive lumberjack. "Welcome to the Market," he said.

They rounded the corner and Willa saw it. An entire aisle, stacked front to back with shining glass panes in gleaming metal doors. Like picture frames, they amplified the wet emerald skin of bell peppers, flaming orange carrots, a rainbow of berries, and every type of mushroom you could name. Further down were the season's last tomatoes, obese squashes, and herbs like rosemary and parsley. Pumpkins! Opposite the kaleidoscope of produce were shelves upon shelves of bread. Some low and dense, others high and fluffy, wrapped lovingly in waxy parchment. Toward the middle of the lane, people restocked meats. Before Willa could ask, Lock interjected, "Chicken, rabbit, cat."

"Squirrel," Lindon added, licking his lips.

"They share all of this," said Lock. She opened a door and pointed at a cucumber, raised her eyebrows at John.

"Go ahead," he said.

Lock took up the vegetable and crunched into it like it'd already been pickled. She gestured to a spot near the end of the aisle. "All the way down," she crunched, "that's us."

Light from the refrigerators filtered red onto the concrete floor. Rows upon rows of Ichorwulf food, neatly strung in its poly bags, intact and chilled. Willa walked down the aisle and opened a door, letting a cloud creep across it. Here and there, she flipped up the bags to check their labels, and did so down the row. Shutting the final door with a frosty thump, she turned to Lock and Lindon. "The distribution is perfect. O-neg at around seven percent, O-pos at just under forty, A-neg at looks like five or so," she said.

John scooted up and presented a tally jotted on the back of an old coupon book. "AB-pos is high though, almost ten percent. I don't know why they have so much. Should be three, right Willa?"

"Yeah, that's right. It should be three, but it's not too important. We got all the highblood," she said. "How many did we get? It's got to be thousands."

"Just over thirty-thousand units of highblood," Lock answered, letting the number hang in the air. "And I only need a fifth of a bag for the decoy pocket."

Willa felt an overwhelming rush. "With that we can make a hundred fifty–"

"A hundred and fifty thousand fakes, depending on time," Lock interjected. "We'll do it here. Assembly line style. We'll build the bags, put in the decoy blood and then distribute for the lowbloods to top off with their own juice."

"You think Patriot won't come for their truck?" Willa asked.

"Truck ain't throwing out a signal anymore, and even if they thought it was here? No way. Its cargo would be deemed tainted. Motherfuckers are scared of disease. They only fly out here to ditch the infirm." She looked at John. "No offense."

"None taken," he said.

CHAPTER TWENTY-SIX

HYPOTENSION
Low blood pressure.

Using his own saliva as a gentle solvent for the flaky residue of what little blood remained, he'd nearly sucked the tablecloth clean. He swallowed his spit in savored sips as he journeyed from AB Plus into A Minus, the cloth like a baby's blanket at his lips. It had been just enough of a boost to get him upright and out of the house, which was where he was supposed to be. Didn't matter though what he was supposed to be doing, the compulsion to get free of the place wasn't one a person could fight. Had he even tried to fight it? Had he wanted to? He couldn't say to what the impulse was owed; a command from his own mind, maybe. Thoughts came and went, blinking on and off like fireflies. Some he recognized, others he didn't. And while the remnant red had given him some strength, his brain – his entire sense of who he was, really – felt like it was crumbling.

Shit had gone bad, he knew that. He was hurting. Not in a way he'd ever hurt before – not like being cut or punched or sick even. His belly felt alive, like his organs were rearranging themselves. Among the fireflies, one thought kept crisscrossing in his mind. He looked down at the teeth marks on his arm, faded now and nearly all healed. The one he'd pummeled had played dirty and bit him, but he damn sure hadn't seen any golden fangs – as far as he knew, he'd been awake throughout the entire thing, at least up until they got him with that lacer. He ran his fingertips over the skin of his neck and, aside from the wound that the redhead had sewn up, felt no holes, not even scabs. How could he be changing without a proper, bloodsucking bite? The only time he'd faded out was after they'd quit the place with the kids.

The kids. How'd he let them take the kids? They'd cheated, no doubt, involving guns and the element of surprise. A rematch would be in order if he got right and managed to find the sonsabitches. He had been a damned-to-Hell evil scrapper as a kid. The skinniest of the bunch, he'd learned to fight furiously, to play dirty if it came to it – and especially when it didn't. Back at Seychelles, he knew he'd gotten a few punches in, bloodied the one bastard's face into ground beef with his big old knuckles, which felt grand. He'd grown up knowing he could talk his way out of a confrontation, but his hands were weapons and he'd usually felt like using 'em. They were bigger than hands were supposed to be. Some thought it was a gift, that was a fact. The old boys who ran the boxing gym when he was just a sprout used to holler at him from the steps to get in the ring, offering to train him and his heavy hands. He never did take them up; he didn't want to be constrained. He was too busy with all manner of mischief and criminal activity to conduct. Turned out he wasn't the best criminal, though, with half his adult years spent in the slammer. But it did mean more time for fighting.

Where was he again?

He considered his knuckles for a beat, wondered if he still had the knockout power of his formative years.

The headache was getting worse, and with it came odd shifts in perception like he'd taken a hallucinogen, inducing paranoia and quickening his temper, like with the lowland fungi he and his crew had once stuffed into their faces as teenagers so they could travel the astral plane.

The new girl had caught on to his delirium and he'd bolted

from the house before her questions could set him off. It wasn't anything really about her prying, per se, but more so the fact that she was on to his altered state, his fevered distraction.

As he stumble-shuffled ahead, he reflected on leaving like he did. Those children there, the ones the girl watched over now, they were his charges and had been for most of their lives. He'd cared for many of them when their parents gave out from the Trade. There was a time when he would have threatened to kill anyone who so much as suggested they take over for him, even just to lend a hand or give him a breather. Kill. Kill with those heavy hands. Because he'd been given responsibility for them, and he would be their source of stability and their provider, their educator and their guardian. *But that guy was a ghost now, wasn't he?* Just a haunt in that house somewhere, looming, feeling sorrowful and jealous. The man walking through A Minus in the other man's clothes was someone else, and he didn't see those kids the same way. His heart felt brittle and he thought that should make him sad, but it didn't. Maybe he could find a stranger and recount the story so that they might weep in his stead.

He shook his head and sucked on the last faint patch of scarlet, ditched the tablecloth. He looked around to find himself stopped in the center of the street. There was no way he'd have the strength to make it. He'd go snakeshit with starvation before he'd get far enough to launder the money that jingled like Christmas in his pocket.

His eyelids pushed their way down over his prickling eyeballs. He gazed longingly at the ground. Lie down in that yellow grass and be asleep in five seconds. Maybe death would come. He didn't think of it as suicide, just… being done. You tell the Good Lord thanks for the chance even though it didn't go as either of you thought.

The ground did beckon, but his brain said no. The long nap is coming, just not yet.

He set the thought aside for the moment and turned back the way he'd come. His brain was too cramped and energy-starved to think any more about the why of the hunger. An urge came to change direction, and so he did. Ignorant of his destination, he felt compelled by a curious sense of adventure. Where was he taking himself?

It must have been twenty blocks before he finally stopped walking. He didn't make a decision to stop, he just did. Even through the haze of his new perception, he recognized the neighborhood. Southwest corner of A Minus, two blocks from Donor Three. It was surrounded by people. Angry people. Right. *Right.* They were protestors. What were they doing? Protesting something. But what? It was like someone had boxed up his memories for relocation. His vision blurred. Squinting, he watched. There was something he was supposed to be looking for. Or was there? Was he meeting someone? Police drones hovered. Five-O. One or two were parked with officers standing at the crowd's perimeter.

On the opposite side of the street, a man and a woman headed down the block toward the crowd, looking clean. Their clothes weren't too old, might have even been newish. Not a single moth-hole or stain. Oh, and that hair! Shiny. Fluffy. They were O-negs if they were anything.

And they weren't protesters either. No sir. They were braving the crowd to get that money. Look at them. Just full of blood. Bursting. The thought had him slavering like a junky and he speed-walked after them, elbows pumping. As they reached the line of protesters, he grabbed for the man's arm, who pulled it quickly away.

"What do you think you're–"

"Don't want to hurt you, just listen."

"Excuse us!" said the man, pushing his lady friend ahead.

"Hear me out!" he barked, holding up a tricoin worth twenty-five thousand.

"Is that real?" asked the woman, suddenly entranced, her voice gone greedy.

"You know it is. Take it. Feel it."

She did, weighed it in her palm. Her eyes glistened as she exchanged a look with her partner, handed it to him. He did the same. "Is this a trick?"

"Nah. No trick."

"What do you want then? We don't have anything worth this much."

"Hell you don't," he said. "But you can't give it over out here." He guided them to a gravel pathway between narrow buildings, one a boarded-up drycleaners, and the other a small Patriot commissary. "Look at me. I ain't gonna hurt you. Come on."

They walked toward the far end of the alley. "Y'all headed over to donate, right? Got full bags?"

The woman answered this time, "Yeah. So?"

"You O-negs right?" he said, getting a little excited, wiping his mouth.

"Yes," said the man. "How'd you know?"

"Givem bags here then, keep the cash."

The man laughed and offered the tricoin back. "You could buy all the black-market blood in Southern City for that. Come on, Lena."

He grabbed the man's shoulder, a predator's strike in the speed of his hand. "Give me the bags!"

They seemed to melt. "OK, fine. Calm down," said the man, pocketing the tricoin and removing his jacket. The woman did the same.

He felt on fire. Why were they moving so slowly? As they peeled the bags from their arms, his vision suddenly sharpened and he felt he could see every millimeter of each needle as they slid out from the implanted ports, like he was watching through a magnifying glass. Hunger stretched every passing second into an eternity. The needlepoints finally emerged, flinging a microscopic scatter of blood from each, and he rejoiced at the task's completion while raging inside at the miniscule drops of wasted food. "Hurry up!"

The woman flinched and nicked her arm above the port. Rich

O-neg welled from the tiny puncture, spherical and gleaming. He felt recognition. Reunion. From inside the headache a word came to him that he'd never even used: ichor.

He dove onto the pair, ripping the bags from their hands. The man fell under his weight and the woman stumbled back against the alley's brick wall. He put one of the bags into his mouth and bit into it as fiercely as he could, wrenching his neck to tear the poly. Blood poured across his face and into his mouth, over his chin and onto the man below. The woman screamed. He brought the second bag to his lips and repeated, more careful this time to prevent spillage, relishing each viscous gulp. His distraction allowed the man to wiggle himself free and regain his footing.

Hunger waned and his vision centered, broadening the periphery. The headache unwound some and his heart slowed. He sat back on his knees in relief. Felt partly himself again. A nap would top off the perfect meal. He felt like he wanted a cigarette, and then he didn't.

The pair ran for the street. He didn't understand why they would do that. He was tip-top now and they were rich. He used his sleeve to wipe the blood from the bottom of his face and then sucked it from the threads.

As the couple made the mouth of the alley, an authority drone swung around the corner, its girth just wide enough to plug the narrow lane. The man and woman ran up to it, squeaking little cries of relief. The drone landed and two helmeted officers exited.

"Oh, thank God!" cried the woman. "There's something wrong with that man."

He pressed up from the ground and started a slow retreat down toward the alley's far exit. The old him started gaming the situation. Play it off? Start rambling shit at the cops, see if they get tired of him and roll on? Run away? If he went zigzag maybe he could make it without getting laced. The new him was less concerned, for some reason. His belly was full. And he came to the realization that he didn't really care what happened.

"You!" called one of the officers. His voice boomed from an amplifier inside the drone, connected to a microphone inside his helmet. "Don't move. We have you locked."

With their guns trained, he halfheartedly professed his innocence, then remembered he was drenched red.

"Approach the drone. Slowly, sir."

He complied. With his hunger tamped, his wits were less frazzled. *Act reasonable like*. He licked his lips and approached with caution.

The woman became hysterical as he got closer. "He ate our blood bags! He. Ate. Them. He – he robbed us! He's insane!"

Everard gave a maniacal laugh, still feeling the afterglow of food.

The second officer spoke, "How did he rob you? Did he have a weapon?"

"No weapon. He simply attacked us, officer," said the man, calmly re-tucking his own blood-covered shirt.

The officers appeared to make eye-contact through their visors. "What were you and your wife doing in the alley?"

"Can we please focus on the insane person who attacked us and then *ate* our blood-bags?" said the woman, pointing at him.

"Ate, you say?" asked the first officer.

The second officer turned to face the man. "He has no weapon. You came here of your own volition." He smirked. "You were selling. That's illegal, you know. How much did he offer you?"

"This is outrageous!" she cried. "We would never!"

The officer reached into the man's coat pocket and pulled out the tricoin, held it up for the other to see. "That's a lot of money," his voice came through the helmet like a walkie-talkie. "Your blood must be delicious."

The other officer whistled.

"We sold it, so what?" said the man. "You would too for that much. You'd sell your own arm for that much."

The first officer called down the alley on the loudspeaker, "Was it worth it? Was it worth twenty-five thousand, sir?"

He felt his chin for more of the sticky red and sucked on a finger. "Yep. It was, yes," he affirmed with a happy thumbs-up and a crazy grin.

"Hmm." The first officer pulled off his helmet revealing a pale face outlined by a tailored black beard. "It's worse than I suspected," he said.

"What?" the woman asked.

"This person… is a vampire," said the still-helmeted officer, delivering the line as if to prompt laughter from a sitcom audience.

"A vampire?" exclaimed the man, apoplectic. "Are you crazy?"

"No crazy here, sir. I'm sure of it," said the bearded officer, matching the hambone delivery of his partner. He cocked his gun and the second followed suit. "You two wait in the drone," he continued. "For your safety."

The couple eyed the blood-covered man and pulled each other close.

"Go on," said the helmeted officer. "We'll write you up for selling after we deal with him."

When the couple turned for the drone, the officers shot them in the back of their heads. They dropped dead to the concrete, hands still clasped.

Down the alley, he flinched. The laceguns had been virtually silent. Just a little puff of air and he thought he actually saw the disks trail off to the sides of the alleyway after they'd exited the couple's brains. "Shee-it," he said, putting his hands to his red-smeared cheeks

They turned back to him. *Uh-oh.*

Beard holstered his weapon and hailed him, "Hey buddy, you're not supposed to be out here. Explain."

He hardly knew anything anymore. Why was he here? What was he supposed to be doing? Why weren't they shooting him?

Helmet, who was much bigger and more muscular than the other, approached. "Answers. Now. We know there's a shortage, but you can't be sorting yourself in public."

"Uh," he answered. "I came in from…" his mind raced, "… Riversfork, uh, for the conference."

"The conference? You look like shit," said Beard. "Riversfork, you say?"

"I'm not picking up a touchstone on my scans," said Helmet.

"Where's your touchstone?"

His mind raced but hunger's claws were scratching again. He tried to answer their questions, but no words would come out, just a clenched teeth growl of some sort. The noise was animal-like and foreign. He refocused and tried to get his mouth to say something convincing, and the last thing that came before his eyes rolled back toward his brain was, *more O-neg*. He felt his muscles seizing up, all the tendons and ropey bits in his joints going tight.

"He's not from Riversfork," said Helmet.

The other officer dropped to a knee and came in for a closer look. "I can't believe it," he said.

He'd seized up now and collapsed to his side, elbows pinned tight to his ribs, forearms and hands sticking out from his body like a mannequin with the limbs twisted wrong.

"What is it?" asked Helmet.

"Look at him, stupid."

"Yeah, he's sick or something."

"Nah," said Beard. "He's seating."

CHAPTER TWENTY-SEVEN

Mitochondrian
Organelle responsible for cellular respiration, digestion, and energy production.

Sitting in the shed out behind the Bahamas, Lock tapped away on Llydia's screen. She brought up some diagnostics and scrolled through them until a window opened with various functions such as environmental control, autopilot, trim, and pitch assistance. She went down the list, setting them all to *off*. "It's fly-by-wire now," she said. "No hovering or letting off the stick, 'kay Willa? Or kaboom, get it?"

"I get it," Willa answered. The drones' aluminum-air batteries had legendary capacity and longevity, but Lock had no way to recharge Llydia's. They had access to electricity, but drones charged inductively and none of the islands had a pad. They had to conserve what power she had left, and it was beginning to wane.

"Should be more than enough left to get us to my guy with the printers and back," said Lock.

Kathy came out from the back door of the house and entered the drone.

"Kids good?" asked Lock.

"Yeah," answered Kathy. "I think Lindon can handle them. Maybe."

Lock shut the door and flicked her eyes skyward. Willa lifted them off and made for the course Lock had set.

Lock turned back to Kathy. "What else was he doing before he split to launder the coins?"

"Nothing really," Kathy answered. "He was sort of rummaging around. I tried to talk to him but he just acted like I wasn't there."

"He say anything weird?"

"Everything he says is weird."

"Help me out here. What was he talking about?"

"He just kept saying that he was hungry. I made him some oats and offered my last cheese tube, but he wouldn't take it."

"Why the hell not?"

"I don't know," said Kathy. "He said he would just get food along the way."

"That's not like him."

"Why?"

"He doesn't get the food," said Lock. "I get the food or Lindon gets the food. He watches the kids. That's what he does. On the rare occasion he has to run an errand, he's out and back without a side trip for anything, much less food. He hates leaving the children."

Willa spoke up, "Maybe it all got to be too much. I mean, losing the kids and all."

"I've known him for a decade," she said flatly. "He's never disappeared on me and we still have a house of children. No. He didn't just give up."

"He had two tricoins he was supposed to launder, though, right?" asked Willa.

Lock's jaw tightened. "He wouldn't steal from me. He wouldn't steal from those kids. Maybe… maybe somebody mugged him. Hurt him."

Willa didn't disagree. Everard loved the children unconditionally. But from what she had learned of the man, he'd lived a life that seemed to attract trouble. Who knew what might happen to someone trying to launder fifty K in the lowbloods.

They flew into AB Minus and over a series of industrial complexes big enough to cover entire city blocks.

Lock directed Willa to one of the largest warehouses with a series of square shafts leading down from the roof. Willa brought them in low and Lock pointed to the shaft furthest to the left. "That's it. That one."

Willa maneuvered Llydia over the center of the shaft, then lowered them down into it, concealing them from all angles except from directly above.

"What is this place?" Willa asked as the drone landed.

"Where Patriot makes The Box."

"What?" Willa exclaimed. "I thought we were meeting your associate to get the printers?"

"Yeah, that's what we're doing," Lock answered.

"This is a Patriot facility, Lock."

"Anyone else you know that has industrial printers laying around?"

"This was your plan?" exclaimed Willa. "To steal printers from Patriot?"

"Willa, dangit. *Jethrum* is stealing printers from Patriot. He's gifting them to me on account of he grossly underpaid me for Claude's cooler bag. He owes me a favor and we criminals help each other out when we're not screwing each other over."

Willa was flabbergasted. "You brought us to a Patriot facility to steal Patriot printers!"

"My plan, Willa, was to get our tricoins laundered and buy already-stolen printers from my associates, but Everard's gone AWOL with the money, hasn't he?"

Willa crossed her arms in frustration.

"You ready, Kath?"

"Yep."

"I didn't know we were coming to Patriot," said Willa shaking her head. "This is too dangerous for her."

"She's the only one small enough to crawl through the incinerator clean-out," said Lock.

"Incinerator?" Willa exclaimed.

"Relax. It's not even on."

"Jethrum hid the printers in the incinerator?" asked Willa.

"Don't be crazy. That's just where we've landed."

"*Inside* the incinerator?"

"You want to use the employee parking lot?" Lock said. "Besides, it's not really the incinerator itself, just the smokestack right above it." She knelt. "Alright, Kathy, let's move. The printers should be somewhere near to the cleanout door on the other side. I'm guessing Jeth probably concealed them."

Kathy hit Lydia's hatch. The chamber into which they'd landed was scorched black cinderblock. A gigantic chimney. The smell of ash came damp and cold into the drone and Willa prayed that meant the incinerator was dormant, or, better, defunct. The outline of a metal door on two hinges made its impression in the soot.

Lock punted the small hatch with the toe of her combat boot, then knelt and held it open as Kathy slithered through. "Hurry now."

Kathy's feet disappeared. Seconds ticked by. Willa began to panic. "How do you know this thing won't turn on while she's gone?"

"I don't know that."

A swell of frustration bubbled in Willa's throat. Lock's plans always had a distinct by-the-seat-of-her-pants improvisational element to them. And here they had Kathy involved again. Willa dropped to the little cleanout door and pushed it open, saw only blackness on the other side. "Lock, what if this thing fires up?"

"Well, it'd probably shear about a hundred pounds of paint off old Llydia, but we'd get out fine."

Willa opened her mouth to retort but was interrupted by the loud clank of the hatch. A long box marked THE BOX – FAMILY OF SIX slid into the drone, followed by another. Willa pulled them in and stacked them by the bench. Kathy began to climb back through, but recoiled as a jet of hot gas blasted up from below. The tiny door slammed shut.

"Shit!" yelled Lock. With Llydia's door still open and a plume of smoke racing up the walls, she yanked on the stick and took the drone straight up, scraping the sides on the way out.

"What are you doing? Kathy's still in there!" cried Willa.

"We can't be!" she answered as they exploded from the chimney like a cannonball.

"We have to get her!"

"She's smart. She'll get herself out," said Lock, as she calmly banked the drone. "We'll circle back and pickerup."

"We cannot lose her!"

"I know that!"

White smoke billowed from where they'd been parked moments before. They made a wide circle over the facility. Willa's fingers clawed the frame of the tiny window as she watched the ground.

Lock ascended to get a better view and brought Llydia around toward the back of the building where workers loaded pallets of The Box into speedloop cargo pods. As if on cue, Kathy burst from a large door and leapt from the dock. She rolled on the ground, sprang upright just as quickly, then sprinted out toward the street. Patriot gave chase.

"There she is!" called Lock.

Kathy raced into the neighborhood, leading her pursuers through a labyrinth of alleyways and side streets, before ducking into a toolshed. Willa's mouth went dry. Her nails dug further into the rubberized window trim.

"We gotta get her fast," said Lock, nervously. "They'll have drones up any minute."

The security detail stormed by Kathy's hiding spot.

"Sit there for a sec, kid," Lock hoped aloud.

Kathy burst back into the alley, headed in the opposite direction.

"Shit!" exclaimed Lock. "Too soon!"

The security team reversed direction.

Anticipating Kathy's vector, Lock flew ahead and set Llydia down in the mouth of another lane just ahead of the running girl. They flung open the door as she sprinted by.

"Kathy!" called Willa.

She skidded to a stop and slipped on the wet ground. Willa reached out from the door as Kathy scrabbled upright. A man flew in from the side, crushing her to the ground. Willa leapt out and tried to pull the man away. More rushed them, guns trained. Lace whispered by. Kathy's hands fired like pistons into the man's face and throat, bloodying his nose, but he managed to keep her pinned through sheer size. Lock latched onto Willa and yanked her back into the shelter of the drone. Willa screamed and struggled. Rays of light burst from the walls as holes popped across Llydia's body. Lock jerked her skyward and closed the door.

Willa beat her fist against the window. "No!"

Lock took Llydia around the facility's perimeter. Below, the men dragged Kathy into the building.

Willa pounded again and again. "No! No, no!"

"We'll get her back, Willa." She leveled the drone. "I promise!"

"You brought her here and you left her!" Willa cried.

"If we stayed another second, it'd be all of us! Don't be stupid!"

"There had to be another way to get those printers! We had to do it your way! Jethrum could have hid them somewhere else, but you had to make it into some grand adventure! Everything is just a game to you!"

Lock spoke quietly. "That's not true, Willa."

"I should have stopped you the second you brought up letting her go in by herself. You just *used* her. And I let you!"

"Don't give me that. You let her play teen mom in front of a twenty-ton truck just fine. But now that shit's gone sideways, you're having second thoughts," she said. "Stay on task."

Willa seethed. "There must have been another way."

Lock stared Willa down. "There wasn't. This was the only way to get those printers out. Get it through your head. Or don't. I don't care. But don't blame me for it." She eased the stick toward Bad Blood. "Like it or not, Willa, the plan worked. Those printers are how we're gonna save your boy. And my kids. And get Kathy back!"

Willa wanted to scream, but stopped herself short. Lock was that awful combination of stubborn and always right. The type of person that never changed their mind, while expecting others to change theirs. And she always had to get the last word. Willa resolved to end it. There was no changing what had already happened.

CHAPTER TWENTY-EIGHT

APLASIA

With regard to blood, it is the deficiency of red cell production in the marrow that leads to a low red blood cell count.

The corner of Lock's mouth was stretched over the fat end of a carrot and she moved it side to side like an army general with a cigar. Willa observed from a nearby table, disgusted, itching for Lock to bite off a chunk and get it over with.

One of the printers was already up and running, spitting out poly-ceramic bags into a wicker basket at twenty per minute. Once Lock had the second printer going – and barring any setbacks – they'd have a hundred thousand of them in about twenty hours. More would be better, but they didn't have time. Distribution had to take place the following evening when they could justify crowding the streets. Halloween hadn't been celebrated in years, but they figured to resurrect something close to it for one night as a cover to hand out the counterfeits under the guise of trick-or-treating. Anyhow, with so few of the neighborhood's cameras in operation, it was unlikely to raise Patriot's suspicions.

Willa watched everything happen as if she was on the other side of glass. Paralyzed. How many children could she lose and still function? In the rush of activity over the last days, she'd been distracted enough to keep pushing, but now in the stillness, reality was dawning. There was no way for them to get inside the Heart and even if they managed it, they had no way of knowing if the bag hack would work. She was tired. Life was piling up. And now she was trapped, handcuffed to this woman who would treat a child like an expendable foot soldier; a means to an end. Maybe Kathy *had* been the only way to get the printers. So what? Willa didn't care; she was a child. There was a line and they'd crossed it. More than once.

Willa eyed the door at the opposite end of the old supermarket. On the other side of it stood a parking lot that hadn't seen an actual car in thirty years. Beyond that was the rest of Bad Blood, the edgelands, and finally, endless fields of silicorn that stretched to the horizon. How hard would it be to muster the will to open the door and start walking? She'd never been to the sky wall before. Perhaps she could get close enough to see it with her own eyes before the rest of her gave out.

They didn't talk about Kathy. There was nothing to say. The plan was all they had left. Succeed, and they get her and the others back. Fail and they don't. They had to presume that she was back in the system. A repurposed child that would go back up for adoption at Patrioteer. Privately, Willa considered that the best-case scenario. Because there was another, worse outcome. If Patriot figured out who Kathy was, who she'd been, and what she'd been groomed to be, it was unlikely they would put her out for general adoption. If anyone recognized her as Ellen Olden, she might already be gone, taken into the lair of the Claret maybe, wherever that was. The girl's unhealed half finger was a giant red flag that could seal her fate.

Lock entered some schematics on the second printer's interface, and it glowed to life. She stepped behind it and unwrapped a heavy billet of raw poly she'd obtained, then hefted it into the machine. After that, she dumped a scoop of ceramic powder into a hopper on top. The printer slowly chewed the poly, what looked like a giant, semi-transparent stick of colorless butter and ejected the first bag. Lock inspected it, then cracked the small cooling element installed inside.

"Oh dang!" she exclaimed, dropping the bag, "that's chillier than I thought – hey Willa, can blood freeze?"

Lock's ability to focus on something other than the children was infuriating. Willa ignored her.

"Hey. Willa. Can blood freeze or not?"

Willa stared at a line of newly arranged work benches, not wanting to answer, but succumbed to her natural compulsion to provide information where a void existed. "About twenty-six point six degrees Fahrenheit."

Lock sucked on her thumb where she'd touched the element. "Well I hope these are calibrated alright. They had to be a little colder to keep the decoy blood from spoiling."

Lindon and John took baskets of newly printed bags to an assembly line manned by Bad Blood's residents, who routed them to the appropriate stations along the refrigerated section. There, the decoy pockets were filled with highblood. Willa found herself wandering down the line, unable to tamp her awe of the operation's magnitude and organization.

John came alongside Willa with one of the baskets. "This was all your idea, huh?"

"Of course not," said Willa. "I don't know anything about printers."

"Yeah. But using blood as a *weapon*? That was you."

"It was there for anyone to see. I just happened to see it, that's all."

"I have a question," he said, standing next to a basket as it filled. "The decoy pocket is only at one end of the blood bag. What if the reapers scan some other part of it?"

"They won't," said Willa, chuckling as her mind conjured visions of her lazy ex-coworkers. "Well, some might, but most won't. Here, look." She bent to the basket and selected a fresh bag. "You wear the bag like so." She held it up to the outside of John's bicep, needle end down, with the decoy pocket inside toward the top. "All phlebotomists pull the bags from the donors the same way, fingers between the bag and the skin, thumb down." She demonstrated the move. "The most natural motion once you've got the bag is to flip it on the way to the scanner, so the top end of the bag becomes the bottom, see?"

"Mmhmm," John nodded.

"The end with the decoy is what receives the needle probes. Now, company rules say we're supposed to change it up from donor to donor. You know," she mimed, "scan the sides, the top, all of that. But nobody does that except for new hires and," she tossed the bag into the now full basket, "stubborn old ladies."

"Why didn't the company crack down, make the reapers change it up?"

"You need highblood for a bag hack, John. Where would the lowbloods get it? What highblood would give it over so lowbloods might profit? I don't think it ever happened but once. And that was when Lock sent Everard through my line a few days back. It's never really been that much of a concern."

"So, we're just hoping they all continue to be derelict in their bag scanning."

"And they will," she said, pushing the overflowing basket to the side and sliding an empty one underneath the printer's output chute. "Sure as the sun will rise."

"You're that confident?"

Willa recalled Lock saying that technology was only part of a hack; because human beings were at the front and back of it, everything still came down to human nature. Weaknesses in technology are predictable because humans are predictable. She wasn't wrong. "I know these folks, John. Plus, they'll be inundated once people start flooding in. All they'll care about is getting the lines down. Trust me."

"We all do," he said, taking the full basket down to the assembly line.

Willa watched him march away and felt a ripple of shame. How long had the people of Bad Blood been sequestered behind that wall? They were the ones with every justification to be paralyzed by despondency and cynicism. Yet they weren't. There was Lock, moving at full speed and with no sleep, working to make sure they were prepared. Willa, meanwhile, had slowed to a crawl, dwelling in her guilt over the loss of Kathy; blaming Lock, blaming herself.

She let the printer fill the basket, then hefted it against her hip like laundry. Down at the assembly area she grinned at a boy who couldn't have been any older than Isaiah. He smiled brightly as he squeezed a bag to test its construction before passing it down the line. At the end of the aisle, the printers, now warm, were spitting out bags at full capacity. She approached Lock. "What do you need from me?"

Lock tried to avoid spilling a stack of poly butter sticks she held like firewood. "I– we need you back."

Willa came closer, offering her arms, and Lock allowed some of the poly to tumble over to her. "I'm here," Willa said. "Show me how to help."

Lock studied Willa's face like a human polygraph. Seeming satisfied, she gestured for her to follow.

Over behind the printers Lock said, "Turns out these Patriot models are way better than anything we could have gotten on the black market. Whereas a run-of-the-mill machine would have to print the poly bag and the inner decoy pocket separately, these bad boys can do it in one go. Ceramic powder ink. See?" She leaned in, directing Willa to a small window on the side of the machine. She could see a decoy pocket being printed, while at the same time extruders formed the outer bag around it. Willa nodded and went to add some more ceramic powder under Lock's supervision.

"Make sure you keep the little tray there topped up with cooling elements," said Lock, pulling on her leather vest and watching Willa work. "Yeah, see? You got it." She turned for the door.

"Where are you going?"

"Rendezvous with some criminal types," she answered. "Meeting with some of the folks I used to hang out with before I met you." She winked. "Settle a few debts."

"Now?"

"Two birds, one stone, Willa," she answered, huffing at her

goggles and then swirling them with a scarf. "They'll help us with the logistics of bag distribution throughout the other segments and I get square for a whole ledger's worth of favors and debts. If this hack takes, then these guys stand to make *beaucoup* casheesh and I get out of the red."

"What if it doesn't work?"

Lock became suddenly less animated and shrugged. "If it doesn't work it means we've lost the kids, Willa. My creditors want to come calling for their pound of flesh, so be it."

With Lock off trying to get their distribution network in place, Willa toiled with the printers. She had lost count of how much poly she'd fed them, though it was easily enough to fill dozens upon dozens of the wicker baskets. The assembly line had dwindled to a skeleton crew. Others napped on pallets in the building or off in their modules. Her good arm ached from hauling poly billets. It was late. And even though there were no windows, the depth of night somehow made it feel darker inside.

Someone began hammering at the side door. John and Lindon leapt to attention and rushed down the long row of checkout aisles. Willa raced to catch up.

John put his ear to the door. "Who is it?" he called. "Lock, is that you?"

No response.

He got to his toes and slid a thin metal piece to the side revealing a peep hole. Pressing his eyes to the slot, he surveyed the outside. "There's nobody out there," he whispered.

"Let me see," said Lindon. Much taller than John, he didn't need to strain to see out the hole. He looked and turned back. "Whoever it was, they're gone."

Another loud bang.

Willa dragged over an old plastic crate and stepped on top, careful to keep her balance. Lindon held her hand as she stepped onto it to look through the slot. In the distance were the modules of Bad Blood, lit here and there by small strands of lights, flickering dimly on the dribble of power that fed them. She looked to the sky for the telltale red of Patriot drones but saw nothing. She stepped down and sat on the crate. "I can't see anyone. I don't know what's going on."

"Kids," said Lindon with a shrug. "Probably playing a joke. Throwing acorns. They know we're in here working."

"We gotta get back," said John. He shuffled toward the assembly line.

"You OK?" asked Lindon.

"I'm fine. I'll catch up," said Willa.

Lindon followed John.

Willa climbed back to the slot. Seeing nothing, she slammed it shut and pushed the crate back against the wall and sat. She leaned over and gave her calves a rub, massaged her sore Achilles.

A tiny squeak, like an injured bird, came from outside. Willa froze and perked her ears. Like a wheeze, it came again, slightly stronger. And again. A word. Whispered. *Vengeance.*

"Oh my God!" Willa threw open the bolt and yanked the door inward.

Kathy was slumped tight to the door frame, her face matted with hair and a thick lamina of blood. Willa dropped to the ground and cradled her. "What happened?"

Lindon and others raced toward them.

The girl's eyelids bumped languidly open. Willa checked her over for injuries. "Kathy?" She caressed her cheek and the girl roused slightly. Cradled in her left hand was a blood-soaked rag. Willa gently lifted the folds.

An oblong hole trickled red from the center of her palm. Lace wound.

They carried her inside to a cot and dressed the wound as Kathy watched passively. Willa checked her for additional injuries. None. Her pulse was strong even though she was painted from head to toe in blood. Like she'd showered in it.

Willa used wet cloths to scrub the grime from the girl's body until there was a seeping red pile on the floor. She rubbed Kathy's skin until it couldn't take any more, but it held a pinkish tint.

Willa lay down on the cot next to her, warming her in an embrace, though she realized the action might have been more for herself than for the girl. Kathy was safe and alive and Willa's conscience would get a second chance. In the morning, she would find somewhere to get Kathy a shower and go looking for some clean clothes.

Kathy's breathing steadied until she was deep in the trough of slumber. Now and then, Willa thought she heard her uttering the password as if she was still outside, pressed to the bottom of the door.

vengeance

CHAPTER TWENTY-NINE

Metaplasia
An abnormal change in the nature of living tissue.

It was somewhere black. Like sitting under the skirt of a weeping willow blindfolded in the swamp on a summer night. Except without biting flies or skeeters. He had a distant recollection of a man who would have been up at the door, wherever it was, beating the sap out of it and screaming about his rights, and kicking asses until he got someone's attention. Would have raised Hell, that other man, made them regret underestimating him. But not the new man. The new man was starving again, headache grinding like cinderblock teeth, flashing pain in imagined colors swallowed by the dark.

It was like being buried alive, the blackness. Until he saw the rat, that was. For some reason it stood out, glowing red-orange inside the chamber they both occupied. Like his eyes were doing him a favor, telling him where the thing was that couldn't see him back.

He was surprised at the amount of muscle in the little thing and how long it fought while he clamped it in his teeth. It kicked and scratched even after he pulled the backbone free, giving the animal a dorsal fan of its own flesh. He became instantly sick, bathing the struggling animal in his acrid and watery vomit just before it keeled, the sounds of his dry heaving its last perceived experience of the world. He watched it twitch, and as it died, felt jealousy at its freedom.

The whole event had confused. If the rat was toxic to his newfound constitution, why had his eyes called it out to him? Was that part of the curse?

He supposed he'd known somewhere deep down that the varmint wouldn't quash his hunger, but as with the marooned sailors of the *Whaleship Essex* who knew not to drink of the salty ocean, they did so anyway when thirst got to a point. Some urges push till they win.

His brain was crawling. His stomach was empty as a viper's gullet. Other things moved about the cell, highlighted in their telltale glow. Most were small rodents and insects, but he dared not fall upon them, for the curse had given him false vision.

His captors said they would feed him once he'd surrendered over the identities of his co-conspirators, and left him a paper pad on which to turn state's evidence, but he wasn't the surrendering type, and so he told them to kick pebbles along with a barrage of other unpleasantries. He'd tried eating some of the paper, but when it failed to satisfy, he tossed it into the corner of the cell. When they'd left, he'd begged in whispers to be fed.

If those cops meant to kill him, well they best get to it.

The thing inside was eating him, he knew it to a certainty. Tiny pieces of who he was, slowly chewed and swallowed, then forgotten. Knowing he was forgetting but not knowing what was lost was a new type of torture. Until he forgot that he'd forgotten, of course. Worry gave way to confusion, only to be replaced by a sense of vague desolation and finally, indifference.

He tried to remember details of the man who had been, to recall some of the things that might have brought that man pleasure. With enough effort he found some vestiges that were almost too buried to access. He smelled and tasted cigarettes, winced at the heat of a well-earned sunburn, heard the bravado in his voice as it spouted off to authority, felt the joy in providing for and protecting those children. *What were their names?* The memories, if that's what they were, brought him nothing. Not a flutter of emotion or whiff of nostalgia. None of it was real anymore. They weren't his stories. They were someone else's experiences told by somebody else about somebody else – stories of the man who had been before. Myths. Maybe it was all made up.

Maybe none of it was real but the suffering.

CHAPTER THIRTY

Arteriole

Small diameter blood vessel that branches from an artery and leads to capillaries.

Kathy's autumn hair was stained plum black. Lock knelt and lifted away a knot of it while the girl stared into a bowl of John's tomato soup. "You should try to eat, kiddo." Then, to Willa, "You checked her over? Nothing but the hand?"

Willa shook her head. Kathy was fine, physically.

"Sweetie, we're worried about you," said Willa. "You've got to talk to us."

Lock sat next to her, tentative. "Kathy, uh, I think I owe you an apology. I should have found another way to get the printers. You are so grown up that you make me forget sometimes that you're still a kid. I'm sorry."

Kathy's eyes became thick and glossy as she fought to keep her composure. Lock, who always seemed awkward with physical contact, slipped an arm over the girl's shoulder.

Tears poured over the big lashes as if tipped from a glass. Crying became weeping, sorrowful and deep, the years of trauma that she had buried beneath layers of armor releasing with each shaking breath. The separation from her parents, the loss of her home, her adoption by monsters, and everything they'd put her through since. She gulped inhalations from between hitching sobs. It was too much for any child to bear, and Willa marveled that it had taken her so long to break.

The three of them sat together on the makeshift bed for some time. With her face pressed to Lock's shoulder, Kathy's sobbing diminished until her body slacked, wrung out. She pushed slowly from Lock's embrace, her eyes watery and swollen. She wasn't saying something.

Lock furrowed her brow. "What?"

Kathy glanced to the side and Willa followed her eyes to a black poly bag at the foot of the bed. "What is that?" she asked.

Kathy's voice was raw. "Look in it."

Willa retrieved the bag and opened it. Inside were hundreds of tiny metal rods the shape of vitamin pills. She held it open for Lock to peer inside.

Lock poked her fingers inside and gave it a stir. "They look like… are those?"

"Yes," Kathy croaked.

Lock squinted. "Bio-implant beacons?"

"Beacons? For what?" asked Willa.

"Location," Lock answered. "It's what you rid Kathy of when you lopped her pointer."

"Where'd you get them, Kathy?"

"Factory."

"The Box plant? What do they need them for?" asked Willa.

"They don't," Lock answered.

"They were moving children through," said Kathy. "Processing them there."

Willa pressed near, squeezed Kathy's hand. "Was Isaiah there? Did you see him?"

"I don't know him, Willa," she answered. "I don't know what he looks like."

Willa's head slumped. "Of course. Of course, you don't." She sniffled, regrouped. "So… he's got one of these – beacons – in him? Like you did?"

Kathy nodded.

"How in the world did you get out of there?" asked Lock.

The girl gave a tight *no* headshake. She was done talking about it. She eyed the soup. "Do you have a spoon for that?"

Bad Blood buzzed as the day unfolded, with everyone preparing for the distribution of the counterfeit bags. Kathy found her feet again and pitched in as well. A minor setback occurred when one of the printers overheated and caught fire, but the remaining one plugged away, spitting out bags until the last minute.

Lock's associates swooped in to collect their allocations for the lowblood neighborhoods within the other city segments. At the same time, she gave them jailbroken touchstones containing a virus of her own making that would allow the user to alter their phenotype profiles to match the blood bag they'd be turning in. The only difficulty was that the only way to infect all the touchstones in the districts was by touchstone-to-touchstone contact. But they had a plan for that. If they were successful, when people turned in their bags and touchstoned-in at the donor booth, the virus would hop onto the local system and the phlebotomist on duty would see a three-way phenotype match between their booth's display, the donor's touchstone, and God willing, the readout on the harvested blood.

At nightfall, Willa, Lock, and Kathy stood on an unnamed street in front of unnumbered houses in AB Plus, garbed in hastily-crafted costumes: Willa the witch, Lock the pirate, and Kathy, packed inside cardboard boxes to look like some breed of robot that had never existed. It was out of their hands now. They watched as children sprinted from door to door across barren lawns and cracked walkways, with bags painted like jack-o-lanterns swinging on their arms. Even though it was unlikely anyone had any candy to give, the freedom was sweet enough.

Willa imagined Isaiah as one of them, bobbing along in a herd of his cohorts, and felt a tug of sadness. She pushed the thought away. In two days, she'd have him back. She loooked to Lock and then to Kathy. "Either of you have any idea what 'trick-or-treat' really means?"

Kathy's cuboid head pivoted. "You ask for a treat and if they don't have it, they have to do a trick for you."

"No, no," said Lock authoritatively. "You do a trick and then you get the treat."

"Mm, not quite," said Willa. "See, the treat is what everybody thinks about – the trick piece of it got lost over the years. People think it was a choice for the person answering the door, do a trick or give a treat. But that wasn't the case. Trick-or-Treat is a threat. The trick was a consequence of not having a treat to offer. Give that treat or get a trick. And the trick was mayhem. Egg your house. Fill the trees with toilet paper. Blow up your mailbox. That's what it means." She laughed a bit. "When it all started, mayhem prevailed. People got wise and started offering candy to buy peace. That's Halloween."

"There hasn't been much candy out there for a while now," said Lock.

"So here we are with the trick," said Willa. "Mayhem."

"Well, what we're doing is a little bit more than setting a mailbox on fire."

"What's a mailbox?" asked Kathy.

Thrilled by the rare chance to run free through the night, children spread across the lowbloods like wildfire, not in any predictable pattern, but certain to cover the territory in a few short hours. Willa listened to the kazoo babble of their voices muffled on the carried wind and marveled at how it made a place of desolation sound like a place of happiness, even with so few treats to be had.

A flock arrived at a nearby house, sending up cheers of *trick or treat*.

The man and woman who'd come to the door smiled at the gang and seemed to be explaining, as most did, that they didn't have any treats.

After a brief exchange, the children dug in their pumpkins and handed over a pair of empty blood-bags.

The man held one up to the yellow streetlight and Willa saw understanding flash across his face as he noticed the decoy pocket and the wipe-away notation they'd written on it of the phenotype contained within. He nudged the woman and pointed it out. The children offered up a jailbroke touchstone and the couple bumped theirs in turn.

Willa, Lock, and Kathy spread themselves out, to troubleshoot if necessary, and to make sure the children stayed supplied. Willa watched them make their deliveries and saw recognition in the faces of the recipients that this was Something Good. In some places, word had spread faster than the children were able to cover ground, with folks already having shared the touchstone virus, neighbor to neighbor.

As the night came to an end, Willa envisioned the lowest of lowbloods, her people, putting on their bags and tapping needles to ports, smiling while their unwanted essence pulsed them full. Come tomorrow, an army of the poor would march to the donor stations, have their bags removed and scanned by the company phlebotomists, and watch with glee as their blood took the label of something it was not, making it liquid cash for them and poison to any monster that tried to eat it.

Lock had been right when she said their trick was extreme. It was. The trick, should it work, was mass murder.

CHAPTER THIRTY-ONE

Taxonomy
The area of science concerned with the classification of organisms.

The sun hadn't been up thirty minutes, but the normally empty streets were filled with lowbloods. Warm, yellow-orange light infused the washed-out grays of their world with humming vitality, as men and woman, many of whom children trailed like ducklings, headed out to break the boycott. Sitting somewhere in west AB Minus and having not slept a wink, Willa watched from an old lawn chair. People made their way through the streets, washed and clothed in their very best, heads held proudly in the way of the highbloods they portrayed. All day, they traversed the city, going to donor stations they'd seldom frequented so as not to raise suspicions of the phlebotomists they'd seen on a regular basis, and who would be familiar with their blood types. The story was the same across the districts when Willa finally made the long trek south to Bad Blood.

That evening, they congregated in John's module to watch *The Patriot Report*. The host of the show, whose face seemed molded from one of Lock's poly butter sticks, gleamed with excitement as he announced the end of the protests and a return to normalcy.

The lights were low and he spoke in hushed tones directly into the camera. "We are proud to welcome back all of the loyal

Patriots who saw the pirated telecast of our program from the other evening exposed for what it truly was: *Fake News!"* He backed away, holding his arms out to the sides. Two attractive assistants fell into place on each. "A devious ruse designed by lowlifes and traitors to cut off desperately needed blood to the Gray Zones." He gestured to a screen showing purported footage of those suffering in the affected areas. "You will be pleased to know that we have already rooted out the terrorists – and that's what they are, folks, terrorists – who perpetrated this scheme. They will be tried and punished." The two assistants clapped like they'd just won a gameshow washer-dryer set.

Those in the room exchanged looks. Lock shrugged, "They got us, apparently."

The host continued, "We don't negotiate with terrorists, but we do reward loyalty! And that is why we are doubling our incentives for the next two days on all blood types!"

An explosion of confetti poured down around him, settling on the brim of his signature red and gold striped top hat.

"And now for today's numbers. Sit still, folks, because we haven't had a single day like this in some time." He paused as a graphic unfurled across the bottom of the screen. "One hundred and thirty-two thousand!" He shouted, flinging the hat. "What an achievement! Our single largest donation day since Goliath!" A huge waving flag graphic appeared behind him and the State Anthem boomed.

"So, it worked?" asked Willa, as the broadcast continued to the segment-by-segment breakdowns.

"Seems the blood got through, at least," answered Lock. "If your theory about the lack of rigor employed by your former coworkers holds true, then it worked. Otherwise, if those needle probes hit anywhere but the decoy pocket, well then, a bunch of folks just got paid for lowblood. I'll wait for my people in North-By and Crosstown to get back to me, see if they got the highblood prices."

The host placed the hat back on, taking care not to over muss his hair, and approached the camera, almost nudging the lens with his nose. "I want you all to know, from the bottom of my heart – from the bottom of Patriot's heart – just how vital your blood is to those who receive it. Always remember, that your continued support keeps people alive. God bless."

"Turn it off," said Lock.

"Thank you," said John as he closed the feed. "I can't watch that asshole anymore." He palmed the front door of the module and stepped into the dwindling light.

"A hundred and thirty-two thousand bags," said Willa. "How many do you suppose are ours?"

"Most of 'em, you'd think. We ended up just shy of one-sixteen before the printers went kaput."

"I'm nervous," said Willa.

"Me too, girl," said Lock, standing and fogging her goggles. "Go get some rest. Get yourself a shower. I'll do the same when I get back."

"Where are you going?"

"Recon."

"Can I come with?" asked Kathy, who everyone assumed had been asleep in a nearby chair.

Lock looked at her like she was crazy. "I'm headed to scope the Heart, so no. Not after what you've been through. I'll take you to the Bahamas later to help Lindon with the kiddos. You can also keep an eye out in case Everard shows back up." She opened the door and stepped out, then paused. "I'll be back late. Don't wait up."

The door slapped shut and Willa stared at it for a moment before turning to Kathy, who dug her fingers in a bowl of radiant cherry tomatoes. "What?" the girl asked, noticing Willa's glare.

"I want to know how you got out."

"Out of where?" Kathy asked innocently.

Willa narrowed her eyes like she did when Isaiah gave her a load of baloney.

Kathy made a noise like *hmm,* but from a place of annoyance rather than contemplation. She gave her attention back to the bowl.

"I'm serious, Kathy. That building was crawling. How does a fourteen year-old escape and then get drenched in somebody else's blood?"

Kathy settled contentedly into the thin cushions of the old couch. The rest had done her good. Her cheeks were full of color and her eyes were clear, their intensity renewed; perhaps even stronger than before. She cleared her throat and leveled her gaze. "I told them who I was."

"What? Why? Why would you bring that attention to yourself?"

"I was kidnapped, Willa. By you and Lock – don't you remember?"

And then it clicked. "You got them to believe we were forcing you to steal the printers," Willa said, understanding. The girl was smart.

"They didn't know we were after printers. I told them you'd sent me in to steal food."

"OK, but that doesn't explain how you escaped."

"Sure it does." The muffled pop of a tomato exploded inside Kathy's cheek. "They separated me from the other kids while they contacted Patriot. I ended up alone with two of them."

"Two of them?" Willa's stomach grumbled uneasily. "How did you get away from two men?"

"It wasn't that hard." She went back to the bowl.

"You… you… killed them, didn't you?" Willa knew she had but wanted the girl to affirm it. Still, it was hard to say out loud.

"Hmm."

"I was hoping there was another explanation," she said quietly, more to herself than anything.

"Well, there isn't. And they weren't men, anyway."

Willa sat down heavily. "I don't understand, Kathy. You're still a child."

"*Was.*"

"I don't understand."

Kathy sighed. "Remember Scynthia Scallien?"

"Yeah, just a bit," said Willa distainfully. "What about her?"

"We're the same thing."

It was like the floor suddenly dropped away, leaving Willa to flail in space. Weightless, without purchase. All she saw in her mind's eye was the woman's face, that mouth. The maw coming to swallow her whole. The air felt thin on her lips. "But… you said you weren't –"

"No, that's not what I mean. I mean we are both vrae."

Willa had seen or heard the word someplace. "Vray?"

"There are thirteen members of the Claret. A number of them, usually seven, are vrae – *the Lethal*. They make problems disappear."

"I don't understand, Kathy. You're not one of them."

Kathy squashed another tomato between her teeth, letting the gelatinous seeded flesh bathe her gums before sucking it away. "Vrae are identified during childhood, as early as possible, and then trained every day after. They start you off with puzzles and mind games. Then physical activities that become more and more challenging the stronger you get. After a while they introduce new subjects: hand-to-hand, close-quarters, weapons, anatomy, pressure points, melee. You know, the quickest ways to kill people. Two hours every morning and two after school. Dinner. Then another hour. The point is to be – well – sort of like invincible when your training ends. When you're old enough for the Choice, you know what your life will be."

"Scallien wasn't invincible."

"From what you told me, it sounds like Claude got her with a cheap shot," said Kathy.

"You're defending her?"

"Just stating the obvious."

"So, they were going to turn you into an assassin?"

Kathy stopped chewing. "Did."

"But, you're just a child!"

"Stop saying that!" Kathy snapped.

The way she looked at Willa was like a slamming door. She was right. Kathy wasn't a child. Age was one thing, experience another. Her childhood had ended long ago, her innocence replaced by an understanding of the world as it truly was. That life is chaos. That others will take what you do not protect. And that sometimes ending the life of another is the cost of preserving one's own. Lessons children shouldn't have to learn, but that Kathy had first-hand. Willa took her wrist. "I'm sorry."

Kathy stared ahead, chewing another tomato. For a moment, Willa thought she felt the girl softening some, relaxing. Then she muttered, "Cardboard."

"What?" asked Willa.

"Cardboard," she repeated. "An empty Box. That's what I killed them with. It's sharper, stronger than you think. Neck skin is delicate. You'd be surprised. It's like banana peel once you get a hole going. They didn't even realize that their jugulars were open for a good two or three seconds."

Willa couldn't respond. Kathy's mouth unravelled into a grin. She held up her bandaged hand. "Guess it's only fair one of them got a shot off, huh?"

Later, Willa and Lock flew Kathy back to the Bahamas. Lindon had the children in order, but no one had seen Everard. On the return to Bad Blood, Willa found herself entirely occupied by Kathy. "Lock?"

Lock watched out the side window while gently guiding Llydia through the night sky. "Yeah?"

"Kathy told me how she got away."

"Yeah? Killed a few of them, looks like."

"She was trained to kill people."

"Hmmph," Lock snorted. "One of those vrae probably."

"You *know* about them? How?"

"It's all in their little book."

"What book?"

She pointed to the seat. "In the bench, there. Remember? From the Oldens'?"

Willa unhooked her belt and opened the hatch on top. Inside was the red-covered book that had been on the mantel at the home. "When did you take this?"

"Jesper said we were welcome to read it. After he was dead, I figured he wouldn't mind if I did."

"You didn't tell me?"

"I wasn't *hiding* it from you, Willa. We've been busy. I only scanned it anyway. Some strange shit in there. Interesting folks, those Ichorwulves."

Willa sat with the book on her lap. *Arise*. She opened the cover and paged through it. It was modeled more like a novel than a history book. There were chapters and characters, apparently, references to adventures and mystical creatures. "This just seems like a story."

"Dang Willa, you're like the worst counterintelligence agent I've ever known. Of course it's told as a story. Then it's fiction, right? What'd you think they'd do, just spell out who they are and what they're all about? *Attention, here's our vampire manual for being vampires cause we're vampires. Read only if you're a vampire.* Geezwilla."

Surprisingly, Lock's response cut. Willa knew that the woman was right, yet it stung to be confronted with yet another instance of her naivete. That made it all the more frustrating. She'd gone through life accepting it at face value. Oblivious. She closed the book and looked down at her shoes. How could she have been so wrong about so much?

When Willa hadn't said anything for a span, Lock turned to her. "Sorry. Didn't mean to go off there, lady," she said. "Guess I'm just programmed for dishonesty, so I see through the bullshit a little quicker. Look, pretty sure that thing helped me figure out how we're going to get into Patrioteer."

CHAPTER THIRTY-TWO

VASODILATION

The widening of blood vessels due to the relaxation of the vessel walls, resulting in increased blood flow.

It was like going to heaven. When the door opened all the way and the light of God came through it to bath his chilled skin, to purify him, to take him home. Or probably, it was none of that. Life always came back. Was he still alive?

He waited there, a prisoner, curled on the ground, stomach grinding like a mouthful of gravel, thinking that God sure must like to make an entrance. Finally, a shadow filled the door, the silhouette of a man, or at least the deity in human form.

The man who had once been the criminal called Everard pondered how it must look, him there, too weak even to sit, surrounded by the killed but uneaten carcasses of lesser animals. *Lesser animals*. That's a good one, he thought, considering his own state.

The new man said something to the guards. There were two of them who tended to his cell. The tall one who liked to kick him, who he called *Ratshit*, and the short, fat one who sounded like his voice had been pumped through a pig's snout. *Pissbaby*. His own broken face cracked a crooked smile thinking on the propriety of the given monikers.

The guards rolled off and the new man pulled the door to. He sniffed at the air like a dog does when it catches prey on the wind, then stepped in and knelt by his side. "My men tell me we have you to thank for the hack of our broadcast."

"It me," answered the prisoner.

"They say you profess to have been a lone wolf, so to speak. Acted on your own with no help whatsoever."

He grunted affirmatively.

"Well," he went on, "That's very gracious of you to confess. And I commend you on your abilities. That was a lot for one man to do. Steal a drone, plant a device that commandeered and redirected our transmission, shoot down our blood transports at almost the exact same time, hire all of those actors for your little film, and then broadcast it all out from a single home in AB Plus. Amazing! But you say that you acted alone. And you know what?" He patted the man's shoulder. "I believe you."

"Hungry."

"Me too, you have no idea," he said. "Your little prank killed our blood supply. So, congratulations, I suppose, if that was the goal of your stunt. Alliance really bent me all the way over in order to get some of their surplus trucked in." He paused as if waiting for a response.

"Anyhow, good news: the lines broke yesterday, so I expect all will be back to normal in a matter of days," he continued, standing and wiping off his hands. "And yet, it's all so… I don't know… depressing."

The prisoner rolled over and made eye contact with the God-man.

"There you are," he said, smiling widely, teeth shining bright as a camera flash. "It's just that humans are so, ugh, *reliable*. Insipid. Boring. No stomach for the fight. We leave the troughs out and they come stomping back to them after less than a week? Don't get me wrong, this whole prank of yours was a royal pain, as I've detailed, but at least it was a change of pace. Invigorating. A problem we had to solve. And then your people go and cut it short by quitting on themselves. Which brings me to why I am here, really. I'm curious to understand why you fight so hard to remain one of them. Who would want that? We've offered you the opportunity to eat, to be strong."

The man mumbled something.

"What's that, Mr Alison?"

"I said," he croaked, "I'll be one goddamned thing…"

"Go on, I'm all ears."

"… you can't… control."

"How noble of you. Truly." The God-man thought silently for a moment, then paced about some, shoving aside murdered rats here and there with his shining shoes. "I'm called Dagen. And as you'll soon find out, I control everything that can be controlled. Do you know why?" He hesitated only a moment, now accustomed to the non-responsiveness of his prone cellmate. "If we control what can be controlled, we won't create that which we cannot. Does any of that compute in your half-eaten mind?"

He sneered up at this new man Dagen. Spat.

Dagen flew over and took hold of the prisoner by the filthy scruff on the sides of his head. Pulling the man's face close to his own, he growled, "You jeopardized everything and you don't even know it. You have no clue what would have happened to you out there on your own, but I do. I'm grateful, though, I am. I am grateful for your stupid, pathetic desire to remain one of them, and not give in to the animal that grows in your primitive brain, to barter for blood rather than to simply take it from the vein. That allowed us to find you. You almost ruined it all, you disgusting excuse for an Apex." He was speaking now within an inch of the prisoner's face, spittle flying, his hot, humid breath thickening the air in the prisoner's nostrils.

Dagen pressed his forehead hard against his. Anger wafted from his skin in hot waves and the prisoner could feel the man desired to harm him, to kill him. He straddled his chest and widened his mouth awkwardly, allowing the bottom jaw to extend long past where it would normally go. His curled tongue hung long, past a pair of silver-rooted gold fangs that peeked from behind the pearly whites. The prisoner got in his mind the image of a possum yawning, its gaping vermin mouth a festering bed of razor teeth hot with disease, and he knew right then he wanted to kill it.

He bucked violently, arching his back and rolling to all fours. Dagen toppled to one side, laughing. The prisoner pounced on top of him, reversing their positions, and he felt his own jaw loosening, and small slits in the roof of his mouth opening to allow the points to protrude.

"There you go," Dagen said, encouraging. "Do you feel that? That glorious current running through every fiber telling you to feed?"

Drool pooled and dripped from the prisoner's mouth as hunger pushed him to delirium.

"Go ahead," said Dagen, running a finger up the side of his neck. "My carotid awaits."

Whatever it was that pushed from within was firing full blast now, a boiler stuffed with coal and oxygen, roaring up from his stomach. Beholden to the new instincts that drove him, he let go and dove for the thumping artery.

Then everything was black. He heard himself choking. Registered the sudden constriction of his throat.

"There, see?" said Dagen, loosening his grip a measure. "I *can* control you."

The prisoner, starved, exhausted, flopped to the floor where he began to sob.

Dagen stood and straightened his jacket. "A bit of advice: you should take of the food we bring you, so you can be strong when it all ends. I would do the merciful thing now, but I need to make an example of you." He walked through the open door and dissolved into the light.

The prisoner rubbed his throat, in awe of the power the man called Dagen had shown in his grip, and the absolute dominion he'd held over him. Maybe he was God after all.

CHAPTER THIRTY-THREE

HEMOLYSIS
The rupturing of red blood cells and the release of their contents into surrounding fluid.

Willa weaved Llydia through the ancient trees surrounding the Heart. They flew into a clearing just downhill from the building, to where a broad stretch of tarmac came into view. Willa lowered the drone amongst the many others parked there, doing her best to conceal her from wider scrutiny.

Garbed in gowns somehow obtained by Jethrum, they stepped onto the tarmac. Llydia, in her final coat of red and gold, had made the trip with only a few minutes' worth of battery remaining. She looked almost triumphant, sitting there, still miraculously intact after everything she'd been through. Willa said a quiet goodbye, giving her a pat as her door closed. The late afternoon sun peeked through a gap in the gray clouds to paint the Central City landscape in beautiful colors it didn't deserve.

They began up the hill. Willa wore a black dress with curling purple filigree, and Lock a deep turquoise gown trimmed in gold with black lace sandwiched between its many layers. The path was gray cobblestone, groomed on both sides with newly planted calendulas, primrose, pansies and violas. Willa couldn't help but feel like she was clicking down the spine of the Yellow Brick Road's evil twin.

The massive parallelepiped emerged fully over the horizon. Red streamers flecked in gold stretched from the roof toward the ground, while large PATRIOTEER 2067 banners flapped in the breeze above each of the two entrances.

Lock halted at the cap of the hill. "So look. I got some bad news."

"What?"

She pointed to the far left of the building. "Those."

Three refrigeration trucks, just like the one they'd hijacked, sat in a line.

"Oh, crap," said Willa, her stomach twisting.

"We knew this was likely, Willa. At some point our bags *will* be in circulation, but at the moment," she gulped, "it looks like they've got enough to eat."

Panic was rising up. Isaiah was inside, they were sure of that, but only until the end of the conference. Then he and all of the other kidnapped children would be gone forever, taken away to some city across the country. "There's no way for us to get those kids out with the Ichorwulves alive," Willa said. "There's no way." Her knees felt weak and she began to slump. "There's no way."

"Straighten up!" said Lock brusquely. "Right now." She took Willa's elbow and lifted her. "You got no choice. You give up now, and you never see that boy again."

"But what are we supposed to do?"

"We go forward," said Lock, sounding more like the soldier she had been. "It's all we have. Forward."

Willa tried to gather herself, breathed deeply, and stared Lock in the face, looking for some hint of confidence.

"I don't know what we're going to find in there," Lock said, her eyes taking hold of Willa's. "But this is where the path leads. Maybe," she added with a sad grin, "maybe, they'll just let us adopt them."

Willa allowed a weak smile in return, nodded, and did her best to focus on the task ahead.

The monolith sat before them, glowing warmly in the setting sun.

As they neared the southern entrance, Willa stiffened. Lock gave her a squeeze of the arm and she loosened a measure. The doors were tall, angled glass creations, pointed at the top like oversized cathedral windows and faceted all over.

They sat wide open.

Patriot officials and guests clustered about, both inside and out, shaking hands and embracing in happy reunion. None seemed to be guarding the entrance or paying it any mind. This was all consistent with what Lock had predicted based on what she'd gleaned from Olden's book. It wasn't that anyone could simply wander in; in fact, quite the opposite was true. But there would be no touchstone tap, password, or secret handshake. Patriot had a single security measure in place that was impossible to hack. It took the form of a translucent ruby strip that ran in a channel around the threshold, a gatekeeping sensor that would verify if those seeking admission were welcome or not. And Lock was confident that they were already in possession of the keys. Willa wasn't so sure. There was no way it could be this simple, but only one way to find out.

Lock pulled beside Willa, whispered, "We are fine. Don't hesitate. It's suspicious. Confidence." Then she went ahead, lightly taking Willa's hand. "Come dear!" she called in an entirely new-and-cosmopolitan accent.

Willa followed Lock's lead and tried to act naturally. They entered the threshold, the ruby inlay pulsed twice as it scanned them, and they passed without anyone so much as glancing their way. Willa let her shoulders down and adjusted the big bun on top of her head. They were through.

Inside was a great hall that ran from one side of the building to the other, bisected in the middle by another corridor. A massive X. A lush crimson rug covered the gleaming floor and chased up staircases enameled in candy apple. Polished mahogany paneling shone like mirrors down the length of the corridor, reflecting the light of giant golden chandeliers hanging at intervals from above. Domed at the top like jellyfish, their long tentacles glinted with pin-lights at each tip.

An usher swept over from a shining elevator bank on the right, his smile permanent and white. "Ladies, greetings. Welcome to Patrioteer. Will you be observing or selecting?"

Willa went tongue-tied.

"We go back and forth, to be honest," said Lock. "Cold feet and all."

"Oh, I hear you," said the man. "So much to consider. The decision to become a parent!" He pressed his hands to his chest, mimicking serious contemplation. "Not to be taken lightly. Well. Have a program and peruse."

Willa accepted the program, which was heavy with thick pages.

"*Confidence,*" Lock hissed.

The man popped his arm from his sleeve exposing a gold bezeled watch implant. "Just over fifty minutes until the pageant. Selection is tomorrow. Now, down the way, we have a tasting bar and media chamber. If you care to find a seat in the lyceum ahead of the crowds–" he placed the back of his hand to the side of his mouth in a playful conspiratorial whisper, "which would be my advice – then please feel free. Just up the steps to level five, or one of our lifts can take you."

"Thank you," said Lock.

"You ladies have an excellent conference."

"We will."

"Oh," he said, turning back to them, "where are you in from?"

"Riversfork," said Willa.

"Ah, Riversfork," he said with manufactured wistfulness, "lovely." Then he spun and disappeared.

Willa looked down at the program and opened it. Children. Page after page of children; their ages, full blood workup, origin, special talents or skills, as well as "concerns," behavioral, developmental, etcetera. Lock commandeered the book and hustled Willa up the steps. "Come on. We can look at it up there."

"Isaiah's going to be in there."

"So will Sasha, Wren, Ryan, Hali, Lynn, and Jack," added Lock. "Remember?"

They came to a landing three floors above the main foyer, where they were alone. Far below, a crowd gathered at a bar serving tasting flights in tiny chalices. Lock glanced over the rail and cursed, "They've got plenty of blood, goddamit."

Willa took the program and flipped to "W" for Isaiah Wallace, and then to "I" but he wasn't listed. "They've already sold him off, Lock, he's not here." She felt the panic rising in her voice.

"Hush now. The names, remember? Kathy was Ellen, right? They probably change them so they're harder to locate if someone comes looking."

Willa dropped to a step and began at the beginning, turning one page at a time.

"I'll be lookout. Tell me if you see any of my guys."

"I will."

She went through deliberately, spotting a few of Lock's kids and dog-earing the pages. Hali was now Jean, Ryan was Bobby, Sasha was Kristeen. Not halfway through, she saw Isaiah and the tears came, unstoppable. Thomas. He was Thomas now. They knew everything. His medical history. Parents. Where he was born. The name of the doctor that delivered him. Where he'd lived. That he was AB Positive. But on the blood, they went beyond just ABO blood type. There was an entire typing profile for every surface protein and carbohydrate his red blood cells carried. Every antigen. Willa knew a lot, but this information hadn't been part of her training, nor was it written in her workbooks. This was hematology, genetics. The only other notation she recognized was an entry showing Isaiah carried the MNS47 antigen, known as the SARA antigen. And then only because she remembered it as an example they'd given in school about particularly rare phenotypes.

Why were they providing comprehensive blood typing on adoptees? The only reason for listing it that she could see was with the Choice in mind. Once they'd turned him into an Ichorwulf, he would know his phenotype profile in every detail so he could avoid drinking incompatible blood and experience hemolytic death. "They're already treating them like… they're never coming back." A heavy tear popped the page.

"You gotta stop that and fast, Willa. Gonna smear your mascara."

"I'm sorry," she said, quickly stroking the wet from her eyes. There he was, starring into the camera, all the sunshine drained from his face. His cheeks, though, were full and he looked stronger than he ever had living with her. She wanted to scream, to crush and destroy those who had usurped her as his guardian only to sell him to more monsters who would, at the twilight of his childhood, give him the choice to become one of them or to die. "I want to kill them," she said.

Lock fingered Olden's lapel pin. "I know."

They climbed the floating staircase, higher and higher over the swelling crowd and arrived at theater style doors, spaced evenly around a large central chamber. Lock pushed one open and they entered. The opulence of the outer hall was but an appetizer to the feast of luxury inside the lyceum. Fashioned after a great orchestra hall, rows of red velvet seating ascended at extreme angles from a central stage. The seat numbers were black opal set in nacre, across a mezzanine festooned in golden ornamentation.

Another large jellyfish chandelier swam prodigiously in the air high above the central parterre. Framed by the arch of the theater's ceiling, it appeared captive, the undulating lights within giving watery motion to its flowing arms. Down below, others trickled in and took their seats. Another usher breezed over. "Reserved seating?"

Willa shot a glance to Lock. "Uh, we–"

"Not a problem. Mezzanine is reserved seating, so to the gods with you!" he declared with an airy laugh. "Right up top. Last ten rows. Enjoy!"

They made their way up the alpine steps and crossed through a gap in a waist-high wall. They selected two seats near the end of the row and tried to fit in. The theatre filled with sumptuously attired and bejeweled Ichorwulves, husbands and wives, husbands and husbands, as well as wives and wives, and only a small number of singles. One of them, a ponderous woman with a grub-like complexion and an over-feathered hat forced herself down the aisle and wedged into the seat next to Willa. Before long, not a seat remained, with many left standing at the periphery.

The big woman sipped from a tiny grail. "Rumor is that the Claret will be here," she said smiling, exposing her red teeth. "Hope they'll come mingle during the reception."

"Oh," said Willa, trying not to look at the woman's gore-stained mouth. "That's great news. Do you know why?"

"Local Patriot quashed the protests. You heard, I'm sure." She gulped a final swallow and licked her lips. "Even with all that got out: the drones, the ganglion, the *children*. Prevented an uprising. Framed it all as a hoax so all the little piggies would break the lines," she said, winking. "And thank goodness for that! I certainly don't want to go back to the Old Way, do you?"

"No. Certainly not," said Willa. "Far too messy for my liking."

"And too much work. You know... I've never even seen it done," the woman confessed, shifting noisily in her seat. "I'm sure it's terribly difficult. Can you imagine having to wrestle someone down while you drain them? It just lacks – what's the word? Refinement. I like my food prepared ready to eat. I don't want to have to hold it still or talk to it."

"Preach," Lock interjected.

The woman cocked an eyebrow. "And, err, where are you both from?"

"Riversfork," said Willa. "You?"

"New Delphi," said the woman. "O-negs I take it?"

"AB-positive," Willa answered automatically just as the lights began to dim.

"AB-pos? Oh my." The woman straightened her posture and fixed her hat. "I had no idea! What are you doing way up here?"

Willa and Lock exchanged a glance and shrugged as darkness fell.

The jellyfish chandelier made the only light – a dim ache of red that seemed to glow from within. Willa half expected to hear the slow rise of music, an orchestral introduction to match the gravity of whatever was happening, but it remained quiet enough that the large woman's labored breaths might as well have been crashing waves.

A spotlight clicked brightly onto center stage, the gap between the heavy curtains splitting the circle of light. Footsteps echoed until a man emerged, tall with thick black hair and vacation skin, dark pants and shirt pulled snuggly over his narrow physique. A single red stripe ran from the top of his left shoulder down the arm to the end of his sleeve. He stepped casually to the front of the stage.

"It's *him*," said the woman breathlessly. "It's Dagen."

The crowd was frozen in anticipation, too enthralled to applaud.

He spread his arms to the room. "Three thousand years," he said. "And we're still here."

At this, a roar went up and the crowd surged to its feet. The cheering continued until he interrupted it with a finger.

"Oh, please, please. This isn't about me. This is a celebration of all of our shared accomplishments," he said over the cheers. "I am so happy to meet you all, to be in your fine city. My name is Dagen. Thank you for welcoming me."

Another round of applause.

"We gather for Patrioteer each year in order to secure the next generation, and I can tell you from having met these fine juveniles, that no one will leave this conference dissatisfied." The curtains slowly pulled apart behind him. "I know you are all excited to get to the Pageant – and we will shortly – but before we do that, it is the wish of the Claret that I reemphasize the importance of the various protocols we have established to preserve our place in the natural order."

A pair of screens descended from the ceiling and a montage of images flashed as Dagen spoke. "As you know, we were recently compromised by a small and cowardly hacking syndicate." Footage from the pirated *Patriot Report* broadcast rolled silently: blood drones being shot out of the sky, Kathy delivering her monologue.

It paused and he gestured to Kathy, saying, "Many of you knew Ellen, the Oldens' only child. She was taken by these terrorists, who murdered and burned her parents, and then forced her to perform in this... charade."

The crowd grumbled its offense. Dagen continued, along with the video, "Though brief, this broadcast induced protests and an acute shortage across all vintages. Naturally, our teams aired brilliant response propaganda and as you all saw on the *Report* last evening, the boycott was ultimately crushed." Brief applause stopped short by a curt gesture. "You *should* be joyous. This is our lifeline. But you must never let the fact that you live among the livestock dull your sense of self or blur the lines of where you belong in nature's hierarchy. We are living our destiny. It has been so since the first seedling took root."

The video paused just as Kathy sliced the blood bag over the ganglion. Dagen stepped to the edge of the stage. "Some of you panicked during this boycott because you forgot the natural order, failed to remember all that we have done to ensure we remain on top. Our efforts. Our achievements. Over the course of a century we positioned ourselves as captains of industry, forming conglomerates, monopolies, taking control of manufacturing so that we could automate the world in order to rid it of the need for cheap labor, and the necessity of paying for it."

He paused for breath. "This was an arduous and expensive endeavor, but always to an end. The wars brought the Harvest. Automation gave us the Trade. We took the jobs and the food supply lined up to feed us. Like beasts of the field, they march to the corral for their monthly reward." Images of actual cows being fed filled the screens. "When faced with adversity, you must always remember what is axiomatic: livestock rarely stray far from the trough."

Willa's throat clamped in terror. Who was this man, this person who declared his kind's superiority over humanity? How did such a person come to be? She felt called back to her Catholic upbringing, the musty classrooms of her youth. Could this be him? The one that the nuns, with their Catechisms, had spoken of while she mocked them from behind her book bag? The one they were told to fear? Was this some twisted comeuppance for her lack of belief in God's nemesis – to render him in flesh before her? Surely if he were real, then this was him – the embodiment of evil.

"It is with this backdrop that I bring you to my final point. One more thing I must share before we get to our main event. I indulge your patience." The screens went black and curtains closed over them. "The blood trade has allowed us, with discipline and constant vigilance, to maintain the exclusivity of our ranks. Recently, however, that discipline has slipped." A large black box wheeled onto the stage. "What is the Rule of Progeny?"

The crowd boomed, "Grow from within!"

"Not from without," he replied in answer. "We select our future lines here, and here alone. We do not take it on our own to play creator and make new Apex outside of protocol. Control is the key to our survival, our lodestar. It has been like this tracing all the way back to the Prime Mover. If you create in the districts, you open the door to millions. And millions more. And then what? Open war. You remember the lesson of Rome, do you not? The Visigoths? They were nothing before their King Alaric. And how did he rise? Through negligence, carelessness, he was made Apex, turned by a foolish aristocrat for his own enjoyment! Erzsébet Báthory was no different! One of our brightest but – to put it lightly – least disciplined, having to be confined within her own castle until her death. Ever since that costly and embarrassing episode, our grasp on the dual helms of our advancement and evolution has never faltered, and I will not be the one to see the grip slackened."

Whispers sifted through the crowd.

"Secrecy is security. Let there be no doubt: carelessness will not be tolerated. It only takes one, a single Apex who is not of our caste to start a rebellion. Or worse. And you know of what I speak." He strode to the black box, said, "Dagen, Patriot ID octozerosix," causing the door to click open. "Come on out, my friend, you are home now."

Willa squinted to make out the creature emerging from the box so far below, but its complexion and hunched posture were unmistakable. Her silent gasp came synchronous with Lock's.

Everard.

"An interesting case," Dagen continued. "This one seemed determined to avoid taking blood in the Old Way. In one respect, I am impressed – a resilient fellow who held onto his humanity for as long as he could throughout the seating process. Patriot security found him soaking in black-market O-neg just outside of DS3."

Everard was even thinner than when Willa had last seen him. He cowered and flinched, tried to see into the crowd against the blaring lights. His trademark sleeveless white undershirt was filthy and bloodstained. "Hungry," he coughed.

"Yes, I bet you are. And we are all going to enjoy a meal very soon," Dagen said, turning back to the crowd. "And in what can only be a stroke of luck for which we should count ourselves doubly fortunate, this person confessed to the infiltration of *The Patriot Report* stream. Described the means and methods precisely. On his information, we located the home from which the broadcast was made and confiscated the equipment. He confessed the names of all of his co-conspirators, who have been found and eliminated. And we thank him for that." He turned to face Everard and began clapping. "Let us thank him, shall we?"

The crowd began to clap and Willa and Lock forced themselves, painfully, to go along.

"Hungry," said Everard.

"Then let us feed you!" Dagen threw his arms out wide.

Spots of red bloomed across Everard's shirt. Shocked, he considered his torso. The splotches expanded as blood poured from a constellation of holes in his body, put there by laceguns fired from the wings.

"No!" whispered Lock.

His eyes were that of a snared animal after the struggle, not comprehending why, but cognizant of the coming loss. His legs gave and his knees kettle drummed the stage. "Hungry," he muttered once more, before falling dead to the wood.

"I hope that this reinforces my sincerity," Dagen said. "The same fate awaits any Apex who sires against the Rule."

Stagehands rushed out and wheeled the box offstage. Another took Everard by the feet and dragged him away like a set piece.

Willa tried to internalize her breathing, to bury it deep within. She could tell that Lock was doing the same.

"And now, putting all of that ugliness behind us, on to the main event."

Behind him, another curtain pulled open to a large tiered dais and he stepped onto the red carpeting that wrapped it. With his back to the audience, he brought his arms up slowly from the sides, as if calling forth the gentle rise of a symphony, but it was not music that came. Lines of children entered silently from both ends of the platform, with the youngest at the base and the oldest across the top row. Dressed in tailored black, faces clean. The boys had their hair clipped short, while the girls had theirs pulled into tight buns or looping braids sealed with crisp white bows. Willa scanned upward to where she guessed the ten year-olds would be and ran her eyes across the faces in search of Isaiah. A few rows from the top she found him, looking solemn, but confident, almost brave. It's not that she expected him to look defeated, or wanted that, but his cool demeanor made her heart ache. Had he already resigned himself to this new life, or worse, embraced it? Did he think she'd given up on him? Did he wonder if she'd even tried?

"Good evening," Dagen called to them brightly, and they responded loudly in sync. He faced the crowd. "Four hundred and seventy-one of the best the region has to offer. Already well into their education and indoctrination. In order to make your jobs easier, we have begun cotillion to ease their assimilation into a higher lifestyle. Each has also selected an enrichment activity that they will take with them into their new homes. Let us see here." He approached the first row and knelt near a little boy, probably no older than four. "Good evening, son. What is your name?"

"Andr – um, Grant."

"That's lovely. Now tell me, Master Grant, have you chosen an enrichment activity since you've been with us?"

The child's eyes darted all over and then settled as he visibly worked to calm himself. "Yes."

Dagen gave a warm chuckle. "Alright, and what activity have you chosen?"

"I, um, the trumpet."

"The trumpet. Of course," said Dagen emphatically. "The brass family. Very bold. Very bold, indeed, Master Grant." He patted the boy's head and returned to the audience. "I know I preach to the choir when I say this, but when you select one of these children, you give them a chance at a better life. Adoption is an act of kindness, mercy. Charity. No such chance exists for them in the districts."

"No thanks to you," growled Lock.

"What's that?" asked the fat lady.

"Nothing."

Dagen visited with a number of other children, none of them from the Seychelles, but little of what he said registered over the raging maelstrom growing in Willa's head. She wanted to leap over the rail and scream her grandson's name before the lace got her. Then he would know for the rest of his life that she had come for him, even though she had failed. She sat, trying to work up the courage to act. All she had to do was stand up. *Do it Willa. Do it. Do it.*

She was still seated when the Pageant ended and the curtains drew closed. Her eyes remained fixed on Isaiah, willing him to see her until the velvet took him from view.

"With that, we will conclude tonight's formal events. Selection begins in the morning directly after the complimentary morning meal," said Dagen. "I do hope everyone will stay and toast our success in the refectory downstairs."

Willa and Lock got to their feet but were almost trampled by those around them, pushing to get out the doors and down to the ground floor. Casually, they let the others rush by and within a matter of seconds their section was clear.

"We have to find where they're keeping them," Willa whispered.

"We need to go down with the crowd," said Lock. "Us lollygagging already looks suspicious."

Outside the Lyceum, Willa gestured to the lines stretching back from the elevator banks, thinking they might provide a plausible means of delaying their arrival downstairs. They stepped into the line and the big woman from their row turned to greet them, her meaty forearms protruding from scarlet sleeves like untrimmed lamb shanks.

"Whew, all of that really got my appetite up," she said. "I don't know about you, but I'm starving!"

"Us too," said Willa.

"Well, I didn't have the time inside to say it, but it's a thrill and an honor to meet you two."

Confused, Willa wondered if they were being toyed with. "It's a pleasure to meet you as well, Miss…"

"Candice. Candice LaTremaine." She extended a hand with gaudy rings choking puffy fingers.

"I'm Eileen and this is my wife, Pearl," said Willa, taking the woman's fist while catching a glare from Lock about her pre-chosen name.

"Pleasure, Eileen," said Candice. "But, can I ask why you are up here standing in line?"

Willa just shrugged.

"You don't see many AB-positives up in the cheap seats."

"Well, we, uh–"

"So modest, you two!" Candice said, turning to the line. "AB-pos back here!"

The line split immediately to the sides, with all eyes on Willa and Lock standing at the back.

"Oh, there's no need," said Willa.

"Don't be foolish," said Candice, imploring them forward. "Don't tell me you'd pass up the chance to eat first."

"I suppose we wouldn't," said Willa. "Thank you." They started forward through the lane of hungry Ichorwulves, all watching and nodding at them in an apparent show of respect. Willa stepped into the elevator next to an attendant in an exquisitely trimmed uniform. Lock entered behind and turned to the crowd, gesturing them in. But instead of flooding into the elevator so they could get to the meal they so eagerly awaited, they shook their heads politely or mouthed for the two AB-positives to please go ahead.

"Refectory?" asked the liftman.

"Yes... of course," Willa answered.

"Just a moment, please." He disengaged a switch on an old-fashioned style lever and eased the contraption down.

"Been a short while since I've been in a manually operated lift," said Lock.

The man considered her briefly and then answered, "Reminders of the past make it less likely to forget. Here we are."

The doors opened to a sprawling hall as garish as the lyceum. At the center was a fountain, so large and out-of-place that Willa actually did a double take to make sure they hadn't wandered outside. Water dyed tastelessly red flowed over yet another domed jellyfish sculpture, its tentacles peaking from the murk with small spouts at the tips. A chamber orchestra played Prokofiev on a raised stage nearby. Bars were set at intervals down the walls, a wooden stanchion with a plaque next to each displaying the vintages being served.

"What was all that about?" asked Lock. "Treating us like royalty? Are they playing with us?"

"I have no idea. Seems like it," Willa answered.

"Shit."

As the room began to fill, Willa and Lock did their best to make the rounds slowly and turned to point at things whenever anyone threatened to make eye contact. After a few minutes, it was elbow to elbow. Willa began to panic. Lock saw her state and said, "You need some water," and pushed up toward one of the bars.

Through a narrow gap in the dense crowd, Willa captured a

glance at a row of drinks being poured. "Stop," she whispered. "They don't have water."

"Whaddaya mean?" said Lock into Willa's hard stare. "Oh right." She angled her neck to watch the bartender twirling glasses and spinning shakers, but always pouring the same syrupy cocktail. "We need to creep out of here. Find the kids."

"Hey you two!"

They spun around to see Candice, smiling fatly.

"What are you doing in this line? This is O-neg. AB-pos is at the front of the room." She pointed.

"Oh, how stupid of us," said Willa. "I guess we're just tired after a long day of travel."

"This your first Patrioteer, isn't it," said Candice with an empathetic tilt of the head.

"Yes."

"Of course it is!" she declared, hiking her purse into her armpit. "Come on, I'll show you around." A frill of loose fabric around her neck shuddered as she changed course.

They had no choice but to follow. As they moved into the middle of the room, its layout became clear. It was a rounded octagon, with the blood bars spread evenly, one on each wall. They were set upon heavy layers of polished black wood with anywhere from one to three bartenders in crisp slate and gold. Behind them, the wood continued up the wall to the ceiling, elaborately carved and holding a mirror within. The images in the structures were largely indecipherable, though some themes were garishly obvious. War, fire, blood, dominion over the animals, a great burning sun, the worship of a higher power.

At what seemed the "top" of the octagon, which was opposite to the entrance from the elevators, a much larger bar loomed over the entire room. It was higher than the others and its carvings were larger, heavier, and more detailed. Only a few individuals loitered, sipping from ornate grails. Willa read the plaque: *AB-positive*. And suddenly everything clicked. She finally understood just what was going on, why she and Lock were being treated with such deference.

AB-positive was the universal recipient, the one group that could survive on anybody's blood. And here they had all the power.

The sheer simplicity of it. In the districts, it was the O-negatives, the universal donors, who enjoyed relative prosperity due to the higher prices their blood fetched. On the outside, they were the most important to Patriot. The O-negs could feed anyone. *Feed any Ichorwulf.* But on the inside, the roles were reversed, it was the universal recipients who enjoyed the flexibility and ease of living, of not having to rely on anyone to label and constantly monitor their sustenance. It didn't matter to the AB-positives that the rest of the Ichorwulves had lost their sense of smell, their ability to discern upon whom they could feed. The AB-positives could take from anyone. For them, there was no such thing as a bad transfusion. At the end of the day the AB-positives didn't *need* Patriot at all.

All of this seemed to confer upon the few AB-positives who were present a mystique of preciousness, exclusivity. It made sense. At three percent of the population, they were indeed rare. They didn't have to rely on the Patriot machine to survive. They could turn to the Old Way without fear of poisoning. For them, Patriot was a convenience, but at the end of the day, unnecessary. In confessing their blood type to Candice, Willa had unwittingly anointed herself and Lock as VIPs, placing them into the upper echelon of Ichorwulf society.

A commotion echoed from the front of the room; a mixture of hoots, whistles, and applause. The crowd appeared to be parting and there he was, Dagen, flanked by an escort of three men and three women, all lean and muscular. They were immediately distinguishable from the usual Patriot security as they bore no laceguns on shoulder straps. Instead, dark gray scabbards holding short swords hung from their hips. Willa nudged Lock, "Look."

Lock went up on tiptoes and craned her neck to see, then thumped her heels back down. "Vrae," she said.

Dagen jumped up onto the wall of the central fountain and put his hands out. The room fell silent.

"A bit of a surprise for everyone! I come bearing good news: we have received the first wave of the blood that broke the boycott."

The crowd aahed.

"And..." he let the tension build, "we've already pulled Alliance's backwash from the taps! Let's toast over something fresh! Go! Celebrate your birthright! Feed! I will return shortly with the Claret!" He leapt from the fountain and appeared to head out of the room to another round of adoring cheers.

As soon as he had exited, the energy in the refectory was charged. Ichorwulves unceremoniously and enthusiastically emptied their snifters and chalices into the fountains, darkening them further. Glasses shattered across the floor. They streamed like so many red blood cells through capillaries to each of the eight bars.

Candice was barely able to contain the saliva gathering on her lips. She led Willa and Lock briskly to the foot of the broad stairs leading up to the bar for AB-positive. "This is as far as I can go. I've heard AB-pos is simply to die for. Well, it would be if I tried it," she giggled, placing a hand to her bosom. "Enjoy! I'm off to get some fresh."

They began climbing the steps and took in the room. All over, Ichorwulves were guzzling the new blood, no longer bothering to keep it from spilling across their faces. Lock pulled close. "Willa – they're drinking the new stuff and they ain't dying."

Willa made a sweep of the room and saw the same. Her mind raced through all the reasons: maybe the Patriot phlebotomists had suddenly begun to take extra care to randomize their needle punches and had correctly labeled it. She guessed it was also possible that enough legitimate blood had gotten through, diluting the counterfeit portion. They hadn't hacked the entire city, after all. Maybe Patriot put the blood through additional security before serving it. Maybe, instead of killing them, it only caused indigestion.

They were finished. Done. It was the end of the line. Something had gone wrong in the chain of events. She went through it all again in her mind. Claude had made it explicitly clear that his kind were just as constrained by phenotype compatibility as humans, yet all around them, Ichorwulves golloped mis-labeled blood. Willa's throat tightened. They could turn around now, maybe get out alive, but it would mean abandoning Isaiah and the rest. And they'd come too far not to try and find them, at least. To make themselves known to the children they'd tried to save. And that was all Willa cared about now. She knew they weren't getting out alive.

At the top of the steps, she considered the carvings behind the bar. Pictographs suggesting a great migration, a battle surrounding a magnificent tower, conqueror and conquered. The return of a great one, a messiah.

An older man in a black turtleneck with a close-cropped silver beard leaned easy on the bar. "Can I get something for you ladies to drink?" he asked. "They're already pouring fresh."

Willa hesitated and Lock took the mantle of responding. "Sure."

"What'll you have," he asked. "We've got all the vintages up here."

"AB-pos for me," Lock responded, playing the part.

"A purist!" he said, signaling the bartender. "I'm the same way. The others are fine for a change of pace, but at the end of the day, I love my own stuff."

The bartender leaned onto the polished counter. "Ninety-eight-six or chilled?"

"Chilled," said Lock, her lips curling involuntarily.

Nausea crept into Willa's throat.

"And for you, ma'am?" asked the man.

"I'm OK, thank you. Not hungry."

"Nonsense," he said, and turned to the barkeep. "Two."

The bartender lifted a golden, swan-shaped carafe from a chilling dock and poured a long stream into a pair of crystal chalices without spilling a drop. Willa could feel her neck beginning to sweat. Her stomach turned as she envisioned how it would feel to swallow it down and her teeth buzzed in anticipation.

"Are you alright?" said the man, kindly setting a hand on her own. "Do you need medical?"

"No, thank you, I'm fine. You're right," said Willa, finding herself. "It's been a long day. I'm sure I am just hungry."

"I'm sure that's all it is. Big choices ahead." He handed over the glasses and took up his own.

Bubbles slowly surfaced and popped. She knew by sight it was around half a unit.

"To what shall we toast?" he asked.

Willa looked up from the blood. "Our children."

"Bravo," he said, and drank his cup dry.

Willa put the crystal to her bottom lip and tried to find a place in her mind she could go in order to complete the horrible deed. She thought of Elizabeth with that lily, like a tiny shining sun held in her hand, and how as they'd walked, she'd scattered petals of daylight onto the ground all through the gray of the place that she'd once lived. She pictured Isaiah's face, so stolid against the immense fear he must have been experiencing. His strength, her strength. Looking back down at the glass, only a thin film remained. She turned, saw Lock struggling to swallow her serving and tried to communicate telepathically that she should be less obvious.

"Where did you say you were from?" asked the man, absent-mindedly flagging down the bartender.

"Riversfork."

"Ah, Riversfork. What did you say your names were?"

"Well, I'm Eileen Wisdom and this is Pearl."

He laughed, "Pearl Wisdom?"

"You know how parents can be."

"I do… I do." He took another chalice from the bar and wiped the inside rim with his pinky, then sucked it clean.

"And your name?" Willa asked.

"Maxwell MacLaren." He took a swig.

"Those are nice cufflinks," said Willa in reference to the tiny gold Patriot insignias flashing at his wrists. "Do you work for the company?"

He looked at her oddly for just a fraction of a second and then reconfigured his face, concealing his initial reaction. Gently, he set his chalice on the bar and slid it toward the tender. "You flatter me, Eileen."

"How is that?" asked Willa.

His face flattened and the corners of his mouth drew down. "Even I can't pass for fifty, anymore."

"Oh, well I–"

"Patriot executives retire at fifty, Mrs Wisdom," he said, alluding to some apparent common policy. "To give us a few years of leisure before the Silvering. Surely you know that."

"Of course," said Willa, now back peddling. "I meant that I didn't know you had been an executive with the company, that's all. We've only just now met."

Lock's eyes flicked back and forth. She was getting antsy.

"I see," said MacLaren, running the backs of his fingers over his beard. "You know, it's odd that we've only just met, considering that I know all of the AB-pos Apex in my city."

Willa smiled apologetically. "We're from Riversfork, though."

"So am I."

Lock pulled herself close to Willa, saying, "It's been an absolute pleasure, Mr MacLaren, but we have a big decision to make with regards to tomorrow, picking a child and such… we are just worn out."

"I understand," he said, letting his weight tip up against the bar. He casually watched as they began down the steps.

"Let's get out of here," whispered Lock. "Quicker the better."

They made the bottom of the stairs and filtered into the crowd, maneuvering easily through the ravenous feeding horde. They passed the large central fountain and wove toward the exit. A few conference goers seemed to notice their hasty retreat, but paid little mind as they downed chalice after chalice of red. Steps from escape, MacLaren's voice boomed from behind. "But you hardly ate!" The room fell silent.

All around, faces watched as the man descended from the AB-positive bar at the top of the room, two large goblets held aloft in manicured hands. He strode down the stairs, upright and beautiful like a show horse, his white teeth gleaming in his sunbaked face. The murmuring crowd parted before him, creating a straight-line path directly to Willa and Lock.

"Riversfork is a good four hours even by the speediest drone. You'll arrive famished," he announced loudly. "This is a special occasion. Please, take ichor alongside your brothers and sisters." He walked slowly forward, drawing out the moment. Stepping before them, he pushed one of the goblets at Willa. It was wide and deep – a cauldron – filled to the brim. A full unit, probably more.

There was no way she could do it. Even if it was water, it would take her half an hour to drink that much. Nearby, another man put a pewter stein to his mouth and gulped down the contents, tipped it at the ground, and gave a bloody smile.

"Go ahead now, Mrs Wisdom, it's fresh and you're so terribly fatigued from the day."

Willa shut her eyes and put her mouth to the goblet. Her top lip sank into the warm soup and she shuddered, recoiling from the warmth, the taste; repulsed by an atavistic recognition of wrongness.

"What seems to be the matter?" he asked, mocking.

The surrounding throng began muttering, shifting with suspicion, agitation.

Willa's mouth gorged with a coating of thick, pre-vomit saliva. "I'm just – I'm not feeling well."

"Well then, here's your antidote," he said, forcing the vessel upward against her face.

She drank. Huge swallows boiled down her throat like salted iron rust. Her stomach stretched and convulsed. She pushed away from MacLaren and the goblet pounded the floor, splashing the crowd.

She cantered violently forward and released all she had taken, heaving blood as much from her nose as her mouth. It erupted in a froth of bile, leaving behind long strings of red mucus that she struggled to cough free.

"I knew it!" a woman yelled. Wiping her face, Willa turned to see Candice LaTremaine snarling forward. "Those two didn't even recite the Rule of Progeny!"

"Did she get the wrong type?" someone asked innocently from nearby.

"They're AB-pos, there is no wrong type," LaTremaine hissed.

"Oh, I'd say they're the wrong type!" declared MacLaren deliciously. "They're humans!"

Gasps and whispered hysteria filled the air of the refectory. Someone said something about calling security. Willa cast her eyes about for Vrae.

"No," said MacLaren. "No security. Have you already forgotten who you are? Have you already forgotten what Dagen said?" He walked over to Lock and slapped the Goblet from her hands. "I haven't forgotten." He smiled widely as slender golden fangs crept down from behind his teeth. He lifted a foot into his hand and smoothly removed a cordovan loafer, then did the same with the other. His jaw moved in and out, his widening maw as wet and red as freshly torn flesh. He came for them.

Willa leapt backward, pulling Lock by the elbow. The crowd pressed in for a better view of the carnage that was to come.

Candice stumbled suddenly between them, tripping drunkenly sideways, then fell into MacLaren while mumbling something about the Rule of Progeny. She was dripping with sweat – heavy beads of moisture running in pink-tinted trails from her temples and forehead. She coughed. Stopped. Coughed again. Worked to stabilize herself. Finally, she stood still. Her eyes flitted between Willa, Lock, and MacLaren. Then she licked her lips as one does before saying something, and a spout of red burst from her nose, followed by a fat rope of gore from her mouth.

The circle around them widened as Candice lurched this way and that, finally tumbling forward onto her taut, round stomach. More blood emptied from her mouth in thick, heaving pulses that gushed until the supply was exhausted, and her limbs fell still to the floor. MacLaren stared. Willa grabbed Lock's arm and pulled her away.

"What was that?" MacLaren demanded. "What did you do to her?"

Off to the sides, other sounds came. Grunts at first. Throats clearing. Then choking, sputtering. A spray of red painted MacLaren's face. Willa didn't see where it'd come from until a man collapsed into him, heaving blood as he begged for help. MacLaren pushed the man away and wiped his face. He considered his dripping hand and his eyes filled with terror. Others began screaming about diseases, hemorrhagic fevers, plague. Faces that had been content and self-satisfied were now manic, confused, and desperate. A beautiful woman standing nearby lurched a bellyful of slimy plum onto her date. He returned a burgundy volley into her face as they fell together into the water feature. A barricade of the bodies piled to the floor between Willa and Lock and MacLaren. He considered them, then turned and fled.

More writhed than were upright, their mouths erupting gouts of blood like miniature geysers. Willa and Lock stepped and jumped over them as they raced toward the elevator bank. Some crawled after, screamed and roared, but their words came malformed, indecipherable, reduced to gurgles as they drowned in the blood of the poor.

CHAPTER THIRTY-FOUR

Eryptosis
The programmed death of red blood cells.

Lock pounded the elevator button and they rushed in. She kicked the dead attendant to the side and played with the lever until they began upward. Between floors, she disengaged it and the car came to a stop.

"Holy shit, Willa."

"What now? Where are the children?"

"Hell, if we killed all the bloodsuckers, maybe the kids found a way out already."

"But the AB-positives are alive for sure. We didn't get them. You saw MacLaren."

"Fuck him."

"What do we do?" asked Willa.

"I'll go low, you go high?"

"Sure."

Lock jumped on the lever and took the elevator to the second floor, where she leapt out.

"If you find the kids, roll to the tarmac."

"See you there." Willa closed the door and looked at the slot that held the lever. Ten floors. She went to the next floor and the doors opened. It was dark. Absent was the resplendent décor that saturated the rest of the Heart. A short, concrete hallway led from the elevator to another intersection. The setting was tight, claustrophobic. And while Willa didn't suffer from the malady, she wondered if one might catch it.

She stepped cautiously from the elevator and listened. There were a few utilitarian-looking desks and chairs near one wall and a set of cabinets next to an interface, but no people. She dragged a chair over to prevent the door from closing, then walked to where the halls met and checked down the passages. Heavy steel doors were placed at close intervals. Their purpose was unambiguous. A place to keep people. A prison. Cold and cruel. Designed to sap the hope from anyone unlucky enough to be held within.

Willa hoped that if she found the children, they weren't here.

A small dot of blood on the ground told her which passage to take. She knelt down and tapped a finger to it. Wet sawdust. A bit further down was another drop, and another. She walked quickly, following the blood like breadcrumbs. Around a corner, another corridor. But this time it was blocked at the halfway point. The portable cell they'd used for Everard sat at an angle, hastily abandoned. She ran as fast as her ridiculous gown would allow. The box was unlocked. "Everard!" she cried, swinging the door to the side. Empty.

To the left, one of the cell doors sat ajar. Willa palmed it open. Images of Claude lying dead poured in like she'd been transported back into Lock's kitchen. On the floor of the cell, surrounded by small piles of matted fur and hairless tails, lay a second friend reduced to dust. A few feet from where his head had been sat another shining ganglion lying where it appeared to have crawled before the blood dried up. "Oh, Everard," she whispered.

His clothes lay flat to the ground, filled with dust in the rough shape of the man it had once been. She knelt and ran her fingers through it, pinched a bit, wondering if there might be some magic to it, some retained power or life force. It only drifted to the floor, inert. She picked up the ganglion. It was small. Deformed. The word *pathetic* flashed, and she felt instantly guilty. The man had suffered. Maybe his ganglion was small because he'd been newly turned.

Maybe they'd not fed him, and it had shriveled from starvation. She considered his remains spread across the ground. He would have fought the thing until he couldn't any longer. Refused to let it win. That's who Everard was. Right up until they shot him. She held it, almost affectionately, then placed it into her shoulder bag.

Willa stood to leave when she noticed a swatch of white across the cell on a ledge a few steps away. A notepad, no bigger than a touchstone, maybe fifty pages thick, and the stub of a pencil, chewed from the top down. The first, and every page stuffed to the corners with the same word repeated end to end. *Hungry.*

Taking the pad into her bag, she exited the cell and trotted down corridors calling for Isaiah and the other children until she was certain that no one was in the cells, or, at least, no one was alive.

She returned to the elevator, stepped over the chair and kicked it free. The next floor up, the doors opened to an expansive office lobby. Ichorwulves lay where they'd fallen, their heads all aimed toward the elevator. It was like they'd been arranged that way, all facing the same direction, like salmon in a river. Willa guessed they'd panicked when the reaction set in and had made for the exit only to fall shy. She tip-tapped through congealed pools of scarlet vomit and ducked her head into the doors but found no children. Next floor, same story. Finally, on the tenth floor, the elevator opened to an entirely different sort of space. To either side lay Patriot security guards, their shirts glazed with thick bloody mucus, their skin taking on the waxy texture that presaged decomposition. She knelt and pulled a lacegun from rigid fingers that loyally clutched it.

The hall was lined with wall-sized glossy images; the type that she remembered from trips to the museum as a child. Most were early black and whites from the century before her birth, depicting various historical landmarks. Scattered between and around the larger photographs were medical illustrations in simple frames. A pen and ink rendering of the first successful human blood transfusion. The anterior diagram of a human heart. A map of the major veins of the thorax. The photographs were easily recognizable. World War I. World War II. The Vietnam War. As the timeline progressed down the hall, she saw mushroom clouds and devastation from the bombs that had fallen on native soil. 2030: Chrysalis. 2039: Kannikin Redux. 2049: Astrid. 2059: Goliath. The expanding plume of Chrysalis – captured in one blink of a camera's shutter – recalled the flash from Willa's memory, the one she'd carried around for months on scarred retinas. A short statement appeared on a metal placard embedded in the frame.

~ Chrysalis ~
Scythe of the Silvered Rebellion; the blade that turned the once barren earth.

A chill ran down her spine like the caress of skeletal fingers. It was as if the death and destruction of nuclear war were being somehow praised. She leaned in close to read a few lines of print embossed on the poster-sized photograph for Kannikin Redux. She remembered it as the bomb that had led the government, or Patriot – or somebody – to establish the first Gray Zone on the East Coast.

Production on Kannikin Redux was five years in the making, but led directly to a renewed vigor in donation programs, helping to quell the first human resistance.

Five years in the making? Production? Memories flashed to the footage from that bomb: flattened cities, scorched countryside, bodies as cinders frozen right where they'd burned. She looked up and down the desolate hallway and read the plaque next to the photographs of Astrid's aftermath.

M. MacLaren's directorial debut.
By 2049, donation enforcement was a strain on Patriot budget and resources.
The Astrid program paid immediate dividends when PatrioCast pushed it onto all data platforms in May of 2049.

Willa almost dropped the lacegun. MacLaren?

She rushed to the section dedicated to Goliath, the latest – and largest – nuke to have hit in the Gray Zones. There were the usual images – the explosion, the fires, the carnage. But there was another series of photographs with annotations, sketches, and computer renderings. Set on display such as it was, it appeared to document a plan that had gone from idea to fruition. The renderings showed diagrams of an unfamiliar geographic area, with various angles on the explosion, and the spread of destruction all set out in a minute-by-minute timeline. But it wasn't a journalistic documentation of a great tragedy. It was a storyboard.

A voice moaned from far down the hall. Willa steeled herself. A set of red lacquer doors capped the end of the corridor, one of them partially ajar. Another moan. Willa slipped out of her shoes and headed toward it. The floor was slick and she skated across swirling waves of variegated red tiles. The voice came again, low. Miserable.

Willa glanced through the slit of light that came from inside the room and nudged the door with the gun. Around a table that stretched the length of the room lay the executives, or so Willa assumed. The room itself was a shrine to indulgence, all red enamels and gold inlay. The door met some resistance as she pushed it wide. She peeked around it to see a man, eyes vacant and moribund, struggling to belly crawl across the floor. He reached weakly for her ankle, but she kicked him away.

In a supple leather chair next to the head of the table, sat a woman, still somehow upright. Her head was back against the headrest and red tears cut through once pristine makeup. She held her stomach tenderly and glanced to Willa. "Help... please," she groaned. "A-neg."

"What's the matter?" Willa asked, stepping over some of the others.

The woman lurched forward and vomited onto the table.

"Oh," said Willa, "you've had a bad transfusion." The woman coughed and gagged on the remnants of her purge, even wiped the edge of her mouth, primly, as if to correct her lipstick – like she might still be able to keep a dinner date.

Willa looked around again at all the dead, some of whom had already begun their disintegration. Each had a single red stripe running down one arm just as Dagen had, and she realized that this was the Claret.

"Please," the woman mumbled. "I need A-neg."

"Think that will help?"

The woman pointed to a toppled chalice sitting in a puddle. "I only took… a sip… of that. A-neg… please."

A sideboard ran the length of the room on which sat a small cooling vault. Willa guessed the Claret must have had their own meal scheduled before joining the others, toasting to their great wealth and power, no doubt. She opened the vault and thumbed through the bags inside until she found a unit of A-neg. Withdrawing it, she let it roll across her finger pads. Either the bag was legit or Lock's decoy pockets were that good. Well, this way she'd find out for sure. If the woman appeared to regain her strength, she could just shoot her. She selected a clean chalice, returned to the woman, and presented the heel of the bag displaying the label. The woman groaned impatiently.

Willa took up a knife from a pile of emptied bags and wiped it unceremoniously on the woman's sleeve, then pierced the bag so it poured into the cup.

The woman grunted and motioned Willa forward with two fingers. "Just give it to me."

She opened her mouth. Her tongue crept out like a serpent, curling at the end to an anticipatory point. Willa held the chalice in both hands and let a thin stream run down the woman's throat. The scene conjured visions from her childhood, watching baptisms, the priests giving communion. *Blood of Christ – not so much.*

The woman took large, greedy swallows, letting the corners of her mouth spill rivulets down her neck and into her blouse. When the cup ceased dripping, she sat upright, marginally rejuvenated. Willa drew the gun to the ready.

The woman surveyed the room and seemed to see it with fresh eyes, then set her gaze to Willa. "How are you not dead?"

"I'm AB-positive, lady," answered Willa. "Where are the children?"

"The… the children?" she coughed.

"You heard me."

"Wait," said the woman, breathing deeply. "Wait. Who are you?"

"I'm Willa Mae Wallace."

The woman's eyes widened as realization came. "You're not Ichorwulf?"

"I ain't."

Her face was anger and confusion. She shifted uncomfortably. "How did you get in?"

"I had a key."

The woman clenched her teeth and grumbled defiantly.

Willa reached into the bun on the top of her head and used her fingers to separate the locks of hair. The woman shrieked as a ganglion emerged from within. Willa slammed it onto the table and shoved it forward.

"How did you get that?"

"Did you know Scynthia Scallien?" asked Willa. "Say hi."

The woman twisted in her chair, burped, and growled, "Impossible."

"Oh, it's definitely her," said Willa. "Where's Dagen?"

"Gone," said the woman, forcing a condescending laugh through ever shallower breaths.

"When I was first learning phlebotomy," said Willa, "they taught us how to diagnose an incompatibility reaction, you know, a bad transfusion."

The woman squirmed, pawed weakly at her neck. Bloody tears wept from her eyes.

"There are many symptoms, of course. You've got them for sure." She leaned in. "But there is one sign that leaves no doubt. Do you know what it is?"

The woman tried to spit, but the pathetic attempt clung to her chin, a hanging string.

"A sense of impending doom," said Willa.

The woman angled her head backward and opened her mouth wide. Her bottom jaw came loose and she hacked. Neck veins bulged. Golden fangs emerged, stretching long from the roof of her mouth as if trying to escape. Then all tension left her body and her head crashed to the table, embedding the fangs in the polished grain.

Willa dropped the chalice and checked the room for any others living, but most were no longer recognizable.

Lock was bouncing up and down when the elevator doors parted. "They got no clue what hit 'em!"

Willa reached for a bleeding wound on Lock's arm.

Lock brushed her off. "It's nothing. Bit of lace. He got me and I got him. And then I got this." She held up a gun.

Willa presented hers.

"Attagirl. Hey, we gotta roll. The AB-positives skee-daddled. I tagged a few of 'em, but you know I'm only one lady. They'll be back for sure."

"The children?"

Lock shook her head

They ran through the lavish corridor.

"Lock," said Willa, panting as she followed. "All the bombs were fake."

"How? I was there for Chrysalis just like you."

"Yeah, that was the only real one. It was what gave them the idea for the others. People volunteer to give their blood when there's a tragedy. So they just kept doing it, except as movie productions. Astrid, Kannikin, Goliath – all fake."

"Those motherfuckers."

In the now-quiet main corridor, ambient music could be heard. New Age synthesizer played over the sounds of waterfalls and babbling brooks. They came to the giant crystal cathedral doors through which they'd arrived.

Willa pointed outside. "Lock!" On the lawn a small group of conference-goers limped and shuffled away. She tried the doors but couldn't budge them. Lock ran to a panel and began messing with the electronics. She yanked wires from inside, unclipped and re-clipped them, pulled some out wholesale, but the doors held.

"The Locksmith, huh?"

"It's figurative!"

A noise came from down the hall behind them. Willa turned to see a man stepping into the far end of the corridor. He held a short sword. "Lock!" said Willa, pointing. "Hurry!"

He started toward them, his pace quickening.

"Now!" Willa screamed.

Lock struggled with the wires.

Willa aimed the gun and sent a barrage of lace into the doors, spilling glass across the floor. She swung around. The vrae launched into a dead sprint. She fired. He dove to avoid the shot, sliding ahead on his stomach, then leaping to full gallop in one smooth motion. They retreated through the door and onto the grounds. Running, Willa aimed backward and pulled the trigger. Nothing. A blue light flashed on the butt of the gun. She tripped and tumbled into the grass. Lock stood a few paces behind, gun raised. Steady. Three shots fired, evenly spaced. *Piff. Piff. Piff.*

The vrae's momentum carried his limp body across the threshold before sliding to a stop.

"How come that one was still alive?" asked Lock, lowering the weapon.

"Either he didn't eat or he's AB-pos."

"Well he's AB-dead now."

Just down the path, a dying Ichorwulf zombie-shuffled away. Lock fired a shot into his dome. He twitched forward and faceplanted onto the concrete steps. She strode into the night and finished off the few others still standing. "Let's find the kids," she said, turning back toward the building.

Willa didn't move.

"What is it?" asked Lock.

Willa pointed overhead as dozens of lights coalesced in the sky over the Heart. "Someone's coming!"

Drones poured over the rim of the building.

Willa and Lock took off down the hill. The first drone to reach them slowed as it came overhead, pacing them as they ran. Looking up at it, Willa could tell it wasn't a personnel drone at all – just an average commerce drone. Lock yanked her to the side as another smashed into the ground where they'd just been, exploding in a spray of Chinese food. Another dove into the turf just ahead of them, this one full of paint.

"What is going on?" Willa screamed.

Lock helped Willa up and pulled her along. "Someone took control of all the drones in the area! They're just throwing them at us."

"Who?"

"Who? Patriot!" Lock stumbled along with her head craned to the sky. "That one." She pointed to a set of lights high above the rest. "Someone's up there, controlling all these."

Another drone hit right in front of them and they split apart. Lock veered from the path and zigzagged through the primrose.

They continued separately onto the tarmac as drones of every kind pelted the ground. Delivery drones, catering drones, dry-cleaning drones, grocery drones, medical drones, and lawn care drones bombed them from all sides. They ran into the maze of parked personnel drones and used them for cover as they worked toward Llydia. Others began to drop randomly upon the tarmac, a sign that the controlling drone had likely lost sight of them.

"What do we do?" Willa called.

"The MK," said Lock, trotting up to Llydia and opening her door.

"You're going to shoot them all?"

"No," she reached in and took the rifle, "*you* are."

"What?"

"You don't need to hit them or anything," Lock said, snapping a round into the chamber and punching the bolt, "just be a distraction. Give me cover to get Llydia airborne."

A drone slammed down nearby, showering glass and metal over them.

"She doesn't have enough power to get us out of here!"

"I know that." Lock handed the rifle over then checked the smudge. "Well that's dead."

"What are you doing!"

"Look," said Lock, "if I hadn't already blown Llydia's brains out, I could just tell her to kamikaze the puppet-master up there, but on account of she's a zombie, someone's got to pilot her."

"What does that mean? What are you going to do?"

"Get close to him hopefully, put some lace into what's left of Llydia's battery and see what it's like to be a firework."

"No!"

"Stop that," said Lock, bringing Llydia's display to life. The ground rumbled from a nearby impact. She yanked off her wig and her orange curls sprang free. She grabbed her goggles from the joystick and pulled them onto her forehead.

The Patriot drone wheeled into view.

Lock stepped out from Llydia and checked the sky, pointed out the lead drone. "Go across the tarmac, get your bead, and shoot that fucking thing." Then she took Willa's cheeks in her hands and pressed her lips hard to Willa's. Pulling away, she smiled. "A reaper. Who'd have thought?"

Willa's body felt numb, paralysis stitching into her legs and fingers. If she turned away now, she'd never see Lock again.

"Go!" said Lock, jumping into Llydia and throwing the door closed. A postal drone streaked down, cratering to the far side and sending a plume of letters skyward.

Willa lit across the tarmac with the rifle. Another drone smashed nearby, but she kept her cool and ducked behind a compact, single-person sprinter. She set the gun's barrel between the small drone's ducted fans just as the Patriot drone loomed toward Lock's position. All she had to do was pull the trigger, distract it, and give Lock the time she needed to get airborne. She trained her sights.

The drone slowed its circling and settled just above Llydia. Willa scraped a layer of stinging sweat from her eyelids and reset her pupil to the scope. She sucked in a chest full of air, eased it out, and squeezed the trigger. Through the scope she saw the hole. The tiny spray of paint where her bullet punched through the control drone's hull. It spun immediately and flew toward her, bringing a swarm of commerce drones behind. She ditched the gun and leapt to the ground next to a stretch limousine drone as the bombardment renewed. Exploded metal and mechanical pieces peppered her. She crawled around the front of the limo and peeked upward where the enemy drone swept the rows with a searchlight. To the far side of the tarmac, Llydia ascended.

Willa climbed atop the limo, and jumped up and down, screaming, "Over here!" A hulking construction drone thundered down, just missing her. She rolled to the ground and pushed into the small shelter afforded by the limo's oversized motor rack. Scrap rained down. A sliver of shrapnel bit into her cheek. One direct hit and she was done. The seconds dragged.

And then the drone's beam of light checked off. The bombardment ceased. She crawled out from among the destruction and stood. A formation of commerce drones charged across the grounds. They were chasing Llydia. She dodged them, then wheeled about and raced high over the redwoods while the Patriot drone gave chase, spilling streams of lace from four short barrels at its front.

Sparks clattered from Llydia's skin as she slowed at the peak of her climb. The Patriot drone only accelerated upward. Llydia appeared to fall and entered a dive. The pursuing drone dodged nimbly aside as they passed, but Lock had gotten close enough.

The night flashed and for a millisecond it was daytime. The sound was a clap of thunder.

The violent swarm that had been following stopped dead in the air, then fell like iron hail. Willa made for the woods to the northeast as legions of disabled drones hammered down around her. Their explosions chased her into the trees, and she curled up among a gnarl of roots. There in the shallow forest, she watched the last machines tumble from the sky until only the stars remained. Llydia and the Patriot drone had been vaporized.

She pivoted her back to a redwood that seemed to embrace and protect her. Crawling to the side, she glanced behind it. Nothing moved. No machines, Ichorwulves, or children. Just silence. Minutes passed. Sitting back in her spot, she scanned the grounds in search of the Locksmith, who would surely make her gallant return while loudly delivering the tale of her narrow escape and scoffing at anyone who doubted her survival. Though Willa's eyes had seen Llydia crack the sky as Chrysalis once did, and her mind knew the truth, her heart was stubborn.

She scrolled back through the short time she'd known the woman, days that were moving so fast that she'd failed to notice the seedlings of affection germinating within her chest. But now in the still and quiet, it all crashed down. She squeezed the tears from her eyelids and willed her friend to appear. And she spoke her words into the biting air.

I only just found you.

CHAPTER THIRTY-FIVE

Livor Mortis

The fourth stage of death, signified by the pooling of blood in the lower regions of the body postmortem.

It was like having a fire alarm blaring inside her skull, the internal clock that said time was running out to go back in for the children. But she had to be smart. She was alone. Kathy and Lindon were waiting at a rendezvous point inside the districts. No one was coming to help. Willa forced herself to wait in her hovel until she was sure the coast was clear. Patriot didn't seem to be rushing the grounds.

She stood and braced herself against the thick bark. Still shoeless, she began up the hill through the trees on the pine straw mat. Body-shaped mounds of Ichorwulf littered the way – far more than were apparent during their earlier exit from the building. She found one that had carried a lacegun and grabbed it. The wind picked up as she made her way, disbursing the piles to the earth.

Lock's absence was a knife between the ribs. But as she got closer to the Heart, she felt her sorrow guttering. And in its place, the thing that had been her friend's defining characteristic: resolve. She tilted the gun and checked the ammo.

The tranquil music was still playing as she tiptoed through the shattered crystal door. Gun at the ready, she trotted down the corridor toward the far end. At the spot where the vrae had appeared before, she saw no sign of any type of ingress into the main thoroughfare. It was like he'd manifested into being out of thin air. Vampires were one thing. She wasn't ready to believe in phantoms that passed through walls.

"Willa!" A call came from behind.

Kathy rushed in followed by Lindon. Willa ran and embraced them, squeezing them like they were the last family she had. Maybe they were. She clung to Lindon, trying to summon the courage to tell them about Lock. Each time she tried to speak, her voice wobbled and fell apart.

Lindon gave her a squeeze. "I know."

Willa pushed from his chest. "How?"

"She's not with you." His voice and his downward glance said he'd save his mourning for later, when he could be alone with his memories.

"She brought all those drones down," said Willa, gesturing with the lacegun. "Saved me."

"We heard it – saw it – from the rendezvous," said Lindon. "It's why we came. Where are the children?"

Willa shook her head and shrugged. Her voice cracked, "I don't know." She wiped her nose.

"We need to find them," said Kathy, unsheathing the tiny sword she'd taken from the Oldens' and giving it a facile spin. Willa hadn't even noticed she was armed.

"Lock and I swept every floor."

Kathy got a look on her face. "Did you sweep this one?"

"There's nothing on this floor," said Willa, holding her arms open to the stark hall.

Kathy twisted her mouth. "Hmm."

"What?" Willa asked, looking to Lindon, who frowned his confusion.

Kathy meandered toward the place where the passages crossed, gouging the wall's mirror finish with the point of her blade. At the intersection of the corridors, she put her hand to a small metal fixture, and glanced back with a self-assured grin. She brought up the sword, set the tip into the fixture, and plunged it into the wall. The entire corner where the walls met pushed slowly open, revealing a dark interior and stairs that went down.

Willa and Lindon raced over just as Kathy drew the blade back out. The wall started closing and they slipped inside.

"Why do you have a sword?" asked Willa.

"It's a saber. My liuyedao. *The willow leaf,*" she answered, leading the way. "Standard vrae hand weapon."

Red lights pulsed along the stairs as they spiraled down.

"You know how to use it?" asked Willa.

"I'm alright I guess," she said, holding the blade aloft. "I hadn't been training long. Orion was my mentor. We probably killed him though. But that's fine."

The stairs terminated into a similarly dim hallway. It was utilitarian and spare – nothing like the rest of the Heart. A heavy, armored door capped the far end. Willa spotted another metal fixture just as Kathy rushed up to it with the liuyedao.

The mechanism turned a lock. A ray of light from inside cut across Willa's face as the massive steel barrier pulled from the wall. It was a dormitory, its walls lined with tiny bunks.

They rushed inside, almost tripping over more piles of Ichorwulf. Willa noticed how much the room fit Kathy's description of everything she'd seen and experienced during her own captivity. It was warm and comfortable. Immense. And so much more than just sleeping quarters. There were rows of books, an educational corner with screens and a large board for writing, surrounded by a semicircle of little armchairs. Personalized footlockers sat snugly against the foot of each bed.

In another corner was a colossal playset that stretched from floor to ceiling, an open space with all sorts of schoolyard games painted out on the surface. A dozen balls lay where they'd been dropped. VR rigs and haptics hung next to giant video screens. It was what Willa had always envisioned – and feared – a paradise for any child living in the districts.

Only there were no children. Just a man.

He was seated in one of the small chairs meant for a preschooler, head in hands. He certainly didn't seem like an Ichorwulf by external appearances. His clothes were plain – like what you might find in the midbloods.

"Hey!" shouted Willa.

He looked up, seeming unsurprised by their presence.

She shouldered the lacegun. "Where are they?"

The man's face was somber. "They're safe."

"Answer me!" she roared. "Where are our children?"

"They're not yours anymore."

Willa rushed to within a few feet of him, her blood boiling to a vapor. "Tell me!" she cried. "Now!"

"That I cannot do," he said, smiling, holding his hands out to the sides. "I'm unarmed."

She didn't let off the trigger until he had toppled all the way back – she didn't even realize she was shooting him until the soles of his shoes were in the air.

Kathy's mouth hung open in stunned admiration.

"This way," said Lindon.

Willa thought she'd feel something like guilt. She didn't.

Between the playset in one corner and the teaching area, sat a large arrangement of tables and chairs, with what looked like a cafeteria-style serving station set into the wall. Next to that, another set of doors. They flew through them and into the kitchen. Inside were a dozen more dusty mounds. At the back, between large stainless supply shelves, was another heavy security door, this one cracked open. A larger sword was embedded in the wall fixture, a pile of dust on the floor beneath it.

"They must have moved them when the shit hit the fan," said Lindon. He pulled the door open and Kathy slipped inside. As Willa went through, something on a nearby shelf caught her eye. A large container filled to the top with red lollipops.

They were back in another maze of corridors, dark and low like mineshafts. Gun drawn, Willa nudged her way past Kathy to take point. The silence was like being folded into a bolt of felt. They were several stories below ground by this point, and the angled shaft carried them further down.

Lindon broke the silence, "What is this, Kathy?"

She looked back, her usual bravado erased. "I don't know."

After several hundred feet, Willa saw something ahead on the wall. Small and white up near the ceiling. Closer in, they made it out. A modest placard. Plastic with engraved letters showing in black and slid into a cheap metal bracket. Like something from the middle of the previous century. *Archive*. Below it, a simple wooden door.

"There's two more down here," Kathy hollered from a bit farther in. "Archives."

"What do we do? Knock?" asked Lindon.

"No," Willa said quickly. "This could be where all the AB-positives are hiding out." She carefully took hold of the handle and tried to move it. "Locked from the inside." She glanced at the other two. "I think we have to kick it in and surprise them. Unless you have a better idea."

Kathy and Willa looked at Lindon. "Alright," he said, backing away. Willa regripped the lacegun. Kathy switched sword hands and spun the handguard. Lindon puffed his cheeks and blew out his breath. "Here goes." He launched forward and kicked the door in.

It exploded open in a cloud of splinters and dust. Willa rushed inside but found herself in a soupy black with nothing to aim at. Even with the bit of light from the shaft coming through, it illuminated nothing. She inched forward. "Whoa," Kathy said, holding the flat of the saber to Willa's gown and nodding downward. Just in front of them was the start of a broad concrete stairway down.

"Can't see anything," said Lindon, feeling along the wall just inside of the door. "Found it."

Lights thunked on overhead. Dim. Red. Like a dark room.

But their eyes slowly adjusted.

"What the hell?" Kathy blurted.

"Yeah, what the hell?" said Lindon.

It was like an ancient ruin. Or a natural history museum, shuttered because people were too terrified to visit the collection. Relics of unknown origin stood high atop cuboid pillars of polished concrete in the way of dinosaur bones displayed to show them as they had once lived. Only there were no dinosaurs, woolly mammoths, soaring pterosaurs, or tarpit carnivores. Just people... or something *like* people.

Incomplete though they were, dozens of chrome-shining humanoid skeletons were assembled in various attitudes. Some stood, while others were posed on all-fours, their uncanny shoulder blades and hips protruding like those of a jungle cat. At the top of every neck was the one piece that Willa recognized: the Apex Ganglion. Though the ones on display were far larger than Claude's or Scallien's, and certainly Everard's. The small root appendages that grew out from the underside were longer on this lot as well, twining down, over, and around the creatures' metallic spines like wire. More disturbing even than seeing the way the ganglions seemed to have overtaken and altered what had once been human, were the numerous odd-looking growths that reached out from the skeletal figurines like antennae. Long silver projections, no thicker than a chopstick, struck out from spines, pelvises, and chest plates. Even the ganglions themselves wore an uneven halo of spikes like rays of sun. Or the Statue of Liberty before the tides took her back.

"Kathy?" asked Lindon.

"Don't ask me." She skipped down the steps and pulled out a camera to fire a few shots. She reached up to touch one.

"Kathy!" Willa said. "What are you doing? You don't know what these are."

The girl caressed a curving appendage. "Oh, it's really smooth."

"Stop!" cried Lindon. Kathy yanked her hand away. Lindon checked his chin toward the back of the room. Willa turned and squinted. She saw it too.

Movement.

Willa slowly, smoothly, drew the lacegun up to her shoulder, setting her finger just across the trigger guard as she'd seen Lock do. One of the relics shifted, then fell from its perch and hit the floor. Shining bones came free from their moorings and rocketed across the concrete floor, filling the room with the deafening cacophony of bouncing metal. When the clamor faded, a tiny face peeked from behind the concrete pedestal. A little girl. Another arm pulled her back into hiding.

"It's them!" Willa cried, letting the gun clatter to the floor. "Isaiah! Baby! It's safe to come out! We aren't them!" She ran to where the child had appeared. "Sasha! Wren! Hali! Jack! Lynn! Ryan!"

Kathy and Lindon began calling for the children as other faces emerged from deeper within the archive. They shuffled out from the shadows in waves, but they did not rejoice or run to these new people who had appeared. Mainly, their expressions were flat. Drawn. Willa rushed through the growing crowd, embracing any child who came close, whispering *you're safe now,* caressing cheeks and squeezing tender shoulders, all the while searching for Isaiah.

She'd come to the Heart needing to be seen by him, so he would know she'd kept her promise. She tore the black wig from her head and tossed it onto a nearby relic. Then, digging down to the bottom of her bag, she took the hot pink hair in hand, gave it a fluff and pulled it snug.

Kathy and Lindon were like buoys in an ocean of kids, as Willa too was swarmed. With the discovery of the children came an abyssal drop in adrenaline, and she felt the layers of anxiety unspooling from around her body. She hadn't found Isaiah yet, but she would. Tears blurred her vision. She pressed farther in amongst the towering statues. And suddenly Isaiah was everywhere, like a mirage viewed through a kaleidoscope. She thumbed the tears from her eyes and blinked away what remained. The many images of him had gone. All but one. The real one. And with him, Wren, Sasha, Jack, Hali, Ryan, and Lynn.

In a room that felt a shrine to evil's abominations, in the bowels of a palace built upon the backs of the blooded, Willa had come to find her own blood, and found him. She reached Isaiah, swept him close. With their beating hearts pressed together, she allowed her tears to soak into his head.

She took him by the shoulders and checked him over, all the while reassuring and apologizing and explaining, then repeating what she'd already said. The thought occurred to her that she might have been more traumatized than he. Finally, she took a breath and opened her mouth to ask the one question that had caused her so much heartache from the start. But her grandson's face had already answered it. She never had reason to doubt.

CHAPTER THIRTY-SIX

HEMOSTASIS
The process whereby bleeding or blood flow is stopped. The opposite of hemorrhage.

On the way out of Patriot's lair they grabbed anything that might be of use. Lindon, Willa and Kathy slung any lacegun that still held ammo about their shoulders and packed clips of ammunition into bags and pockets. They ransacked the kitchen, ordering the children to pilfer as much food as they could carry. Willa took the container of lollipops.

Their exit from the Heart could hardly be called an escape, as they met no further resistance. What Ichorwulves survived had fled. In the short run, Willa surmised the company would blame blood contamination or an unknown pathogen until they simmered down and realized only the universal recipients among them had lived. At that point, they'd know they'd been hacked. God, she wanted to be able to share it all with Lock.

Leading a procession of some four hundred-plus children through the blood districts at dawn was no cakewalk, even compared to the nightmare that had been Patrioteer. Once the children got over their fear of Kathy's vrae swords, they allowed themselves to be entertained by her basic tricks and stunts. She had two blades now, having nabbed the one they'd found stuck in the wall above the pile of its previous owner. Word of the children spread quickly, and parents stood along the streets like onlookers at a parade hoping to find their own. Willa kept Isaiah close, whispering promises to never again let evil befall him.

Lindon was well acquainted with many of Lock's connections and they were able to find temporary accommodations for most of the children whose parents hadn't yet been located. Willa finally met Jethrum, a tank of a man with a pointed red beard and a face that read like a history book written with sharp objects. As with Lock, he ran a section of the lowbloods, a criminal and caretaker alike, looking after homes packed to the gills with orphans. When Lindon broke the news about her, he'd been inscrutable at first and then punched a hole through the front door. They discussed logistics and Jethrum spent several minutes explaining how they might deactivate the beacons implanted in the children's fingers without the need for amputation.

Home, for now at least, would be Bad Blood until they determined which, if any, of Lock's safehouses were still actually safe. Until then, it was the best place. Patriot was certain to show up at some point, but they hoped it would be after they'd ransacked the districts. The last place Patriot would want to venture shortly after being decimated would be one filled with blood diseases. They wouldn't risk reducing their numbers any further by rushing in to shake down their own quarantine zone.

Willa sat with Isaiah on a bench in one of Bad Blood's communal gardens watching robins pluck berries from a bush. The birds had never left, but she hadn't noticed them in years. Their whistle-clear calls, the ruffle of their wings against the air. And it seemed significant in some way. Like a rebirth. Birdsong. The sound heard when the guns of war fall silent. And for the first time since Chrysalis, Willa allowed herself an easy breath. Peace and normalcy, the objects of hope, felt attainable.

Word was spreading. Kathy's photos, proof of what lived in the bowels of Patriot's heart, were disseminated as quickly as people could send them. They'd distributed some of the lollipops too. Truth was a tumbling boulder and there was nothing Patriot could do to stop it. There would be no more Harvest, no more Trade. No more categorization and ranking of people according to what antigens their blood happened to carry. Willa had no illusions that the path forward would be difficult. Society would begin to rebalance itself. With no authority pressing down from above, factions would rise and fall, protectorates and fledgling governments would vie for territory and control. Some would sputter, others would flourish. The prospect of all of that, even if daunting and a little bit scary, was invigorating. Human life would be in the hands of the humans. It felt like springtime.

And should whatever remained of Patriot decide to make an appearance, they knew how to fight them. There was nothing special about Ichorwulves. They were a little quicker, stronger, maybe, but they died just as humans did. And they were ten times as hungry. You could always starve them out.

That night, surrounded by several children who would become the new sons and daughters of Bad Blood, they met up with John in his module. Curious to see what Patriot was telling the outside world, he turned to the Channel when *The Patriot Report* usually came on, only to find the screen black. No shiny host in top hat and billboard teeth, no bombshell assistants or self-congratulations. No Confetti. Just blackness, and at the center of it, barely large enough to read, were two words flickering in red.

Mos maiorum

Everyone looked to everyone else.

"I mean…" mumbled John, "… my Latin's not so good."

"Tell us," said Willa.

"Uh," he said, squinting at the screen and thinking, "it's something like *ancestral tradition* or… *the way of the ancestors*."

Willa's heart plummeted, her body hollow, her breath still.

"What is it?" asked Lindon. "What's the matter? What is that supposed to mean?"

Willa looked up. "It means *the Old Way*."

Kathy stood, giving her blade a spin. "It means they're hungry."

▽ **PATRIOCAST 3.11.68** ▽

NUCLEAR BLAST IN THE SOUTHEAST!

Hydrogen Bomb *Fifolet*

Crisis –Fusion reaction detected on Southern Coast. Mass casualties reported.

Tap to play video.

Northwestern Gray Zone Update – Acute illness: up. Radiation sickness: up.
Anemia of chronic diseases: up. All cancer categories: up.
Total Units Required last 30 days: 3,708,409
Total Units Provided by Patriot: 2,616,991

Northeastern Gray Zone Update – Acute illness: up. Radiation sickness: up.
Anemia of chronic diseases: up. All cancer categories: up.
Total Units Required last 30 days: 12,087,116
Total Units Provided by Patriot: 11,204,323
#Lives Saved Estimate last 30 days: 12,000
#Lives Saved Estimate year-to-date: 29,000

Southwestern Red Zone – Traumatic injuries: widespread. Radiation sickness: anticipated. Anemia of chronic diseases: anticipated. Cancers: anticipated.

▽ *Patriot thanks ALL DONORS. Your gift matters!* ▽

ACKNOWLEDGMENTS

My wife has read and edited countless drafts and fragments of my various writing attempts for years now, always giving me her honest takes. She has been endlessly supportive along the way, serving as an important barometer to help me gauge feedback and criticism. I say thank you from the bottom of every one of my O-pos RBCs.

It was my mother who put a pen in my hand. It was she who taught me to type, on an actual typewriter, with an actual typing workbook, in seventh grade. It was miserable, those summer months, typing each day for what felt like hours (it was thirty minutes). As a child, she read to me every night, and that imagery still lives unfaded in my memory – the grand adventures of Peter Pan, Huck Fin, White Fang, Meg and Charles Murry. Thanks to my father, who is always quickest to read my work and the first to give feedback. Getting that quick hit from my dad has always been the boon I need to push into that second draft.

My sister, Elizabeth, a writer of children's stories, has been with me each step of the way. We've shared this journey together.

Jess Hagemann, whose book *Headcheese* any fan of horror should read, was one of the earliest to give feedback and encouragement on the first draft. My law partner David Greenstone was enthusiastic and supportive from the beginning, though he did lament the lack of a teenage vampire lust subplot (that's what sequels are for, David!). Jackie Brewer read a draft in three days and gave me excellent notes. Heather Ezell, author of *Nothing Left to Burn*, did an extensive markup and structural edit on an early draft that helped me to focus the story. They say writing a novel is a solitary exercise – and that is mostly true. Finishing one, however, at least for me, was quite the opposite.

An immense amount of research was necessary in order to create this world, but I am far from an expert. If anything, all of that learning simply showed me the breadth of what I don't know. I reached out to a number of professionals for assistance and generally struck out. Apparently cold-calling (or messaging) people to politely ask how one might execute a vein-to-vein transfusion isn't how you garner a response. Thankfully, one person, Dr Joe Chaffin, aka "The Blood Bank Guy," did respond and assisted with a number of technical issues. Specifically, he helped me to portray the anastomosis scene correctly.

Gemma Creffield at Angry Robot championed this story and was the main reason they acquired the book. As the book's editor, she pushed me to give it flesh when what I had initially delivered was a bare-bones plot burner. The characters and settings would not have the dimension they do now absent Gemma's input and urging. I count myself fortunate that she read this story when it came in and for her focus in helping to bring it where it had to go.

Metal bands I listened to while writing this book: Alterbeast, Amorphis, Behemoth, Between the Buried and Me, Black Crown Initiate, Ensiferum, Falconer, Ghost, Gatecreeper, Kvelertak, Mastodon, Pig Destroyer, Power Trip, Ringworm, Russian Circles, Spirit Adrift, Totem Skin, Vault Dweller, Weekend Nachos, Wolfchant, and Zeal & Ardor.

Fancy more apocalyptic monsters?
Why not try
Three by Jay Posey

JAY POSEY

LEGENDS OF THE DUSKWALKER

Read the first chapter here!

ONE

Golden beams of sunlight spilled through the skeletal high rises, and through the concrete and steel network of interlaced highways, bypasses, and rails that once flowed with harried humanity, now devoid of all but the meanest signs of life. Overpasses stacked ten high lay inert, arteries of a city embalmed. The wind was light but weighty with the failing autumn, like the hand of a blacksmith gently laid.

Beneath the lowest overpass, a lone figure plodded weary steps, bowed and hooded, burden dragging behind leaving long tracks in the concrete dust. He paused, raised his head, laid back his hood, and felt the cooling breeze on his sweat-beaded face. His sun-squinted eyes roved over the urban desert before him as he adjusted the straps of his makeshift harness to ease his protesting shoulders.

"I see why you left," the man muttered. He spat, wiped his nose on the sleeve of his knee-length faded olive-brown-mottled coat, and started on his way again.

The man stepped up onto the road, felt his senseThetic boots soften slightly to better absorb the hard shock of the asphalt, cringed at the hollow echo of his cargo scraping across the scarred and pockmarked ground. As he walked, he imagined the city as it might've once been. The endless dissonance of a half-million people packed into five square miles, swimming in an almost tangible soup of electromagnetic traffic. He wondered what traces of personality might still be left, rippling through those invisible fields around him even now.

Progress was slow, but he was close. Another few minutes and at last the man stood before the gates of his destination: a small enclave of survivors set within the dead cityscape. From atop a twenty-foot wall of haphazardly-welded urban debris, a watchman called down.

"What's your business, stranger?"

The man jerked his thumb behind him, indicating the cargo he was dragging. The watchman grunted.

"Yeah, alright," he answered. "Reckon the agent's gonna wanna take a look before you go far."

The man waited in silence as the enormous gates ground open, just wide enough to admit him and his payload. They started to close again before he was all the way through.

"Second street on your right, agent's the first on the left. First floor."

The man nodded curt thanks, and headed to see the enclave's agent. Within the walls, the architecture was unchanged from that outside: tall gunmetal skyscrapers with windows darkened like gaping sockets of a skull, dead flat panel signs forty-feet wide that might once have hawked the day's latest technological fashion. In here, however, there were men, women, and even wide-eyed children, who stared in wonder at this new evidence of life from beyond the wall, walking amongst them. Most of the adults pretended not to notice him, though he felt their sidelong glances and heard the hushed whispers after he passed. Even in days as strange as these, it was unusual to see a man harnessed as he was, hauling such a load: scrap aluminum, worn and scratched, bent into the makeshift but unmistakable shape of a coffin.

The man reached the agent's office, and he paused, steeling himself with a final deep breath of outside air. He'd dealt with agents before, nearly thirty he could recall, and they'd all been the same. Muscle-bound gun-toters with a lot of bark, always itching for a reason to bite.

Mostly ex-military or law enforcement, agents were tough guys who liked the power, and still clung to the outdated notion that order could be maintained even in a desolate society. They had their uses. But the man had little use for them.

He stepped forward, automatic doors sliding smoothly open to admit him, and dragged in from concrete to polished granite. In an earlier time, the office might've been a bank, with all its oak and stone. Or a tomb. Now, it was just a long corridor, leading to an imposing flexiglass cube. The glass was darkly smoked, but the man correctly presumed whoever was inside could see his approach. Still, he strode nearly the length of the corridor, before a sudden booming voice stopped him five paces from the cube's door.

"State your business," thundered the voice, rolling emphatically down the stone hall.

"Bounty," replied the man.

"State your name."

"Three."

There was a pause.

"You got three of 'em in there?"

"You asked my name."

The voice puzzled for a moment. Then–

"Who you got in the box?"

"One of yours."

"Open it."

"I'd rather not."

The voice resumed a more professional tone.

"All collections must be verified and processed before payment will be distributed."

"So open the cube."

A slot opened in the cube, and a sleek metal case slid out, popping open to reveal a cracking rubberized interior.

"Deposit your weapons in the provided secure receptacle."

"I'd rather not."

Another pause. Though it still boomed, the voice sounded flustered.

"You cain't come in here so armed, mister. I don't care who you are."

The man named Three let the straps of his harness slide off his shoulders. They clattered to the floor next to the coffin.

"Then you come out. I'm done dragging."

Three turned around and started back down the corridor.

"Hey!" the voice thundered, "Hey, you cain't just leave that settin' there!"

Three walked on.

"I'll have you arrested if you don't come back!"

He was almost to the exit. There was a whir and a click behind him, and a thin, crackly voice called out from the cube.

"What about your bounty? Don't you want it?"

Three stopped. But didn't turn.

"Come on get this box inside, and I'll see what we owe ya. My back cain't manage it."

Three swiveled on a heel, and returned to the cube. There, a bent old man who looked like he weighed less than his age tottered and leaned against the now-opened door. A stimstick dangled precariously from his lower lip, glowing with casual indifference. Three grabbed the straps off the floor and hauled the coffin inside the cube. The old man followed him in.

"Don't know why you folks gotta make things difficult for *us* folk. Times is rough enough without undeserved meanness."

The cube interior was a stark contrast to the cavernous entryway. Nearly every available square inch was stuffed with various devices, blinking and humming and whirring, and it was easily fifteen degrees warmer inside than out. There was a desk of sorts in the middle of the room, with a plush recliner behind it, and an overturned plasticrate that Three assumed served as a seat for rare company. From within the cube, the flexiglass was clear, and the granite corridor stretched off to the glass exit at the far end.

"So who'd you git?" the agent asked.

"Nim. Nanokid out of the Six-Thirteen."

The agent's eyes twitched back and forth as he internally accessed the appropriate file.

"Alright. Looks like fifteen-hundred."

"Four thousand."

"Nah, only fifteen for dead."

"I didn't say he was dead."

The agent looked up into Three's eyes, mouth open slightly, but he swallowed whatever question he'd been about to ask, and instead took a drag on the stimstick. He turned and rummaged through a pile of gadgets on his desk, dragging out a slender rod, pewter-colored, without any apparent seams or separate parts, which emitted a pleasant hum. This he pointed casually at the coffin, grunting after a moment with some mix of satisfaction and disdain.

"Well, that's him in there alright," he said, turning again to fish around in his desk drawer. "Pointcard's OK?"

Without waiting for an answer, the agent produced a translucent green card and swept it through a slotted device, which clicked once and beeped cheerily. He extended it to Three.

"Hard, actually," Three replied, hands in his coat pockets.

The agent's slight shoulders slumped almost into non-existence.

"I don't keep that kind of Hard just layin' around. No more than a thousand any given day."

The pointcard trembled in the agent's still-outstretched hand, in vague hope that this strange man from beyond the wall would take it and disappear. Three could tell he disturbed the agent. The wrinkled old man stared at him like he didn't belong there, like he was some alien thing wedged in the wrong reality. The agent shivered.

"I'll take the thousand now, and come back for the rest."

The agent pushed the card a little closer.

"Might be a day or two."

"I'll wait."

The agent let out a weary sigh. He rummaged in, under, and around the electric clutter of his office, until he located an ancient lockbox, secured with physical biometrics. After running his bent and knobby fingers over the touchpad, the box hissed open. The agent opened it just wide enough to slip his hand in, counted out twenty nanocarb chips, and handed them over to Three with some reluctance. Three glimpsed more Hard in the box, but made no comment, sized the agent up instead: dilated pupils, thin sheen of perspiration, colorless ring around tensed lips.

"Sorry I frighten you," Three said without apologetic tone. He leaned his head to one side and cracked his neck audibly, watching the old man carefully. The agent laughed, too suddenly, too loud.

"What? I ain't scared of ya, don't ya worry about that."

Lie, Three thought.

"I lived plenty enough years to see things a lot worse than you, friend."

That was true. Three lowered his head in the barest hint of a bow. Whatever the agent's reason for withholding a portion of his stash, Three decided, he was an honest dealer. Probably owed someone. The agent got back to business.

"Gimme your SNIP, I'll pim ya when I get the rest."

"I'll come back tomorrow."

The agent's eyes narrowed slightly.

"Be easier if you just gimme the SNIP."

"I'd rather not."

"Figgered that," the agent snorted. "Well, gimme two days, I'll have the rest for ya then. Late afternoon."

Three unfastened his coat to pocket the payment, revealing a mammoth pistol crouching in a holster on his vest, coiled like some predator hungering to pounce. The agent's eyes bulged at the hardware, but he quickly diverted his attention. He kicked at the coffin.

"'Preciate the work you done," he said half-heartedly. "Dunno why you had to do him like that, though."

Three adjusted the pistol, then refastened his coat, concealing it once more.

"You will when you open it."

Three nodded to the agent, and swiveled back down the stone corridor. As Three walked away, the agent watched him briefly, then, on a sudden whim, picked up and aimed the humming rod at his back. The agent frowned slightly, shook the rod, and pointed it again, more purposefully. His frown deepened, eyes narrowed with some undefined emotion. A thought occurred, and wide-eyed he fumbled over himself to seal the flexiglass cube, as Three stepped back out onto the street.

The honey-colored liquid swirled gently in the finger-smudged squat glass on the table in front of Three. It was his fourth of the afternoon. Still he waited for the comforting blanket of alcoholic haze to embrace him. He leaned forward, resting his face in his hands, and his elbows on the table, felt it shift slightly to the right, and wondered briefly if it were the table or himself that had wobbled. Was this the wobbly table? Or had that been yesterday? Yesterday? Yesterday. It was the second day since he'd met with the agent. Payday.

Three let out a weary sigh, ran his hands back over his shaved head, feeling the stubble of a few days' growth, then massaged his temples, probably throbbing though he couldn't be sure. It was like this when he didn't have a job; something to find, someone to bring in. The restlessness was setting in, the need to move. To hunt. It was the third day in the same town. Might as well have been a month. There were benefits to being a freelancer, but down time wasn't one of them.

From his corner booth, he had a commanding view of all the critical angles. The booth itself was U-shaped, tucked in the front corner of the bar, a natural blind spot from the entrance. Temprafoam, covered in some cheap imitation of a much sturdier textile, it was adequate comfort and gave him all the room he needed, and best of all required no reservation, deposit, or record of stay. He sat with his feet propped on the bench opposite, with his coat bundled around his hardware on the perpendicular seat that completed the U. His eyes involuntarily swept around the bar, taking stock of his surroundings, the way they had two minutes before. Habit.

But everything was the same. Same hazy atmosphere. Same chattering regulars. Same bartender. The bartender was a lean man, lean like he'd been a foot shorter and stretched to his current height, and fidgety. He was never completely still, fingers always working the air when they weren't cleaning glasses or pouring drinks. Three guessed the bartender was splitting time between customers and some fantasy app, but didn't want to guess the type.

He took another swig of his drink, then casual interest in the door. Instinct. A moment later, a woman entered pulling a small boy along behind her. She was bent at an awkward angle, clutching her long coat closed tight around her with a balled fist pressed hard to her side. Colorless, sweating, desperate. Damp shoulder-length brown hair plastered to her forehead. Wild brown eyes darting around the room. The boy was blond, vibrantly pale, with eyes deep sea-green and natural, the mesmerizing kind the Money would've paid top Hard for at the height of the market. Three guessed him perhaps five years old. The boy trembled with the frightened silence of a child who's been told everything's alright, but knows it isn't. His shocking innocence swept through the bar: fragile, beautiful, a snowflake drifting amongst ash.

Three lowered his eyes back to his glass, kept the woman and boy in his peripheral awareness. She moved from patron to patron, urgent, pleading, waved off impatiently. Three shut his eyes and drank deeply the remaining honey-liquid from his glass. He set it back on the table with a dull crack, felt the table shift again.

Good, he thought with a half-smile. Table, not me.

When he opened his eyes, she was there.

"Please ..." she began. Three's gaze flicked to the door behind her. In the next instant, it swung open, and she whipped around to face it, inhaling sharply. Whoever she was expecting wasn't there. Just a pair of teen Skinners blowing in off the street. She clenched her eyes, bent over Three's table, dropped a fist to support herself.

Three watched her hazily, felt his eyes float to the boy. The boy ran his hand slowly, methodically, back and forth along the edge of Three's table, tiny fingers wrapped around some scavenged plaything: a model of an ancient shuttlecar with a few flecks of yellow paint where bare metal hadn't yet worn through. He fixed Three with a wet, penetrating stare, and never looked away.

Three reached in his vest pocket and flicked a pair of nanocarb chips onto the table, a hundred Hard. The woman opened her eyes, stared down blankly at them, then back up at him, shaking her head.

"No," she practically whispered, teeth catching her bottom lip for an instant in an almost imperceptible struggle to maintain thin composure. "We need help."

"You lose something?" Three heard himself ask heavily. The fog was settling nicely now.

"What?"

"Did you lose something?" he repeated, with overemphasized precision.

"No, I–"

"Looking for someone?"

"What? No, we're just–"

"Then I can't help you."

The woman straightened, and looked back to the door, but didn't leave. Three glanced to the boy again, found himself staring into deep green pools, fascinated. The boy seemed equally intrigued by Three. The woman made one more attempt.

"I'm not asking you to help me," she pushed the boy to the front. "Look, will you help him?"

"I'm not being rude, ma'am. Just honest."

Three tilted his glass on the table, signaled to the bartender for another. Still the woman stood, chewing her lip, pressing her fist to her abdomen, while the bartender jerked his way over and refilled Three's glass to the brim.

"Take the money," Three said, sipping from the glass, feeling the warmth roll down his throat, filling his chest with dull flame.

"Mama," a small voice peeped next to the woman. "Mama, let's just go."

The woman stared vacantly, at the door, at the table, at the Hard.

"Go on," Three said. "I've got plenty."

"Mama, please, can we go now, can we go?"

Without a word, the woman swept the two nanocarb chips up off the table and into her pocket, then whirled and tugged the boy along behind her to the bar. She spoke animatedly with the bartender, who directed her with various twitching gestures towards the back. The boy never took his eyes from Three, not until he vanished with his mother into a back room and, Three assumed, out again into the streets.

Three downed a good half of his glass, felt a faint satisfaction waft through, like the smoke-wisp of a just snuffed candle, knowing he'd helped some local skew and her runt, and hadn't even been annoyed when she hadn't thanked him. A hundred Hard was probably more than she'd make in a week of nights under sweaty Joes who couldn't afford even C-grade sims.

"Hold my table," Three called to the bartender, hauling himself out of the booth to take care of the growing pressure in his bladder that he'd just noticed.

In the stall, he watched in a sort of drunken lucidity the stream splashing onto the stainless grate, knowing somewhere below it was being absorbed, filtered, broken down into useful parts for biochem batteries, or solvent, or cooking. He chuckled aloud at the thought of his fellow patrons out there drinking his recycled urine.

But then the sudden image of the boy's sea-green eyes cut short his personal amusement, and Three couldn't shake the feeling that there was something in them he should've noted, something he missed that was important, or would've been if he'd noticed. He was still rolling it over in his thickened mind when he stepped back out to the bar and felt the twinge, the automatic heightening of senses he'd learned to trust even when he didn't know why.

He continued to his table smoothly, seemingly unconcerned, knowing any change of intent might draw unwanted attention, and slid into his booth, absorbing at a glance the altered environment. The adrenaline surge burned away all traces of the alcohol-induced mist he'd spent the afternoon cultivating. The bar was nearly the same; same hazy atmosphere, same regulars, same bartender. The regulars weren't chattering now. The Skinners had a new companion.

He was tall; taller than the bartender, broad-shouldered, with long, stringy dark hair like tendrils down his back. His face was skullish, skin stretched taut across sharp features, unnaturally smooth despite other, more subtle signs of age. Thin hands, tapering to long, dexterous fingers. The eyes were the key: a slight wrinkling at the edge, with thirty more years of life in them than the rest of the man's build suggested.

Genie, Three guessed. Dangerous.

He'd run afoul of a couple of Genies before, humans who through extensive genetic engineering, or outright tampering, had attained preternaturally advanced talents or skills. It was a mistake Three didn't plan to repeat. The trouble with Genies was you never knew what about them had been enhanced. The eggheads were never a problem. Others, though, could be lethal. Judging the tall man at the bar, Three guessed he was a strength tweaker. Could probably crush a man's skull in his massive hand.

The man spoke few words, but each brought forth a torrent of information and gestures from the Skinners, as they tripped over one another trying to convince him of their eagerness to help. They both looked terrified. Three hadn't drawn his notice, but the newcomer wasn't interested in him anyway. One of the Skinners motioned to the back of the bar, and shortly after, the tall man exited by way of the front door, without so much as a glance in Three's direction. After several tense moments, one of the regulars mumbled something that drew laughter from the others at the bar. Normalcy rebooted, a programmatic hiccup resolved.

Three reached for his glass, half-empty when he left, now half-full. The boy's eyes burned before him, innocent, unaccusing. There was no doubt the tall man was after the woman; the boy. Veins in the tall man's temples had bulged slightly as he left the bar. Anger. Three knew in his heart that the tall man meant harm to those two. He shook his head: not his problem.

A hundred Hard, Three thought. That'll go a long way, if she's smart.

He picked up his glass, swirled the slightly viscous liquid. Unappealing now. He wanted to want to drink it, but instead just watched it spin and settle. Over the rim of his glass, on the far side of the table, something caught his eye. A small model shuttlecar with chipping yellow paint.

He left the glass.

"How much do I owe you?" Three called to the bartender, standing and gathering his things.

The bartender looked his way, puzzled.

"For the drinks," Three explained.

"Your woman-friend already paid," the bartender answered. "Nice tipper, too."

Silence descended upon the bar as Three made ready, patrons goggle-eyed at this last brazen assault on their day-to-day routine. They'd all assumed Three was a drunken drifter. Now, he was checking the cylinder of his pistol and holstering it, sliding a slender-bladed short sword into its sheath at his lower back.

Three threw his coat on over his hardware, and wordlessly flowed out onto the street, in pursuit of a deadly man he didn't know for reasons he couldn't understand.

We are Angry Robot

angryrobotbooks.com

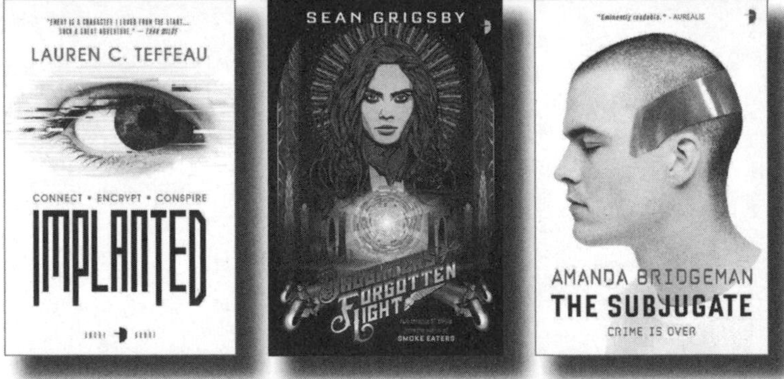

Silent Hall
N.S. DOLKART
Among the Fallen
N.S. DOLKART
A Breach in the Heavens
N.S. DOLKART
Science Fiction, Fantasy and WTF?!
THE BULLET-CATCHER'S DAUGHTER
ROD DUNCAN
UNSEEMLY SCIENCE
ROD DUNCAN
"ELIZABETH BARNABUS WILL ENTICE READERS FROM THE FIRST PAGE."
THE CUSTODIAN OF MARVELS
ROD DUNCAN
@angryrobotbooks
PAIGE ORWIN
THE INTERMINABLES
MOONSHINE
JASMINE GOWER
"RARE AND PRECIOUS... COMPELLING AND TRUE."
AN OATH OF DOGS
WENDY N WAGNER

DARIUS HINKS
the Ingenious
CAMERON JOHNSTON
THE TRAITOR GOD
HEROISM COULD GET A MAN KILLED
CAMERON JOHNSTON
GOD OF BROKEN THINGS

The INSTITUTE for SINGULAR ANTIQUITIES
S.A. SIDOR
The INSTITUTE for SINGULAR ANTIQUITIES
THE BEAST OF NIGHTFALL LODGE
S.A. SIDOR
KAMERON HURLEY
THE LIGHT BRIGADE

JAINE FENN
HIDDEN SUN
SHADOWLANDS BOOK I
JAINE FENN
BROKEN SHADOW
SHADOWLANDS BOOK II
SHADOWBLADE
ANNA KASHINA